THE COURTESAN

Silently the girl took the scarlet kerchief from around her neck, and reaching up on tip-toes, wiped his features with it gently, before handing the silken stuff to him to continue the process. As she stood there close to him, throat and shoulders largely bared above the open-necked and brief white line bodice, the man could not but be much aware of the warm honey-hued loveliness of her, and the deep cleft of the richly-swelling firm young bosom. Mary was indeed, beyond all question, physically as well as mentally, no longer anybody's child — and the sooner he came to terms with the fact, almost certainly, the better for him.

The Courtesan

Second in The Master of Gray Trilogy

Nigel Tranter

CORONET BOOKS
Hodder and Stoughton

First published in Great Britain in 1963 by Hodder and Stoughton Ltd.

Coronet edition 1973

Second impression 1990

Printed and bound in Great Britain for Hodder and Stoughton paperbacks, a division of Hodder and Stoughton Ltd., Mill Road, Dunton Green, Sevenoaks, Kent TN13 2YA (Editorial Office: 47 Bedford Square, London WC1B 3DP) by Cox & Wyman Ltd., Reading.

ISBN 0-340-17838-8

PRINCIPAL CHARACTERS

In order of appearance

(Fictional characters printed in *italics*)

Mary Gray: supposed daughter of David Gray, but actually of his half-brother, Patrick, Master of Gray.

David Gray: illegitimate eldest son of 5th Lord Gray; land steward and schoolmaster.

PATRICK, 5TH LORD GRAY: Sheriff of Forfar. Strong in the Kirk party.

Mariota Gray: wife of David, daughter of the Bishop of St. Boswell's; mother of Mary.

KING JAMES, THE SIXTH OF SCOTS: son of Mary Queen of Scots; became first monarch of the United Kingdom.

LUDOVICK, 2ND DUKE OF LENNOX: second cousin of King James; near heir to the throne, son of Esmé Stuart of D'Aubigny, former Chancellor.

JOHN, EARL OF MAR: Keeper of Stirling Castle; boyhood companion of King.

The LADY MARIE STEWART, MISTRESS OF GRAY: daughter of Earl of Orkney, wife to Patrick.

SIR JOHN MAITLAND OF THIRLESTANE: Chancellor of Scotland.

PATRICK, MASTER OF GRAY: son and heir of 5th Lord Gray; former Master of Wardrobe, and former Acting Chancellor; condemned for treason and banished, 1587.

The LADY JEAN STEWART: younger sister of Marie.

PATRICK LESLIE: Commendator of Lindores Abbey; later 1st Lord Lindores; married the Lady Jean.

Mr. ROBERT BOWES: Queen Elizabeth's resident envoy at Scottish Court. Later knighted.

MASTER ANDREW MELVILLE: Principal of St. Andrews University and Kirk leader.

5

LORD ROBERT STEWART, EARL OF ORKNEY: one of King
    James Fifth's many bastard sons. Former Bishop of
    Orkney; uncle of King; father of Lady Marie, Mistress
    of Gray.
GEORGE, 6TH EARL OF HUNTLY: Chief of Clan Gordon;
    principal Catholic nobleman.
JAMES STEWART, EARL OF MORAY: known as the Bonnie
    Earl. Son of another of James Fifth's bastards. Nephew
    of the Regent Moray.
The LADY ELIZABETH, COUNTESS OF MORAY: wife of
    above; daughter of Regent Moray.
SIR WALTER RALEIGH: courtier, diplomat and explorer.
QUEEN ELIZABETH OF ENGLAND.
FRANCIS HEPBURN STEWART, EARL OF BOTHWELL:
    son of one more of James Fifth's many bastards, and
    nephew of Mary Queen of Scots' third husband, Bothwell.
ANNE, PRINCESS OF DENMARK: wife of King James the
    Sixth.
MASTER DAVID LINDSAY: the King's chaplain.
Peter Hay: page to the Duke of Lennox.
GORDON OF BUCKIE: a laird of Huntly's, who struck down
    the Earl of Moray.
The COUNTESS OF ATHOLL: Lady-in-waiting, daughter of
    1st Earl of Gowrie, wife of Earl of Atholl.
The LADY BEATRIX RUTHVEN: Lady of the Bedchamber;
    sister of above.

Chapter One

THE girl picked up the much creased and battered looking letter, smoothed out the folds, and began to read the dashing, sprawling handwriting. She knew that she ought not to be reading it; but equally she had known that she was going to do so from the moment that she caught sight of the broken-sealed paper lying there on the table. She had seen the ship-master from Dundee handing it to her father in the castle courtyard that morning – and had cried out then, was it from her Uncle Patrick? David Gray had turned away abruptly, thrusting the letter deep into an inner pocket of his doublet, jerking a rough negative. And few people ever found it in themselves to be either rough or negative with Mary Gray.

Her slightly pouting red lips silently formed the carelessly vigorous letters into words as she read – such different writing from her father's own neat and painstaking hand, so much more difficult to read. Yet how vividly it spoke to her of her Uncle Patrick himself; all the gallant, mercurial, laughing brilliance of him, casually masterful, shatteringly handsome – beautiful indeed, the only man that she had ever seen who could be so called and yet remain indubitably and essentially masculine. If there had been a mirror in that purely functional modest chamber in the north-west flanking tower of Castle Huntly – which of course was unthinkable in a room solely her father's – Mary Gray would have had little need to conjure up any mind-picture of the writer of that letter, as she spelled out the words, for what she would have seen therein would have served better than any such year-old memory, better than any painted portrait however expertly limned.

The girl knew that she was quite fantastically like the absent Master of Gray, and in more than mere features, colouring and expression – embarrassingly so to a great many who saw her, though never to herself. Mary Gray was not readily embarrassed, any more than was her Uncle Patrick.

7

Slightly but gracefully built, at fifteen she was nevertheless already showing more than the promise of a lovely and challenging young womanhood – for women as well as men ripened early in the vehement, forcing days of James Stewart the Sixth, and of Elizabeth Tudor. Dark, of a delicate elfin beauty, she was exquisitely made alike in face as in figure, great-eyed, lustrous, with that highly attractive indeed magnetic expression, unusual as it is apparently contradictory, which seems to combine essential, quiet gravity with a more superficial gaiety, even roguery. Mary Gray left none unmoved who saw her; that would be her burden as well as her guerdon all her days. Only some few women are born with that fatal stamp upon them – including that lovely and unhappy royal Mary after whom she had been named.

The girl read with a sort of still absorption.

'My good and respected D.,

Will you hear a sinner's plea? I write in all humility, not to say trepidation – for you did not answer my last. It is important that you heed me now, I assure you. Important for your upright self, for both dear M.'s, for whom – dare I say it? – you will not deny me some mede of devotion if not responsibility? Even for our noble progenitor – whom, however, God may rot if so He wills!

Heed then, good D. The glorious and utterly accursed lady whose price was above a ruby will, within a three-month, meet her deserts. This beyond a peradventure. The two most catholic have decided it at last, and all is in train. Your humble debtor has the ear of H.C.M., if not of H.H., and is satisfied that this time justice will be done. These eyes have indeed looked on the ready-forged sword of that justice, and are content. Here is no plot, no conspiracy, but invincible persuasion sufficient to the task. More than sufficient, craft replacing craft, *nota bene*. You have doubted my word times a-many, D. Doubt it now at your peril. You are a deal less dull than you seem, and it will not have escaped you, I vow, that H.C.M. is testatory heir to that other unfortunate lady, against whom the fates waged such unrelenting war. Now, great as must be our gratitude to this paladin, I judge that you will agree with me that an

8

overdose of good things is seldom a kindness. Moreover we have our errant young friend J. to consider. Accordingly certain precautions will be advisable.

Here they are. Inform our blustering northern cousin H. of all this forthwith. Urge that he brace himself, and swiftly. Likewise S. and the C. and others of that kidney. A month must suffice them. Then, only when they are ready, inform young J. But not his tutor and servitors, lest the lad be unduly distracted. J. to write to H.C.M. offering a mutual arrangement, satisfactory to both – pointing out, needless to say, that short of some such convenient understanding, it might be necessary for him to go to the thrice-damned woman aforementioned. He will take the point, I have no doubt.

This should serve, I think. See to it, D – and swiftly. Not for my sake but for all you hold dear – lest the office be set up on Castle-hill! Do not doubt the choice before you.

My own M. would send you all too much of love, I fear, if she knew that I wrote. She is well, as am I.

Do not withhold my worship and devotion from those whom I also hold so dear and on whom I pray God to smile – though your stern Reformed God never smiles, does He? Who knows, I may see them, and your own sober visage, sooner than you think. Salutations.

P.'

Mary Gray had worked her way once through this peculiar epistle, and, wide brows wrinkled slightly, was part-way through a second reading, when a sound from the open doorway drew her glance from the paper. David Gray stood there, frowning, lips tight, a more formidable figure than he knew.

The girl did not start guiltily, nor drop the letter. She did not even look discomposed. That had ever been the problem with her from earliest childhood – how to assert parental authority and suitable sway over one so strangely and basically assured, so extraordinarily yet quietly judicial, so patently quite unassertively master of herself and her immediate situation. Even my Lord Gray himself did not attempt to impose his imperious will on her; indeed, he had always spoiled her shockingly.

9

'What do you mean by reading that letter, girl?' David Gray demanded, jerkily. 'It is not for such eyes as yours. Is nothing private to me, even in my own chamber? Can I not leave my table for two minutes, but you must come prying, spying? I did but go to speak to the foresters . . .' He stopped. Not for him to explain to this chit of a girl. 'Put it down, child! Think you that all my affairs must be business of yours? I will have you know otherwise, 'fore God! I lock my door from such as you?'

He went on too long, of course – and knew it. Too much school-mastering, too much the petty tyrant as my lord's steward. At the clear and unwinking regard of those deep dark eyes, he cleared his throat loudly and rubbed his clean-shaven chin.

She ignored all that he had said – or perhaps not so much ignored as listened to it, considered it, and dismissed it as irrelevant.

'What does Uncle Patrick mean, Father, by the lady whose price was above a ruby? He calls her accursed. And the ready-forged sword of justice? I think that I understood some of his letter – but not that. Nor this, where he writes of craft replacing craft? What means that? And who is H.C.M. and H.H.? And all those others? "Both dear M.'s", of course, means Mother and myself. But these others? Tell me, if you please.'

There it was, the almost imperious demand, none the less infuriating for being quite unconscious, quite devoid of any undutiful intent, any impertinence, yet ridiculous, insufferable in a girl still in her teens. So might a born queen speak and look – not the bastard daughter of a bastard, however lofty the standing of three of her grandparents. Davy Gray's problem, self-assumed, for fifteen years. Or one of them.

The man stepped over to the table, and took the letter out of her hands. He was a stocky plain-faced youngish man – extraordinarily young-seeming to play the father to this burgeoning beauty. At thirty-two, indeed, he showed no single grey hair, no sign of thickening about the belly, no physical corroboration of the staid man of affairs, the schoolmaster, steward of a great estate, father of three, the man who had shortly rejected King Jamie's proffered accolade of knighthood but a year previously. Somewhat blunt-faced, heavy-browed, strong-jawed, grey-eyed, his hair worn short, and dressed in simple and well-worn homespun doublet and breeches and tall riding-boots, he looked perhaps a harder man than he was. Swordless despite his position of steward to the fifth Lord Gray, his father – and despite all the notable swording that was credited to him in days not so long past – he looked like a man who might be seeking the sober, the settled and the respectable rather before his time, and by no means always finding it.

'I shall tell you no such thing,' he said. 'On my soul, did you not hear me? I said that it was not for your eyes. It is naught to do with you.'

'It is from him. From my Uncle Patrick.'

'Aye.' For some reason his glance dropped before hers. 'Aye, more's the pity! But what he speaks is of no concern of yours, child. Nor . . .' David Gray sighed heavily, 'nor of mine either, indeed. Nor of mine!'

'Surely it is, Father? For I think that it concerns the King. 'Young J.' – that is King Jamie, is it not? Who else would he name our errant young friend J.? He is to be informed after these others. It is what he is to be informed that I do not understand.'

'God be good, Mary – I . . . I . . .!' Her father swallowed. 'Have done, girl, I tell you. Will you never heed what I say? You are too young. Fifteen years – a mere child . . .'

'At fifteen years you married my mother, did you not? Carrying me within her.' That was calmly, factually said.

David Gray drew a deep quivering breath, blinking grey eyes quickly, but found no words.

She went on, as calmly. 'I am not a child any more, Father. I am a woman now. You should know that.'

'I know that you are an upstart, saucy malapert, a hussy, a baggage! And that my letters are no concern of yours, d'you hear?'

'This letter greatly concerns my Uncle Patrick.' She paused on the name, and then repeated it carefully. 'My Uncle Patrick. Therefore it concerns me, does it not?'

David Gray opened his mouth to speak, and then closed it again. He turned away from her, and took a few paces across the bare wooden flooring to the window, to stare, not down into the cobbled courtyard of the great castle, but out over the wide, grassy, cattle-dotted levels of the Carse of Gowrie and the blue estuary of Tay beyond, gleaming in the brittle fitful sunlight of a February noon stolen from spring. South and south he gazed, as though he would look far beyond Scotland, beyond England even, to sunny France or Spain or wherever his damnable, disgraced and yet beloved half-brother presently spent his banishment. And however hard he frowned, his grey eyes were not hard, at all.

In three light running paces, Mary was at his side, her hand on his arm, her lovely face upturned to his wistfully, all winsome tenderness now. And in such mood no man whom she had yet encountered could resist her.

'Forgive me, Father,' she said softly. 'You are my true father, my only father. And always will be. You have my devotion always. You know it. But . . . I must know of him. I cannot help myself, you see. What concerns him, I must know. Do you not understand?'

'Aye.' Licking his lips, David Gray turned to her, and his arm slipped up around her slender shoulders. His voice shook a little. 'Aye, lass. He is . . . what I can never be. Well I know it. And you are so like him. So . . . so devilish like him, child. Sometimes I am frightened . . .'

'I know,' she whispered: 'I know it. But never be frightened, Father. Never – for me. There is no need, I think.'

He considered her, all the quality of her that made him feel like a plough-horse beside a Barbary, a bludgeon beside a rapier; that made her unassuming country wear of scarlet homespun waisted gown, aproned and embroidered underskirt and white linen sark or blouse, in fact as simple as his own attire, apear as apt and as strikingly delectable as any court confection. He sighed.

'Aye, Mary – you are a woman now, in truth. Folly to shut my eyes to it. Yet, all the more you need guidance, counsel, protection, my dear.'

She nodded her dark-curled head, accepting that. 'But not from Uncle Patrick, I think?'

He hesitated a little before answering her slowly. 'I would that I could be sure of that.'

She searched his face intently. 'Mother says that you

always have been less than fair to Uncle Patrick,' she observed. 'Do you think that is true?'

'Your mother knows him less well than I do, girl.'

'And yet . . . you love him, do you not?'

'Aye.' Sombrely he said it. 'Although it might be better – better for us all, I think – if I did not.'

'No.' She shook her head decidedly, rejecting that. 'No.' Then she smiled again, in her most winning fashion. 'You love me, and you say that you love *him*, Father. Yet you will not explain his letter. To me. When he says not to deny me and Mother his worship and devotion. And responsibility also, does he not say?'

David Gray ran a hand over brow and hair. 'Och, Mary, Mary – the letter is an ill one, a dangerous one. Better that you should know naught of it . . .'

'But I do know some of it. Much of it, I think. I know that it concerns King Jamie, and therefore that it must concern us all, all Scotland. And if young J. is indeed the King, then will not the accursed woman be the Queen of England? Elizabeth? And will not that make the other unfortunate lady, on whom the fates waged war, our own good Mary the Queen, whom Elizabeth murdered? If I know all this, is it not better that I should know the rest? And I know that it is dangerous, for does he not say to doubt it all at your peril?'

'That is not the danger that I meant,' the man said. 'But let it be.' He shook his head over her again. 'I' sooth, you are shrewd, child. Quick. Sharp as a needle. Your . . . your father's daughter, indeed!' He shrugged. 'I suppose, yes, having gleaned so much you may as well learn all. Mayhap it will teach you something . . . something about the Master of Gray. That you ought to know.' He spread out the letter. 'But . . . this is for your ears alone, mark you. You understand, Mary? No one else must know of it. Do not discuss it, even with your mother. She knows of the letter, but not all that it portends. She has ever misliked secrets. Nor would she understand much of it, besides. She frets. Some things it is better that she should not know.'

'*I* do not mislike secrets,' the girl said simply. 'And can keep them.'

He glanced at her sidelong, almost wonderingly. 'That I

13

believe. Else I would not tell you this.' He tapped the much-travelled paper, soiled by the tarry paws of seamen and heaven knew what furtive secret hands in France or Spain or Italy. The missive bore no address.

'Patrick – your uncle – has not changed in a year,' he said heavily. 'Nor ever will, I believe. Ever he must dabble in affairs of state. It might have been thought, to be condemned to death for treason and only to have escaped with his life by the breadth of a hair, that he might have been cured of such folly. But, no. A few brief months after his banishment for life – eight months, no more – and he is back at it. I suppose that to have ruled Scotland in all but name is too much for him to forget, to renounce . . . although he said that never did he wish to bear the rule. And that I think he meant, in truth. And yet . . . I do not know. I cannot understand him, what makes him what he is . . . '

Gently she brought him back to the letter. 'He says that the accursed lady will meet her deserts within three months, does he not? What is this of a ruby? A price above a ruby?'

'That is Elizabeth Tudor, yes. The ruby was one that he sought to buy her with. A great gem. Elizabeth had ever a passion for such things. It was Mary's of course – our own Queen's. Sent her by the Pope, years before. First he used it to discredit Arran, when he was Chancellor, and then he took it to Elizabeth. She accepted it . . . but she did not keep her side of the bargain.'

'He bargained it – this jewel – for Queen Mary's life?'

David Gray looked out of the window again. 'No. That is not what Patrick bargained for, I fear. Something . . . other! But that is an old story. He mentions it here only that I should know for whom he speaks. This letter – I know not where he writes from. The last was from Rome . . . '

'And you did not answer him.'

'No. I . . . it was better that I should not. Better for all – himself also, I think.'

'You mean that it is dangerous? To deal with one who is convicted of treason? If the letter should come into the wrong hands? The King's hands? That then you would be endangered?'

'No, it is not that . . . '

'But that is why Uncle Patrick writes as he does, is it not? In this strange concealed fashion. So that you shall not be implicated . . . ?'

'It is not for fear of implicating *me* that Patrick writes so! Indeed, he means that I *shall* be implicated – very much so. He would avoid evidence – written evidence he fears. He has tasted of its dangers, already! Written evidence can condemn, where nimble wits and a honeyed tongue would otherwise save. It is himself that he seeks to spare – not me!'

'But he is safe. In France. Banished . . .'

'Aye – so it might be thought. So Scotland thinks. But . . . does he not say that we may see him sooner than we think? Where he may be, even now, the good Lord knows! I know not where he writes from – notably, he does not say. The last letter was from Rome – but clearly he has been in Spain but recently. And what he has seen and heard in Spain convinces him that Queen Elizabeth's days are numbered.'

'Spain? Not France? Always it was France, was it not, Uncle Patrick dealt with. The Duke of Guise and the Cardinal of Lorraine? Our Queen Mary's cousins. I thought that it would be these, perhaps, whom he meant by the two most catholic . . . ?'

'No. The two most catholic are just what he says – H.C.M., that is His Most Catholic Majesty, the King of Spain; and H.H., that is His Holiness the Pope of Rome. It is of these he speaks. They have decided it, he says – decided that justice, as he calls it, will be done, and that Elizabeth of England will meet her deserts.'

'For killing our Queen?'

David Gray's heavy brows lowered in a band across his face. 'I would not swear, child, that such is what *he* means by justice – whatever Spain and Rome may mean. Would that it was. Rather, I think, it is because Elizabeth betrayed *him*, broke their wicked compact over Queen Mary, and denounced his part in that vile execution to Chancellor Maitland and the Council of Scotland. For that, I think, he will never forgive her. Elizabeth, I vow, made a dangerous enemy the day she wrote that letter betraying the Master of Gray.'

The girl drew a long breath. 'You do not sound . . . as though you loved him,' she said.

15

'You do not understand, Mary. Indeed, how could you? Himself I love. Patrick, my brother.' His lips tightened. 'My half-brother. The noble brother of my lord's bastard! I cannot help myself. We have been very close, always. Strangely, for we could scarce be more different. Himself I love, then. But what he is, and what he does, I hate! Hate and fear, do you hear me? Hate and fear.' The paper was trembling a little in those strong hands. It seemed as though almost with relief he came back to it, back to the letter. 'In Spain, then, Patrick saw sufficient to convince him that Elizabeth's days are numbered. It can only have been the ships, the great armament, that King Philip is long said to have been preparing. Armada is the word that they use for it – a great fleet of galleons, and great armies of men, to invade and subdue England. There has long been word of it, rumours – but Patrick must have seen it with his owns eyes, and have been satisfied that it is great enough, powerful enough, to serve its purpose. The downfall of Elizabeth's England. Beyond a peradventure, he says. For him to be sure, the armament must indeed be vast and very terrible. And nigh ready to sail, since he says within a three-month. Unless . . . '

'Invasion of England – before the summer!' Mary said, with slight difficulty. 'So soon. Yet a year too late!'

'Eh . . . ?'

'To save Mary the Queen.'

'Aye. That is the truth. One short year. Or, perhaps . . . I do not know . . . but perhaps there is a reason for that. It may be that Philip of Spain prefers to invade England with Mary safely dead rather than invade to save her life. In her testament she named him, not her son James, as heir to her two kingdoms of England and Scotland, you will mind. She did it, I think, more as a threat to make Elizabeth keep her alive, than as her true desire – for when we saw her at Wingfield Manor only a year before her death, she spoke most warmly of young Jamie – warmer than he deserved, 'fore God! Still, she died leaving Philip of Spain her heir, by this testament – and now he is prepared to claim his inheritance!'

'And Scotland? Surely that could never be? Not here . . . ?' The girl's great eyes widened. 'Is that what Uncle Patrick means when he says that . . . ? Here it is . . . He says "you will

16

agree that an overdose of good things is seldom a kindness. Moreover, we have our young friend J. to consider". He means, then, that Scotland must be saved. Saved from King Philip and his invasion. That is it?'

David Gray nodded. 'Something of the sort, he suggests. Although not all would say, I think, that it was for the *saving* of Scotland! He would have me inform the Early of Huntly of all this – that is "our blustering northern cousin H." of course. With the Earl of Erroll, the High Constable, and the Lord Seton, and others of the like kidney. In other words, the Catholic lords. These to brace themselves – to muster their forces, to arm. Then, and only then, when they are ready and assembled, to inform King Jamie.'

'Why that? Should not he be the first to be told?'

Her father smiled, but not mirthfully. 'We are dealing here with the Master of Gray, child – not some mere common mortal! The King then to write to Philip of Spain – or to send an ambassador, belike – offering a treaty of alliance, to aid in the invasion of England. On the condition, need I say, that Scotland is left free. Assuring him that a Scottish army is assembled and waiting. And, of course, to add that if Philip refuses to agree, he, James, will be compelled to inform Elizabeth of all – even to join forces with her. Which assuredly would much distress His Most Catholic Majesty.'

The girl swallowed. 'I . . . I see.'

'That is your Uncle Patrick! That is what the letter means. Scarcely apt intelligence for a chit of a girl?'

'Perhaps not.' She took the letter and gazed down at its curiously untidy yet vital, forceful handwriting. 'But I do not see, Father, why you say that it is no concern of yours, either? Is it not of the greatest importance?'

'He would have me esteem it so, I agree.'

'But is it not, indeed? For us all? For all Scotland?'

'I do not know.' David Gray moved away from the window, to pace up and down the little bare room. 'It could be – indeed, probably it is – but one more of his many conspiracies. A plot for the furtherance of his own affairs. Like so many.'

'But . . . the invasion of England! That is no private plot!'

'No. But what he would have transpire here in Scotland

might well be, girl. He would have this done *now* – this of Huntly and the rest. Philip of Spain's armament, this Armada, may not be so near to sailing as he says. There have been rumours of it for long. He could be using the threat of it for his own purposes. To stir up trouble again in Scotland. He knows that Huntly is a firebrand, ever ready to rouse the north . . . '

'Yet he writes this not to my lord of Huntly, but to you, Father.'

'Aye. Huntly, the great turkey-cock, would not make head nor tail of such a letter! Patrick would use me – use me as he has done before, times without number. I had thought that we had done with such. I *have* done with such, by God! I'll no' do it – I will not!' The man thumped clenched fist on his table as he passed it.

Thoughtfully, gravely, the girl looked at him. 'How can you say that?' she asked. 'He declares roundly that this is no mere conspiracy. Not to doubt him. The King, and the whole realm, must be endangered if the Spaniards invade England. None can question that, surely? Uncle Patrick has pointed a way of escape, has he not? For Scotland. How can you refuse your aid? If not for his sake, as he says, for the King's sake. For all our sakes.'

'I can – and do! You hear?' Almost he shouted at her – which was markedly unlike David Gray: 'I will be entangled in no more of Patrick's plots and deviltries. I swore it – and I will hold to it. I have seen too much hurt and evil, too much treachery and death, come of them. No – I will not do it.'

She shook her dark head slowly, and turned back to the paper in her hand once more. 'What is this about an office?' she enquired. 'An office to be set up on Castle-hill? Here, does he mean? This castle . . . ?'

'No. He means the Holy Office, so called. The Spanish Inquisition. Set up on the Castle-hill of Edinburgh. He would chill my blood . . . '

'The Inquisition!' Mary Gray stared at him now, wide-eyed, something of the terror of that dread name quivering in her voice. 'Here? In Scotland? No – oh, no! That could never be! Not . . . that!'

Her father did not answer her.

She came over to him almost at a run. 'Father! Father – if that could happen, the Inquisition here . . . then . . . then . . .' She faltered, gripping his arm. He had never seen her so moved. 'You would never stand by and see that happen? Anything would be better than that, surely? You – a true Protestant? You cannot stay your hand from what he would have you do – from what this letter says, if that could be the outcome? You cannot!'

'Mary – can you not understand, child?' he cried. 'Cannot you see? What Patrick here proposes could well *bring* that very evil about! Bring the devilish Inquisition to Scotland, to Edinburgh. You talk about saving Scotland – about Patrick saving Scotland, thus. Do you not perceive, lass, that this is in fact most like a conspiracy to overthrow the Reformed religion in Scotland? The Catholic lords are to muster and arm. Secretly. Not until they are assembled is the King to be told. Not even then the Chancellor and the Council – that is what he means by James's tutors and servitors. The Protestants around the King are not to know of it. Until too late. Think you that this Catholic army will do the young Protestant King's biding? He will become its prisoner. Then James is to make a secret alliance with Catholic Spain. Against Protestant England. Do you believe that the Kirk could ever agree to that? So the Kirk will have to be put down – by Catholic arms. What will remain, then, of Protestant Scotland? Would the Catholic lords keep out Philip's Inquisition? *Could* they? Do you not see what it means?'

She stood still, silent.

'It is not easy, straightforward,' he went on, sighing. 'Nothing about Patrick Gray is ever easy or straightforward.'

'Yet you cannot leave it thus, Father,' she said. 'You cannot just do nothing.'

'What can I do? Other than act as he demands? Which I will not do.'

'You could tell the King, could you not? Without telling the Catholic lords. He used to rely on Uncle Patrick's advice in matters of state. Is the plan itself not a good one? Apart from putting Scotland in the power of the Catholic lords. If it was the *Protestant* lords who armed and assembled instead? The King could still treat with Spain, with an army at his back. It is a sound policy, is it not? The only way to preserve the realm in this evil pass? Uncle Patrick has the cleverest head in Scotland – often you have said it. Use it then, for Scotland's weal, Father. But . . . use your own likewise. Let it be the Protestant lords who arm – but otherwise the same.'

It was the man's turn to stare. Almost his jaw dropped as he considered what was proposed – and who proposed it. Was this the infant that he had petted and played with? The child that they had brought up? What had they nurtured, Mariota and himself?

'You . . . you do no discredit to your sire, I think,' he said, a little unsteadily.

'It is best, is it not? That you should go to the King?'

'It is not, i' faith! I cannot go to the King, girl. His last words to me, yon day at Holyroodhouse, were that he wished never to see my face again. Nor Patrick's either. An ill and graceless breed, he named us . . .'

'The same day that he would have made you knight?'

'Aye. But that was before I had abused him. I spoke him hard that day – as no subject should bespeak his prince. No base-born subject in especial . . . like Davy Gray the Bastard! I threatened him sorely. The King. For Patrick's sake. He will never forget it, will James Stewart. I have cut myself off from the King.'

'If you told him that the safety of his realm depended on hearing you? The safety of his person – for it is said that he is heedful for himself? Surely he would see you.'

'You do not understand, Mary. Kings are not to be approached thus. I cannot see him, or speak with him, without he summons me . . .'

'But, Father – even I used to speak with the King. He said that I was a bonny lass, and that he liked me well. He thanked me for being kind to Vicky – to the Duke of Lennox.'

'That was different, lass. Then your Uncle Patrick was a power in the land. Acting Chancellor of Scotland, and Master of the King's Wardrobe. I was his secretary. We were part of the royal Court. Ever about the King. Now . . . ' He spread his hands. 'I cannot speak with James without he summons me. And that he will never do.'

'The King, it is said, is not one whose mind cannot be

changed . . . !' she began when her quiet voice was drowned.

There was a great clattering of hooves, clangour of armour, and the shouting of commands, from close outside. Man and girl moved back to the window. Through the arched doorway under the gatehouse streamed into the inner courtyard of Castle Huntly a troop of heavily-armed riders mounted on the rough garrons of the country, shaggy and short-legged but sturdy horses whose hooves struck sparks from the cobblestones of the enclosed square and echoed back and forth from the tall, frowning walls of great soaring keep and flanking-towers. Amongst them all, conspicuous because of the height of his handsome Flanders roan, rode a heavy florid man of middle years, dressed in richly embossed half-armour, black and gold, dark doublet and trunks, and long riding-boots. On his massive greying head was clapped a flat old-fashioned velvet bonnet instead of the more fashionable high hat and plume – the only man there not wearing a steel morion helmet.

Throwing himself down off his horse, this paunchy bull-like man started to shout as soon as his boots touched the cobbles – and at his bellowing, all other voices soever fell discreetly silent.

'Davy! Davy Gray – to me, man!' he roared. 'A pox on you – where are you? Where in hell are you skulking, i' God's name? Poring over dusty books and papers, I'll be bound . . . ' He glanced up at the round north-west flanking-tower, and perceived the figures at the window. 'There you are, damn you! Down with you, man. Would you ha' me stand waiting your pleasure like some carle frae the stables? Me – Gray! Did you no' hear my horn? Are you deaf, man – as well as heedless o' my affairs and well-being . . . ?'

'My lord sounds as though restored,' David Gray said to the girl, drily. 'His gout is improved, undoubtedly – and therefore he must needs burst a blood-vessel with his shouting!' But he raised a hand to the window in acknowledgment of the summons, and folding the letter, tucked it away carefully in his doublet, and turned to the stairway – but not in any urgent haste.

The fifth Lord Gray's voice neither awaited his arrival, nor lessened its volume. 'And where is my moppet? Where a pest's

21

Mary – my ain Mary? God's mercy – is this a house o' the dead, or what? Must Gray come to his ain, and naught but doos and jackdaws greet him? Mary!' he bawled. 'Mary Gray – haste you, lass. Would you hide frae me? Bairnie – where are you?' Although the noise of him had nowise diminished, the tone and tenor had altered significantly; almost there was a chuckling, wheedling note in the vociferation now, if that can be imagined, distinctly ridiculous in so notable a tyrant.

Smiling gently, the girl turned to follow her father down the narrow winding turnpike stair. And for all her curious calm and serenity of manner, she tripped lightly as might any child.

When she emerged, my lord was hectoring her father in front of all the fifty and more grinning men-at-arms. ' . . . trees down all along the Inchture road, dykes broken and beasts straying! But two nights gone, and I come back to this, Davy Gray! I make you steward o' half the Carse, the more fool me, and here's you roosting in your tower moping over papers . . . '

'Last night's storm was notably strong, my lord . . . '

'What of it, man? Must trees lie where they fall because o' a skelp o' wind? And my beasts stray, because you canna keep your nose out of books and parchments?'

'I have men clearing the trees and mending the dykes,' David declared, his voice flat, nor noticeably apologetic. 'I set them to the home parks first, believing that you would have it so.' His glance flickered over the ranks of armed retainers. 'If your lordship would travel with a wheen less of escort, more men there would be for clearing your trees!'

'Insolent, on my soul! *You* to speak me thus! You – a chance by-blow!'

'Exactly, sir. But *yours*! And with my uses – where secrets are to be kept!'

Father and son eyed each other directly, choleric yet shrewd pig-like eyes in that sagging, dissipated face, meeting level grey ones. This was an old battle, almost a formality indeed, something of a game to be played out.

'The godly business of the Kirk prospered at Perth, I hope, my lord?' the younger man went on, as evenly. 'Knowing its import, we scarce expected to see you home for a day or two yet. Or, should I say, a night or two?'

The other frowned, black as thunder, but before he could

speak, a trill of laughter came from the small tower doorway where Mary stood watching.

'Was the Lady Murray unkind, Granlord . . . or just unwell?' she called, dark eyes dancing. 'Or perchance did her husband come home oversoon from the Court?'

'God be good – Mary, you . . . you ill-tongued hussy! You shameless baggage!' my lord spluttered, but with the frown vanished from his heavy brows like snow before the sun. He went limping forward, all jingling spurs and clanking steel, arms wide, ridiculous. Into them the girl came, not running, indeed with a sort of diffident hesitancy of pace, so at variance with her dimpling, smiling assurance as to be laughable, and was enfolded, swept up off her feet, and chuckled and crooned over. 'Och, lassie, lassie!'

She gurgled something into his neck above the steel gorget.

'Lord – it's good to have a grip o' you! You're the bonniest sight these eyes have seen in a score years!' he told her, nuzzling his gross empurpled features in her hair.

Her laughter pealed out. 'Bonnier than the Lady Murray? Bonnier than the Provost's wife at Dundee? Or Mistress Moncur? I have not her great paps, Granlord!' And she kissed him full on the lips.

'Och, wheesht you, wheesht you, wench! The randy wicked tongue o' you!' her grandfather gasped. 'Damme, you're a handful! Aye, God – an armful is nearer it, eh? An armful getting, I swear!' And he squeezed her comprehensively.

She bit his ear, quite sharply, so that he yelped.

David Gray looked at his father and his daughter from under puckered, downdrawn brows. Always this was the way of it – always it had been. The child, conceived in shame, born in disgrace, fathered on himself, could do what she would with this bellowing bull of a man, one of the proudest, most arrogant and powerful lords of all the arrogant strutting nobles of poor Scotland, where none other could do anything. She alone, of all within his wide orbit, not only seemed to have no fear of him, no revulsion, but actually seemed to love him, taking outrageous liberties with him, as he with her. Sometimes he feared for her in this also – for David Gray cherished no illusions as to his potent sire's character and appetites, pillar of God's Reformed Kirk as he was. The great stot, drooling over her, pawing her . . . aye, and letting her call him Granlord, that silly childhood name she had given him. Why did she never act so with himself, Davy Gray – who would give his right hand for her, his life indeed, any day? Who had cherished her and brought her up, and loved her as that sodden, whoring wind-bag of a lord could never conceive? Himself, her father – at least, in all but blood – she seldom hugged and laughed with and rained kisses upon.

Abruptly, the stern, sober, soft-hearted Davy Gray swung on the watching leering ranks of my lord's unmannerly and uncouth men-at-arms, and waved a peremptory hand at them.

'Off with you! Away with you!' he commanded. 'Gawping idle gowks! There are trees to be cleared. Dykes to mend. Cattle to herd. And see you look to those beasts, your horses. That they are rubbed down and baited. No watering till they are cooled, d'you hear? The brutes are lathered wickedly. Ridden over hard, and for no need. Horseflesh is scant and dear . . .'

'Hark at him!' my lord hooted. 'The right duteous steward . . . now!'

'He looks to your affairs very well, Granlord,' Mary Gray said, gravely, shaking the older man's arm. 'Well do you know it, too. Better than ever did old Rob Powrie.'

'As well he might! Did I no' pour out my siller to put him through yon college at St. Andrew's? Him, and that . . . that graceless, prinking jackanapes, that simpering Popish coxcomb who . . .'

'Hush, my lord!' The girl's voice went cool, aloof, and she sought to withdraw herself from her grandfather's embrace. 'That is an ill way to speak of one who . . .'

'Who has brought shame on my head and hurt on my house, girl!'

'Who is your son and your heir. And could a coxcomb and a jackanapes have raised himself above all others to be the King's right hand in Scotland?'

'Eh . . . ?' Lord Gray looked at her askance. 'What way is this to talk to me, child? I . . . I . . .'

'Your Uncle Patrick was never highly regarded in this his own home, Mary,' another voice said, tightly, from behind them. 'Save . . . save perhaps by me! You know that.'

Unnoticed by the others, a woman had come across the courtyard to them from the main keep, a very lovely woman, and still young. Tall, auburn-haired, high-coloured, a satisfying, well-made, deep-bosomed creature, she had fine hazel eyes that were wide and eloquent and anxious. Those eyes, ever wary, questioning, prepared to be startled, like the eyes of a deer, told their own story, despite the determined resolution of an appealingly dimpled soft round chin. Even yet they could turn David Gray's heart over within him, in an access of protective affection, however hard he might seek to disguise the fact. Compared with the inherent calm and composure of her daughter, Mariota Gray was essentially the child, the uncertain one. Lovely as they both were, indeed, mother and daughter resembled each other in little or nothing.

'Woman – hold your tongue!' my lord barked. 'How should you ken aught o' the matter? Who are you to judge – save, belike, between your legs!' He snorted coarsely. 'And there, nae doubt, Patrick's regard is high, high!'

Flushing hotly, and biting a quivering lip, Mariota turned to her husband, instinctively, those gentle eyes quickly filmed with tears. David Gray spoke harshly, set-faced.

'My lord – I'd urge you to mind that you speak to my wife!'

'D'you think I forget it, man? Waesucks, yon's no' a thing any o' us could forget, I swear!'

'Then I'd have her spoken to with the respect that is her due. And mine. Or . . . '

'Aye, then . . . or? Or what?'

'Or you can seek a new steward, my lord.'

'Ho, ho! So that's it, by God? Hoity-toity, eh? I can, can I?'

'You can, yes. Nor find one so cheap, who will save your precious siller as I do. Nor write your letters to certain proscribed and banished lords!'

His father's swiftly indrawn breath all but choked him.

Both women turned to him, as quickly – Mary keen-eyed in speculation, her mother unhappy, alarmed.

'No, no, Davy!' Mariota cried. 'Not that. Pay no heed to it . . . '

'I heard him. Not for the first time. And paid heed. As I urge my lord to do now!'

Mary spoke. 'Granlord – you are tired. From your journey.

25

And hungry. I can hear your belly rumbling, I vow! Come you. Mother and I will have your table served before you have your harness off. Come.'

Lord Gray looked from her, past her mother, to his son, and meeting David's eye directly, swallowed audibly.

'Och, be no' so thin-skinned, Davy!' he said huskily. 'You're devilish touchy, man, for a . . . a . . . Houts, Davy – let it be, let it be.' The older man flung his arm around the girl's slender shoulders. 'Aye, lassie – you have the rights o' it. As usual. Come, then – and aid me off with this gear. Aye, and feed me some victuals. Thank the good Lord there's one with some wits in her head . . . !' And muttering, the Lord Gray stalked off limping towards the guarded doorway of the great keep, Mary seeking to match her pace at his side.

David Gray muttered also – more to himself than to his bonny agitated wife. 'Patrick! Patrick Gray!' he whispered. 'Still you can do it. Set us all by the ears. Every one of us. Wherever you are. Still you pull the strings, be it from France or Spain – and we dance! Damn you – are we never to be quit of you?'

But that last was breathed on a sigh.

It was evening before Mary Gray saw her father alone again, with my lord safely carried to his bed in a drunken stupor, and the girl on her way to her own little garret chamber high within the keep's dizzy battlements. On the corkscrew stone staircase they met.

'I know how we must gain the King's ear, Father,' she said, without preamble. 'With Uncle Patrick's tidings. I had thought that my lord would be able to speak with the King. He is great with the Kirk and the Protestant lords. But he is so bitter against Uncle Patrick . . . ' She took David's arm. 'You have not told him, I think? Of the letter?'

'I have not. Nor shall. But what of it, girl? It is no concern of yours.'

She ignored that. 'Moreover if Granlord has been writing letters to banished lords – that is what you said, is it not? To banished and proscribed lords? Or, since he writes but ill, you wrote them for him? That could be treasonable, could it not? So my lord may not stand over well with the King, after all.

26

Any more than do you, Father. So . . . '

'Lord!' the man gasped. 'What has come into you, child? All this of statecraft and affairs of the realm! Grown men's work, lords' work – not lassies'. Put it from you, Mary. Forget that you ever saw yon letter. Off to your bed, now . . .'

'Somebody must do something, Father,' she insisted. 'And I know what to do.'

Uncertainly he stared at her, by the smoky light of the dip that he carried, flickering in the draughty stairway and casting crazy shadows on the bare red stone walls.

'We must tell Vicky,' she said. 'And he will tell the King. Vicky Stuart, the Duke of Lennox.'

David Gray blinked rapidly, and moistened his lips. He did not speak.

'Is it not the best way, and the surest?' she went on. 'Vicky liked me well. And King Jamie likes Vicky. He is closer to the King than is anyone else, he says – even the Chancellor. And he sides with the Protestants – though he knows not the difference in one belief from another, I vow! And he was brought up a Catholic, was he not?' She smiled.

The man pinched his chin. 'All this may be true, girl. But . . . the Duke is ever at the King's side. To reach him will be as difficult, belike, as to come to the King himself. And he is young, little more than a laddie – young even for his years . . . '

'Is that not all the better, Father? He will do as I say.'

'As *you* say! You flatter yourself, child, do you not? Lennox likes you well enough, in a way, I dare say. You are bonny, and you played together as bairns, yes. Although, then I mind, you thought him dull . . . '

'He still is dull,' she agreed, frankly. 'But he is kind and honest.' Mary Gray's dark eyes gleamed amusedly. 'And he says that he would die for me!'

Her father gulped. 'Die! For you? Lennox? What . . . what nonsense is this, mercy on us?'

'It is not nonsense, Father. At least, he swore it on his heart and the cross of his sword!'

David Gray sought for words. 'I . . . I . . . you . . . Dear God – he must be clean daft! Duller even than we knew! But this would be but child's talk – when he was a laddie indeed?

Bairns playing together.'

'Not so. It was not long since. And does he not write it anew, in each letter?'

'Letter . . . ? Lennox? The Duke writes letters . . . ?'

'Indeed, yes. He is a better writer than a talker is Vicky! He writes very well.' She laughed. 'As do I, of course, likewise.'

The man shook his head, completely at a loss. 'You? How can this be? Letters! You . . . you are cozening me, child. How can you write to the Duke? 'Tis more bairns' make-believe . . . '

Almost pityingly she regarded him. 'It is the truth.'

'But . . . how could *you* send letters? Have you a messenger, a courier? You?'

'No. But Vicky has. Indeed, he uses the King's couriers, and so do I.'

'On my soul, Mary . . . you . . . ' Her father had difficulty with his respiration. 'You use the King's couriers? For your exchange of letters? You – Mary Gray – and young Ludovick of Lennox! Lord – this is beyond all belief!'

'Why should it be? It is very simple, Father. The King, or the Council, are ever sending couriers to the Master of Glamis, that is Lord Treasurer, at Aldbar. Or to the Sheriff of Forfar. Or to my Lord Ogilvie at Airlie. These must needs pass here. Vicky, who is on the Council likewise, gives the man a letter for me, also. He leaves it at the mill at Inchture. Cousin Tom there brings it to me. I leave mine at the mill for the courier to take up, on his way back. Could aught be more simple?'

The other's head wagged helplessly. 'I' faith, it is beyond me! Beyond all. Tom Affleck in it, too – and therefore his father. Whom I shall speak with, 'fore God!' David Gray's own mother had been Nance Affleck, the winsome daughter of the miller of Inchture. 'And does it . . . does it stop at writing letters, girl?' he got out.

'Oh, no. We meet. But only now and again. Not so oft as Vicky would have it, I assure you.'

'You . . . meet!' Easy simple words to make such a croaking over. 'He was here – Lennox was here – three months past, yes. On his way to my Lord Innermeath at Redcastle . . . '

'He was here last week,' the girl amended demurely. 'We

28

have an arrangement. The King is often at Falkland, hunting. Vicky can ride to Newburgh in little more than an hour, he says, from Falkland, cross the ferry to Erroll, and be here in another hour. He rides fast horses – the King's own. It takes him but little longer from his own castle of Methven, the other side of Saint John's town of Perth . . . '

'Damnation – will you be quiet, girl! I care not how long it takes him, how he comes hither to you! Do you know what this makes *you*, child? You – our daughter? Meeting secretly with the second man in the realm, the King's cousin? You, a common clerk's daughter – at least, in the eyes of men. A bastard's daughter. It makes you a . . . a . . . ' He stopped, regaining partial control of himself somehow – and it was seldom indeed that David Gray required to do that. 'You have not . . . ? He has not . . . ? Och, Mary lass – he hasna . . . ?'

Calmly, almost sadly, she met his urgent demanding gaze. 'He has not had me, no – if that is what you mean.'

'Thank God for that! But, the danger of it, the folly . . . '

'There is no danger, Father. He is gentle, simple almost. When we meet, *I* am master – not Vicky. Always it was so.'

His mouth opened, and then closed, as he considered her. She had David Gray silenced.

'So, you see – it will not be difficult. Whether the King is at Falkland or Stirling or even Edinburgh, I shall have a letter to Vicky in but a few days. We shall meet, and he shall bring me before the King. He will do as I ask, never fear. And so Uncle Patrick's warning shall not be lost. Nor the Protestant cause either. It is the best way, the only way – is it not?'

'God save us all . . . !' her father prayed.

'Yes. But we must do our own part also – so good Master Graham says, at the kirk. We cannot just leave Uncle Patrick's letter to God, can we?'

'Would that I knew, girl.'

'But we do know. You said yourself, did you not, that in Spain Uncle Patrick must have seen sufficient to be sure that Queen Elizabeth's days are numbered? Seen with his own eyes. Therefore Scotland is endangered also. And must act if this realm likewise is not to fall to the Spaniards. So that *we* must act. And quickly.'

'I vowed . . . ' he began, but wearily.

'Yes, Father – I know. But *I* did not. Is it not most fortunate?'

Chapter Two

THE four riders sat their fidgeting, steaming mounts within the cover of a thicket of scrub birch and holly, and waited. The cover was to shield them from view, not from the rain, for the shiny holly leaves sent down a cascade of heavy drops upon them with each gust of the chill wind. It was no better a day for hanging about in wet woodland than it was for hunting – but King Jamie cared nothing for the weather so long as there were deer to chase. In season and out of season – as now – day after day, storm or heat or snow, he must hunt the heavy woodland stags, in what had become little less than a mania with him – to the sorrow and discomfort of most of his Court, who would have preferred more seasonable and less active entertainment.

The riders looked out, across a broad grassy ride, to the reed-fringed border of Lindores Loch. Their stance was a strategic one, and had been as carefully chosen, at short notice, as the difficult circumstances would allow. All day they had been moving across trying and broken country, hill and bog and forest, seeking to keep in touch with the royal hunt, without being seen or scented thereby – no easy task, for James, with some reason, had a great fear of being ambushed or attacked on such occasions, by some coalition of his ambitious and arrogant nobles, and always sought to maintain a screen of armed guards in attendance. The watchers were now, wet and weary, on the skirts of rocky Dunbog Hill, in north Fife, fully seven miles from the King's palace of Falkland. The hunt had killed for the third time near Inchrye, and as the light was already beginning to fail, James would be satisfied. He did not like to be out in the dark, being much aware of the forces of darkness, human and otherwise. Almost certainly the royal

30

party would return to Falkland this way. The steep hillside and Lindores Loch would confine the cavalcade to this woodland track before them. So declared the groom, sent by the Duke of Lennox. The man had been ferrying back and forth between his master and the little party of three all day, to keep them informed and to have them in readiness and available when and wherever the energetic monarch should make his final kill. It had been a testing time for all – and not least, undoubtedly, for Ludovick, Duke of Lennox.

David Gray glanced at his daughter. Tired she must be, inevitably, but she at least showed no signs of it. Upright, alert within her enveloping cloak, she sat her stocky mud-spattered garron, even humming a little song to herself, eyes gleaming like the raindrops that glistened on the dark curls escaping from her coif, eager and watchful still despite all the similar waits and false alarms of the day. Almost, she might be enjoying herself. Which was more than her father was doing – or either of the Duke's men, by the look of them.

The situation did not fail to bring to David's mind that other occasion, six years earlier and distinctly similar to this, when he had waited, hidden likewise, for another of James's hunts, near Ruthven in Perthshire, waiting to effect a rescue of his youthful monarch from his cynical captors of the Raid of Ruthven. The Master of Gray had been behind that venture also – had indeed planned it all from far-away France. He himself had been merely the fool, the poor puppet, who carried it out, with thanks from none! Nor did he anticipate either gratitude or satisfaction from this day's work – save perhaps in the mind of this strange girl whom he called his daughter and whom he now wondered whether he knew at all. David Gray waited by Lindores Loch, not only against his inclinations but really against his better judgment.

'Vicky said that the men-at-arms will come first, as they ride back to Falkland,' Mary declared. 'We are to let them past, before coming out – else they might attack us and the King be alarmed. I hope that he and Vicky are not too close behind the soldiers. It may be difficult, a little . . . '

Her father nodded grimly. He had never seen this entire project as anything else but difficult. At their early morning secret rendezvous with the young Duke, he had impressed upon them the need for quite elaborate care and planning. James was as nervous as an unbroken colt, and sensed treason and violence in every unusual circumstance – as indeed he had reason to do. So many attempts had been made on his person, in his twenty-one years, as on his executed mother and assassinated father before him, that such wariness was only to be expected, and precautions highly necessary. The wonder was that he should persist with this incessant hunting, which provided opportunities for the very attacks that he dreaded.

'Let us hope that the Duke keeps his wits – and uses them,' David said. 'As well that he is less excitable than his royal cousin!' He turned to the other of the two attendants, Lennox's tranter or under-falconer. 'Your master is to have his hands bare, is he not, if all is well? As signal for you to ride out. If he is gloved, you are to remain in hiding?'

The grizzled servitor nodded. 'Aye. We dinna move if he is wearing his gloves.' These two men were known to the King, and dressed in the Duke's livery, bearing his colours of red and white. It was hoped that they would not alarm the apprehensive monarch as they issued suddenly from cover.

'I hope that we shall be able to see him clearly – and he us,' Mary said. 'That there is not a throng round the King, so that we cannot see ... '

'Och, never fear, lassie,' the tranter assured. 'My lord Duke kens fine what's needed. He decided it, did he no'?'

'It is not what the Duke does, nor yet the King, that so much concerns me,' David Gray observed. 'It is the men-at-arms, in front. And people about the King. If the guards hear you, and turn back. Or if the others rush out from behind, fearing an ambush ... ? I do not want the lass here embroiled in any clash or tulzie ... '

'Na, na, master – dinna fret, man. They all ken the Duke's colours. Ken us, too. Dand, here, has been riding back and fore to the Duke all day, has he no'? They'll no' be feart at him and me and a lassie, just. Eh, Dand?'

The short dark groom appeared to be otherwise preoccupied. 'Och, quiet you!' he jerked. 'I heard them, I think ... ' He was gazing away to the right, through the tracery of the dripping branches.

They all strained their ears.

Sure enough, the faint beat of hooves, and even the slight jingle of arms and accoutrements could just be distinguished above the sigh of the trees in the wind. Waiting was over, at last.

Riders appeared on the track to the right, northwards. They came at a jog-trot, two by two, for the track was not broad. Although dressed proudly enough in the red-and-gold of the royal livery, they looked jaded, weary, spume-flecked from the mouths of tired and hard-ridden horses. A score of them, perhaps, they rode loosely, slouched in their saddles, witness to the exhausting service of their restless and anxious master. None appeared to be examining the track before them with any great vigilance, much less scanning the flanking woodland.

In a few moments, they jingled past the hidden watchers without a glance in their direction.

The latter need not have worried about the King coming too close on the heels of his escort. There was a distinct interval before the next group of riders appeared – and then it was three huntsmen, leading each a garron on which was tied the carcass of a stag, their burdens jouncing about with the uncomfortable trotting pace.

'The kill coming *before* the King!' David exclaimed. 'Here is a strange sight! I hope that he comes. That he has not delayed. Or gone some other way, perhaps.'

The tranter pointed. 'Yonder's the reason, master. See yon last beast? The head o' him! Fourteen points if he has a one, I warrant! A notable kill. His Grace will be right pleased. He'll no' be able to keep his eyes off yon stag, will Jamie. Aye – there he is now. I've seen him do the like before, mind. He'll be proud as Auld Hornie! Aye – he'll be in good fettle this day, will His Grace.'

'Good!' Mary commented. 'See – Vicky rides beside him. And his hands are bare.'

Two horsemen came trotting no great distance behind the third and most heavily-laden garron, with, at their backs, the beginning of a lengthy and motley cavalcade emerging into view round a bend of the woodland track. They made a markedly different impression from that of the previous riders, this pair – or indeed from those who followed them. They looked very young, for one thing, little more than boys, beard-

33

less, slight, and with nothing jaded about their appearance. Richly dressed, though less than tidy, and superbly mounted on identical lathered black Barbary horses, they rode side by side, with nothing of the aspect of weariness that afflicted the men-at-arms in front or the generality of the straggling if colourful company behind, even though they were inevitably travel-stained, mud-spattered, with clothing disarranged, like all the others. Yet there was but little of similarity about themselves – indeed they contrasted with each other in most respects. Where one was trim and and slimly upright, sitting his mount almost as though part of it, the other sprawled loosely, in an ungainly, slouching posture that was as unusual as it was undignified. Neither youth was handsome, nor even conventionally good-looking; but the upright one was at least pleasantly plain, whereas the other's features were almost grotesquely unprepossessing, lop-sided and ill-favoured generally, only the great expressive, almost woman-like eyes saving the effect from being positively repellent. James, by the grace of God, King, was singularly ill-endowed with most other graces.

His companion, while paying respectful attention to the other's seemingly excited talk, was looking about him keenly, watchful. His glance kept coming back to the projecting clump of evergreens and birches ahead.

As the huntsmen and the laden ponies swayed and ambled past, the grizzled falconer raised his hand. The groom nodded. Together they urged their horses forward. Between them, Mary Gray was only half a length behind. As she went, her father muttered a brief God-be-with-you. He himself remained where he was.

James was not so deep in chatter as to fail to notice the trio the moment that they emerged into view. He jerked his spirited black in a hasty dancing half-circle, as quick as thought, sawing at the reins, his words dying away in immediate alarm. 'Vicky! Vicky!' he got out, gasping.

Lennox was almost as prompt in his reactions. 'My own lads it is, Sire,' he called loudly, reassuringly. 'Never fear, Cousin. It is but Patey and Dand, see you. And they have found a lady for us, by the Mass!' Ludovick Stuart seldom remembered to adhere to only Reformed oaths.

'Eh . . . ? Oh, aye. Aye. So it is. Patey, aye – Patey and yon Dand. A . . . a p'plague on them – jumping out on me, like yon!' the King gabbled, slobbering from one corner of a slack mouth. He had been born with a tongue just too large for his mouth, and had the greatest difficulty in controlling it, especially when perturbed. He was peering; James was not actually short-sighted – indeed he saw a deal more than many either desired him to see or knew that he saw – but he was apt to peer nevertheless. 'It's no' a lady, Vicky – it's just a lassie,' he declared. 'A lassie, aye – wi' your Patey and Dand.' That came out on a spluttering sigh of relief. Majesty drew up his thin, skimped and twisted body in the saddle. 'What . . . what is the meaning o' this, eh? They're no' to do it. I'll no' have it, I tell you. I . . . we'll no' abide it. Jumping out in our royal path like, like coneys! Who is she, man?' That last was quick.

'A friend of mine, Sire – and of yours. An old friend of yours,' the Duke assured, waving Mary forward. 'I crave your permission to present . . .'

'I ken her fine,' the King interrupted. 'She's no friend o' mine. She's the lassie o' yon ill man Gray!' He sniggered. 'I didna say his daughter, mind – just his lassie! No friends o' mine, any o' that breed o' Gray.'

'You are wrong, Sire.' Clearly, unflurried, the girl's young voice came to them, as she rode up, her attendants having dropped back discreetly. 'It is only because I *am* your Grace's friend, your true friend, that I am here.'

'Na, na. I ken the sort o' you – fine I do. Ill plotters. Treasonable schemers. *Both* your fathers!'

'Sire – what she says is true,' Lennox asserted urgently. 'It is to do your good service that she is here. I would not have countenanced it, else.'

'Aye – so *you've* countenanced it! This is your work, Vicky? I'm no' pleased . . . we are much displeased wi' you, my lord Duke. We are so. We had thought better o' you . . .'

'Do not blame Vicky, Highness. Do not blame the Duke,' Mary pleaded. 'I greatly besought his help. For your Grace's weal. For the weal of your realm. It is very important . . .'

'Does this young woman annoy your Grace? Shall I have her removed?' a deeper voice intervened. Behind them the

35

long cavalcade was in process of coming up and halting, not so close as to seem to throng the King but not so far off that the front ranks should miss anything that was to be seen or heard. The speaker, a big, red-faced, youngish man, too elaborately dressed for hunting, searched the girl's lovely elfin features boldly, calculatingly. 'You may safely leave her to me, Sire . . . '

'Not so, my lord of Mar!' Lennox said, his open freckled face flushing. 'The lady is a friend of mine. She has private business with His Highness.'

'That is for His Highness to say, sir.' The Earl of Mar looked slightingly at the younger man. Ludovick Stuart was just sixteen, and by no means old for his years, a snub-nosed, blunt-featured youth, not nearly so sure of himself as he would like to have been, and an unlikely son of his late brilliant and talented father, the former Esmé, Seigneur D'Aubigny and first Duke, Chancellor of Scotland. Mar, nearly ten years his senior, did not attempt to hide his disrespect.

James plucked his loose lower lip, and darted covert shrewd glances from one to the other. 'Oooh, aye. I'ph'mmm. Just so,' he said, non-committally. At twenty-one he was already an expert at playing his nobles off one against another, at waiting upon events, at temporising so that others should seem to make decisions for him – for which they could be held responsible afterwards, should the need arise. His survival, indeed, had depended on just such abilities. With the ineffable Master of Gray out of the country, Queen Elizabeth of England's astute and well-informed advisers, Burleigh and Walsingham, believed this extraordinary, oafish and tremulous young man, so often considered to be little more than a half-wit, to possess in fact the sharpest wits in his kingdom.

Mary Gray spoke up again. 'His Grace's safety is in no danger from such as me, I think, my lord,' she said. 'Could a girl drag her King to Ruthven Castle – even if she would?'

King James's suddenly indrawn breath was quite audible – as indeed might have been Mar's own. She took a risk in naming Ruthven Castle in such company and in such a place. But a calculated risk. It had been when out hunting, as now, from Falkland Palace six years before, that the King had been attacked, forcibly abducted to Ruthven and there held prisoner by a group of power-hungry Protestant lords. And John, Earl of Mar, had been one of those lords. The Ruthven Raid was not a thing that had been mentioned at Court for quite some time, James preferring not to be reminded of those days of humiliation – and others equally wishing them forgotten.

'M'mmm. Ah . . . umm.' The King peered at her from under down-drawn brows, gnawing his lip. His head was apt to loll at curious angles, seeming to be too big for his ill-made body, too heavy for the frail neck that had to support it. Now it drooped forward, and served His Majesty fairly well to hide those great tell-tale eyes of his. 'Ruthven, eh? Aye . . . Ruthven. Yon was an ill place. Aye.' He swung round in his saddle abruptly. 'Eh, Johnnie?'

'Er . . . yes, Your Highness. Indeed it was. Certainly – most certainly . . . ' The red-faced earl was assuredly redder.

'Aye. I mind it so – mind it well.'

'It was my father who gained Your Grace's freedom from that toil, was it not?' the girl went on, gently pressing her advantage. 'He was none so ill a friend then. And would be again . . . from another danger.'

'Eh? Danger?' The King's voice squeaked. 'What danger? Fiend seize me – tell me, lassie! What danger?' That word could ever be guaranted to arouse James Stewart.

'I would prefer to tell Your Grace in private.'

'Private. Aye, private. My lord of Mar – leave us. Leave us.' James waved a suddenly imperative hand.

Mar cast a narrow-eyed vicious look at Mary, curled his lip at Lennox, and bowing stiffly to the King, swung his horse's head around savagely and trotted back to the waiting throng.

'Ride on a little, Cousin,' Lennox advised.

'Now, girl – this danger. Speak me plain,' the King commanded.

'Yes. It is danger for your person, your throne, for your whole realm,' she told him earnestly. 'From Spain.'

'Spain, you say? Tcha, lassie – what nonsense is this?'

'No nonsense, Sire. It is the King of Spain's invasion. His Armada . . . '

'That for the King of Spain's Armada!' James snapped long, strangely delicate fingers. 'A bogeyman he is, no more! Yon Philip has talked ower long o' his Armada. Forby, his

37

invasion is no' for me.' He leered. 'It is for my good sister and cousin, Elizabeth – God preserve her!'

'Yes, Sire. Elizabeth first. But who thereafter? When King Philip has England? Mary the Queen, in yon testament, left him heir to Scotland likewise, did she not?'

James all but choked. 'That . . . that . . . God's curse upon it! Foul fall you – it's no' true! It's lies – all lies. A forgery it was, I tell you! A forgery.' Gabbling, he banged his clenched fist on the pommel of his saddle. 'Never say yon thing in my hearing – d'you hear me? I'll no' have it! She . . . my mother . . . she never wrote it, I swear. A plot, it was – a plot o' yon glowing fiend out o' hell Walsingham, Elizabeth's jackal! I ken it – fine I ken it!' The last of that was scarcely coherent or intelligible, as the King lost control of his tongue, and the saliva flowed down unchecked in a bubbling stream.

Wide-eyed, startled by this passionate outburst, even sickened a little by what she saw, Mary instinctively drew back in her saddle, glancing quickly at Lennox. That young man stared distinctly owlishly at his cousin, and produced neither mediation nor guidance.

The girl, small chin firming, did not further flinch. 'That may be true, Sire – but King Philip holds otherwise. We have word, sure word, that he intends to have Scotland as well as England.'

'Then the Devil burn him! Roast and seethe him everlastingly! Precious soul o' God, I . . . I . . . ' With an obvious effort James controlled himself, if not his twitching mouth and flooding spittle. 'Folly!' he got out. 'This is folly! D'you hear, girl? All folly. For Philip willna win England – much less Scotland.' He rounded on Lennox. 'You, Vicky – you ken it's folly! He shouts loud, does yon Philip – but he'll never reach London. Na, na – he's been shouting ower long, the man. His Armada's all but boggarts and belly-wind! For years he's been threatening it . . . '

'A great fleet of ships, Sire, takes long to build, does it not?' Lennox pointed out.

'Tcha! These ships are but spectres, I warrant. And didna the man Drake burn a wheen o' them no' that long past . . . ?'

'Drake could not burn spectres,' his cousin pointed out reasonably.

'Houts, man! Forby, doesna Elizabeth build ships, too? She is a hard woman yon – but she kens how to hold her ain. Soul o' God, she does! She builds fine ships, too – bonny ships . . .'

'Will they be ready in three months, Your Grace?'

'Eh . . . ?' James goggled, as much at the calm factual way that the girl asked it, as at the question itself. 'Three . . . three months?'

'Yes. For that is when they will be needed. So says my Uncle Patrick. The Master of Gray.'

'A-a-ah!' The King's breath came out part-sigh, part-snort. 'So that's it! Yon limb o' Satan! Yon apostate knave! Yon . . . yon arch-traitor!' His eyes darted and rolled with seemingly enhanced urgency, as though their owner looked to see the Master of Gray materialise there and then from behind some tree, from the very ground at his feet. 'So he is in it, eh? Where? Where is he? Here's a plot, then – a black plot, if yon one's in it. You'll no tell me otherwise . . .' The royal gabble faltered and died in a harsh croak, as James abruptly raised a padded arm, and jabbed a pointing, trembling finger. 'Who's yon?' he demanded, out of his incoherences. 'Guidsakes – who's yon? There's a man in there – a black man in yon bushes. Watching me! Hiding! It's . . . it's a plot. Treason! God be good – treason, I say!'

He was pointing straight at David Gray in the thicket, as his voice rose towards panic. His questing glance was proved none so short-sighted: their move forwards, away from the throng of courtiers, had in fact brought the trio into a position that partly invalidated the cover of that thicket.

'No treason,' Mary said quickly, but quietly still. 'That is but my father. Davy Gray, whom you know well.'

'Davy Gray! Davy Gray! A rogue, then! A base-born limmer! A knave . . . watching me . . . !'

'Not so, Sire. But the same man who saved you from Ruthven!'

'He means no ill, Cousin,' Lennox put in. 'He but brought his daughter. That she might warn you of all this . . .'

'What does he hide for, then? Yonder. Peeking out at me? Spying on me?'

'He but waits for Mary, here. You have forbidden him your

royal presence, he says. So he could not come before you himself . . . '

'Have him out, then. Here wi' him. I'll no' be spied on, I tell you . . . '

At the Duke's wave, David Gray rode out from his bushes, slowly, reluctantly, set-faced. Doffing his humble blue bonnet, he came up to them, inclined his bare head stiffly to his monarch, and so sat. But not humbly. That was Lord Gray's constant complaint against this by-blow of his; he was never suitably humble, in any circumstance. Sometimes indeed he seemed to have more unseemly pride than even the nobly-born Grays, soberly stern as he was. He did not speak, now.

James seemed to find it difficult to look at him directly. 'Well, man – well?' he said impatiently. 'What's the meaning o' it? Hiding in there like a tod in a cairn?'

'Twelve months back, Your Grace – less – you said that you never wished to set eyes on me again.' David answered evenly. 'I would not seek to oppose your wishes – in that, or in any other matter.'

'Haughty-paughty yet, man! Aye, you were right ill-mouthed yon time – rude and unbecoming in a subject,' the King declared, plucking at lip and chin. 'You were aye a hard uncourtly man, Davy Gray – dour and frowning.'

'No doubt, Sire. But at least I was honest in your service. More than others who were . . . more courtly. And you used to trust me.'

'More fool me, maybe! When it came to the bit, Davy Gray – who did you serve? Your king or yon traitorous knave, Patrick Gray?'

'It was for my brother's life, Highness. In the end, a man must do his all to save his brother.' He paused briefly. 'Or . . . his mother! Must he not?' Directly his level grey eyes sought to meet and hold the other's liquid flickering gaze.

James however looked away, anywhere but at his questioner, his sallow features flushed. 'You . . . you presume, by God! Greatly you presume!' he stammered. 'As you did yon time. I could have had your head for yon, man. You threatened your king. Yon is . . . is *lèse-majestié*, I tell you. Aye, and it was misprision o' treason too, man!'

40

David swallowed. 'No doubt, Sire. Perhaps I misjudged my duty.' He managed to make his voice no less stiff than heretofore. 'Others have done that likewise – in the matter of Your Grace's royal mother in especial! But I am seeking to redress it now. Redeem my loyal duty. As is the Master of Gray . . .'

'Yes, yes – what o' this? Come to your point, man.' Hastily, the King interrupted him. 'What is this folly? The lassie prating o' His Majesty o' Spain and his ships. Some talk of three months . . . ?'

'That is the time that my brother says, Your Grace. I have just received a letter. From Spain, I take it. He says that within a three-month England will indeed be invaded. He says that with his own eyes he has seen King Philip's preparations, now all but ready, that they are enough. Beyond a peradventure, he says. Invincible, he calls this Armada. And all is in train. Within three months he assures, Elizabeth will be under attack.'

'Houts, man! We have heard that sort o' talk before. In plenty.'

'Not from the Master of Gray, Sire. Say what you will of him – did you ever know Patrick to make a mistake anent matters of fact? Was his information ever wrong – whatever his policies?'

James explored his nostrils with nervous fingers. 'Maybe no', maybe no'. You say he has been in Spain himsel', the ill limmer?'

'Yes. He has seen it all with his own eyes, he says. Satisfied himself. Spoken with the King of Spain, indeed, it seems . . .'

'Treasons, no doubt, then – treasons, for a surety!'

'At least he would have me warn Your Majesty.'

'Aye – but why, man? Why?' Shrewdly the King peered. 'He doesna love me, does Patrick Gray! He loves nane but himsel', I swear. If he's that close with Philip? And he's a Papist, as all men ken. And banished my realm for his treason. Eh? Why warn me?'

David hesitated, moistening his lips. 'I do not search his reasons, Sire – only the facts. That this invasion endangers Scotland as well as England.'

Mary Gray spoke. 'Is that not your answer, Your Grace? That he can still love *Scotland*?' she asked simply.

'Eh . . . ?' James frowned, wriggling in his saddle. '*I* am Scotland,' he said.

No one spoke.

Into the pause the beat of hooves sounded, as the escort of men-at-arms belatedly came pounding back along the track, to discover what had happened to their royal charge. James waved them away again, peremptorily. At the other side, the clustered seething company of his lords and ladies and courtiers kept up an unceasing hum of talk and conjecture as they gazed inquisitively, suspiciously, resentfully, at the little group beside the monarch. The Earl of Mar in especial looked and sounded angry, not minding who perceived it apparently. Undoubtedly he had not forgotten Davy Gray and his part in the rescue of Ruthven.

James grimaced at the colourful noisy throng and turned his puffed and padded shoulder on them. 'Forby,' he said, returning, with one of his lightning changes, to his former querulous, weasel-like probing. 'Why did he no' write these tidings to me, mysel', man? Tell me that. He's aye writing me letters, is Maister Patrick.'

David stared, at a loss. 'He is . . . ? Patrick? He writes to *you*? To the King? Still, Sire . . . ?' Incredulity was evident in every word of him.

'Aye, he does.'

'But what . . . ?' He bit his lip, pausing. A subject could scarcely demand of his King what even his half-brother might write to the monarch – though the brother had been condemned to death by the same monarch less than a year before, and only had his sentence reduced to banishment for life by a hair's-breadth, through certain unseemly pressure on the part of the present questioner. David wagged his head helplessly. 'Patrick . . . is a law unto himself, Your Highness,' he said.

'Aye. The last letter was from Rome. Wi' a message from the Pope himsel'. Ooh, aye – your Patrick rides a high horse, for a felon! Vaunty as ever! He sends me advices, whispers, intelligences, from a' the Courts o' Europe. Aye – and in return would have Dunfermline back! Guidsakes – he has the insolence, the shameless audacity, to demand the revenues o' Dunfermline Abbey be returned to him! For his decent upkeep and reasonable dignity, as he names it! God in Heaven – was there ever sic a man?'

Involuntarily, David Gray exchanged glances with his daughter – though whether she recognised the enormity, as well as the vital significance of this revelation, he could not know. The Commendatorship of the Abbey of Dunfermline, once the richest church lands in all Scotland, the prize plum for all the hungry Scots lords after the Reformation, had eventually and most skilfully been acquired by Patrick, Master of Gray at the downfall of Arran the Chancellor. At his own downfall, in turn, they had been the main price that had had to be paid for the necessary intervention of the powerful Earl of Huntly on his behalf, David acting as go-between. Huntly was now Commendator of Dunfermline, and held its rich revenues. That Patrick should be working to get them back, though a forfeited exile, and so soon, not only indicated an extraordinary impertinence and double-dealing, but showed that he was seeking to conduct a campaign against Huntly, his own relative, with the King. Yet, this letter that had brought them here to the Wood of Lindores, had as its ostensible purpose the saving of Scotland by means of Huntly and his Catholic colleagues. Or at least the implication of Huntly in a Catholic rising, to control the King, dominate the land, and engineer a strategic alliance with the Catholic King of Spain. Could it be . . . could it be, after all, only a conspiracy? A deep-laid and subtle device to discredit and bring down Huntly, and so win back the riches of Dunfermline? Good God, it was possible – so possible, with Patrick! David Gray, frowning blacker than he knew, sought an answer, racking his wits. He needed time – time to think this thing out, to winnow down through the dust and chaff to the secret inner core of his brother's intention. Heaven save him – he had to think . . . !

His daughter gave him a moment or two, at least. 'If Uncle Patrick wrote to you from Rome, Sire,' she said, 'then that would be before he went to Spain. Before he saw the Spanish ships. Therefore he could not tell you of it.'

'Houts, lassie – why write to *you* to warn me, then? Why no' send the letter to me, the King? There's an ill stink in this somewhere, I swear. I smell it . . .'

The girl looked from her father to Lennox, and received no help from either. 'Would your Grace have believed it?' she asked.

'A pox! If I believe not him, why should I believe you, with his tale, woman?'

'Because the Master of Gray knows that you will esteem my father honest. Whatever he said to you yon time. All men know David Gray as honest, do they not?'

So artlessly, apparently innocently, entirely naturally and yet authoritatively did she come out with that, that she left her hearers, somehow, with no option but to accept it. They stared at her – her father longest.

'So it is true,' she added, with a sort of finality. 'And there is little time. But three months.'

'Aye – three months. This three months . . . ?' Majesty nibbled his fingernail. 'Little time – if it is true. What can I do eh? What can I do in three months?'

David found his voice. Whatever his brother's real intentions, they must go through with this now. The substitution of a Protestant instead of a Catholic muster at arms would prevent any involvement of Huntly anyway – and so wreck Patrick's plot, if that indeed was his aim. 'The Master of Gray, Sire, has his suggestions to make,' he said. 'For Your Grace. Have I your permission to put them?'

'Suggestions, eh? From *him*? Aye, man – out wi' them. Waesucks – what does the rogue suggest?'

David cleared his throat. 'The project is simple – and, I think, the wise course in the circumstances, Sire. Possibly the only course that could save your realm in the event of a successful invasion of England. It is that you call upon the lords to muster their forces, the Protestant lords of course. Within the month. The Spanish ambassador will quickly acquaint his master of the fact. Then you send a message or an envoy to King Philip, suggesting a secret treaty of alliance against England. On the condition that Scotland is left free and unassailed. Offer a Scottish expedition over the Border at the same time as his Armada sails, to weaken Elizabeth's arms. And, if Philip should reject this – then the word that Your Grace would be forced to inform Elizabeth of all. And to send your assembled forces to join her own . . . in the

44

defence of the Protestant religion!'

'Good God in Heaven!' Lennox exclaimed.

King James seemed considerably less startled. 'A-a-aye!' he breathed out. 'So that's it! Guidsakes – it sounds like Patrick Gray, to be sure! Aye, i'ph'mmm. Here's . . . here's notable food for thought. 'Deed, aye.' Keenly he peered at David. 'But the Master's a Papist, we a' ken. Here's unlikely Popery, is it no'?'

The other looked away, in his turn. 'My brother, I think, has never taken matters of religion with . . . with quite the seriousness that they deserve,' he said.

James actually giggled. 'Aye.' He nodded the large top-heavy head. 'I can believe that.' He glanced over towards the restive throng of his followers in the hunt, growing the more impatient as the rain grew heavier. 'We'll have to think on this. Think closely. It's no' that simple, mind. The lords . . . they'll likely no' be that eager to muster their strength. It's costly, you ken – costly. No' without I tell them what's to-ward wi' Spain. And then yon woman . . . then my good sister Elizabeth would hear o' it in a day or two. She's right well served wi' her spies, is Elizabeth.' The great unsteady, luminous eyes narrowed. 'A pox – I canna ken which o' a' these pretty lords there will be writing to her frae my ain house o' Falkland this night!' And he gestured towards the overdressed company. 'Or how many! For she pays them better than she pays me, the auld . . . ' He swallowed, adam's-apple bobbing. 'How am I to get the lords to muster, without I tell them this o' Spain – and have Elizabeth champing at my door?' The King of Scots suffered under the major handi-cap of having no sort of standing army of his own, other than the royal guards, so that he must depend for any real military force upon the feudal levies of his haughty lords.

It was Mary Gray who answered him promptly, simply. 'Tell them that you fear a *Catholic* rising, your Grace. In favour of the King of Spain's plans.'

Her father caught his breath. Here was thin ice for even light feet.

'Aye. Uh-huh. Well, now . . . ' James paused. 'But . . . would they believe it?'

'They would, would they not, if the Catholic lords did

45

indeed likewise muster? If your Grace was to write to my lord of Huntly and the other, privily, that they muster quietly. In case . . . in case perhaps of a Protestant rising to aid Protestant England against Spain.'

All three of her hearers made strange noises. The Duke of Lennox's plain and homely face was a study as he stared at the girl. King James's high-pitched laughter burst out in a whinny. David Gray chokingly protested.

'Mary – be quiet, child!' he exclaimed. 'What fool's chatter is this? Have you taken leave of your wits . . . ?'

'Na, na, Davy!' the King chuckled. 'Leave her be. It's nane so foolish, on my oath! Sakes, it's easy seen whose daughter this is! I can see profit in this – aye, I can.'

'And dangers too, Your Grace. Dangers of civil war. With your realm an armed camp. Both sides facing each other, sword in hand.'

'Och man, if it came to that, some small blood-letting, a few lords the less, might no' be just a disaster for my realm, you ken!' The monarch licked his lips. 'But – och, that needna be. I could keep them apart. Huntly and the Catholics are mainly in the north. I could have the Protestants assemble in the south – along the Border.' James smote his wet knee: 'Aye – along the Border! And how would our good cousin and sister o' England look on that? Wi' Spain threatening? Guid lack – I might even win Berwick back! And never a shot fired!'

'Your Grace will do as you think best. But I would advise that you muster only the Protestant lords,' David said heavily. 'Lest you light a bonfire that you canna douse!'

'Aye, well. I'ph'mmm. We'll see . . . '

'Cousin, the lords would rise – the Protestant lords – fast enough, I vow, if it was to make a sally to avenge the Queen your mother's execution. Over the Border.' Young Lennox made his first contribution. 'Have I not been asking for such a thing this six-month past? *Ma foi* – I myself will raise and arm five score brave lads for such a venture! Marry that to this matter of the Spaniards, and do you not shoot two fowl with one arrow?'

'M'mmm. Well, now . . . '

'Why, yes,' Mary nodded. 'Then, with your army on the

Border, Sire, are you not well placed? No need, surely, to draw sword at all – to shed blood. If the King of Spain will treat with you, all is well and Scotland is safe. And you will have Berwick again, no doubt. He will know that you are assembled ready, and could march south to Queen Elizabeth's aid. So he will indeed treat, I think.' She paused for a moment. 'And so, I think, will Queen Elizabeth.'

'God's Body – you are right, girl! So she would, I swear.'

'Yes. But . . . ' Mary looked, with touching diffidence, at her father, and smiled, at her most winsomely appealing. 'I am only a lassie, I know, and understand little of affairs of state. But . . . would it not be wise to have my lord of Huntly and some of his Catholic forces with you, Sire – lest while you are away over the Border, maybe, with the Protestants, the Catholic lords should indeed arise and seize Scotland?'

The three men took some seconds to assimilate that. James found words first – or rather, he found a guffaw which rose and cracked into a less manly tee-heeing.

'Save my soul – here's a right Daniel! A bit female Daniel! Lassie – I should have you at my Court. I should so . . . !'

'No, Sire – you should not!' Harshly, almost in a bark, that came from David Gray. 'My daughter's place is in my house – not in any Court. I have seen enough of Courts! She is young – a mere child. However forward, malapert! She is but fifteen years . . . '

'Och, she's no' that young, man. At fifteen was I no' ruling Scotland? And without a Regent. And . . . and you could come wi' her, Davy. I'd owerlook yon time. I'd . . . we would exercise our royal clemency, maybe, and admit you back to our Court and presence. Aye . . . '

'No, Sire. I thank you – but no. I am a simple man. I do very well as a schoolmaster and my lord's steward. I know my place. And Mary's. *Her* place is in my house, with her mother.'

'But Master Gray,' Lennox exclaimed. 'Here is a notable opportunity . . . '

'For whom, sir?'

'For her. For Mary, *Mon Dieu* . . . '

Mary Gray silenced the Duke with a touch of her finger on his wrist. She looked at the King, however. 'Your Grace is indeed kind. But my father is right, I am sure . . . '

'Of course I am right, girl! God grant me patience! Your Grace – have I your permission to withdraw? We have done what we came to do – acquainted you with my brother's tidings and advice. The matter is no further concern of ours.'

'Aye, Master Davy – you may go. I . . . we are grateful. Grateful, aye. For your tidings. We shall consider it well. Closely. And take due action.'

'The Chancellor . . . ' Mary whispered to her father, but loud enough for the other to hear.

'Eh . . . ? Ah, yes – the Chancellor.' David frowned. 'Sire – my brother also has it that it would be best, safest, if Your Highness dealt with this matter yourself, without informing Sir John Maitland, the Lord Chancellor. Especially the letter to King Philip. I take it that he believes that the Chancellor would not approve.'

'Aye. Belike he wouldna, Sir John! The more so if he kenned that Patrick Gray was at the back o' it! They never loved each other yon two, eh? We'll see, man – we'll see. I canna promise you anything, mind. It's a matter o' state . . . '

'Exactly, Sire. For myself, I care not which way it goes. It is no more concern of mine. Nor of Mary's. Our part is done.'

'Just so, just so. Aye. Off wi' you, then. Time, it is. Johnnie Mar is glowering there black as a Hieland stot! Hech, Vicky – you'll hae to think o' some matter to tell him we've been discussing on. Some matter to do wi' Lord Gray, belike. Aye, maybe anent his Sheriffdom o' Forfar. That will serve . . . ' The King held out his not over-clean hand. 'Our thanks to you, then, Master Davy. And to you too, lassie. We are indebted to you, and . . . and shall weigh it generously against your former misdeeds. Aye. You may leave our presence.'

Stiffly indeed David leant over to offer but a token kiss of the royal fingers. Mary was more suitably dutiful, even warm. As she straightened up in her saddle, she said quietly. 'I greatly thank Your Grace for asking me to your Court. It is true that I am too young, as my father says. But . . . would you not be better served to have back my Uncle Patrick to your Court? Much better. He is a clever man . . . '

'A plague on him – too clever by half! Tush, lassie – enough o' that! Yon one will serve me better in France or

48

Rome or Spain itsel', than here in my Scotland. Be off wi'
you.'

'Come, Mary.'

'I shall accompany you some way on your road, Mary?'
Lennox suggested.

'Not so, my Lord Duke,' David jerked. 'Your place is with
the King – not with my lord of Gray's steward and his brat!
Besides, I am very well able to look after my daughter, I
assure you – *very* well able!' Reaching out, he took the reins
of Mary's garron, and pulled his own beast's head round hard.
'Your servant, Sir . . . and my lord Duke!'

'Farewell, Vicky!' Mary called, as they trotted off.

Her father clapped his blue bonnet back on his wet head.

Past all the staring supercilious courtiers they rode, northwards, the man gazing straight ahead of him, the girl eyeing
the chattering fashionable throng with frankest interest,
unabashed.

It was not until they were well past and on their way, alone,
towards Lindores village and the Tay, that David spoke. 'I
do not know what to make of you, Mary – on my soul, I do
not!' he said.

'Must you make aught more of me than you have made
already, Father?' she asked fondly. 'Some would say, I think,
that you have wrought not ill with me hitherto – you, and
Mother . . . and Uncle Patrick!'

David Gray uttered something between a groan and a
snort. 'God help me . . . !'

Chapter Three

THE Lord Gray came home to Castle Huntly in a gale of wind
and the worst of tempers. For three weeks, three solid weeks,
he had been away kicking his heels down in the Borderland,
along with many another Scots lord, whilst his wretched men
ate and drank themselves silly in armed but pointless idleness,
by royal command but at *his* expense – men who should have

49

been hard at work rescuing the hay crop from the sodden far-flung grasslands of the Carse of Gowrie, hay for the vast herds of cattle that were the very basis of my lords prosperity. It was mid-July. The wettest and wildest spring and early summer in living memory. There would be the devil to pay for it next winter, in lack of forage and starving beasts, with the hay lying flattened and uncut, or rotten and mildewed – and the corn harvest like to be as bad. Seventy-five men of his, seventy-five able-bodied men, wasting their time and his substance amongst those damnable mist-shrouded bog-bound Border hills, on the commands of a crazy young half-wit King, who feared Catholic risings, Spanish invasions, and God alone knew what else!

Lord Gray had come home with fully half his force, king or no king. And those that he had left behind in Teviotdale were the most useless of his band, moreover – as was the case with many of the other feudal contingents, the majority of the lords being in a like state of impatience and fulmination, almost revolt. James, the young fool, had forbidden any worthwhile activity, even cattle-raiding, any forays across the Border – although that is what they understood that they had been there for – and nibbled his finger-nails instead, afraid of the English Lord Dacre's Northumbrian levies hurriedly raised to face them, afraid of the Governor of Berwick's garrison, afraid of the Catholics in the west under the Lords Maxwell and Herries who were supposed to be threatening the English West March, afraid of what the madcap Earl of Bothwell might do in these circumstances – afraid indeed of his own shadow. Waiting for his envoy back from Spain, it was said, delayed by storms; waiting for the supposed Spanish invasion of England; waiting for the gold that Queen Elizabeth had hastily promised him for keeping her northern march secure and denying his ports to Spanish ships; waiting, Christ God, for anybody and everybody to make up his royal mind for him!

In such case was the Kingdom of Scotland this deplorable summer of 1588, with its monarch a drooling ninny, the lords made fools of, and the so-called Spanish Armada a myth and a Popish fable. At least, such was my lord of Gray's profound conviction.

It required all of Mary Gray's soothing charms to make him even bearable company for the rest of his household and dependants at Castle Huntly in the next few days.

Those days brought tidings and rumours to the Carse of Gowrie that gave even Lord Gray second thoughts, however – whether he admitted them or not. First came the word that the Earls of Huntly, Erroll and Montrose had risen in the north, with, it was said, as many as five thousand men – though that might well be an exaggeration – and had taken over the direction of the towns of Aberdeen, Stonehaven, Banff and Elgin, expelling the provosts and ministers of the Kirk and installing Catholic nominees of their own. Then, only two days later, they heard that O'Neill, Earl of Tyrone, revolting against Elizabeth in Ireland, had landed in person in the Western Isles, and was there urging the Highland chiefs to raise a clan army to make cause with him – Catholic, of course – that was to link up with Huntly in the east. That this Irish move should have coincided so closely with Huntly's seemed unlikely to be mere chance – and the linking of the name of Logan of Restalrig with the business, no Highlander, no Catholic, but cousin and erstwhile bravo of the exiled Master of Gray, set at least some minds furiously to think. King James's reluctance to venture over the Border into England with his distinctly unruly force, was to be considered now in a new light. There were even whispers that the Crown had all along been privy to the entire business; it was noteworthy that it was the Kirk that whispered thus – and in far from dulcet tones. On the other hand, it could not but be recognised by all that, had not the Protestant lords been providentially assembled at this time, there would have been little or nothing to prevent the combined Catholic forces from turning southwards and taking over the kingdom. King Jamie might be owed some small thanks for this, accidental though it could have been. Even Lord Gray had to acknowledge that.

The next news made Lord Gray wish even – without saying so – that he had been perhaps a little less hasty. It was that the King, as counter to the northern situation presumably, and as something to occupy the remnant of his Protestant forces, had personally marched them westwards along his own Border, to attack, capture and destroy the great castle of

51

Lochmaben in Annandale, ancestral home of his heroic predecessor Robert Bruce and now held by the Catholic Lord Maxwell as hereditary keeper. As a politic gesture he had hanged its captain and six other Maxwells. Whatever the reasons for this flourish, James's first military exploit – and it was variously reported that it was to please Elizabeth, who, with no Armada appearing, it would be wise to keep well-disposed; that it was to keep the Kirk quiet; that it was to warn Huntly and the Northern Catholics not to move too far south – whatever the reasons, the Lord Gray could have wished to have been present, for Annandale was a rich land, and the sacking thereof could hardly have failed to be profitable for those engaged.

It was all difficult and confusing in the extreme. A man could scarcely tell which way to turn, to best advantage.

Then, on the very last day of the month of July, something more substantial than tidings and rumours reached Castle Huntly. All that boisterous day ships, great ships such as had never before been seen in Scottish waters, were to be observed all along the east coast, heading northwards in ones and twos and straggling groups, before an unseasonable south-easterly gale, weather-worn, battered, sails rent and shredded, top-hamper askew. One great galleon indeed, limped in through the gap in the long roaring sand-bar of Tay, and let down her anchor off Lord Gray's castle of Broughty which guarded the estuary, the rich colours and banners of Castile torn but still flying proudly from her soaring aftercastle and broken foremast. She sought provisions, water, care for her wounded, and time to effect repairs. My lord was sent for in haste the dozen miles from Castle Huntly. He found a Spanish marquis, a round dozen dons, and no fewer than two hundred soldiers of the Duke of Parma's Netherlands army aboard, as well as the crew, all armed to the teeth, though with many wounded and much damage apparent, not all of it caused by the storm. The *Santa Barba del Castro* had, it seemed, put into the Tay in error, mistaking the estuary and assuming that Dundee town was Aberdeen.

My lord was in something of a pickle. Nominally at least he was a staunch Protestant and a strong supporter of Christ's Reformed Kirk. These were notorious Papists, and therefore

52

anathema. On the other hand, he was not sure whether they were in fact allies of his King or enemies, at this precise moment – depending on whether Philip was treating with James or not. James admittedly was anxious to accept a large sum in gold from Elizabeth for denying port facilities to the Spaniards – but then it was well-known that the gold had not yet been paid, and the Tudor woman's promises were markedly unreliable. Moreover, this galleon mounted three tiers of cannon on either side – fifty-two guns, fully five times the number available on Broughty Castle's battlements – and disposed of more armed manpower than Gray could raise in a month. He compromised, therefore, very sensibly, supplying provisions and water, and timber for rough-and-ready repairs, but permitting no landing of wounded and only two days anchorage – thereby enriching his coffers by a sizeable quantity of gold ducats and some quite excellent silver plate.

So Scotland became aware that the long-delayed and much-dreaded Armada of Spain was in fact over, a thing of the past, a cloud dispersed – and unlike neighbouring England which went crazy with joy, did not know whether to be relieved or disappointed. As details gradually became known, and the size of the disaster to Spanish arms was assessed, so grew the realisation that England, the Auld Enemy, released at last from the bogey and spectre that had haunted her for years, was likely to prove a still more arrogant and dangerous neighbour than heretofore, and Elizabeth more interfering than ever. King Jamie saw his promised gold melt away for sure, and the English dukedom with which Elizabeth had also tempted him at the same time evaporate into thin air. Even the public and long sought-for announcement that he was evident, lawful and only heir to the said ageing Queen, now that Mary his mother was dead, was clearly postponed once again. The deceived and ill-used young man left his Borders and returned to Holyroodhouse and his capital in a state of deep depression.

At Castle Huntly, at least, there was no such depression. My lord had done better out of the Armada than most. David Gray heaved a profound sigh of relief, for not only was the threat of Spanish interference removed, but civil war likewise, for Huntly and his friends in the north promptly saw the light of reason and dispersed their rising as though it had never been. The Irish-Highland venture still went on, but that was far away. His brother Patrick's conspiracy, if such it had been, was surely brought to naught, exploded, blown away on the south-easterly gale – for which the good God be praised! And Mary Gray each night at her maidenly bedside thanked the same much-invoked God that the Holy Office and Inquisition would not be established on the Castle-hill of Edinburgh – but besought Him fervently at the same time that He would bring her Uncle Patrick home to Scotland just as quickly as it was celestially possible. Ludovick, Duke of Lennox was adjured likewise to entreat the Thrones of both Heaven and Scotland in the same cause. Patrick Gray it was who had brought the ten-year-old Ludovick from France to James's Court on his spectacular father's death.

Alas for the prayers and devotion of youth and innocence – the Master of Gray's stock had seldom been lower, his acceptability in circles of government more improbable. The Armada might almost have been entirely his own invention, and the unusual gales which had first delayed the fleet for six weeks, then harassed it in the narrows of the Channel, putting it at the mercy of the lighter and better-handled English ships, before finally breaking it up in major disaster and sending its dispersed vessels scudding north-about right round Scotland and Ireland as the only way of getting back to Spain – these gales might have been of the Master's personal devising. James, mourning his lost gold and duchy, even his unpaid pension from Elizabeth not received for months, was in no state to lend his ear to even Vicky's pleas. Instead he listened rather to the creaky voice of his wily lawyer-like Chancellor Maitland, who had lain notably low during all these alarms and excursions and now emerged again, like a tortoise from its shell, for the proper running and weal of the realm. And the King had spoken truly when he had declared that the Chancellor and the Master of Gray did not love each other. Sir John Maitland, as all at Court knew, never ceased to bewail that the beheading of the said malefactor had not gone off as planned – as *he* had so efficiently planned. And that was the bastard Davy Gray's fault.

Almost it seemed, indeed, as though God Himself was

54

against the unfortunate exile in foreign parts. Only a short time after the Armada fiasco, the powerful de Guise brothers, Henry the Duke and Cardinal Louis, Archbishop of Rheims, full cousins of the late Mary of Scotland, were assassinated by order of Henry Third of France. These had been Patrick Gray's potent protectors and supporters for years, the source of much of his influence, employment and funds on the Continent. Without their far-reaching Jesuit backing, Europe was going to be a very different place for their gallant and handsome protégé.

If the Reformers' stern God was going to take a denominational hand, of course, then the Master of Gray was not the one to fly in the face of destiny. Not even his worst enemy had ever suggested, however he might miscall him, that he was apt to do such a thing . . . once destiny made its intentions reasonably clear. Destiny might always be gently aided and piloted, however, along its chosen course, contrary though that might be, by a philosophical and agile-minded man. Such a man as Patrick Gray.

Mary Gray came to her father one golden morning that autumn, when he was superintending the placing and building of the numerous round oat-stacks of the belated corn harvest, in a sheltered stackyard nestling beneath the tall upthrusting crag out of which rose the red-stone walls of Castle Huntly, high above the flat carselands. It was the sort of work that David Gray enjoyed – much better indeed than schoolmastering; with all the local lairds, whose children he taught along with my lord's more recent brood, equally busy rescuing their corn and glad of even youthful help, lessons had been postponed with mutual relief. Her father now stood atop a round half-built stack, in shirt-sleeves, doublet discarded, hair untidy, face, chest and bare arms coated with oat-dust, catching the heavy sheaves that were tossed up to him from the laden two-horse wains, and building them into position on the steadily growing stack. He laughed and joked with the workers, and even sang snatches of song, as he laboured.

Mary looked up at him affectionately. This was as she loved best to see her father, working carefree and effective in the good honest toil of the fields and woods. Clearly he ought to have been a farmer; all his learning and experience of affairs seemed to bring him little or no satisfaction. He was more truly grandson to old Rob Affleck, miller of Inchture, than son to my lord of Gray. And yet . . . she knew also that he would have made a better lord for Castle Huntly than did Granlord, or even, it might be, than Uncle Patrick would make one day. She loved him, up there, all strong, confident, cheerful manhood. She felt loth indeed to interrupt and bring him down. But the matter might be urgent.

'Father,' she called. 'A lad from Kingoodie – Tam Rait, it is – came seeking you. With a message. There is somebody there asking for you.'

'Eh . . . ?' David paused in his rhythmic toil, and wiped back an unruly lock of hair from his brow with the back of a dusty hand. 'At Kingoodie? Sakes, lassie – if anybody wants me from Kingoodie, they can come here for me!'

'Yes. But . . . ' She moved closer to the stack, as near to her father as she could get. ' . . . this is a woman, Tam says. A lady.'

'A lady?' The man stared down at her. 'At Kingoodie? A few salmon-fishers' cots and a fowler's hut!'

'Yes. She is at Tam's father's cottage. And asking for Master David Gray. To go to her there, forthwith. I said that I would tell you.' Roguishly she laughed. 'I asked him if she was handsome – and by his face I deem that she is! And something more than that, maybe.'

'M'mmm.' He frowned.

'Tam said that she had told him not to tell anyone but your own self. But . . . well, Tam Rait could not keep a secret from me!' The girl's eyes danced. 'I did not tell Mother.'

Her father coughed. 'Well . . . ' he said. He jumped down from the stack, already rolling down his shirt-sleeves, and called for one of the men to take his place. He picked up his old torn doublet. 'I . . . I am but scurvily clad for visiting ladies,' he said doubtfully. 'Even at Kingoodie. But if I go home first . . . '

'Mother will undoubtedly be much interested,' she finished for him. 'I think that we should just go from here, do not you? It will save time, too.'

'We?' her father asked, brows raised. 'I can find my way

to Kingoodie, Mary, without your aid!'

'Oh, yes,' she agreed. 'But I promised Tam Rait that I would bring you myself. And at once.'

'Promised . . . ? Houts, girl – be off with you! I'll manage my business, whatever it is, without you. Or Tam Rait!'

'Would you rather that I went home to Mother?' she asked, innocently.

He looked at her, sidelong. 'You are a – a shameless minx! Yes, go home, girl. What should there be here to alarm your mother?'

'I do not know, Father. Only . . . Tam says that the lady who was asking for you so secretly is big with child!'

David Gray swallowed. He looked away, and ran a hand over his mouth and jaw – thereby smearing the sweaty dust thereon into still more evident designs and whorls. He moistened his lips.

Silently the girl took the scarlet kerchief from around her neck, and reaching up on tip-toes, wiped his features with it gently, before handing the silken stuff to him to continue the process. As she stood there close to him, throat and shoulders largely bare above the open-necked and brief white linen bodice, the man could not but be much aware of the warm honey-hued loveliness of her, and the deep cleft of her richly-swelling firm young bosom. Mary was indeed, beyond all question, physically as well as mentally, no longer anybody's child – and the sooner that he came to terms with the fact, almost certainly, the better for him.

Unspeaking they turned and walked side by side towards the stackyard gate where David's horse was tethered.

'I shall ride pillion at your back, very well,' Mary mentioned, as he made to mount the broad-backed shaggy garron.

Without a word he leaned down, and arm encircling her slender waist, hoisted her up behind him.

To the admiring grins of the workers – for the beast's broadness meant that the girl's shapely legs, long for her height, were much in view – they rode off.

They had to go a bare three miles across the reedy levels of the flood-plain of the Tay, marshy cattle-dotted pasture, seamed with ditches lined with willow and alder and the spears of the yellow flag. Taking a track which followed the coils and twists of the Huntly Burn, they headed almost due westwards until they reached its outfall at the low weed-girt shore. Turning along this by a muddy road of sorts, presently they came to a few lonely cot-houses and turf-coated cabins, where there was a rough stone jetty, boats were drawn up on the shingle, and nets were hanging up to dry on tall reeling posts. Kingoodie, where my lord obtained most of his salmon.

Their approach had not gone unobserved, and a youth emerged from one of the houses and waved to them. As they rode up, behind him in the low doorway, a lady stooped and came out.

She made a strange picture, materialising out of that humble stone-and-turf windowless cottage that was little better than a hovel, a beautiful youngish woman, stylish, assured, dressed in travelling clothes of the finest quality and the height of fashion, carrying her very evident child with a proud calm. Grey-eyed, wide-browed, with finely-chiselled features and sheer heavy golden hair that was almost flaxen, she had a poise, an unconscious aristocracy of bearing most obviously unassumed.

'God be praised – Marie!' David Gray cried, and leapt from his horse in a single agile bound, leaving his daughter to slide down as she could – a strangely impetuous performance for that sober, level-headed man, rash indeed in front of witnesses.

'Davy! Davy! Davy!' the woman called out, part-laughing, part-sobbing, and came running, light-footed enough considering her condition.

Wide-eyed, Mary Gray stood by the garron, watching.

David halted before he reached the newcomer, seeming to recollect discretion. Not so the lady. She ran straight up to him, to fling herself against him, arms around him, to bury her golden head on his dusty chest. Something she said there, but what was not clear. He raised a hand, a distinctively trembling hand, to stroke her fair down-bent head. So they stood.

At length she looked up. 'Oh, Davy,' she said, blinking away tears from grey eyes almost as level and direct as his own. 'How good! How fine! To see you again . . . to feel you . . . good, strong, solid, unchangeable Davy Gray! Let me look at you! Yes – the same, just the same. You have not changed one whit . . . '

'It is but a year, Marie,' he said, deep-voiced. 'Fifteen months . . . '

'Ah – you count them also! Fifteen long months.'

'Aye. Long, as you say. I . . . I . . . ' He shook his head, as though consciously denying himself that train of thought and emotion. 'Is all well? How came you here? Patrick . . . ? And you – you are well, my lady?'

'Well enough, yes. Can you not see it, Davy? Larger than ever I have been! Well – and in the state all good wives long to be, so they do say! Do you not congratulate me?'

'Aye,' he nodded. 'I am happy to see it – happy indeed.' Gravely, unsmiling he said it. 'I was sorry . . . about the other.' The Mistress of Gray had miscarried in a storm-tossed ship on her way, with her banished husband, to exile.

She searched his face. 'No doubt,' she said. 'But . . . there is young Mary. Good lack – she is . . . she is liker . . . more than ever she is like . . . '

'Aye,' the man agreed briefly. 'How, and where, is Patrick?'

'Mary, my dear,' the woman called out, and leaving David's side moved over towards the girl. 'On my soul, you are lovely! A child no longer. A woman – and a beauty! Let me kiss you, poppet.'

Mary curtsied prettily before the other reached her, and then embraced her unreservedly, returning her kisses frankly. 'How nice you are, Lady Marie,' she declared. 'What a splendid surprise! And the baby – how wonderful! She gurgled delightedly. 'Will it be my cousin – or my brother or sister?'

'Mary . . . !' David Gray protested, shocked.

The Lady Marie Stewart, Mistress of Gray, laughed musically, mock-ruefully. 'Lord – I do not know, Mary! I do not. But, I vow, if it is like you at all, then I shall be happy.'

'Thank you. And how is my Uncle Patrick?'

'He is well, And sends you his love and devotion. As well he might! I left him at Dieppe, where he put me on a ship . . . '

'He put you on a ship?' David demanded, coming up, and dropping his voice heedfully, glancing around them for listeners. 'Patrick sent you here? Alone? From France?

'Yes. I suppose that he sent me. Though I wished to come. I was pining for home. And determined that my son should be born in Scotland. It is a boy, you know – I am sure of it. Do not ask me how I know. But . . . he will be called Andrew, and he will be heir to Gray. It is only fitting that he should be born here. Wise, too – that there be no doubts, with my lord . . . !'

'Even lacking his father?'

'Even so. Although . . . who knows, his father may not be so far away by then, God willing. And Patrick scheming!'

'M'mmm,' David said, frowning.

'But how did you come here, Lady Marie?' Mary asked. 'To Kingoodie?'

'I shipped on a Scots trading vessel. Bringing wines and flax. To Pittenweem, in Fife. Faugh – the smell of her! Hides she had carried before, from Scotland to France. Do I not stink of them yet? From Pittenweem I bargained with a fishing skipper to bring me round Fife Ness and put me ashore secretly in the Tay, as near to Castle Huntly as might be. I arrived last night, here. And these good folk have treated me full kindly.'

'Kindly! Dod Rait should have brought you straight to the castle. It is but three miles. Instead of keeping you, wife to the heir of Gray, in this cabin . . .'

'Not so, Davy. They know not who I am, for one thing. I could not come to Castle Huntly. My lord would scarce welcome me, I think! Would he? I am the wife of a condemned and exiled felon, banished the realm. I must go warily indeed. It was you that I had to see – you whom I knew would guide and help me.'

'Aye – that I will, to be sure. But . . . was it wise to come, my lady?'

'Wise! Wise! Is Davy Gray doubting already? Is that my welcome? Would you that I had stayed away?'

'No. But there are hazards – grave hazards. Patrick's credit is low, my lady. The Armada business . . .'

'There are hazards in living, Davy – in breathing! And it is to improve Patrick's credit that I am here, see you. But . . . am I to be my lady to you again? Would you keep me at a

60

distance? Was it not Marie that you named me, Davy when first you beheld me? I thought I heard it. Am I not your good-sister. And before I was that – your friend?'

'Aye. You are kind.' David Gray could look very grim at times. 'But you are the Lady Marie Stewart, daughter to the Earl of Orkney, and own cousin to the King.' That was true. Her father, the Lord Robert Stewart, former Bishop and now Earl of Orkney, was one of King James Fifth's many bastards, brother on the wrong side of the blanket to the late Mary Queen of Scots. 'You are a great lady. And I am . . . '

'Stop! We all know what you are, Davy Gray! The proudest, stiffest-necked man in this kingdom!' She shook her coifed golden head, but smiled at him warmly nevertheless. 'The man who bought my husband's life, when no one else could, at great cost to himself. I have never had opportunity truly to thank you for that, Davy.' She laid a hand on his arm. 'I do now. I do, indeed. And, alas, need your help once more.'

'It is yours, always.'

'Yes, Davy dear. I know it. Like, like a warm glow at my heart that thought has been, many a weary day.' She mustered a laugh. 'Patrick says, indeed, that you are the only man who could make him jealous of his wife . . . !'

David's face was wiped clean of expression. 'That is no way to talk, your ladyship,' he said evenly. 'Nor this any place to talk, at all. Come – can you mount my beast? In these fine clothes? And in your, your present state? Mary can ride behind you, holding you. And I will walk, leading the beast. It will be quite safe, I think. I will send for your baggage later.'

'Lord – of course I can ride, Davy! I am not that far gone. But five months. Do I look so monstrous? But . . . where will you take me?'

'To Castle Huntly. Where else?'

'But I cannot go there. Surely you see it? Anywhere but there. My lord always was out of love with Patrick. Now, he will have none of him, or his, I swear. And I will not come begging his charity. Or any man's. Save . . . save perhaps yours, Davy Gray!' She shook her head again. 'Besides, it would not do. Lord Gray is a notable pillar of the Kirk. Though no Catholic myself, I will be held to be one for Patrick's sake. To harbour me at Castle Huntly could do my lord

61

much harm – you all, perhaps. I thought to go to my half-sister's house – Eupham, that is married to Mark Ogilvie, of Glen Prosen. If you could help me to win that far . . . '

'We go to the castle,' David interrupted her bluntly.

'But, Davy – what of my lord . . . ?'

'Allow me to deal with my lord! That Patrick's wife, bearing Patrick's child, should seek shelter in her need anywhere but at Castle Huntly is unthinkable. Leave my lord to . . . to his steward!'

'And your Mariota?'

David was a little less definite. 'Mariota will, will rejoice to see you,' he said.

'I hope so, yes. But . . . ' She shrugged and sighed. 'She is well? How does she, the fair Mariota?'

'She is well – and in the same state as you are!'

'Oh!'

'Yes. Now – we will take leave of the Raits here. How much of belongings have you . . . ?'

So presently the trio were pacing across the flats of the carse, the Lady Marie mounted with Mary Gray behind her and the man leading the garron. Ahead, the great towering mass of Castle Huntly reared its turrets and battlements above the plain like a heavy frown in stone, even in the golden sunlight. To its presumed future mistress it seemed less than beckoning.

'My lord has been away at Foulis Castle these two days,' David informed her. 'But he will be back tonight.'

'Then I had rather be gone by then,' she said.

The presence of a number of stamping, shouting men-at-arms in the castle courtyard, when they arrived, indicated that Lord Gray had in fact returned home earlier than anticipated. As David aided the Lady Marie to dismount, young Mary slipped down and ran on ahead, and in at the main door of the keep.

Mariota came hurrying down the winding stone stairway to welcome them, in consequence, greeting the newcomer with a sort of uneasy kindness, all flustered surprise, bemoaning her own unsuitable attire, that she had had no warning, my lord's untimely arrival, exclaiming how bonny was my lady, how tired she must be coming all that way from France, how sad to be parted from dear Patrick, and was he well, happy? All in a breathless flood.

Marie kissed her warmly. They made a strange contrast, these two, both so very fair to look upon, but so very different in almost every respect. David considered them thoughtfully, rubbing his chin. Into the chatter of exclamation and half-expressed question and answer, he presently interrupted, gently but firmly.

'Up with you,' he declared. 'Here is no place for talk. Let the Lady Marie in, at least, my dear. She will be weary, hungry. She needs seating, comfort, refreshment. Up the stairs with you. Our rooms are on high, but they are at your service . . . '

'Indeed!' a hoarse voice challenged heavily. The Lord Gray had appeared on a half-landing just above, a stocky massive figure, a furred robe thrown hastily over and only part-covering his dishabille. At his broad back, a hand tentatively within one of his arms, was his grand-daughter. 'In my house, *I* say what rooms are at whose service! Bring the lady into my chamber, Davy!'

Marie sank in a curtsy. 'Greetings, my lord,' she said. 'I hope that I find you well? I am but passing on my way . . . elsewhere . . . '

'Aye,' he answered shortly. 'No doubt.'

'I think not,' David put in quietly, evenly. 'Patrick's wife does not pass Castle Huntly!'

'Eh . . . ? Fiend seize me – who are you to speak?'

'One who esteems the name and honour of Gray, sir. And, since we are privy here, and all of a family as it were – your eldest son!'

'Damn you, you . . . !' My lord all but choked, unable to find breath or words.

Mary found them. 'We knew that you would wish to honour the King's own cousin, Granlord.'

'Ah . . . ummm.'

'And very beautiful, is she not?'

'Wheesht, child – hold your tongue!' her grandfather got out, but in a different tone of voice. 'A pox – but I'll be master in my own house, see you!' He jabbed a thick accusatory finger, but at David. 'Mind it, man – mind it, I say!' He turned on Marie. 'How came you here? And where is yon graceless popinjay that has bairned you? If he it was!'

'Yes, my lord – he it was,' Marie answered without heat, even smiling a little. 'I carry your heir. I would have thought that you would have rejoiced to see it. I am new come, by ship from Dieppe, secretly – where I left Patrick.'

'Thank the good God he's no' here, at least! Why are you come, woman?'

'I have good reasons, sir. One, that you would wish the heir to Gray to be born where you could see it, I believed. Not in some foreign land. Was I wrong?'

The older man grunted. 'A mercy that you came secretly, at the least,' he said, after a moment. 'None know that you are here, then?'

'None who know who I am.'

'My lord – the Lady Marie is tired. Unfit to be standing thus. In her condition. She must have food and wine . . .'

'I am very well, Davy. I seek nothing . . .'

'I said to bring her into my room, did I no'?' Gray barked. And turning about abruptly, he went stamping back up the stairs.

As David took Marie's arm, to aid her upstairs, she held back, shaking her head. 'No, Davy,' she declared. 'I had liefer go now. Away. It is as I thought. This house is no place for me. He is set against Patrick, and therefore me . . .'

The man did not relax his grip, and propelled her forward willy-nilly. 'You will stay in this house,' he said grimly. 'It is your right. He will do as I say, in the end. For he needs me, does my lord of Gray! I know too much. Come, Marie . . .'

'And do not take my lord too sorely,' Mariota advised, biting her lip. 'He has a rough tongue, and proud. But he is not so ill as he sounds. And . . . I think that he loves Patrick at heart, more than he will say.'

'Forby, he loves beautiful ladies!' Mary added, with a little laugh. 'So smile at him, Lady Marie – smile much and warmly. And he will not withstand you long!'

'Tut, girl . . . !' her father reproved.

They went upstairs together, three of them turning in at

my lord's private chamber just above the great hall of the castle, and Mariota proceeding higher to collect viands and refreshment for the guest.

The master of the house stood at the window of a comparatively small apartment, the stone floor of which constituted the top of the great hall's vaulted ceiling. It was snug, overwarm indeed, for my lord liked a fire here summer and winter in the fireplace with the elaborate heraldic overmantel showing the Gray arms of rampant red lion on silver, carved in stone. Skins of sheep and deer covered the floor, and the stone walls were hung with arras, again embroidered heraldically. Gray gestured towards one of the two chairs of that room without leaving the window, for Marie to sit down.

'Patrick?' he jerked, not looking at her. 'Is he well enough?' And lest that might seem too mawkishly solicitous, 'And what follies and mischiefs and schemes is he up to in France or Rome or whatever ill-favoured land he's plaguing with his presence now?'

'He is well, yes,' Marie answered. 'And as for his schemes ... well, Patrick is Patrick, is he not?'

'Aye!' That came out on an exhalation of breath that was something between a groan and a sigh. He turned round to stare at the young woman now. 'Why did he send you here?' he demanded directly. 'I ken Patrick, God pity me! You didna come without he sent you. And he didna send you just to drop your bairn in front o' me, where I could see it! Na, na. He doesna care that for me, or mine!' The older man snapped his fingers. 'Unless for my gear and lands.'

'I think that you wrong him, my lord,' Marie told him quietly. 'But at least credit him with the desire that there should be no doubts about the birth of the heir of Gray.' She smiled a little. 'And that not on account of your lands and gear! Believe me, sir, great as these may be, Patrick looks for greater.'

'Eh ... ?'

'He is determined to win back the Abbey of Dunfermline and its revenues, from the Earl of Huntly.'

'Christ God – the more fool he, then! The prinking prideful ninny! He'll never do that.'

'He will try, my lord, without a doubt.'

David, frowning, spoke. 'I mislike this,' he said. 'I mislike it, for many reasons. It is folly, dangerous, flying too high. But it is less than honourable, too. And it brings me into it. For he used me to offer Dunfermline to Huntly. I made the bargain for him – Dunfermline for his life. Dunfermline for Huntly to get me into the King's presence, so that I could bargain with James also! Now, to go back on it . . .'

'Faugh!' his father interrupted him scornfully. 'Save your breath, man! Patrick's no' concerned with honour, or keeping bargains, or aught else but his own benefit.' He swung back on Marie. 'But here's idle chatter. He'll no' get back Dunfermline – that's sure. And dinna tell me, woman, that he sent *you* here on such fool's errand? You!'

'No,' she agreed patiently. 'That is not part of my errand. That he must look to himself – if he can win back to Scotland It is to intercede with the King to permit his return – that is my duty.'

'Ha! Now we have it. And near as much a fool's errand as the other! You'll no' manage that, I'll vow! He's banished for life, is he no'?'

'What decree the King has made, the King can unmake,' she asserted. 'And *I* am not banished. If I can come to my father in Edinburgh, he will bring me into the King's presence.'

'To what end, woman – to what end? The King's cousin you may be – in bastardy – but that winna serve to gain Patrick's remission. You pleading for him on your bended knees, weeping woman's tears? Think you that will move our Jamie? Or the Chancellor? And the Council? Condemned by the Council o' the Realm for highest treason and the death o' the King's bonny mother, think you that tears and pleas will bring him back? None want him here. You'll need a better key than a woman's snuffles to open the door o' Scotland again to Patrick Gray!'

'That key,' she told him calmly, 'perhaps I have.'

All gazed at her – and Mariota's entrance at this moment with food and wine was greeted with considerable impatience by my lord. It was pushed aside peremptorily.

'What mean you?' Marie was challenged. 'How can you have anything such? What is this?'

'The King's marriage,' she answered.

There was silence in that overheated chamber.

'Patrick has been busy,' she went on, but levelly, factually, almost wearily. 'He has not wasted his time abroad. He has been working for a match between James and the Princess Catherine, sister to King Henry of Navarre.'

'Patrick . . . ? The King's matching?' my lord gobbled. 'Devil slay me – what insolence! What effrontery!'

'Navarre . . . !' David exclaimed. 'But . . . what of the Danish match?'

'Patrick believes this better, of more worth. Henry of Navarre is the Protestant champion – whilst the Danish royal house is known to be unsure in its religion, inclining back towards the old faith . . . '

'God's Body – is Patrick concerned now for the Protestants! What next, woman?'

Marie ignored that. 'Moreover, Navarre will be heir to France. And Patrick believes the King of France to be sickening.'

She had them silenced now.

'And the King of Scots married to a sister of great France is a different matter to him married to the daughter of little Denmark'

That was not to be denied. David, somewhat abstractedly, began to offer refreshment to their guest, while his father hummed and hawed.

'This . . . this is scarce believable,' the latter got out. 'That Patrick should dare fly this high – a condemned man!'

'Flying a high hawk never troubled Patrick,' David said. 'No doubt we were foolish to believe that he would change just because he was banished. But . . . how much substance has this project, Marie? What says King Henry of Navarre? Does he even know aught of it?'

She nodded. 'Patrick has been closeted with him more than once. He is agreeable, it seems. The matter has reached the stage of considering the worth of the dowry . . . '

'Precious soul o' God – and King Jamie kens naught o' it, woman?'

'That is why I am sent, my lord. To apprise him of it. Of its . . . advantages.'

David noticed the tiny hesitation on Marie's part before she used that term.

'Aye. But what makes Patrick believe that this ploy will win him back into the King's favour?' his father asked. 'A big jump that, is it no'? Agile jumper as he may be!'

'Perhaps, sir. But Patrick does not seek to take it all in one jump, I think. He has kept all in his own hands, thus far – so that, if James is interested, it will be necessary for Patrick himself to come here to Court to discuss it. And once back in the King's presence, Patrick does not fear but that he will stay there. He swayed James before, readily enough; he does not fear that he cannot do so again.'

My lord could only wag his bull-like head. 'The devil!' he muttered. 'Cunning as the Devil himself! I' faith – he almost makes me misdoubt my own wife's chastity!'

'Marie,' David said carefully. 'We have heard the advantages of this project. But I think that there are disadvantages, are there not?'

She looked at him for a moment steadily, before she answered, level-voiced. 'Catherine of Bourbon is ugly, crooked and no longer young,' she said. 'Moreover, few I think, would name her chaste.'

'Oh, no!' That was a young voice, in involuntary urgent protest, as Mary Gray broke the hush. 'Not that!'

The Mistress of Gray looked down at the goblet of wine in her hand, and said nothing.

David considered her thoughtfully, rubbing his chin.

My lord produced something between snort and chuckle. 'Houts!' he said. 'No insuperable barrier to a royal match, yon! Forby, she'd no' be getting aught so different hersel' – save maybe in years! Jamie's no' that much o' a catch!'

'He is the King of Scots, Granlord,' the girl demurred in quiet reproach.

'Aye, God help him!'

'You will not acquaint His Grace of this? Of the Princess's . . . quality?' David asked, in a moment or two.

The Lady Marie's answer was to put her hand into a brocaded satchel-purse that hung from the girdle of her travelling-gown. From it she produced a miniature portrait, painted on ivory, within a delicately gemmed frame. She handed it to

68

David. It showed a young woman, oval-faced and pale, richly dressed and bejewelled, almost dwarfed within a high upstanding ruffed and pearled collar.

'She looks none so ill,' he said, passing it to his father.

Faintly Marie smiled. 'A Court painter may flatter,' she observed. 'And that was painted ten years ago, at the least.'

My lord was admiring the diamonds round the frame. 'Potent persuasion this!' he mentioned. 'And the dowry? What of that?'

She shook her head. 'Of that I have no knowledge. It would be necessary for Patrick himself to come to Scotland to discuss it.'

'Oh, aye. I'ph'mmm. No doubt. So he baits his trap, the miscreant!' Lord Gray took a heavy limping pace or two about his chamber. 'Cunning, artful, I grant you. If this match should take place . . . ! France! It would be a great matter for the realm. For Scotland. For us all. Aye – and for Patrick Gray!' He turned on Marie. 'How comes it that he is so close with Henry of Navarre?'

'Patrick has a nose for . . . for keys! Keys that will open doors. And a powerful colleague in Elizabeth Tudor. The Protestant lioness and the Protestant lion!'

'Elizabeth!' David exclaimed. 'The Queen? You mean . . . you mean that he deals with Elizabeth still? After all that has happened? Elizabeth, who betrayed him?'

'He writes to her, or to Burleigh, or to Walsingham, each week.'

'But . . . but this is scarce to be believed! He hates Elizabeth. She played with him, led him on, and then worked his downfall. With Maitland and James. Elizabeth, that monument of perfidy – his chiefest enemy!'

The young woman shook her head. 'That is not how Patrick views it, Davy. For him, it is all the game of statecraft. He does not cherish friends or enemies. He does not measure injuries done to him . . . nor that he does to others. He uses the cards that come to his hands – *uses*, you understand?' She sighed a long quivering sigh. 'Would it were not so! God – would he were as other men! But he is not. He is . . . Patrick Gray. And I am his wife. I married him knowing him. Elizabeth betrayed him, yes – but had he not betrayed her beforehand? They are

69

of one kidney. But she is Queen of England, and therefore an important card in his game indeed, to be played if he can . . .'

'But the Armada of Spain! That was to destroy her? That he built his hopes on . . . ?'

'Did he, do you think? Another card in the same game, Davy.'

'A card that went sore agley, 'fore God!' my lord snorted. 'I'm hoping this new card o' his, this Navarre match, isna like to go the same way, eh?'

Marie looked at him coolly, directly. 'You hope . . . ? You approve of the venture then, my lord? Of the attempt that I am here for?'

'Me? I didna say that, did I, woman? *Me* approve? Na, na — I said no such thing,' the older man blustered. 'An unlikely day it'll be when I approve o' any plot o' Patrick's! But . . . if Elizabeth o' England is behind this match, it's no' to be taken lightly. And Navarre *is* heir to France, right enough. The French king is young. But if he is ailing . . . ' He coughed. 'And I am a good Protestant, forby!'

Marie smiled slightly.

'Aye, then.' My lord seemed to make up his mind. 'I'll see that you get to my lord of Orkney your father's house in Edinburgh. I'll no' take you, mind — for thanks to Patrick my credit's no' high at Court. But I'll see that you win there. Davy here will take you, belike. Till then, you can bide here.'

She inclined her golden head. 'Thank you, my lord. This is generous indeed. More generous by far than I looked for. Or Patrick either!' She met his shrewd little pig's eye. 'But I shall not burden you with my awkward presence for long, I assure you — for the sooner that I can reach the Court, the better. For this . . . this estimable royal project.'

'Aye. So be it.'

She turned to David, and found him eyeing her strangely, intently, almost sorrowfully, with little of gladness or elation in evidence over this happy change in her immediate fortunes. At his look she bit her lip, and mute appeal shot with some sort of pain clouded her clear grey eyes. She said nothing — nor did he.

It was Mary who spoke. 'May I see the picture, Granlord?' she asked, and slipped over to take the miniature portrait from

70

her grandfather. She looked at it closely, and then from it to the Lady Marie.

'No!' she declared briefly, softly, but with a strange finality.

'I am sorry,' Marie Stewart said – and sounded as though she meant it.

Chapter Four

THE new heir to Gray was born in the icy mid-January of 1589 – not at Castle Huntly but in the somewhat raffish and ramshackle establishment of the Lord Robert Stewart, Earl and Bishop of Orkney, in the old eastern wing of the Palace of Holyroodhouse which King James allowed his carefree but never debt-free, permanently impecunious, illegitimate uncle. No festivities were held, no bonfires lit on the hill-tops flanking the wide Gray lands in the Carse of Gowrie, as was normal on such auspicious occasions. The Lord Gray had reverted to his former attitude towards his daughter-in-law, and would have none of her.

Undoubtedly my lord was disappointed. The worthy, hopeful and ingenious scheme for the Navarre match had come to nothing. Admittedly it was still being mooted in certain quarters and Queen Elizabeth had declared herself in favour. But James himself had become quite definitely opposed. Which was very strange, for at first it had been quite otherwise. When the Mistress of Gray had arrived at Holyroodhouse in October, it had not taken long for the entire Court to buzz with the exciting news that King Jamie was veering away from the proposed Danish match and was much intrigued with this new notion of marrying the sister of the man who was heir presumptive to France and might very well shortly be king thereof. James indeed began drawing elaborate heraldic doodlings and designs incorporating the Lilies of France into the Royal Arms of Scotland, and calculating the shining possibilities of himself, or at worst his heir, succeeding eventually to the throne of France as well as that of England – since Henry of

Navarre, although married for seventeen years, had no legitimate children. James was even said to have made up a lengthy and romantic poem to dispatch to the lady.

Then, all of a sudden and without warning, all was changed. James lost interest. Word spread through the Court that the King had discovered that Princess Catherine was in fact old, ugly, crooked and of doubtful morals. Whence and how this intelligence had reached him was not known, although it was noted that the Duke of Lennox, who, being half-French himself, had at first been strongly in favour of the match, quite abruptly became as strongly against it, James following suit. Indeed so offended was the King that he went further, and promptly reverted to negotiations with Denmark once more – where, as it happened, King Frederick, having given up Scotland, had pledged his elder daughter the Princess Royal to the Duke of Brunswick in the interim; however, he still had his younger daughter, the fourteen-year-old Princess Anne available. She was prettier than her sister, too, he pointed out – though naturally the dowry would be smaller in consequence.

So Lord Gray's hopes of credit and profit through being intimately connected with a resounding Franco-Scottish union faded almost entirely.

The Master of Gray perforce remained an exile. But it was a very near thing. Letters of recall from the King and the Chancellor were in fact bringing him home to Scotland, when suddenly they were countermanded without explanation. Had bad weather not kept his ship storm-bound at Dieppe, he might indeed have beaten the ban. As it was, he did not allow receipt of the royal edict, which reached him actually on shipboard, wholly to demolish his plans, for by February information reached Scotland that the Master was in London, and apparently cutting high capers at the Court of Saint James.

The ageing Lord Burleigh, Lord High Treasurer of England, wrote a letter to Sir John Maitland, Lord High Chancellor of Scotland, to the effect that that realm would much benefit by the speedy return of the talented Master of Gray, and suggesting that the said excellent Chancellor should advise his royal prince to that effect.

The royal prince maintained, as so frequently was his habit, a masterly inactivity.

There was further correspondence – a deal of it now, a flood. Sir Frances Walsingham, Principal Secretary of State to Elizabeth, and the most sinister figure in Europe, wrote to Mr. William Ashby, English Resident at the Scots Court, desiring him to urge King James to countenance and receive back to favour the notable Master of Gray, whose love for His Majesty was as well known as his services were assuredly valuable. Archibald Douglas, lifelong enemy of Patrick's, and Scots Resident at the Court of Saint James, informed Chancellor Maitland by letter that he truly believed the Master to be far changed in his fashions and moreover filled with goodwill towards the said Chancellor to whom he might be of considerable use if he was permitted to return home. Sir Christopher Hatton, Lord Chancellor of England, wrote to the Vice-Chancellor of Scotland, Sir Robert Melville – he refused to have anything to do with Maitland – indicating that Patrick, Master of Gray had an excellent head for figures and that he had put certain financial proposals before himself which, if he was allowed to bring them to fruition might well greatly advantage King James and his realm. Lord Howard of Effingham, Lord High Admiral of England, wrote to the Earl of Bothwell, Lord High Admiral of Scotland thanking him for his belated congratulations on the defeat of the Armada, and in a postscript recommending to him the useful Master of Gray with whom he was sure he would have much in common.

Chancellor Maitland's prim lawyer's mouth was almost permanently down-turned these spring days of 1589, and his royal master nibbled urgently at his ragged nails, wagged his great head, and sought the patience of the Almighty God whose earthly vassal and vice-regent he was. Doing nothing can tax even the most expert, at times.

At the end of April, Queen Elizabeth herself had occasion to set her royal hand to paper. Walsingham's minions had been successful in intercepting letters from the Earls of Huntly and Erroll and other Catholic lords to the King of Spain and the Duke of Parma, lamenting on the defeat of the Armada and promising to share in another attempt against England, provided 6,000 Spanish troops were landed in

Scotland. Elizabeth's reaction was vigorous, clear and by no means restricted to diplomatic terminology. Was ever a realm plagued by such neighbours, she demanded? Was this to be borne? Good Lord, she wrote, her quill spluttering ink, methinks I do dream! No king a week could bear this! Was James a king indeed? Her last paragraph, however, ended on an abruptly different note. Obviously her well-beloved but youthful cousin of Scotland could do with more sage counsel and seasoned advice about his government and realm, and to such end she could not do better than recommend the return of Patrick, Master of Gray, of whose good intentions, probity, and agility of mind she was now heartily assured. With this admonition she committed James to God's especial care and guidance.

That young man, sorely tried, took himself away for a prolonged bout of hunting in Ettrick Forest.

Lastly the Master of Gray himself wrote to his monarch, privily, and enclosed the letter in one to his wife. Significantly, it was addressed from no farther away than Berwick-upon-Tweed. After assurances of his undying devotion and loyal service, he mentioned that while in London, having had some conference with Queen Elizabeth and sundry of her ministers, he had been deeply shocked to learn that His Grace's pension from that princess, negotiated by himself a year or two before, was much in arrears and moreover sadly inadequate to the situation. He had certain proposals for the rectifying of this deplorable state of affairs, consonant with the dignity of all concerned, and believed that he had convinced Her Highness and her Lord Treasurer in the matter. It but remained to lay his proposals before His Grace. Moreover, in a purely personal matter he craved the royal indulgence. His son and firstborn, whom as yet he had not had the felicity to behold, was now four months old and notably in need of christening. It was suitable that the boy should be received into Christ's true and Reformed Kirk of Scotland, for the eternal salvation of his soul, a ceremony at which he, the unworthy father, had perhaps understandable ambitions to attend. If His Grace would exercise his royal clemency so far as to permit the devoted petitioner to be present at such a humble ceremony, this would surely provide a suitable occasion to discuss the aforementioned financial matter, and also the additional suggestion that he had made to the Queen of England that Her Highness might decently invest her heir and successor with an English dukedom as token and earnest of responsibilities to come. Etcetera.

No mention was made of the Princess Catherine of Bourbon.

James, by the grace of God, King of Scots, Duke of Rothesay, Lord of the Isles, and Defender of Christ's Reformed Kirk, saw the light belatedly – in the warm glowing reflection of English gold pieces as well as in the saving of an innocent young Catholic brand from the burning. He capitulated, inditing a note in his own intricate hand, permitting his right worthy and traist friend and councillor Patrick, Master of Gray to re-enter his realm of Scotland forthwith. He personally appended the royal seal – omitting to inform the Lord Chancellor – and despatched it by close messenger to Berwick-upon-Tweed.

It was exactly two years, almost to the day, since the royal sentence of beheading for high treason had been reluctantly commuted to banishment for life.

The great banqueting-hall at Holyroodhouse presented a scene of which Mary Gray, at least, had never seen the like. In the hall at Castle Huntly she had witnessed many an exciting and colourful occasion, but never on such a scale and with the atmosphere of this one. It seemed to her, from her point of vantage in one of the raised window-embrasures which she shared with her father and mother and a life-size piece of statuary, that there must be hundreds of people present – not one hundred or two, but many. Every hue of the rainbow shone and revolved and eddied before her, jewellery flashed and glittered in the blaze of a thousand candles. The noise was deafening, everybody having to shout to make themselves heard, so that the music of the royal fiddlers and lutists in the ante-room was almost completely drowned. The smells caught the throat – of perfumes and perspiration, the fumes of liquor and the smoke of candles. The cream of Scotland was here tonight – the Protestant cream, that is – by royal command and in its most splendid apparel. Chancellor Maitland, in sombre black, who must pay for it all out of a chronically impoverished Treasury, frowned sourly on one and all from beside the high double-doors at the top end of the vast chamber. Few heeded him, however, for his frown was part of the man.

The small Gray party was very quiet and dully-clad compared with the rest of the gay and confident throng, in their best clothes as they were although none would call dull the flushed and ripe comeliness of Mariota Davidson, a mother for the fourth time, all tremulous wide-eyed unease; and Mary's lip-parted, utterly unselfconscious excitement, wedded to her quite startling elfin attractiveness, drew innumerable glances, admiring, intrigued, speculative and frankly lecherous. As for David, his frown almost matched that of the Chancellor as he partly hid himself behind the statue that had been one of Mary the Queen's importations from her beloved France – for too many of the faces that he saw here tonight he knew, and had no wish to be recognised in turn. All this had been his life once, all unwillingly – and he had hoped, indeed sworn, never to tread the shifting-sands of it again. They were in Edinburgh, at the Lady Marie's earnest request, for the christening on the morrow; and here tonight only to please the urgent Mary, who had engineered a royal summons for them through Ludovick, Duke of Lennox.

Abruptly the din of voices was shattered as, from the top of the hall, a couple of trumpeters in the royal livery blew a fanfare, high-pitched, resounding, challenging. Chancellor Maitland stepped aside, and footmen threw open the great double doors. From beyond strode in the Lord Lyon King of Arms, baton in hand, with two of his heralds, brilliantly bedecked in their red-and-gold tabards and plumed bonnets. This, it appeared, was to be a state occasion.

Behind paced, preternaturally solemn and looking extraordinarily youthful, the Duke of Lennox, newly appointed Lord High Chamberlain, a position once borne by his father, not quite sure whether to wield, carry or trail his staff of office. Dressed in plum-coloured velvet, padded and slashed, he took very long strides and appeared to be counting them out to himself. At evidently a given number of paces, he halted, turned, cleared his throat in some embarrassment, and then thumped his staff loudly on the floor.

76

Mary Gray gurgled her amusement.

In the succeeding hush they all heard the King sniffing, before they saw him. He appeared beyond the open doorway presently, shambling in a hurried knock-kneed gait, almost a trot, peering downwards and sideways as he came, fumbling at the stiffening of his exaggeratedly padded trunks. He was over-dressed almost grotesquely, in royal purple doublet barred with orange, stuffed and distended about the chest and shoulders inordinately, pearl-buttoned and hung with chains and orders. His lolling head seemed to be supported, like a joint on a platter, by an enormous ruff, soiled already with dribbled spittle, whilst round and about all this he wore a short but necessarily wide cloak, embroidered with the royal monogram and insignia, edged with fur, and boasting a high upstanding collar encrusted with silver filigree. To top all, a fantastically high-crowned hat, fully a score of inches in height, ringed with golden chain-work and festooned with ostrich feathers, sat above his wispy hair. The effect of it all, above the thin and knobbly legs, was ludicrously like an over-blown and distinctly unsteady spider. It could now be seen that the reason for the regal preoccupation was the extraction of a handkerchief from a trunks pocket, less than clean.

A woman giggled, and somewhere from the back of the throng came a choked-off guffaw. Then, as the monarch came shuffling over the threshold, Lennox bowed deeply, if jerkily, and thereupon the entire concourse swept low in profound obeisance, the men bending from the waist, the women curtsying, remaining so until James spoke.

'Aye, aye,' he said thickly. 'I . . . we, we greet you warmly. Aye, warmly. All of you. On this, this right au – auspicious occasion.' His protruding tongue had difficulty with the phrase. 'You may stand upright. Och, aye – up wi' you.'

With a very audible exhalation of breath the noble company relaxed again, amidst an only moderately subdued murmur of comment and exclamation, not all of it as respectful as the occasion might have warranted.

'I do not like his hat,' Mary mentioned judicially. 'It is too high, by far.'

'Hush, you!' her father told her, glancing around uneasily.

'Yes. Is not Vicky ridiculous with all that padding?'

'Ssshhh!'

Servitors brought in a gilded Chair of State, on which the monarch sat himself down. The Chancellor moved up on one side of it, Lennox to the other, while the Lord Lyon stood behind. The music resumed, and so did the noise and chatter, while certain notables were brought forward by the heralds, and presented by either Lennox or the Chancellor. James, fidgeting, extended a perfunctory nail-bitten hand, eyed them all sideways, and muttered incoherences. He kept glancing from Lennox to the far end of the room, it was noted, impatiently.

Presently, while still there was a queue of candidates for presentation, James leaned over and plucked at his cousin's sleeve, worrying it like a terrier with a rat. 'Enough, Vicky – enough o' this,' he whispered, but loud enough for all around to hear. 'On wi' our business, man.'

Lennox nodded, waved away the queueing lords, and thumped loudly on the floor again with his staff. The musicians in the ante-room were silenced.

'My lords,' he said. Clearing his throat again, and as an afterthought, 'And ladies. His Grace has asked . . . has commanded your presence here tonight for a purpose. An especial purpose. A notable undertaking. His Grace is concerned at idle talk that has been, er, talked. About his royal marriage.' Ludovick ran a finger round inside his ruff. 'Unsuitable talk and inconvenient . . . '

'Aye – blethers, just. Blethers,' the King interrupted, rolling his head.

'That is so, Your Highness. To still such talk . . . ' Lennox swallowed. ' . . . such blethers, His Grace has been at pains to, to prove otherwise. Quite otherwise. In his, ummm, royal wisdom he has decided to seek the hand . . . '

Sir John Maitland, pulling at his wispy beard, had stooped to the King's ear. James, nodding vigorously, reached over to tug at Lennox's sleeve again. 'Heir,' he said. 'Our royal heir, man.'

'*Mais oui*—the heir. *Pardonnez-moi*,' the Duke observed, little harassed. 'His Grace, recognising the need for an heir, not only to this throne and realm, but that of England also,

78

has decided that this matter should be arranged. Arranged and settled forthwith. Accordingly, he has chosen and elected to seek the hand of that Protestant princess Anne, daughter to the illustrious King Frederick of Denmark in, in . . . '

'In royal and holy matrimony,' James finished for him enthusiastically, producing a lip-licking leer that went but curiously with the phrase. 'I've wrote a rhyme . . . we have turned to the Muse in this pass, and have indited a poem. Aye, indited a poem, I say . . .' He began to search within his doublet, muttering.

There was an uncomfortable pause.

'His Grace has written this poem. To the Princess,' Lennox went on, far from confidently, as the search produced much but no papers. 'A, h'mm, noble poem, setting forth in verse, good verse, excellent verse, his royal offer for her hand. To convey this to the lady, it is decided . . . '

'Och, mair'n that, Vicky – mair'n that! I've expounded on her beauty – for she's right bonny, the lassie. And on her virtue and chastity – for she's but fourteen years, and no' like to be much otherwise!' The royal whinny of laughter tee-heed high. 'No' like . . . no' like . . . ' James gulped, and went on hurriedly. 'As to her wit – och well, I'll teach her that mysel'.' He looked down, as at last he managed to extract some crumpled papers from his doublet, breathless now from the contortions inevitable in a hunt through his over-padded and stuffed casing. 'Here it's. Aye – this is it. I'll read it to you. To you all. For it's good, mind – as good as any I've done. Guidsakes – there's no' that many crowned monarchs could write the like! No – and fewer, I'll be bound, who could put it down in the Latin and the Greek as well, forby! You see, I dinna ken if the lassie kens our Scots tongue. Belike they dinna, in yon Denmark. So I've wrote it out in all three. Aye – well, I'll read it to you. I've named it *The Fond and Earnest Suite and Smoking Smart of James the King*. Aye. I'll read the Scots first . . .' Quite carried away, James got to his unsteady feet, smoothing out the crushed papers.

The great company did not actually groan, of course, but the restraining of such in a hundred throats, and the stirring of innumerable feet, sounded like the moaning and rustling of a lost wind in a forest.

Lennox at one side and Maitland at the other, moved in on the King, whispering.

'The Marischal, Sire!'

'The Ambassador . . . !'

'Eh . . . ? Ooh, aye. Uh-huh. I forgot. Aye.' Somewhat crestfallen, the sovereign looked down regretfully at his epic, tipped his tall hat forward over his brow to scratch at the back of his bulging head, sighed audibly, and sat down again. 'Hae them in, then,' he said.

The Duke resumed. 'In order that His Grace's intentions and royal suit be worthily and courtly presented before the Princess and His Grace of Denmark, it is the King's pleasure that an embassage carrying suitable gifts shall . . .'

'And the poem, man – the poem!'

'And the poem, of course, Sire. An embassage shall depart for Denmark forthwith. Tomorrow indeed, if wind and tide serve. This embassage shall consist of my lord the Earl Marischal and a noble retinue, with Master, er, Herr . . . with the Danish envoy. They now wait without. His Grace will now receive them, read to them his poem, entrust them with its delivery and the royal gifts, and wish them God-speed.' That all came out in something of a spate, as though a lesson learned and thankfully got over. Lennox thumped the floor loudly. 'In the name of King James – admit the King's guests.'

James himself, craning round his Chair of State, signed to the trumpeters to render a flourish.

At the far end of the great hall, double doors were thrown open. To the ringing echoes of the fanfare the colourful concourse seethed and stirred, as some pressed backwards to open a lane, an avenue, down the centre, and others pressed forward the better to see.

After a moment or two of delay, in through the doorway walked a single man, unhurriedly.

'Waesucks!' came a croak from the Chair of State. 'Christ God be good!'

Something between a shiver and a shudder ran through the entire chamber, electric, galvanic. Chancellor Maitland reached forward, gropingly, to steady himself against his master's chair. Lennox looked the merest boy, his heavy lower jaw dropped.

Silence descended, complete but throbbing.

In that silence the only sounds were the steady, deliberate, yet almost leisurely click-click of high-heeled shoes, punctuated at regular intervals by the tap of a stick.

All eyes were riveted on the walker – almost to be described as a stroller. As well they might be. Of medium height, slender but graceful, the man was dazzlingly handsome, with a radiance of good looks that could only be called beauty – redeemed, however, by a basic firmness of line from anything of femininity. Cascading wavy black hair, worn long, framed a noble brow above brilliant flashing eyes. The delicately-flared nostrils of a finely-chiselled nose matched the wicked curving of a proud scimitar of moustache, to balance a warmly, almost sweetly smiling mouth. A tiny pointed beard enhanced the firm but never aggressive chin.

If the tension in that great room was such that all seemed to hold their breath, the same could not be said of the spectacular newcomer, by any manner of means. Unselfconscious, urbane, confident yet with a sort of almost gently mocking deference toward the Chair of State, he moved without haste between the lines of silent watchers, dressed dazzlingly yet simply, all in white satin save for the black velvet lining to the miniature cape slung negligently from one shoulder, the black jewelled garter below one knee, the black dagger-belt, and the black pearls at each neat ear. His spun silk white hose, half as long again as any other in that place, lovingly moulded an excellently-turned and graceful leg almost all the way up the thigh, to disappear into the briefest trunks ever seen in Scotland, verging on indecency back and front; across shoulders and chest hung the delicate tracery of the chain and grand cross of some foreign order of knighthood.

Almost as much as the man himself, and his elegance, it was the staff that drew all fascinated eyes – and the manner of its use. Tall, shoulder-height indeed, slender as its owner, white as ivory save for its deep black ferrule and bunch of black ribbons at its top, it was as different from the Chamberlain's thick rod-like stick of office as it was from the Lord Lyon's short baton. Never had any of his watchers seen such a thing. Nor such casual but extraordinarily effective flourish as the way in which its owner walked with it, swinging its ribboned head forward in an eye-catching wide figure-of-eight movement at every second pace, so that its ferrule made one loud and authoritative tap to each of the two lighter tap-taps of the notably tall-heeled satin-covered shoes. It was impossible not to compare it with Lennox's awkward handling of his own stick.

Some few of the company, who had been close enough to notice the little Gray party in their alcove, turned now to gaze from the newcomer to Mary Gray, eyes wide. To say that Mary's own dark eyes were wide and shining would be a crass understatement. She stood on tip-toes, lips parted, bosom frankly heaving, one hand convulsively clutching David's arm. That man stood as though graven in stone.

It was a long apartment, with fully a hundred feet of floor to cover between the lower doors and the position of the throne-like chair. King James and his immediate supporters therefore had ample time to adjust themselves, to cope with the situation, to give orders to heralds and servitors, even to summon the Captain of the Guard standing nearby. That they did none of these things was strange, a token of the depth of their surprise perhaps, or an involuntary tribute to the calm assurance of the new arrival. James blinked owlishly, jaw going slack, lips twitching. He half rose to his feet, gripping the arms of his chair and crushing the papers of his poem, and so waited, almost crouching. Maitland tugged at his beard, glanced right and left uncertainly, and then, stooping, began to whisper agitatedly in the royal ear – and was completely ignored. Lennox merely stared – although something like the beginnings of a grin appeared at the corners of his wide mouth.

There was some slight commotion back at the bottom end of the room, where a group of gesticulating individuals, one actually bearing a sort of banner, had appeared at the still-open doorway – but no attention was paid to them. All eyes were fixed on the progress of the man in white. He reached a point two or three yards from the Chair of State, paused, and smiling brilliantly, placed his staff, with an elaborate brandish, slant-wise against his delectable person, and extending one foot behind him, sank low in the most complicated genuflexion King James had ever received. His smile advanced to what was almost silent laughter as he held this extraordinary stance, head up, regular white teeth gleaming, eyes dancing. He did not speak before the monarch.

James found words, if incoherent, ill-formed ones, as he sank, or rather shrank, back into his chair. 'Guidsakes, Patrick man . . . you shouldna . . . this isna right. It's no' correct. Where . . . how did you come here, this way? I didna . . . we gave you no summons, man – no royal summons. It wasna you we were looking for . . .'

'Alas, Sire – do I disappoint, then? Heigho – and me foolishly hoping, believing, that after all these weary months of absence from the sun of your royal presence, I might win the bliss of a regal smile, the kind accolade of your kingly generosity!' The Master of Gray's voice was in tune with the rest of him, attractive, warm, lightsome, musically modulated – and clear for all the room to hear as he straightened up. 'Ah, me – is it not to be so? Alack-a-day – must I return banished, Your Grace, to outer darkness? Where I have dwelt so long? When you so raised my poor hopes . . . ?'

'I didna. I didna do that, man. Na, na. You mistake me. You werena to come here. No' to our Court and presence. And I . . . we are employed, see you. Busy. Aye, transacting business. Important business. We were looking to see the Marischal. And yon manikin frae Denmark . . .'

'The Marischal, Sire? Why, I saw my Lord Marischal back there on the stairs. As I came up. Throng with business, he looked, too, i' faith! Laden with packages and merchandise, like any packman! Never fear, Sire – he is about your palace somewhere . . .'

'Yon were my royal gifts to Denmark,' James protested, spluttering. 'I'll thank you, Master o' Gray, no' to name my favours and offerings to the Lady Anne of Denmark as merchandise!'

Patrick Gray's laughter held a gay and carefree note. 'Is that what it was, Sire? Here's felicity, then – here's joy! Is it permitted for a most humble and unworthy subject to congratulate his sovereign on his happy choice?'

'Aye, it is, Patrick – it is,' the King nodded. He glanced up, risking a brief direct look. 'But it was no' *your* advising, mind! You were for a mare frae another stable, eh? Nor ower nice anent her parts and aspect, I'm told. In especial her teeth, man – her teeth!' James produced something between a snort and a snigger.

The other inclined his dark head. 'I but considered Your Highness's interests in the matter of a large dowry. And a notable alliance with the power of France. And the lady is . . . kind. But, Sire, 't'was only a notion. Your own choice must be the joyful choice of us all. And the Princess Royal of Denmark no doubt is a notable-enough match. Even for the King of Scots.'

'Aye.' James coughed. 'But . . . it's no' just the Princess Royal. No' now. It's her sister. The Princess Anne. Anne, it is.'

'Anne!' Something like consternation showed on the Master of Gray's expressive features. 'Only the *second* daughter! For you – king of a greater realm than Denmark. To be King of England, also . . . !'

'Och, well – it wasna to be helped, see you. He'd given the other lassie to Brunswick. Elizabeth, they call her . . . '

'Brunswick! A mere German dukedom! Dear God – on whose advising was this done, Sire? For but a second daughter! The dowry? What of the dowry?'

The King licked slack lips. 'The Marischal is to see to that, Patrick . . . '

The Chancellor came to the rescue of his master. 'Highness,' he broke in. 'Suffer not this insolence! It is intolerable. This man is a convicted felon, an arch-traitor, condemned for highest treason. Sentenced to the axe for the death of your royal mother. Of Your Grace's undue mercy rather than wisdom he was spared – but banished your realm for life. Here, against your commands and those of your Council, he has returned to Scotland. He has the effrontery to force himself into your royal presence. The dignity of your crown and throne, Sire, requires not only that he shall not be heard, but that he be warded securely forthwith. Committed to the castle, to await his further trial. Permit that I summon the Captain of the Guard to his duty, Highness.'

'Aye. Oh, aye, Sir John. Nae doubt you're right, man – nae doubt. But bide a wee – just bide a wee. Master Patrick's done ill to break in this way, to intrude – aye, to intrude. But it's maybe no' just necessary to ward him . . . '

'Sir John was ever a great one for the warding, Majesty,

was he not?' the younger man observed pleasantly. 'Like the laws of the Medes and Persians, he changeth not. Even when circumstances are notably changed. God keep you, my Lord Chancellor. I hope that I see you as well as you merit?'

'Highness – this is not to be borne!' Maitland exclaimed. 'The verdict of Your Grace and Council cannot be set aside . . .'

'Cannot, Sir John? Cannot, eh? Cannot is no' a word to be used to anointed monarchs, man. What we have said, we can unsay. What we decreed, we can un-decree. No' that I'm saying that we'll do that, mind. We shall hae to consider . . .' James darted glances between the two men. 'Consider well . . .'

'Exactly, Your Grace,' Patrick agreed. 'And there is so much to consider, is there not?' He lowered his voice confidentially. 'The matter of your royal pension, for instance. My negotiations with Her Grace of England.'

'Aye, Patrick – what o' it?' The King sat forward, eager now. 'How does she say, the woman? It hasna been paid – no' a plack o' it. No' since you left, man . . .'

'Sire,' the Chancellor interrupted heavily, harshly. 'It is inconceivable that this question, the matter of Your Grace's royal dealings with the Queen of England, should be traded and chaffered over by an outlawed miscreant! Her Grace would never countenance such a thing. This man but seeks insolently to cozen Your Highness . . .'

'You forget, Chancellor, that it was Master Patrick who arranged my pension with Elizabeth in the first place. Aye, maybe you forget it – but I dinna.' The King pointed a nail-bitten finger at the Master of Gray. 'Would you seek to cozen me, man? Would you?'

'Your Grace must be the judge of that,' Patrick declared simply. 'I would have brought the tokens and proofs of my, er, trade and chaffering with me into this your chamber, Sire – save for its weight. Gold, you see, is heavy stuff!'

'Gold!' James cried. 'Gold, you said. You have it with you, man? You brought me gold?'

'Only a token payment, Sire. Not the entire pension. I convinced the lady, I believe, that three thousand gold pieces would be a more suitable and worthy pension for her heir than two. It is but the extra thousand that I brought with me, I fear.'

The King gulped and swallowed convulsively – but even so the saliva flowed copiously down his doublet. 'A thousand gold pieces! Extra! God's splendour – the pension is increased, you say? You have a thousand gold pieces for me, Patrick man? Here? Is it the truth?'

'Outside. In your own palace, Sire. In my Lord of Orkney's lodgings. The rest is promised within the month.'

James was so moved that he got to his feet and reached out to grip the Master of Gray's white satin arm, his poem falling unnoticed to the floor.

Sir John Maitland's sallow features were wiped clean of all expression. He actually moved back a little way from the Chair of State. He knew when, for the moment, he was beaten.

Without seeming to fail in support of the royal grasp, Patrick stooped low to retrieve the fallen papers. To do so he had to use the long staff as prop, so that the ribboned top of the thing was just under the King's nose. James blinked at it.

'You've . . . you've done well, Patrick,' he said thickly. 'I . . . we shall accept the gold from our sister, gladly. Aye, gladly. It's no before its time, mind. But you've done well. And . . . and yon's a bonny bit stick, you have. I've never seen the like.'

'The latest folly at Versailles, Sire. His Grace of France uses one such. You admire it? Then it is yours. Take it.'

'Eh . . . ? Me?' Flushing with pleasure, the King reached for the staff. 'Thank you, thank you. Man, it's a bonny stick. But . . . ' He giggled. ' . . . I'll no' ken what to do wi' it, Patrick.'

'I will show you, Sire. Privily. It is very simple. When you can spare the time. There are other matters for your royal ear, also, when you can spare the time. This dukedom . . . '

'Ooh, aye – I'll spare the time. I've plenty time.'

'Perhaps then, Sire, you will graciously spare a little of it tomorrow? To attend the christening of my son?'

'M'mmm. Oh, well – maybe . . . '

'I was hoping, Highness, that you would consent to be godfather to the boy.' That came out a little more hurriedly than was usual in the utterances of the Master of Gray. 'Since he is, in blood, second-cousin to Your Grace. And in order that his reception into the true Kirk and Protestant faith may be . . . unquestioned. Alas, my own faithful adherence has been so oft and shamefully doubted by my ill-wishers! And you are God's chosen and dedicated Defender of the Faith, are you not?'

'Aye, I am.' James was very proud of that title.

'For the saving of the innocent mite's immortal soul . . . '

'I'ph'mmm. Ooh, aye. Well . . . maybe. Aye maybe, Patrick. We'll see.' The King was twisting and poking the staff this way and that.

'Your Grace – I am profoundly, everlastingly grateful!' Patrick bowed low, to kiss the royal fingers. And, straightening up, 'You dropped these papers I think, Sire.'

'Oh, aye. My poem. M'mmm. For the Princess Anne. I wrote a poem. For the Marischal to take wi' him to Denmark. Aye . . . my Lord Marischal. He's down there yonder waiting yet, the poor man. And the wee envoy frae Denmark. Vicky – my Lord Chamberlain – summon the Marischal again, man.'

The Duke beat his tattoo on the floor once more, and gestured to the heralds, who in turn moved down to usher in the impatient and injured party at the door. The buzz of excited talk and comment from the company hardly sank at all, now – although some laughter sounded.

James sat himself in his chair again, but clung to his new staff, which he laid across his knobbly knees. Patrick strolled over to Lennox, smiling warmly, to grasp the youth's padded shoulder.

'Vicky!' he declared. 'It does my heart good to see you again – I vow it does! And Lord Chamberlain too, i' faith! On my soul, you are a grown man, now!'

The Duke looked at the other with a frank, almost doting admiration. 'I thank you, sir,' he jerked. 'It is good to see you also.'

James, close by, did not miss the admiration in his young cousin's tone – and glowered his jealousy. 'Quiet, you!' he comanded. 'The Marischal . . . '

Patrick and the Duke of Lennox exchanged conspiratorial grins, and stood side-by-side waiting, as the little procession, that was the object of and reason for the entire assembly, approached. Indeed, the Master of Gray appeared to have become an integral and prominent part of the proceedings and royal committee of reception.

George Keith, fifth Earl Marischal of Scotland, a tall soldierly figure in early middle age, dressed it would seem rather for the battlefield than the ballroom, came first, looking angry, with at his back his standard-bearer carrying the red, gold and white banner of his house and office. Next strutted a tiny dark bird-like man, the Danish Envoy, richly but sombrely dressed. Behind followed perhaps a dozen lordlings, lairds and pages, bearing a variety of boxes, chests, parcels and bundles.

Coming near to the Chair of State, the Marischal bowed stiffly, his splendid half-armour creaking and clanking at the joints. The little Dane bobbed something remarkably like a curtsy, fetching titters from the body of the company. The others variously made obeisance.

At a cough from James, Lennox suddenly recollected his duty. 'Your Grace's embassage for Denmark,' he announced.

'Aye,' the King said. 'We greet you well, my Lord Marischal. And you, Master . . . er . . . Bengtsen. Aye, all o' you.'

'Sire — we are here by your royal command,' Keith declared, his deep voice quivering with ill-suppressed ire. 'We have been waiting . . . we were misled! Yon man Gray . . . he misdirected Master Bengtsen, here. Aye, and sent these others off. Down to your stables, Sire. His wife kept me in talk . . . '

'Ooh, aye, my lord — just so,' James acknowledged, head rolling but eyes keen. 'Nae doubt. A . . . a mischance, aye. A misadventure. But nae harm done . . . '

'But, Sire — it was very ill done. 'Fore God, it was! I am not to be made a fool of . . . '

'Na, na, my lord — never think it. The Master o' Gray wouldna ken what was toward. New come to the palace. You'd no' intend any offence — eh, Patrick man?'

'Indeed no, Sire,' that man assured, pain at the thought and kindliest bonhomie struggling for mastery on his beautiful face, in his whole attractive bearing. 'If I have transgressed against my lord in some fashion, I am desolated. I tender profoundest apologies. But . . . I must confess to be much at a loss to know wherein I have offended?'

'Damnation — you made a mock of me, did you no'?' the

Marischal seethed. 'You named Skene, here, a pedlar! You sent Master Bengtsen to the other end o' the house, and these others to the stables! Deliberately, I swear, in order to . . .'

James, leaning forward, banged his new stick on the floor reaching it out almost to the speaker's feet, and then made a poking motion with it at the earl's middle. 'Enough, my lord – enough!' he protested, his voice going high in a squeak. 'You forget yoursel'! We'll hae no bickering in our royal presence. Aye.' He rose to his feet. 'Now – to the business. I . . . we now, my Lord Marischal, solemnly charge you to convey these our gifts and liberality to the Court of our cousin King Frederick o' Denmark, in earnest and in kindly pledge o' our love an affection. Aye – that's towards himsel', you ken. But more especial towards his daughter, the Princess Anne, wi' whom it is our intent and pleasure – *pleasure*, mind – to ally oursel' in holy and royal matrimony. In token o' which, my lord, you will gie to the said lady this poem and notable lyric which I have wrote wi' my ain hand. Aye.'

With a curious mixture of urgency and reluctance, James thrust the crushed papers into the earl's hand.

Blinking, Lennox cleared his throat. 'Sire – are you not to read . . . ?' he wondered.

'No.' That was a very abrupt negative for James Stewart. His glance flickered over to the Master of Gray, however, and away. Poets were scarce indeed about the Scottish Court – but Patrick Gray was a notable exception.

The Earl Marischal, the arranged programme thus further disrupted, eyed the papers doubtfully, glanced around him, and then, for want of better to do, bowed again.

'Aye, then,' the King said, scratching. 'I'ph'mmm. Just that.' He seemed, of a sudden, desirous of being finished with the entire proceedings. 'Er . . . God speed, my lord. And to you, Master Envoy. To all o' you. Aye. God speed and a safe journey. You will convey the Princess Anne to me here, wi' all suitable expedition. Expedition, you understand. Tell her . . . tell her . . . och, never heed. You hae our permission to retire, my lords.'

'But . . . the gifts? The presents, Sire . . . ?' the Marischal wondered.

'Och, I ken them a'. Fine.' James waved a dismissive hand. 'You may go.'

Schooling their features to loyal if scarcely humble acceptance, the bridal ambassadors proceeded to back out of the presence – a trying business, with a long way to retire and all the gear and baggage to manoeuvre. James let them go only a bare half-way before he rose and hurried over to the Master of Gray.

'Man, Patrick,' he said, turning his back on the assemblage at large. 'This o' the dukedom? Think you . . . think you she means it, this time? Elizabeth?'

The handsome man smiled. 'I think that Her Grace meant it . . . when I left her, Sire,' he said gently. 'It is for us to see that she continues to mean it!' He gave just the slightest emphasis to the word us.

'Aye. She . . . she seems to think highly o' you, Patrick. Why?' That last came out sharply.

There was nothing sharp about the reply. 'Your Grace – I have not the least apprehension. Not a notion!'

'U'mmm.'

It was some little time before Patrick Gray was able to detach himself from the King and from the many others who came clustering round him – the ladies in especial. It was noticeable, of course, that quite as many others did not cluster around him, or greet him in any way, other than by hostile stares, muttered asides and coldly-turned shoulders – amongst these some of the most powerful figures in the land, such as the earls of Mar, Glencairn, Atholl, Argyll and Angus, the Lords Sinclair, Lindsay, Drummond and Cathcart, the Master of Glamis who was Treasurer again, and numerous black-garbed ministers of Christ's Kirk. One man who dithered betwixt and between, in evident perplexity and doubt, was the splendidly-attired Bishop of St. Boswell's, Andrew Davidson. Towards him, Patrick cast an amused smile, but by no means sought the cleric's company.

Dancing in progress, the Master of Gray threaded his graceful way through the throng, greeting and being greeted, all amity and cordiality, but not permitting himself to be detained for more than moments at a time. As directly as he might, he made for the raised window alcove wherein he saw his wife standing, with three others.

As he came close, those in the near vicinity moved aside, as by mutual consent, to allow him space. Scores of eyes watched, intently, curiously.

The newcomer's eyes were intent also. After a swift, searching initial glance up at all four occupants of that embrasure, he gazed at one and one only – young Mary Gray. For once his brilliant smile faded – which was strange, for the girl was beaming, radiant.

None in that circle spoke. Never, surely, were a man and a woman so alike – and yet so different.

'Mary!' the man got out, throatily, almost hoarsely.

'Uncle Patrick!' the other cried, high, clear and vibrant, and launched herself down off that plinth and into the white satin arms.

David Gray stared straight ahead of him, grey eyes hooded, lips tight. The Lady Marie reached out a hand to press Mariota's arm.

They kissed each other, those two, frankly, eagerly, almost hungrily, as though unaware of all the watching eyes. They were in no hurry. There was no pose here, no seeking after effect, no calculation. It could have been this, rather than anything that had gone before, that had brought the Master of Gray across most of Europe, moving heaven, earth and hell itself to make it possible. Long they embraced, elegant, magnetic man and lovely eager girl – as though magnets indeed held them together.

Then Patrick as with an effort put her from him, at arm's length. But still he could not take his dark eyes off her face. For once he had no words to speak.

'Oh, it is good!' Mary said, for both of them. 'Good! Good!'

He nodded, slowly, as in profound agreement. Then, still holding one of her hands, he turned to face the others.

'I rejoice . . . to see you,' he said, the so eloquent voice unsteady, uncertain. 'All of you.'

His half-brother inclined his head.

'Oh, Patrick – Patrick!' Mariota exclaimed, breathlessly. 'Thank God! It has been long. So long.'

'Aye, long,' he agreed. 'Too long. You are very beautiful, Mariota my dear. I had almost forgot how beautiful. And how warm. Kind. And Davy . . . Davy is just Davy!'

'Aye,' that man said. He stepped down, to hold out his hand. 'Aye, Patrick.'

Still holding Mary to him, the Master slipped his free hand from his brother's grasp and up around his wide shoulders, there to rest. 'God help us – what a family we are!' he murmured.

The Lady Marie laughed, though a little tremulously. 'You see, Mariota,' she said. 'Those three will do naught for us. We shall have to climb down from here as best we may – for these men scarce know that we are here!'

The ladies were assisted to the floor, and more normal greetings exchanged. Mary was agog, however, for information, for explanations, for secrets.

'Uncle Patrick,' she demanded, just as soon as she had opportunity, dropping her voice conspiratorially. 'How did you do it? You were not expected until tomorrow. How wonderful was your entrance here! How did you affect it? Did you know? Know that it was all arranged for the Danish mission? Did you?'

He touched her hair lightly. 'What think you, my dear?'

'I think that you did! I think that you conceived it all – and deliberately upset all the King's plans. So that you should be the one to whom all looked – not the King. And not the Marischal. I was sorry for my Lord Marischal. And the little Danish man. That was scarcely kind of you, Uncle Patrick. But . . . I think that you are very brave.'

'M'mmm,' he said. 'You appear to think to some effect, young woman. What else do you think, eh?'

'I think that King Jamie, though he may seem to have been won, though he smile on you now, will not love you any the better for this night.' She shook her head seriously, dancing roguery gone. 'He planned all, that he might read his poem for the Danish princess. To us all. For he esteems himself to be a notable poet, does he not? But then, you came. You upset all – and he dared not read it. For he knows full well that you are a much better poet than is he. I think that he will not readily forgive you for that, Uncle Patrick.'

'Say you so?' The Master of Gray fingered his tiny pointed

beard. 'It may be so. Perhaps you are right. It may be that I was a trifle too clever. Who knows? I can be, you know.'

'Yes,' she nodded gravely. 'As in the matter of the Navarre lady.'

His finely arched eyebrows rose. 'Indeed!' he said. 'Mary, my heart – what is this? What has come to you? Here is unlikely thinking for, for a poppet such as you! What is this you have become, while I was gone?'

'I am . . . Mary Gray,' she told him quietly, simply.

Into the second or two of silence that followed, both Mariota and her husband spoke.

'Do not heed her, Patrick,' her mother declared, flushing. 'She is strange, these days. Foolish. Perhaps it is her age . . .'

'She is no longer your poppet, brother – or mine!' David jerked. 'What she has become, I know not. But . . . she concerns herself with things a deal too high for her – that I do know. Nonetheless, Patrick – she is right in this, I fear. The King will not love you the more for this. And you have made an enemy of the Marischal – when you have enemies enough.'

'The Marischal, Davy, is off to Denmark tomorrow – and by the time that he wins back to Scotland, it will matter not.' The Master, speaking softly, guided his little company into a corner where at least they might not be overheard. 'It was necessary, see you, that I should be received back at Court – and be seen by all to be so received. Before my enemies could know that I was here, and could work against me with the King. James did not summon me to Court – only permitted my temporary return to Scotland – and that reluctantly indeed. For the christening. Tomorrow. So I wore out relays of cousin Logan of Restalrig's horses getting here tonight. I am here before the courier who brought me the King's letter could himself win back! Think you that Maitland and the rest of the Protestant lords would have permitted that I be received? By tomorrow night, I swear, my body would have been floating in the Nor' Loch, rather! And an outlaw, none could be arraigned for my death. But now – I am received, admitted, one of the elect once more! They dare not touch me now – not openly. I have the King's ear, the King's protection . . . for so long as he needs something that I can give him. One thousand golden guineas! And, he is to pray, more to come! A deal of good money – but cheap at the price, I vow!'

'Cheap . . . ? The price? What price? To you? It is Elizabeth's money . . .'

The Master's laughter was silvery. 'Why, Davy – I thought that you at least would know our Elizabeth better! That gold was hard-earned – but not from Elizabeth of England. It came from less lofty sources – at no little cost to me. Methinks that she will not deny credit for it one day, nevertheless! Heigho – we cannot have chicken-soup without immersing the chicken! Cheap at the price I esteem it, yes – and moreover have we not achieved a royal godfather for young Andrew! Which also may have its value, one day. But . . . enough of this whispering in corners. It looks ill, furtive. And I am never furtive, am I – whatever else I am, God help me! I see my lord of Mar eyeing me closely. He grows ever more like a turkey-cock, does Johnnie Mar.' The Master of Gray was of a sudden all smiling gaiety again. 'See – it is a pavane that is being danced. I am partial to the pavane. In good company. Now – which of you ladies will do me the honour . . . ?'

It was at Mary Gray that he looked.

A moment or two later they moved out together to the stately measures of the dance, eyes in their hundreds watching, dazzling satin and humble lawn. Mary Gray danced like a queen.

Chapter Five

A bare three weeks after Patrick Gray's dramatic return to Scotland, the country was in a turmoil. The Catholics had risen again. All of Scotland, north of Aberdeen, was said to be in revolt, and the Earls of Huntly and Erroll declaring that they would march south forthwith and would be in the capital to rescue their King in a week or so. The departure of the Earl Marischal for Denmark was said to be the immediate cause of this; he was the Protestant's strong man in the north, and co-lieutenant with Huntly for the King's rule in those vast and unmanageable territories. There appeared to be more than just this in it, however, for the madcap Earl of Bothwell, with the assistance of the turbulent and widespread Border clan of the Homes, had assembled what amounted to an army near Kelso, and threatened to march on Edinburgh from the south should the royal forces move north against Huntly. This was curious, for Bothwell and the Homes were no Catholics. What was their objective in this affair was not clear – though it was assumed that the downfall of Maitland the Chancellor and his friends from their positions of power around the King, must be the aim. There were those in Court and government circles, nevertheless, who did not fail to point out that, equally curiously, the Master of Gray, only two or three days after his son's christening, had disappeared off in the direction of the Borders, ostensibly to visit his disreputable cousin Logan of Restalrig and his aunt, the former Lady Logan, now married to the Lord Home – and had been away for a full week.

However, base suspicions on this score were lulled, if not altogether scotched, when, on word of Bothwell's threat reaching Edinburgh, Patrick, newly returned to town, sought audience of the King – and, strangely enough, of the Chancellor. He urged that a strong and vigorous gesture be made forthwith against the unruly Borderers, whereupon, he vowed, Bothwell would not actually fight. Moreover, he was able, loyally and almost miraculously, to warn King and Chancellor of a nefarious conspiracy to seize their persons, by certain ill-willed folk about the capital – who, when arrested and suitably put to the question, admitted that such had been their aim, and were thereafter satisfactorily hanged. Since James had an almost morbid dread of such plots, and Maitland was a deal more at home with clerkly administration than military action, the Master's advice was taken, if doubtfully, and a force of the levies of Protestant lords in the Lothians hurriedly assembled. And lo, as prophesied, Bothwell's force, which had meantime reached as near as Haddington, seventeen miles from Edinburg, promptly melted away, shrinking, it was reliably reported, to a mere thirty horse.

Flushed with this demonstration of the value of firm action, the King smiled upon the useful Master of Gray, and called upon all leal lords, the Kirk, and his faithful burghs, to provide him with a sufficiency of armed men to march north to deal with the much more serious threat of the Catholic rising, at the same time issuing a proclamation ordering all men to forsake the service of the Earls of Huntly, Erroll and Bothwell, on pain of treason.

This Catholic threat had indeed cast its shadow elsewhere than on the Court and Capital. Dundee was the nearest large Protestant city south of Aberdeen and of Huntly's domains. When reports of Catholic columns reaching as far south as Bervie and Montrose, and of raiding Gordon bands pouring down the Angus glens, began to reach Dundee, the Provost and magistrates and ministers of the kirk of that God-fearing city perceived the need for drastic action. Walls were hastily repaired, gates strengthened, citizens called up. Dudhope Castle, the town's fortress, was stocked and garrisoned, and a deputation sent hot-foot to call upon the Lord Gray to urge that Broughty Castle, the key to the city from the east and seaward, be likewise garrisoned and put in a state of defensive readiness forthwith.

My lord, in some agitation and with no little reluctance – for his castle of Broughty, for one reason and another, was not in a good state of repair – and the expense of doing what was necessary would undoubtedly fall wholly upon his own pocket – agreed to see what could be done. In no sunny frame of mind, and at the almost feverish pleadings of the Provost and Sir John Scrymgeour, the Hereditary Constable of Dundee, he set off for Broughty, hailing David Gray his steward along with him.

This was the distinctly involved and dramatic situation prevailing when, the very next morning, on a sunny and sparkling July day, the Master of Gray, with his wife and baby son, attended by only two servitors belonging to Marie's father, returned, unexpected and unannounced to his birthplace, one-time home, and presumably future seat of Castle Huntly, after an absence of years – for he had been estranged from his father for long before his trial and banishment. In the absence of my lord and Davy, Mary Gray greeted them, and joyfully, all laughter and delight. She explained that her grandfather and father had been at Broughty Castle since the day before, and it was not known when they would be back. Patrick announced that, much as he would have preferred to stay at Castle Huntly with herself and her mother, it was his father that he had come to see, and as the matter had some urgency, he would ride on to Broughty forthwith. Mary, despite the attractions of cosseting and cherishing the baby Andrew, declared that she also would ride to Broughty with him – her Uncle Patrick nowise objecting. The Lady Marie was glad enough, apparently, to remain with Mariota, having ridden from Megginch that morning.

Pensively the two women watched the man and girl ride off eastwards, thinking their own thoughts.

The larks carolled, the sun shone, the countryside basked, and Patrick Gray seemed to have not a care in the world this fine morning. He was barely out of earshot of the castle gate-house before he began to sing. He had an excellent lightsome tenor voice, and plunged straight into some gay and melodious French air which seemed to bubble over with droll merriment. It took only a few moments for Mary to catch the lilt and rhythm of it, and to add her own joyful trilling accompaniment, wordless but effective. Thereafter they sang side by side in laughing accord, clear, uninhibited, neither in the least self-conscious, caring naught for the astonished stares of the villagers of Longforgan or the embarrassed frowns of the two Orkney servants who rode well to the rear as though to disassociate themselves from the unseemly performance in front.

After the village there was a long straight stretch of road before it reached the coast at Invergowrie, and with a flourish Patrick smacked his horse into a canter. Not to be outdone, Mary promptly urged her own mount to a round gallop, passing the man with a skirled challenge, hair flying dark behind, her already short enough skirt blown back above long, graceful legs. Shouting, the Master spurred after her, gradually overtaking, until neck and neck they thundered together, raising a cloud of brown dust all along a couple of miles of rutted highway, whilst cattle scattered in nearby fields, folk peered from cot-house doors and the grooms behind cursed and made pretence of keeping up.

Just short of Invergowrie they pulled in their frothing beasts to a trot once more, the girl panting breathless laughter and

97

pulling down her skirt. Patrick reached out, to run a hand down her flushed cheek and over her shoulder and the heaving curve of her young bosom.

'We are sib . . . you and I . . . are we not?' he said.

'Indeed, yes,' she agreed, frankly. 'Would it not be strange if we were not . . . since you sired me?'

'M'mmm.' Sidelong he looked at her, silenced.

She turned in her saddle. 'You did not think that I did not know, Uncle Patrick?' she wondered.

'I . . . I was uncertain. Your father . . . h'mmm . . . my brother, Davy Gray – he has never said . . . '

'Not to me. But I knew, years ago. Many made sure that I knew.'

'Aye, many would! But . . . ' He smiled again. 'God bless you – it was the best thing that ever I did, I vow!'

'A better would have been to wed my mother, would it not?'

It took him a moment or two to answer that. 'Perhaps you are right, my dear,' he admitted, quietly for him. 'I . . . I do not always choose the better course, I fear.'

'No,' she agreed simply. 'That I know also.'

Again the swift sidelong glance. 'You are like me, child, God knows. But . . . in some ways, curse me, you're devilish like Davy also! Like your, your Uncle Davy.'

She nodded seriously. 'I hope so, yes. For he is the finest man in this realm, I do believe. But . . . he is Father, not Uncle Davy. He, he fathered me, whilst you but sired me, Uncle Patrick. There is a difference, is there not?'

The Master of Gray looked away, his handsome features suddenly still, mask-like. 'Aye,' he said.

They rode in silence, then, through Invergowrie, and kept down by the shore-track thereafter to avoid the climbing narrow streets and wynds of hilly Dundee.

As they went, they could see men busily engaged in building up the broken town walls, and at the boat-harbour others urgently unloading vessels.

'It is an ill thing when people must fear their own folk, their own countrymen, because of the way that they worship the same God, is it not?' Mary observed. 'I do not understand why it should be.'

'It is one of the major follies of men,' her companion acceded. 'A weakness, apparently, in all creeds.'

'Yes. A weakness that, they say, you use for your own purposes, Uncle Patrick. Is it so, indeed?'

He puckered his brows, wary-eyed – for Patrick Gray seldom actually frowned. 'I must use what tools come to my hand, my dear.'

'For your own purposes, always?'

'For purposes that I esteem as good, child.'

'Good for whom, Uncle Patrick?'

'Lord, Mary – what is this that you have become? You talk like a minister of the Kirk, I swear! How old are you? You cannot be more than just sixteen – for I am but thirty-one myself! Here is no talk, no thoughts, for a girl. You should be thinking of other things at your age, lass. Happier things. To do with clothing and pretty follies. With lads and wooing. With courting and marriage, maybe . . . '

Directly she turned to face him, clear eyed. 'Like King Jamie, perhaps?'

Patrick touched mouth and chin. 'The King's wooing is of rather more serious import, my dear. So much may depend upon it. An heir to the throne, the peace and prosperity of the realm, the weal – perhaps even the lives – of many.'

Gravely, almost judicially, she inclined her head. 'That is what I thought, yes. That is why, Uncle Patrick, I sent word to the King about the Princess of Navarre.'

'You . . . what?'

'I sent word to the King. Through Vicky. Through the Duke of Lennox. Vicky does what I say, you see. I sent him word that the lady was ill-favoured and old and would bed with any. As the Lady Marie told Father.'

'Precious soul of God – you! It was you? You who turned James against the match? After all my labour, my scheming . . . !'

'Yes.'

'But this is beyond all belief! That you, *you* my own daughter, should think to do such a thing! And why? Why, in God's name?'

'Because it was not good. Surely you see it? The Lady Marie is true and honest. She would not lie – not to Davy

99

Gray. If the Princess is bad, and old, and ugly, then she should not be Queen in Scotland. King Jamie is but ill-favoured himself. With an old and ugly queen, would not the Crown be made to seem the more foolish? Weak, when it needs rather to be strong? If she is old, it might be that there would be no child, no heir to the throne. And that is important, is it not? Did you not just say so? Moreover, if she is but a whore, it could be that if a child there was, none would know who sired it. I think that would have been but an ill turn to Scotland, Uncle Patrick. So I sent word to Vicky. And that the little picture was ten years old, and a flattery.'

The Master of Gray let his breath go in a long sigh. He did not speak.

'I am sorry that you are angry,' she went on, reaching over to touch his arm. 'Do not be angry. Was what I did wrong?'

Slowly he turned to consider her, all of her, vital, lovely, pleading, yet somehow also compassionate, forbearing, so unassumingly sure of herself. Swallowing, he shook his head.

'I am not angry,' he said. 'And, Heaven forgive me, you were not wrong!'

Mary smiled then, warmly, nodding her head three or four times as though in confirmation of what she already knew.

They were not much more than half-way to Broughty Castle, but already they could see it rearing proud and seeming defiant on its little peninsula that thrust out into the estuary four or five miles ahead. Something of a fortress this, rather than an ordinary castle, the Grays had used it for generations, in conjunction with another at Ferry-Port-on-Craig on the Fife shore opposite, to command the entrance of the Tay, thus narrowed by headlands. Theoretically it was for the defence of Dundee and other Tay ports, but in fact had been used to levy tolls and tribute from all shipping using the harbours – a notable source of the Gray wealth. My lord's father, the fourth lord, had shamefully surrendered it to the English under Somerset nearly forty years before, during a disagreement with the Queen Regent, Mary of Guise; and my lord himself, two years later, had gained his limp and almost lost his life seeking to retake it. The damage done then, by cannon-fire, had never been fully repaired – hence the present crisis.

As man and girl rode on along the scalloped coast, presently Mary began to sing again, a sweetly haunting melody of an older Scotland still. Patrick did not join in now, but he eyed her, time and time again, as she sang, wonderingly, thoughtfully, calculatingly – and when her sparkling eye caught his own, he mustered a smile.

It was seldom indeed that the Master of Gray did not set the pace in any company that he graced.

They came to Broughty Craig two hours after leaving Castle Huntly, and found it as busy as an ant-hill, with men re-digging the great moat which cut off the headland from landward, shoring up timber barricades against the broken battlements, filling in gaps in the sheer curtain-walling with its many wide gun-loops. It was a more gloomy frowning place than Castle Huntly, less tall but more massive, consisting of a great square free-standing tower of five storeys, immensely thick-walled and small-windowed, rising from an oddly-shaped enclosure, almost like a ship, which followed faithfully the outline of the rocky headland itself, this latter also provided at its corners with smaller round flanking towers. Around three sides the sea surged, and under the stern ramparts the harbour crouched – the ferry harbour, which was another source of my lord's revenues, since none might come and go across the estuary to St. Andrew's, without paying a suitable tax. Other ferries were effectively discouraged.

The newcomers found David in the courtyard superintending the hoisting of heavy timber beams up the outer walling to the dizzy parapet-walk at top floor level, doublet discarded and sleeves uprolled like any labouring man. He stared at his spectacularly clad brother, astonished, and then curtly ordered him to wait, and safely out of the way, while the delicate process of hoisting was completed. Then, running a hand through his sweat-damp hair, he came over to them.

'What brings you here, Patrick?' he demanded. 'My lord is here. Within. Talking with your brother Gilbert, and the Provost . . . '

'What of it, Davy? May a man not call upon his father, on occasion? Even such a father as ours? And Gibbie – Lord, I have not seen Gibbie for years. Eight years. Ten. He will be a man now, also, of course.'

'He is laird of Mylnefield, and a burgess and bailie of Dundee.'

'All that? Young running-nosed Gibbie! It makes me feel old, I vow! Well, well – let us within.'

'Patrick – think you it is wise?' David sounded hesitant, uneasy. 'My lord – he is in no sunny mood. With all this expense . . .'

'The more reason that she should be gladdened by the sight of his missing son and heir – if not his firstborn, Davy! Besides, I can save our skinflint sire some of this foolish expense – ever the sure road to his heart! Come.'

Patrick led the way in at the door of the keep, Mary and David following. The girl slipped her hand within her father's arm.

'Uncle Patrick is not afraid, Father,' she murmured. 'So why should you be? He has faced more terrible folk than Granlord, I think.'

'It is not your Uncle Patrick for whom I am afraid, girl!' David answered briefly, grimly.

They heard voices from the great hall on the first floor, and mounted the worn steps thereto. The place was less large than might have been expected, owing to the great thickness of the walls, and only dimly lit by its small deep-set windows. Moreover it was but scantily furnished with a vast elm table in the middle of the stone-flagged floor, and a few chairs and benches. My lord had always least liked this castle of the many that he had inherited – partly no doubt on account of the shattered knee-cap, won here, that he had carried with him for forty years – and maintained it was only a keeper-cum-toll-gatherer and a few men, none of whom used this great central keep. It was cool in here however, at least, after the mid-day July heat outside – although the musty smells of bats and rats and damp stone caught the throat. Two men sat, with tankards in their hands but all attention, at the great table, and the third limped back and forth before them, declaiming vehemently.

At sound of the newcomers, my lord looked around, though he halted neither his pacing nor his harangue at first. Undoubtedly the dim lighting denied him identification – although the younger of the seated men got slowly to his feet, staring at the doorway. Probably it was this that made the nobleman glance again, and he perceived at least Mary Gray there, with Davy and the superbly dressed visitor. His heavy sagging features lightened, and if the growl did not go right out of his voice, it developed something of a chuckle.

'Ha – my poppet! My ain pigeon! Is that yoursel', lassie? What brings *you*, like a blink o' sunshine, into this thrice-damned sepulchre o' a place? Eh? And who's that you've got wi' you bairn . . . ?'

'Can you not see, Granlord? Is not this splendid?'

'Does blood not speak louder than words, my lord?' Patrick asked pleasantly. 'I rejoice to see you well. And active in, h'm, well-doing.'

'Christ God!'

'Scarce that, my lord – just your son Patrick!'

The older man groped almost blindly for the support of the table. His thick lips moved, but no sound issued therefrom. Mary ran to his side, to take his other hand.

Patrick and David came forward. 'It is some years, sir, since we have had the pleasure, is it not?' the former went on, easily. 'You wear well, I see. And is that Gibbie with you? Brother Gibbie – a man now, a sober, respectable, man, I vow – and scarce like a Gray at all, at all! Greetings, brother. And to you, Mr Provost.'

My lord smashed down his fist on the table-top. 'Silence!' he barked, though his voice broke a little. 'Quiet, you . . . you mincing jackdaw! You mocking cuckoo!' As Mary tugged at his arm, whispering, he shook her off roughly. 'Fiend seize me – what ill chance brings you here? How dare you darken any door o' mine, man?'

'Dare, sir? Dare? Why, I am a very lion for daring. That at least I inherit from my sire – if naught else. Yet!' Patrick smiled. 'I dare, my lord, because I would see you, have word with you – who knows, even possibly come to terms with you!'

'Never, curse you – never! I told you yon time – never did I want to see your insolent ninny's face again. I meant it then, by God – and I mean it yet!'

'My lord . . . ' David began, but Patrick silenced him with a gesture.

'My face, sir, may not please you – since it is vastly unlike

103

your own . . . which no doubt contents us both well enough! But, I had thought that you at least would wish to look on the face of your eventual heir. The seventh Lord Gray, to be. You did not grace his christening. So I have brought him to Castle Huntly, that you may see him there.'

'Then you may take the brat away again – and forthwith!' the older man returned. 'I want no more sight o' him that I do o' you, d'you hear? I ken you, you crawling thing, man! First you would come to me hiding behind a woman's skirts. Now, behind a suckling's wrappings. I'll no' . . . I'll no' . . .' The Lord Gray all but choked to silence, his face congested, purple, his heavy jowls shaking. He staggered a little, and the hand which reached out for the table again trembled noticeably.

Mary ran back to his side, to hold him, biting her lip.

The Master's slender ruffled wrist was gripped strongly, as in a vice. 'Enough,' David said, low-voiced but commanding. 'He will take a hurt. He is your father – and mine. Enough, I say.'

Patrick slowly inclined his handsome head. 'Very well,' he murmured. And louder, 'These family pleasantries over, then – I come to business, my lord. Private business, and pressing.' He turned to the two men at the other side of the table. 'Mr Provost – you will excuse us? You too, Gibbie, I think. Yes – go please.'

Both sitters rose, the younger, thin, dark-featured, long-chinned, frowning. 'Sir . . . Patrick . . . !' Gilbert Gray protested. 'This is . . . this is insupportable! You'll no' treat me like a lackey . . . and in my father's house!'

'Lord, Gibbie – I treat you like I do the Provost, here. With great respect, but scarce requiring your presence in the private business, affairs of state, that I have to discuss with my lord. So – off with you both to somewhere else.'

The Provost, a fat and perspiring bald man, ducked and bowed and mumbled in alarmed reaction to the authoritative, indeed imperious, orders, moving hastily if sidelong towards the door. Gilbert Gray, almost involuntarily did likewise, but more slowly and looking to his father.

My lord was staring glassily straight ahead of him, breathing stertorously, aparently heeding none of them.

104

As they reached the door, however, Patrick suddenly stopped them with a snap of his long fingers. 'Stay, Provost – a moment. You may as well hear this first. Before you go. You may spare your worthy citizens their unnecessary labours, man. Their hammerings and stone-masonry and running to and fro. Likewise, my lord, your distressing activities here. There is no need for such extremities. All unnecessary. Huntly is not coming south.'

They stared at him, all of them.

'Tut – do not gawp! You have jumped at shadows. Your panic is superfluous. Save yourself further troubles, gentlemen. And expense. Huntly will not move. His outliers will retire on Aberdeen by nightfall. Already they will have turned back. There is no danger to your douce town of Dundee.'

'But . . . but . . . ?'

'How do you know this, Patrick?' David jerked.

'I have my sources of intelligence, Davy. As you know.' Patrick smiled. 'Moreover, the King and a great Protestant host, filled with holy and Reformed zeal, will be beyond Strathmore and Jordan . . . or the Esk . . . by this! I left His Grace at Perth yesterday noon, rumbling martial thunderings from lips and belly. So there is naught to fear.'

'My lord . . . honoured sir . . . ,' the Provost gabbled. 'Is this . . . is this sooth? You are assured o' it . . . ?'

'A pox, fellow – do you doubt my word! You?'

'Na, na – och, never that, sir! Never that . . . '

'Then be gone. And you, Gibbie. Every minute will save money, will it not?' It was perhaps noteworthy that though the Master of Gray dismissed his lawful brother thus cavalierly, he did not make any similar gesture towards his bastard half-brother. Nor, for that matter, towards young Mary. Turning his elegant back on the pair from Dundee, he addressed his father, who appeared to be recovering. 'Perhaps you should sit down, my lord,' he suggested. 'That we may discuss our business in . . . ' – he glanced around him distastefully – ' . . . in such comfort as this rickle of stones allows.'

'I have . . . no business . . . to discuss . . . wi' you!' my lord rasped throatily, harshly – 'Now, or ever.' He did not move from his stance by the table.

'Ah, but you have sir, I assure you. On a matter close to

105

your heart, I vow. Siller, my lord – siller! Sillibawbys, merks and good Scots pounds! Sink me – have I not already saved you a pretty purseful by this intelligence that I bring? You no longer need spend a plack on this rat-ridden ruin. Send all your drudges home. And let your pocket thank me – even if naught else does!'

From under heavy brows his father gazed at him, like a bull dazed and uncertain. 'This . . . is certain? About Huntly? And the King? We are safe, now?' he got out.

'Now – and before. You never were in danger. Huntly makes a demonstration – that is all. For, shall we say, a variety of excellent reasons. He never had any intention of descending upon the south. The King of Spain, God preserve him, has sent Huntly a consignment of gold ducats, and he must make pretence of using them to good effect. Moreover, Huntly does not love my lord of Bothwell, and considers that his wings needed clipping. This achieves it. So King Jamie marches valiantly north, and will enjoy a notable, a resounding victory – since none will oppose him. Oh, some Highland caterans will be slaughtered and a few Aberdeen burghers hanged, no doubt, for dignity's sake – but Huntly will speak loving peace with His Grace, and some few of the ducats will belike find their way into Jamie's coffers . . . '

'God's death – what mad rigmarole is this?' his father cried. 'Are you crazed, man?'

'Hardly, sir! Do you really think it? Indeed, I humbly suggest otherwise. For, you see, good is served all round is it not? Elizabeth of England, perceiving the great stresses and dangers King Jamie lives under, in preserving the sacred cause of Protestantism, must needs increase her contributions towards the upkeep of a stronger and truly loyal guard in this happy realm. The matter is vital – for the Reformed faith, you understand. Already, indeed, the couriers are on their urgent way to London, to that effect. Heigho – all things work together for good, as I say, do they not?'

My lord was speechless.

It was David Gray who spoke, in a whisper. 'So soon!' he said. 'So soon! We are back where we were, i' faith! Nothing is changed. The . . . the Devil is come back to Scotland!'

'Come, come, Davy – you flatter me! Besides, no harm is

done. Quite the reverse, I vow. Are not all advantaged – or nearly all? Which brings me, my lord, to the matter of our business – so that *we* shall be advantaged also. The matter concerns the Abbey of Dunfermline.'

'A-a-ah!' Lord Gray said, despite himself.

'Exactly! I intend, you see, to recover my commendatorship and the revenues thereof. George Gordon of Huntly has enjoyed them quite sufficiently long for any small service that he effected. He is proving stupidly obdurate, however. Always George was stupid – do you not agree? And our Jamie is something of a broken reed in the matter, I fear. Indeed, I suspect His slobbering Grace. So, I propose to sue George for Dunfermline in the High Court. And believe that, with a little forethought and judicial, er, preparation, I shall win. For Huntly has few friends amongst His Grace's judges – who are all good Protestants, of course!' Patrick sighed, a little. 'Unfortunately, such processes of law cost money. Siller, my lord – siller. A commodity of which I am, at the moment, somewhat short, more is the pity. Hence this approach . . . and your good fortune, sir.'

His father gaped like a stranded fish. 'You . . . you . . . ? Me . . . ? Siller . . . ?' With difficulty he enunciated consecutive words. 'Ha, you gon plain gyte, man? D'you think to win siller frae me? *Me?*'

'I do, naturally. And for good and excellent reason. I do not come to you out of mere, shall we say, family affection and esteem, my lord – admirable as are such sentiments. This is a matter of business, of lands and heritable properties. Heritable, I pray you note, is the significant word. Since, one day in God's providence, I or my son shall inherit from you the Gray lands, merest foresight and common prudence indicates that it is to you that I should offer Balmerino. So that, heigho, in the said God's time I shall have it back again! Balmerino, my lord – Balmerino!'

Lord Gray was so much moved that he groped his way round the table, Mary supporting him, to sink into one of the chairs. He never took his eyes off his beautiful son – although from his expression the sight appeared to afford him only extreme distress.

Well might the Master harp on that word Balmerino, of

107

course. Balmerino Abbey, or the ruins thereof, with its little town and port, lay almost exactly across the Tay estuary from Castle Huntly. Its lands were extensive and fertile; more important however, from Lord Gray's point of view, was the fact that owing to the shallows and shoals of the firth at this point, its port commanded the ship-traffic of the upper reaches of the estuary. Taken in conjunction with the Broughty Castle and Ferry Port toll barriers, it could completely dominate all trade, internal as well as external, along the entire causeway, with a judiciously-placed cannon or two. Long had the Grays looked across at Balmerino in North Fife with covetous eyes. Its possession could vastly increase their revenues.

Patrick answered his father's unspoken question. 'I have arranged with Sir Robert Melville an exchange of Balmerino for the Dunfermline pendicle of Monimail near to his own lands of Melville. When I win back Dunfermline, Balmerino will be mine. Or rather, yours, my lord – for one thousand silver crowns. A bargain, you will admit!'

His father uttered a groan of sheerest agony.

'You perceive, my lord, how necessary it is that I come to you, rather than to any other? Balmerino is worth a score of times more to Gray than to anyone else in the kingdom. Am I not a dutiful son, after all?'

'No!' the older man croaked. 'No! No!' he banged fist on the table time and again.

'But yes, sir. You would not throw away Balmerino for a mere thousand pieces of siller?'

His father was grimacing strangely. Undoubtedly it was the hardest decision of that nobleman's life, striking to the very roots of him. But he made it. 'Damn you . . . no! Never!'

Patrick was still-faced, curiously blank-looking for a moment. But only for a moment or two. 'I am sorry,' he said, then, shrugging.

"I . . . I vow you are, foul fall you!'

'But, yes. I would be as foolish not to be so, as are you in throwing this aside, my lord. Blinded by . . . by whatever so blinds you. I can get the money elsewhere, to be sure – but not so profitably for Gray.'

'Then get it, man – get it! For you'll no' win a plack frae me. All your days you've wasted and devoured my substance.

You'll do it nae mair. You can beg for crusts in the vennels o' Edinburgh, for a' I care, d'you hear? You and your woman and your brat can starve . . . '

'Oh, Granlord – no!' Mary cried.

'Here are but doubtful fatherly sentiments, my lord! You scarce ever doted on me, I think – but it seems . . . excessive. What new ill have I done to you since last we met, I pray?'

The other rose slowly to his feet, with something of dignity now. 'You butchered your Queen,' he said. 'You were the death o' the bonny Mary, that I loved well.'

There was complete silence in that dim and musty chamber, for seconds on end.

It was young Mary who broke it. 'It is not so, Granlord,' she said urgently. 'Not so. He went to save her, and could not. That is not the same. Queen Elizabeth it was who killed our Queen. Not Uncle Patrick. He was not able to save her. But then, neither was Father. Neither was Sir Robert Melville, who went too. None could.' Her young voice seemed to echo desperately round the gaunt vaulted cavern of masonry, pleading.

None of the men either looked at her nor answered the question behind her words.

'Why must you be so hard on each other?' she asked. 'So cruelly hard?'

'Mary – it would be better, I think, that you should leave us, child.'

'No. No, Father. Do you not see . . . ?'

My lord spoke through her pleas. 'Go!' he commanded – but not to the girl. 'Go, Judas – and never let me see your false face again! I want nane o' you – nane, d'you hear? Judas!'

The muscles of the Master's features seemed to work and tense. For once, there was little of beauty or attractiveness to be seen thereon, as glittering-eyed, ashen-lipped, he faced his father. 'For that word . . . you will be sorry!' he got out. 'Sorry!'

'Go . . . !'

'Oh, yes – I shall go. But first, I will have my rights from you. What you will not give in love and affection, even in decency, you will yield as of right. For I am Master of Gray

109

– heir to this lordship. I have never asked for it before – but I demand it now. I want my portion.'

My lord belched rudely. 'That for your portion, man!'

This crude coarseness seemed to have the effect of steadying the younger man, of enabling him to revert to something of his usual assured air of mastery of any situation. 'I think not,' he said, actually smiling again. 'The heir to Gray has certain rights, beyond the mere style. I have not sought them of you . . .'

'Any such you ha' forfeited long since. You ha' squandered my siller . . .'

'I refer, sir, not to your precious siller, but to more enduring claims. My patrimony. Properties. You have, I understand, settled Mylnefield on Gibbie. Brother James, I am told, has Buttergask and Davidstoun. William is in Bandirran. I am not wholly uninformed, my lord. Myself, I require the heir's portion.'

His father was breathing deeply, purpling again. 'Curse you – you'll get nothing! Nothing, I say. Knave and black-guard that you are! I . . . I . . .' Of a sudden, my lord's heavy features seemed to lighten a little. 'Or . . . aye, I have it! That's it. Your portion, my bonny Master o' Gray! You have it, man – you're standing in it! *This* is your portion – all you'll get, while I am above the sod! Broughty Castle!' Hooted harsh laughter set the older man coughing. ' 'Tis yours, Patrick – all o' it, yours, by God!' he spluttered. 'See to it, Davy. The papers and titles – to Patrick, Master o' Gray, in life rent, Broughty Castle. The building only, mind. No' a stick or stone else. No' an inch o' land. No' a penny-piece o' the tolls. A rickle o' stones you named it, Patrick? Aye – then take it, and I pray to God it falls on your scoundrelly head and makes your sepulchre!'

Pushing Mary aside roughly, the Lord Gray stalked heavily past his sons without a further word or glance, and out of the arched doorway to the winding stairs.

Tears were trickling down the girl's face from brimming dark eyes, though she made neither sob nor sound.

'I shall build up these crumbling wall, I tell you – raise new towers and battlements. I shall root out these mouldering boards and rotting beams. I shall open up these wretched holes of windows, and let in air and light. I shall hang these bare walls with Flemish tapestries and cover the floors with carpets from the East, and furnish these barren chambers with the finest plenishings of France and Spain and the Netherlands, such as not another house in this realm can show!' The Master of Gray was striding back and forward across the uneven bat-fouled flagstones of Broughty Castle's hall, set-faced, eyes flashing. 'I shall make of this stinking ruin a palace, I swear! A mansion which every lord in the land shall envy. Where the King will come to sup and wish his own. I shall make it so that Castle Huntly seems a hovel, a dog's kennel, by comparison, and its proud lord shall come here seeking admission on his bended knees! I swear it, I say – and swear it by Almighty God!'

'Uncle Patrick – don't!' Mary Gray said. 'Please don't. Please.'

David and the girl were watching the extraordinary, almost awesome spectacle of the most handsome man in all of Europe, the brightest ornament of the Scottish scene, the most talented gallant in two realms, in the grip of blind unreasoning bitter hurt and passion, tormented, distraught. Helplessly they watched him, listened to him, anguish and sorrow in their own eyes – for they loved him, both. Mary had never seen the like, although she had witnessed some shocking, savage scenes in that strange and contentious family. David had his arm around the girl's shoulders, holding her; he indeed had seen the like before – and it turned his heart sick within him.

Patrick Gray changed his tune. He stopped his pacing, and began to curse. Tensely, almost softly, but fluently, comprehensively, he commenced to swear in breath-taking ingenious ferocity.

David Gray acted. Leaving Mary, he strode up to his brother, grasped him by both elegant padded shoulders, and with abrupt violence shook him as a terrier shakes a rat. 'Quiet!' he commanded. 'Quiet, I say. Patrick – be silent! Mary – by God, mind Mary!'

The evil flow was choked back, partly through sheer physical convulsion, partly by a real effort of will. Gasping and panting a little, the Master stepped back, and the scorching fury in his gaze at his half-brother faded. Slightly dazed-seeming, he moistened his lips and shook his head.

'I . . . I apologise,' he said thickly. 'My thanks, Davy. I . . . Mary, my dear – forgive me. If you can.' He looked over to her, and the change in his expression was quite extraordinary.

She came to him, then, wordless, to take his hand.

'I think . . . that I lost my head . . . just a little,' he said, jerkily. 'Unedifying in the extreme, no doubt. Davy . . . well, Davy knows me. Too well. But you, Mary lass, should have been spared that. It shall not occur again.'

'Granlord was very cruel,' she said. 'But he was hurt, too. He torments himself in believing so ill of you. In thinking you capable of so much evil.'

Over her head, Patrick's dark eyes met David's grey ones. 'And you, child, see me rather as an angel of light?'

'Oh, no,' she told him, simply. 'Not so. I know that you can do ill things. Uncle Patrick. Very ill. As in the matter of the Princess of Navarre. And the plot for the Catholics to gain the King and all Scotland, before the Armada invasion of England. But I am sure that you are not as my lord thinks. That you do much good, as well as ill. We all do ill things as well as good, do we not?' Seriously, she put it to him. 'I think that the good that you do, Uncle Patrick, will be better than most. Just as the ill is . . . is very ill.' For Mary Gray, that last was hesitant.

'Thank you, my dear,' the other said, shaking his head, and clearly moved. 'I do not know that many would agree with you!' And again he met his brother's level gaze. 'But thank you.' He raised her small hand, and brushed it with his lips. 'I believe that you are . . . very good for me. God keep you so. But . . . a moment ago, girl, you spoke of a plot? A plot, you said. Before the Armada of Spain. To gain the King and Scotland for the Catholics. This is . . . interesting.' His glance swivelled round to his brother. 'What did you mean by that, Mary?'

"Just that I saw your letter. The strange letter that you wrote to Father.'

'Indeed. It was not meant for such eyes as yours.'

'No. But I perceived that the writing was yours, Uncle Patrick. So I must needs read it.'

His brows rose. 'I see.'

'Yes. It was a very clever letter.'

'But . . . you saw it as a plot? A Catholic plot.' Still it was at David that he looked.

That man nodded.

'But it showed excellently well the way to save the realm,' the girl went on. 'Had the King of Spain triumphed in England. So . . . we told King Jamie, as you said. But that . . . that the Spanish Inquisition should not come to Scotland . . . ' Mary bit her lip. 'Lest the Office be set up on Castle-hill – that was how you wrote it, was it not? That there should be no chance of that ill thing, we told the King that it was the Protestant lords who should be assembled. First. Otherwise the same as in your letter, Uncle Patrick.'

The Master actually stopped breathing for many seconds together.

'Was that wrong?' she pressed him. 'It was not what you intended. We did you hurt in that, perhaps? But . . . we could not countenance a Catholic plot. Could we?'

'God . . . help me! What . . . ?' Patrick swallowed. 'What is this?'

David answered him, harshly, throatily. 'This is your daughter, Patrick. Your own flesh and blood. Risen up in judgment. Something that has stolen upon us all unawares. You could dispose of her mother as you would, you and my lord – but this is beyond you. Beyond us all.'

The other stared.

'Do not think ill of me,' Mary said – and it was to them both that she spoke. 'What I did was for the best. In all else it was as you advised, Uncle Patrick. And the King believed that all came from you. That you advised the mustering of the Protestant lords. So, you see, your credit stands the higher with him. He esteemed you Papist before – but this would cause him to doubt it. In that you are advantaged, are you not? It may be that he was the kinder to you at Holyroodhouse yon night, because of it. And why he attended Andrew's christening and stood godfather.' She nodded, as though to herself, satisfied. 'You see it, Uncle Patrick?'

It was Davy Gray who expostulated. 'Child – this is no way to talk! Subterfuge and guile and, and chicanery! Leave you that to others, 'fore God!'

'It is but the truth, is it not, Father? So it has come to pass . . .'

Patrick interrupted her, laughing, in a sudden return to something of his old gay assured self. 'Ha – do not chide her, Davy,' he said. 'Here is a pearl beyond all price, indeed! The wisdom of dove and serpent combined! And all in the comeliest small head and person that we are likely to find in the length and breadth of this kingdom! Do not rail at what the good Lord has wrought!'

'You – *you* to talk thus?'

'To be sure. Why not? Since it seems that I may claim some of the credit! And I need all the credit that I may summon up, do I not, Davy? I think . . . yes, I think that Mary and I might run very well in harness. I must think more on this. For, i' faith, I'd liefer have our young Mary as my friend than my enemy!'

'That you will have always, Uncle Patrick,' the girl declared gravely. 'But it would be easier if you were a Protestant again, rather than a Catholic, I think.'

'In the name of Heaven . . . !' David Gray exclaimed.

'Exactly, Davy – exactly! But, come,' the Master said, in a different tone of voice. 'It is time that we were hence. I do not know whether my esteemed and noble father will be returning forthwith to Castle Huntly – but I would not wish Marie to be the object of his further attentions in his present state of mind.'

'God forbid!' his brother agreed. 'You left her at the castle?'

'Yes. I must get her away from there, and under some more hospitable roof.' Patrick looked about him, grimacing. 'Since I may scarce bring her here. Yet.'

David nodded. 'I am sorry,' he said. 'Sorry for all of it. But sorriest for Marie, who deserves better things.'

'Aye. Deserves a better husband belike?' Patrick shot a quick look at the other. 'A husband such as the upright Davy Gray, mayhap?'

'That is ill said, brother,' David observed, even-voiced. 'Marie deserves better than any man I know. Remember it, I charge you! Come, then – we waste time here.'

There was no sign of my lord or Gilbert Gray or the Provost of Dundee outside. Already the workmen had abandoned their various tasks and were leaving the place.

As the trio mounted and rode off over the drawbridge and the half-dug moat towards the village and harbour, Patrick turned in his saddle and looked back.

'A task,' he said softly, as to himself. 'A notable task. And expensive. But worth it, I think. Aye, worth it.'

'You mean to do it, then? Still? To go ahead with it, Patrick? Restore this great ruin?' David asked. 'That would be folly, surely?'

'Folly?' His brother smiled. 'Living is folly, and dying the only true wisdom, Davy, is it not? But there is folly — and folly! This folly might well make a fool of still greater folly. We shall see. But . . . I shall be obliged for those papers and titles that my lord mentioned, Davy — before he changes his mind!'

Chapter Six

DAVID GRAY paced the floor of his own little circular chamber in the north-west flanking tower of Castle Huntly, set-faced. Once again he held in his hand a letter — and once again it was in his brother Patrick's dashing handwriting. When he had recognised the writing, even when the missive was still in the courier's hand, his heart had sunk; for Patrick's letters seldom left their recipients as they found them, unmoved or uninvolved. This one was no exception.

It was addressed from the Laird of Tillycairn's Lodging, The Canongate, Old Aberdeen, and dated 27th July, 1589 — three weeks after the clash at Broughty Castle. This was no coded nor cryptic letter like the last, but it made its demands, nevertheless. It read:

'My excellent Davy,
    But a few days after we left you, His Grace summoned me here to Aberdeen. I was intrigued to know for why. I

have been reappointed to my old and useful position of Master of the Wardrobe – though not yet to the Council, as is my greater requirement. But that will come, no doubt.

The reason for my summons north would appear to be, not so much that His Grace and the Chancellor cannot bear to be without my presence, as that they seem to hold unwarranted and base suspicions as to my activities and whereabouts when I am not under their eyes! I wonder how they came to gain the whisper that I had hastened south to the house of my lord of Bothwell whenever I left them at Perth that day? A strange calumny, was it not? But with its own usages. Since now I am secure at Court – in fact, in the Wardrobe! Take note, Davy – *fama nihil est celerius!*

All here is triumph and rejoicing. Even the poor, damned Catholic rebels rejoice, so felicitous is the occasion and so clement the royal victor. As previously arranged. The Battle of the Brig o' Dee will, I doubt not, go down in our realm's history as unique – in that scarce a blow was struck, our martial monarch's very presence striking terror into the hearts of all Catholics, heretics, and enemies of Christ's true Reformed faith! Huntly, Erroll, Montrose and the others have yielded themselves up to gracious Majesty – who, I rejoice to say, agrees that mercy should temper justice quite signally. So all is contrition, love and merriment indeed – save for the good Chancellor, who would have preferred a few heads to fall – with our eloquent prince preaching the Reformed evangel with potent zeal. I, of course, am one of his most promising converts. As young Mary so shrewdly advises.

The which, Davy, brings me to my prayer and request. I would crave you to permit Mary to come to Court. I well know your own mislike of such, but I think, if you are honest – and always you are notably that, are you not? – that you will admit that she is as though born for the Court. Fear not for her safety. I shall watch over her well, I promise you, as though – why, as though she were my own daughter! She will, of course, lodge with us, and Marie shall cherish and protect her. You need have no fears on that score. Although, think you not, Mary may be well able to protect herself?

116

Do not dismiss this plea in selfish haste, Davy. There is much to commend it. Mary will be good for me, I think. There will be a Queen again in Scotland ere long, and Maids of Honour and Ladies in Waiting are already being selected. This comes within the province of my Lord Chamberlain – and I understand that Vicky is not without his own plans in the matter. So, dear brother and self-appointed keeper of my conscience, should you think to refuse to let Mary come, as I pray, consider well how a royal summons could *command* her to attend at Court. My way, I ween, is the more suitable. I swear that if she likes it not, or if it is anyways in her interest to leave, she shall return to your good care forthwith.

Consider for her, Davy – not for yourself. The Court returns south for Edinburgh tomorrow. A sennight at Holyroodhouse for a Council and the trial of the miscreants. Then Falkland and Majesty's beloved stags. Let it be Falkland for our Mary, brother.

I send my devotion to you all.

Patrick'

In a rounder and less spectacular hand was added, at the foot:

'Bear with us please, Davy dear. And guide Mariota to allow Mary to come. Even though it cost you both dear. Award the child her destiny. She might take it in her own hands, else.

Marie'

So David Gray paced his floor. He had got over the worst of it now, the pent-up fury, the hot resentment, the wrathful denial. David was just as much a Gray as either his father or his half-brother. The hurt, the pain, was with him still; but his head was cooler now, his reason functioning. Yet his expression grew the bleaker as he paced.

Could he hold her back? Should he? That was the question. Which way lay his duty to her? She was a child no more – but surely she yet required protection? More than ever, perhaps. And, God help her – what sort of protection would Patrick afford her? Marie, yes – but Patrick! And yet – did she have a deal of protection here at Castle Huntly? Watch for her as he would? She came and went as she wished. She could twist every man and woman in all the Carse around her little finger. Including her grandfather. My lord would not relish this. Indeed, he would forbid it if he could. But . . . was that not to the point? The old man had always doted on her – but now did so unpleasingly. Lasciviously. As a woman, no longer as a child. And where women were concerned, he was without scruple. He was not good for Mary . . .

And if young Lennox worked up on the King to summon her? As Patrick might well put him up to if he did not think of it himself? There could be no holding her then against the royal command. Better surely that she should go freely, and in Marie's care, at least.

But Patrick! As sponsor for the girl into that wicked, deceitful and corrupt world? Patrick, the falsest schemer and liar and betrayer of them all! And her father, save in name. . . .

David came to stare out of his window. The leaves were already beginning to turn on the elms and birches, though not on the beeches and oaks, barely August as it was. So short a summer. Not that he saw any of them. He saw only a lovely, elfin face, great-eyed, wistful, grave, and true. And another, attractive also, smiling, handsome, and false. So like the other; so like.

It was the likeness that tipped the scales. Not merely the likeness of feature, of lineament. It was the inborn assurance, the air of breeding, the indubitable yet unpretentious quality of prescriptive right, that each wore like a casual easy garment. Something that was no more to be ignored than denied. Both had been destined by something more than mere birth for the great world of rule and power and influence. Who was Davy Gray the Bastard to say it nay?'

Sighing heavily, the man crushed that letter in his strong hand, and went downstairs to seek Mariota.

Mary Gray came to the royal burgh of Falkland on the eighth day of August. It proved to be a notably smaller place than she had imagined, a little grey huddle of a town, all red pantiled roofs, tortuous narrow streets and winding steeply-sloping alleys, crouching under the tall green cone of the easternmost of the Lomond Hills, and quite dominated by the turreted and ornate palace. This, although of handsome architecture, was itself of no great size for a royal residence, and the entire place, with the Court in residence, gave the impression of bursting at the seams. With David as escort, the girl had to force her garron through the throng that choked the constricted streets and wynds, a motley crowd of gaily attired lords and ladies, of lairds and clerics, members of the royal bodyguard and men-at-arms, grooms and foresters, hawkers and tranters, hucksters and pedlars, townsfolk, tradesmen and tinkers. People hung out of every window, as though being squeezed out by the press within, laughing and shouting to folk in the street, or across their heads to the occupants of windows opposite. Horses were everywhere, for the main business of Falkland was hunting, and followers might require three and four mounts in any hard-riding day. Hay and oats to feed the many hundreds of beasts crammed all available space, wagon-loads and sled-like slypes coming in constantly from the surrounding farms further jammed the congested lanes, together with flocks of cattle, sheep and poultry to provide fare for the suddenly trebled population. The bustle was indescribable, the noise deafening – more especially as the church bells were tolling clamorously, it was said for a witch-burning – and the stench was breath-taking, particularly of dung and perspiration and pigs, this warm August day. Mary was no stranger to the crowded streets of Dundee and Edinburgh, but this concentration in little Falkland was something new to her.

Pushing patiently through the press, David shepherded his charge, with her bundles of belongings, towards the lower end of the little town, where the palace reared its twin drum towers, its elaborate buttresses and stone-carved walls above gardens, pleasances, tennis-courts and the wide island-dotted loch. Mary, all lip-parted excitement and gleaming eyes, assumed that they were making for the palace itself, when her father turned his mount in at a narrow vennel called College Close, just opposite the great palace gates. Thence, through a dark and ill-smelling pend, they came into a sort of back court of small humble houses, jumbled together, in one of which they found the Mistress of Gray installed, with the baby

119

Andrew. It took Mary a little while to realise, even after the first fond greetings, that this was where she was going to dwell meantime, in this low-browed and over-crowded rabbit-warren. Not that she was foolishly proud or over-nice in the matter; it was just not what she had anticipated in this business of coming to Court.

The Lady Marie, strangely enough, was quite delighted with these lowly quarters. It seemed that King Jamie's passion for hunting was rued by his courtiers not only because of the everlasting cross-country pounding and prancing but on account of chronic lack of accommodation at Falkland, where earls had to roost in garrets and bishops crouch in cellars. The French ambassador was, in fact, lodging next door, and Queen Elizabeth's new resident envoy, Mr Bowes, across the tiny cobbled yard. Only the Duke of Lennox's good offices had got the impoverished Grays in here, this being the house of his own under-falconer, Patey Reid, whose acquaintance Mary had already made one day by Lindores Loch.

'My sister Jean is here with us also,' Marie told them. 'She is chosen one of the ladies to the new queen. She and Mary will share this tiny doocot of a room in here, under the roof – and no doubt will fill it with laughter and sunshine! For Jean never stops laughing, the chucklehead.' Her expression changed, as she turned directly to David. She laid a hand on his arm. 'So you have brought her, Davy,' she said. 'You have made your sacrifice – as I knew that you would. Never fear for her, Davy dear – we shall watch over your precious one.'

'That is my prayer,' the man said heavily. 'I require it of you, Marie, by all that you hold true and dear.'

'Yes. So be it.'

'You will send me word immediately should anything threaten her? Anything, or anybody. You understand?'

'I do. And I will, Davy.'

Mary came and clasped him, laying her dark head against his broad chest. 'Why do you fear for me so, Father?' she chided, but gently. 'Think you that I am so weak? Or so simple? Or very foolish? Or that I cannot think for myself?'

'No,' he jerked. 'None of these. But you are a woman, young and very desirable. Men, many men, will desire you. Will take you if they can. By any means, lass – any means.

And at this Court means are not awanting, examples evil, and consciences dead. Dead, do you hear? You must be ever on your guard.'

'That I will, Father – I will.' Mary smiled then, faintly. 'But so, I think, should be some of the men you name, perhaps!'

Laughing, Marie threw an arm around each of them. 'And that is the truest word spoken this afternoon, I vow!' she cried. 'Lord – I know one who already walks but warily where this wench is concerned! One, Patrick, Master of Gray!'

'Aye. May he continue to do so, then – or he will have me to deal with!' his half-brother declared, unsmiling still. 'Where is he, Marie?'

'Closeted with the English envoy. Across the yard yonder. As so often he is.'

'M'mmm. With Bowes? I see. Then you will give him my message, Marie. He will know that I mean it.'

'You will not wait, Davy? Stay with us? Even for this one night . . . ?'

'No. You forget perhaps, my lady, I am a servant and no lordling. My lord of Gray's servant. My time is not my own. My lord does not so much as know that we are here. He would never have permitted this – and it may be that he is right. I must be back to Castle Huntly this night – or Mariota will suffer his spleen . . .'

'Very well, Davy.'

They went down and out of the pend with him, to bid him farewell and watch him ride off with Mary's garron led behind, a sober, unsmiling, formidable man whose level grey eyes nevertheless gave the lie to most of what he appeared to be. There were tears in the Lady Marie's own eyes as she watched him go. Mary Gray's were not so swimming that they did not note the fact.

Coming down the narrow vennel from the street were three gallants escorting on foot a young woman whose high-pitched uninhibited laughter came before them to rival the pealing bells. One was but a youth, one a young man, and the third somewhat older; all were over-dressed. David's two horses, in that narrow way, inevitably forced them, from walking four abreast, to leave the crown of the causeway for the guttered side of it, choked with the filth of house, stable and midden. Whereupon the two younger men shook their fists at the rider, cursing loudly, but the older took the opportunity to sweep up the lady in his velvet arms and carry her onwards – albeit staggering not a little, for she was no feather-light piece. Moreover neither his pathfinding nor his respiration was aided by the fact that he likewise took the opportunity to bury his face deep in the markedly open bosom of his burden's gown, so conveniently close. Whereupon the laughter pealed out higher than ever.

Davy Gray rode on without a backward glance.

Breathless and stumbling, the gallant precipitately deposited his heaving, wriggling load almost on top of the Lady Marie, and would have fallen had he not had the girl to hold him up. He sought to bow, but the effort was ruined by the eruption of a deep and involuntary belch; whereupon his charge thumped him heartily on the back, all but flooring him once more. The vennel rang with mirth.

'This, my dear, is my young sister Jean,' Marie informed, unruffled. 'Did I not tell you that she had an empty head but excellent lungs? Of these gentlemen, this, who is old enough to know better, is Patrick Leslie, the Commendator-Abbot of Lindores. The child there is my lord of Cassillis my nephew, and far yet from years of discretion. Who the other may be, I do not know – but he does not keep the best of company!'

'That is Archie, Marie,' the Lady Jean Stewart announced, giggling. 'Archie Somebody-or-Other. Very hot and strong! Like me!' She was a tall, well-made young woman, high-coloured, high-breasted, high-tongued, bold alike of eye and figure and manner, dressed somewhat gaudily in the height of fashion – an unlikely sister for the poised and calmly beautiful Marie. 'Who have we here?' She was staring now at Mary. As indeed were her three escorts.

'Somebody whom you are going to love, I think, Jeannie. Mary Gray.'

Mary sketched a tiny curtsy, and smiled. 'My lady.'

Impulsively the Lady Jean went up to her and threw her arms around her. 'Lord – how like him you are!' she ex-. claimed. 'You are lovely. I am crazed over him – so I shall be crazed over you, I swear!'

'Gray . . . ?' Leslie jerked. 'This, then, is . . . ?'

'Someone for such as you to meet only when you are sober, my lord Abbot!' Marie declared firmly. 'Be gone, gentlemen.' And, turning Mary around, with an arm about her shoulder, she led her forthwith back through the dark pend. Jean Stewart followed, laughing, leaving the three men gazing after them, distinctly at a loss.

Patrick Gray, roused by all the laughter and shouting, came out of another little house in the yard as they crossed the cobblestones, a tall bland-faced and richly-dressed gentleman at his side. Mary restrained her impulse to run into his arms, and dipped low instead to the gentleman, before searching Patrick's face from warmly luminous dark eyes.

The Master of Gray, who had been starting forward, likewise restrained himself, actually biting his lip. Which was not his wont, for seldom indeed did that man require to amend or adjust his attitude, his comportment. Marie perceived it, with something like wonder.

'My dear,' he began, and paused. 'I . . . this is my brother's child. My half-brother, Mr Bowes. Mary Gray. Of whom I have told you. Come to Court. Mary – Mr Robert Bowes, Her Grace of England's envoy.'

'Ah? So! I congratulate you. Congratulate you both!' The tall suave man bowed, his smooth pale face unsmiling. Mary, meeting his glance, decided that his eyes were both cold and shrewd, and that she did not like him. 'Master Davy we know. And the Bishop of St Boswells we know likewise. His grand-daughter, I think?'

Patrick raised one eyebrow. 'You are well-informed, sir,' he observed lightly.

'As you say,' the other acceded. 'And as is necessary.'

'I believe that the Bishop of St Boswells would scarce thank you, sir, to remind him of the fact,' Mary said, without emphasis but seriously. 'Nor would such as I think to disagree with him.'

Patrick drew a quick hand down over his mouth, as his eyes gleamed. Lady Marie smiled, and her sister whinnied laughter.

'Indeed!' Mr Bowes said. 'Ummm . . . ah . . . is that so?'

Demurely Mary moved over to the Master's side, and rising

123

on tip-toe, kissed his cheek. 'I hope that I see you well, Uncle Patrick?' she asked.

The man tossed discretion overboard, swept an arm around her slender waist, and lifted her off her feet to kiss her roundly. 'Bless you, Mary lass – you see me vastly the better for the sight of you! Mr Bowes, I pray, will excuse us?' And nodding to the envoy, he reached out for Marie's arm also, and led them all over to their own little house.

Queen Elizabeth's representative looked after them thoughtfully.

All Falkland, it seemed, had been talking of the masque for days. Other intriguing matters occupied busy tongues of course – the King's unaccountable leniency towards the Brig o' Dee rebels, Huntly in especial, allied to his notable harshness towards my Lord of Bothwell; the rumours that Huntly was indeed a convert to Protestantism; the highly indiscreet behaviour of the young Countess of Atholl. The masque, however, maintained pride of place. It was being devised and was to be staged by the Master of Gray – and undoubtedly nothing like it had been seen in Scotland since those spectacular days of nearly ten years before when Esmé Stuart of Lennox Duke Ludovick's father, and the young Patrick, had ruled the land in the name of the boy King James. Details were being kept a close secret, but it was known that, weather permitting, it was to be held out-of-doors on the night of the ninth, and that outrageous requests had been made to shocked Reformed divines to pray that it did not rain. Who was paying for it all was a matter for much speculation – for the Master himself, having been stripped of all his properties at his trial, was known to be in dire financial straits, and the King certainly was much too fond of gold to waste any of it on such nonsense.

Mary Gray's arrival only the day previous would not have precluded Patrick from inserting her conspicuously into the scene somehow, had not Marie put her foot down firmly, declaring that, knowing her husband, this affair was unlikely to be a suitable launching into Court life for the girl, and that also, any so early thrusting of her into prominence might seem ostentatious and unseemly. Reluctantly he bowed to his wife.

In another matter he was adamant, however. Mary should

be dressed as she merited – or he was not the Master of the King's Wardrobe! One glance at the girl's best gown, extracted from her bundle, assured the need of his services, however gentle he was towards her susceptibilities in the matter, and however hard he was on the Lady Jean for her shrieks of laughter at the thought of anything so simple and plain being worn at Court. So, since time was short and the royal wardrobe not yet geared to the proper provision of clothing for women, the King's tailors and sempstresses were brought over to the falconer's house to adapt and cut down one of Marie's own dresses. Mary was almost overwhelmed by the situation – but not sufficiently to prevent her from selecting quite the least elaborate and unaffected of the choice before her, a creation of pale primrose satin, closely moulded as to bodice, with little or no padding on shoulders and sleeves, a high upstanding collar rimmed with tiny seed-pearls to frame the face, and skirts billowing out from padded hips, slit to reveal an underskirt of old rose. Marie recognised the unerring instinct and taste, however much her sister might decry this as feeble and exclaim over more ambitious confections. The neckline provoked a further clash, Mary being quietly insistent that it was much too low for her, an attitude which both Jean and the dressmakers declared to be patently quite ridiculous in that bosoms were being bared ever more notably each season – and this gown was fully three years old. No prude, Mary nevertheless maintained her stand, hinting that a little mystery at her age could be quite as effective as any major display, especially if display was otherwise the order of the night. Jean eyed her more thoughtfully, then. A yoke of openwork, diaphanous lace was therefore contrived, which had the desired effect, by no means hiding altogether the shadowed cleft of firm young breasts while at the same time intimating a suitable modesty – and which Jean cheerfully pointed out could conveniently be whisked out and discarded when the evening really got into its stride.

Marie smiled her slow smile from the background.

The evening sky was cloudy but, since rain withheld, Patrick declared this to be all to the good, providing a more effective dusk to screen preliminary activities and better to show off the fireworks. Patrick took a vociferous Jean away with him early, in noisy company. Mary, in due course, with Marie, found herself being escorted over to the palace gardens by the English ambassador and one of his gentlemen, Mr Thomas Fowler, a broadly-built Yorkshireman whose small round eyes lit up at the sight of the girl and who, while conversing with her politely enough in his strangely broad-vowelled lazy voice, almost seemed to devour her nevertheless with his busy unflagging gaze. Mr Bowes himself did not prevent his own glance from sliding very frequently in Mary's direction, the Lady Marie noted. The young woman's combination of modest discretion, youthful eagerness and calm assurance was as singularly engaging as it was unusual. She made no enquiries about the Duke of Lennox.

The gardens presented a kaleidoscopic and animated scene that set Mary actually clapping her hands, to the amusement of her companions. The shrubberies and fruit trees were hung with myriads of coloured lanterns of every hue and size and shape, and a double row of hundreds of pitch-pine torches blazed right down a long arboured rose-walk that led from the great gates directly to the lochside. Up and down this weirdly illuminated avenue, as well as on the grass and amongst the trees, the gaily-dressed crowd sauntered and eddied, presenting an ever-changing chequer-board of light and shadow, of pattern and colour and movement. Shining fabrics, gleaming bare shoulders, glittering jewels, and the motion of long silken hose, swaying skirts and glinting sword-scabbards, made a fairyland scene. Two great bonfires flamed at either end of the balustraded terrace between the long north front of the grey palace and the loch, casting ruddy leaping reflections on the dark water. Music drifted from hidden groups of instrumentalists near and far.

Mary, wide-eyed, seeking to miss nothing, yet careful to heed her escort's rather difficult conversation and suitably to greet those to whom the Lady Marie presented her, moved down to the loch, a broad shallow expanse of water, reed-fringed and dotted with many little islets. Here were tables laden with cold meats, cakes, sweets and fruits and flagons of wine and spirits – from which a pack of the royal wolf- and deer-hounds, as well as lesser dogs, were already being fended off by anxious servitors.

A fanfare of trumpets announced the King's arrival on the scene. James, clad in an extraordinary superfluity of velvets, fur, ostrich-feathers, gold-lace, filigree-work and jewellery, came down the steps from the palace, preceded by his own torch-bearers and heralds and followed by his great nobles, high clergy and ministers of state. Lolling his head in all directions, he waved an apple that he was munching towards sundry of the bowing and curtsying guests, but paused for none. Straight down across the grass to a sort of roundel or bastion of the lower terrace he hurried, throwing excited gabbled and unintelligible remarks over his grotesquely padded shoulders to his almost running retinue. At the roundel he gave his apple to the red and perspiring Earl of Orkney, his uncle and Marie's father, grasped a torch from one of the bearers, and promptly applied it to a large and ornamental rocket erected there especially on a wooden stand. Distressingly, in his trembling haste, James knocked the firework off its stand as he lit its fuse. Fumbling, he stooped to right it, thought better of it, and agitatedly signed to the torch-bearer to do so instead. That unfortunate hesitated in some alarm, but at his monarch's imperious urgings, gingerly picked up the spitting spluttering object, holding it at arm's length, to return it to its stand. Unhappily he held it fuse upwards, and thrust it thus on to the stand, leaping back therefrom immediately as though scalded. But even as James, voice rising in a squeak, pointed out the error, with a sudden whoosh the fuse ignited the charge and the thing went off. Sadly, of course, it went downwards, not upwards. It struck the paving of the roundel in a shower of sparks, and proceeded to dart and whizz and zig-zag furiously, unpredictably, like an angry and gigantic hornet, amongst the royal, noble and ecclesiastical feet, with notable effect. King James danced this way and that, cannoning into his supporters, seeking to get out of the way and the range of the erratic missile. Inevitably his entourage blocked the way of escape from the roundel – though not for long. Yelling with fright the King cursed them, and in as wholehearted and unanimous retiral as had been seen since the Rout of Solway Moss the flower of Scotland scrambled and scampered out from that corner of the terrace, stumbling over one another, leaping the fallen, some actually throwing themselves over the balustrade, more than one landing in the shallows below with a splash. Fireworks were as yet something of an unknown quantity in Scotland, and this rocket a large one – indeed the signal rocket for the entire masque. The monarch and the torch-bearer vied with one another to be second-last or better still, out of that distressingly confined space, and had only partly achieved this object when the unpleasant pyrotechnic blew up with a loud bang, exploding a galaxy of coloured stars about the heads and shoulders and persons of the royal retinue. King Jamie's screech could be heard shrilling above the uproar, mingled with the yelping of one of the shaggy wolf-hounds which somehow had got a proportion of the burning phosphorus embedded in its coat, and went bellowing through the gilded throng into the night.

The noise was quite phenomenal, what with the shouts of the fleeing, the cursing, the plethora of commands, pleas and invocations, the baying of hounds and the vast and unseemly mirth of the scores not actually involved – in which, it is to be feared, Mary Gray's girlish laughter pealed high and clear.

Higher and clearer still, however, above all the babel and confusion below, rose the pure and silvery note of a single trumpet, turning some eyes at least upwards towards the topmost lofty parapet of the palace's flag-tower. Here a cluster of lanterns had been lit to illuminate the royal standard on its staff, and beneath it, standing balanced on the crenellated paparet itself, an extraordinary partially-robed figure, luminously painted, with gleaming helmet sporting wings, a staff with an entwined serpent in one hand and a voice-trumpet in the other, notably large white wings also sprouting from bare heels. This apparition, through the speaking trumpet, announced in high-flown terms to all mere mortals there below that he was Hermes or Mercury, messenger of the gods, and that to their unworthy earth-bound eyes would presently be revealed the fairest and greatest of all the heavenly host, Zeus himself, in search of love. Another ululant trumpet-note, and the vision pointed outwards, lochwards, commandingly, and thereupon faded into the darkness as his lights went out.

It is to be feared that less than the fullest of attention was paid to this supernatural manifestation, in the circumstances.

Indeed no great proportion of the company was able to hear what was said on account of the noise below, where a more terrestial potentate was providing his own commentary, and earls, lords, bishops and dogs were in loud process of reinstating themselves in their own estimation. Even amongst those who received the announcement from on high, it produced only a mixed reception, guesses at the identity of Hermes vying with the loud assertions of a dark-clad divine near the English ambassador's party that this was shameful, a work of the Devil, sheerest paganism if not what worse, popery.

In consequence, no very large proportion of the assemblage at first perceived the dramatic developments proceeding a little way out on the loch. Hidden lights came on, one by one, amongst the many islets about one hundred yards out, lighting up the dark water; and out from behind a long and artificial screen of reeds and osiers and willow-wands there floated a silver galley rowed by hidden oarsmen, ablaze with lights. On a raised daïs at the stern stood a tall slender woman, rhythmicall brushing her long fair hair. It did not take a great many moments, thereafter, for this lady to draw most of the inattentive and preoccupied eyes in the sloping gardens in her own direction, for she was entirely naked, apart from a silver mask over her eyes, her body glowing greenish-white with luminous paint – although certain prominences were picked out in scarlet. Crouching at her feet but otherwise unclothed likewise save for masks, were three maidens, who stretched up willowy waving white arms towards their principal in adoration.

Music swelled from the islands as the silver galley moved slowly in towards the watching throng.

A great gasp swept the company, and out of it everywhere voices arose in wonder, admiration, speculation and condemnation. There was a notable surge down to the actual waterside, to shorten the distance between viewers and spectacle. The Kirk raised an almost unanimous shout of righteous indignation. King James sufficiently forgot recent misfortunes to call 'Bonny! Bonny!' out across the water in a cracked high-pitched voice. Everywhere men and women were disputing as to the probable name of the lady with the hairbrush. Mary, clasping her hands together, gazed raptly, almost forgetting to breathe. Nearby a group of men were loudly asserting that they could identify at least two of the masked maidens, offering detailed reasons for their beliefs, the Abbot-Commendator of Lindores being particularly vehement that he would recognise the high globe-like breasts of Jean Stewart of Orkney anywhere and in any light.

Another trumpet note from aloft presaged the announcement that Leda, Queen of Sparta and daughter to King Thestios of Aetolia approached. As a revelation this scarcely satisfied most of the company. The ladies present, at least, managed on the whole to withdraw their gaze in order to scan their neighbours to see, if they might, who was missing.

Then, as another and more orthodox rocket soared skywards from one of the islets, a great clashing of cymbals rang out, followed by much-enhanced musical accompaniment suddenly loud and martial, seeming to fill the night – not all of it immediately in time and key. And from behind every islet and the screen of greenery burst forth brilliant cascades of scin-tillating light, streams of blazing darts, fans of soaring sparks, shooting stars, flaring fizgigs that burst on high to send down showers of shimmering tinsel. Loud explosions succeeded, with lightning flashes, to drown the music and shake the very ground. On and on went this dazzling percussive display, to the amazement and delight of the watching crowd. Or perhaps, not quite all of it, for though the head-shakings of the divines could be taken for granted, Mary at least heard still another reaction. Just behind her, Mr. Bowes muttered to Mr. Fowler that this was altogether too much, that they might have known that the fellow would overdo it, and did he think that silver crowns grew on trees? To which Mr. Fowler replied something that Mary did not catch save for the last broad phrase to the effect that Sir Francis might not scan the account too close so long as the goods were delivered in good shape.

Mary neither turned round nor showed signs of listening.

As the bangings and thunderings mounted to a crescendo, quite battering the ear-drums and overwhelming all other sound, they were abruptly stopped short, cut away, finished quite; the sparkling, spraying fireworks also. And into the throbbing, almost painful, silence that followed, thin strains of sweet and gentle music gradually filtered. Out from the sud-denly silent and darkened islands sailed into view a great swan, calm, tranquil, immaculate. The sigh that ran through the waiting gathering was as though a breeze stirred a forest.

The swan, lifelike, white as snow, graceful, with noble wings part-raised and arching, glowed with lights without and within. It might be perhaps five times life-size and appeared indeed to be coated with gleaming real feathers. Slowly, serenely, it came sailing shorewards, towards the waiting galley, its propulsion invisible, a mystery. The lady on the daïs turned to watch its approach, stilling her brushing, the maidens likewise. These were no more than thirty yards from the shore now, and receiving their mede of admiration, some gallants being actually up to their knees in the water the better to show their appreciation.

As the swan, unhurried, came up to the silver galley, the trumpet sounded once more, and Hermes announced his father Zeus, Ruler of the Heavens, Giver of Laws, Dispenser of Good and Evil, and Source of all Fertility. Up from between the arching white wings rose a glowing male figure, perfectly proportioned, poised, naked also save for a golden fig-leaf and a celestial pointed crown. Hair was lacquered silver to mould the head as in a smooth gleaming cap; at the groin too hair was silvered, otherwise body and face were clean-shaven. In one hand he held the dumbell-like symbol of the thunderbolt. No mask hid these beautiful, smiling and confident features. Patrick Gray was ever his own mask.

As the cymbals clashed again, Zeus leapt lightly from the swan up on to the daïs of the galley. Low he bowed to Leda, who drew back, while the arms of the kneeling damsels waved in undulations about them both. Then, as the music sank to a low, rhythmic and seductive melody, the man commenced an extraordinary dance sequence. With but a few feet of platform on which to perform, he moved and twisted and insinuated himself amongst the white shrinking bodies of the women, at once suppliant and masterful, coaxing, pleading yet assured. Sinuously, gracefully determined, fluid in movement but wholly masculine, he postured and spun and circled, in sheerest desire, yet in perfect tune with the tempo and mood of the languorous melody. The maidens' fluttering, waving arms reached up and out to him, seeking to draw him away, to protect their mistress, stroking at his legs and thighs and belly

131

in part-restraint, part-caress; but he would have none of them, spurning their silent urgings, his very body eloquently flicking away their anxious lingering fingers, concentrating all his frank and potent manhood on the more mature fullness of the tall, fair Leda.

One by one the younger women sank down level with the rush-strewn platform in defeat and rejection, throwing the central figures, pursued and pursuing, into high relief. And now the tenor and tone of the dance subtly altered. Pleading faded from the man's gestures, and command began to reinforce his coaxing. He was smiling brilliantly now, and every so often his fingers lighted on and loitered over the smooth flesh that no longer shrank from him. For the woman was cold no longer, but turning to him, commenced to respond to his vehement though still courtly advances. Quickly the movements of both grew more sensuously desirous, more blatantly lustful, above the bare backs of the low-bent girls, as the beat of the music mounted hotly. Tension could be sensed growing avidly amongst the watching company.

With every motion of man and woman working up to a controlled frenzy, the climax came suddenly. Holding up the golden thunderbolt that he had made play with suggestively throughout, Zeus twirled it in triumphant signal, pulling Leda to him by a hand on her swelling hips. Then he tossed the thunderbolt high, away from him, so that it fell with a splash into the water. The cymbals clanged and throbbed, and, a little belatedly presumably, firecrackers exploded their dutiful thunder. A cloud of pink smoke rose from the body of the galley, to envelope the daïs, billowing and rolling, while the throng peered and fretted impatiently. When it cleared at last, it was to reveal the three damsels sailing away in the swan, waving swan-like white arms in mocking salute and farewell, while on the galley the two principals were posed in close and striking embrace, the woman bent backwards, hair hanging loose, bosom upthrust, the man leaning over her, lips fused to hers, one hand cupping a full breast, the other holding aloft her mask. Despite its felicity, it must have been a difficult pose to maintain.

Loud and long sounded the applause, tribute and exclamation – with a certain amount of rueful complaint that Zeus's head still enfuriatingly prevented the face of Leda from being seen and identified.

In a final fanfare of trumpets, all the lights were extinguished somewhat raggedly, and the two luminous-painted bodies now glowed ghostly and indistinct. There came a woman's breathless squeal from the galley, and then the clear mocking note of the Master of Gray's silvery laughter floated out across the dark water.

Not a few eyes turned thereafter to look at the Lady Marie, Mistress of Gray.

She was smiling, and offering Mary a sweetmeat.

The great voice of Master Andrew Melville, Kirk leader and Principal of St. Andrews University, could be heard declaiming to the King that these last ill sounds were the most lascivious and ungodly of all the disgraceful display – to which James answered obscurely in what was thought to be Latin.

Torches now sprang into ruddy flame on the galley, and it was seen to be rowing directly towards the land. Its high curving prow grounded on the reedy shore, and hitherto unseen oarsmen, mighty ordinary-seeming, jumped out into the shallows to run out a wide plank as gangway from the daïs to the beach. Down this, hand in hand, and bowing, smiling, strolled Patrick Gray and the still unclothed lady – the latter, however, once again safely masked, indeed with a veil over her face also.

There was a near-riot as spectators hurried close, shouting questions, comment, witticisms, demanding the lady's name, making shrewd suggestions – all manner of suggestions. Only the torch-bearers and oarsmen kept a way open for the couple, less than gently, reinforced by Patrick's own laughing requests that they make passage to the King's Grace. Sauntering unblushingly, unashamedly forward, the pair made barefoot, and bare all else, across the grass to where James stood doubtfully, plucking at his lower lip.

'Och, Patrick – this is . . . this is . . . och, man, man!' His Majesty faltered, his darting glance afraid to linger on the lady's charms at such close range.

'This, Highness, is Queen tonight from another age and sphere and clime. Spartan indeed, as you will perceive – though thank the good God it is a warm night! Eh, my dear?'

133

'Sire!' boomed Master Melville. 'You canna tolerate this. This scandal. You'll no' give your countenance further to this disgraceful ploy, sir? This . . . this shameless strumpet!'

'The Lady Leda has naught to be ashamed of . . . that I can see!' Patrick rejoined lightly, but ignoring the divine. 'Can Your Grace discern any imperfection?'

'Eh . . . ? Na, na. Och – no' me, Patrick. Be no' so sore, Master Melville. Other days, other ways, mind. 'Tis but a dramaturgy, see you – a guizardry, no more. And a bonny one, you'll no' deny. Aye, wi' a right notable exode. Erudite, Patrick – most erudite. A credit to your scholarship, man. I'll say that.' James tapped Patrick's bare arm. '*Vita sine litteris mors est*, eh? Aye, and *hinc lucem et pocula sacra!*'

'Precisely, Sire. Therefore, *vivat Rex! Fama semper vivat!*'

Delighted, James chuckled and nodded. 'Ooh, aye. Just so. *Vivat regina*, likewise!' He glanced more boldly at the lady, in high good humour now. James dearly loved Latin tags, and much approved of those who would exchange them with him. 'So we'll hope that she'll no' catch her death o' cold, man. Do I . . . do I ken the lady?'

'Not so closely as I would wish, Sire!' Leda answered for herself, giggling behind a hand raised to lips to disguise her voice.

'Hech, hech!' James whinnied, reached out a hand, thought better of it, and coughed. 'Aye. Well. I'ph'mm.'

'I have a notion, Sire, 'tis the Countess of Atholl,' the Earl of Mar suggested, at the King's side. 'I wonder if her lord is sober enough to know? Where is he?'

'I think not. The hair is unlike. So is . . . so is . . . I would suggest the Lady Yester,' Lord Lindsay put in.

'Na, na, man,' Orkney objected, chuckling fatly. 'The Lady Yester's borne bairns, and this quean hasna, I'm thinking. I jalouse the Lady Borthwick.'

'Gentlemen, gentlemen!' Patrick intervened, but easily. 'How undiscerning you are! And how ungallant! Do none of you respect a lady's, h'm, privacy? Master Melville, here, I swear, is better disposed. Indeed he will be eager to assist, I think! May I borrow your cloak, sir?' Without waiting for permission, Patrick twitched off the good dark woollen cloak that the Principal wore over his sober habit, and flung it around the gleaming shoulders of the lady in almost the one graceful movement. 'Off with you, sweeting!' he said, and patted her bottom with genial authority.

As Principal Melville spluttered and protested, Leda dipped a brief curtsy to the King, kicked an impudent wave at the noble lords, and turning, ran off towards the palace in tinkling laughter, the clerical cloak flapping around her white limbs and seeming to make her distinctly more indecent than heretofore. Quite a pack of eager gentlemen ran after her.

'*Vera incessu patuit dea!*' Patrick murmured.

'Ho! Ha!' James guffawed. 'Apt! Right apt, 'fore God! Man, Patrick – it has been a notable ploy. Aye, and I'm . . . we are much diverted. We thank you. Your wit's none blunted, I warrant.'

'Your Grace is gracious . . . '

At the King's elbow Orkney spoke, low-voiced. 'It's a wit we could well do with on the Council, Jamie,' he said. 'We're no' that well founded in wit, yonder, I'm thinking!'

Mar overheard, and frowned, glancing at Lindsay and Glencairn. 'Your Grace . . . ' he began, but James overbore him.

'Aye , my lord – you are right. I was thinking the same. Certes, you are right. Patrick – we will have you on our Council again. Aye, we will. We'll welcome your advices there – eh, my lords? We ha' missed our Patrick's nimble wits and nimble tongue, to be sure. You are commanded, Master o' Gray, to attend our Privy Council henceforth, as before.'

'Your Grace is good – most generous. And I all unworthy . . . '

'Aye. Well. I'ph'mmm. Now – as to yon guizardry, Patrick. Wasna Leda mother to Castor and Pollux? Aye, and Helen. The fair Helen. You could ha' shown us these man. Another time, maybe – aye, another time. And I am wishful to see the swan. It was bonny . . . '

Presently the Master of Gray came strolling through the company that now concentrated largely on the laden tables, still naked save for his fig-leaf, but totally unconcerned. His progress was slow, for practically all the women present seemed intent on speech with him – whatever might be the reaction of their menfolk. His passage was accompanied, indeed, by an

135

almost continuous series of shrieks, squeals and giggles, a situation which by no means appeared to embarrass him.

Almost breathless, he arrived at last at the little group which contained his wife and Mary, composing his laughing features to gravity, and carefully straightening both crown and fig-leaf with a flourish. 'Lord,' he exclaimed, 'never have I had to carry such weight of affection and esteem! Never to receive so many kisses and, h'm, even warmer tokens of enthusiasm, in so short a space! 'Pon my soul, I had no notion how many fair aspirants there were for the part of Leda!'

'No doubt but you will take note . . . for the future?' Marie observed gently.

'Exactly, my dear.'

'You were very adequate, Patrick. As always you are in such matters.'

'My thanks, heart of my heart.'

'But it would be a pity if you were to contract a chill in your exposed parts, would it not? Or to discommode or distress Mary here.'

'M'mmm.' Patrick turned to the girl – indeed his glance had all along tended to slide to her face. 'You . . . you were not outraged, my dear? Offended?'

'No,' she assured him simply. 'Should I have been? You are very beautiful so. I like you lacking your beard. But you should have stayed on your boat, Uncle Patrick.'

'Indeed?'

'Yes. You were king there, were you not? Here you are but a spectacle.'

Almost audibly the man swallowed, and Marie raised a handkerchief to her face. 'You . . . think so!' he got out.

'If your boat had come to the shore and waited, instead of you coming to King James, he would have come to you. On the boat. And all others after him. To touch you and be close to you both. It would have been a more fitting triumph I think. And the lady remained a queen and not become a trollop.'

'God save me!'

'Yes. Would you like a cloak, Uncle Patrick? I am sure that Mr. Fowler here would lend you his.'

'I . . . no. Not so. That will not be necessary.' The Master was clearly disconcerted. 'I thank you. I am not cold.'

'Nevertheless, Patrick, I commend Mary's advice,' Marie put in, seeking to keep her voice even and her face straight.

'Very well.' He was almost short. 'You, sir, have no complaints?' That was thrown at Mr. Bowes who stood a little back. 'Anent my procedures?'

That suave man inclined his head. 'It was featly done, sir. A notable achievement,' he said smoothly. 'Although . . . perhaps as much might have been achieved with less expenditure of costly fireworks?'

'Would you scrape . . . !' Patrick stopped, and then shrugged. 'At least it achieved its object,' he ended lightly again. 'I am restored to the Council.' And bowing sketchily to them all, he strolled away.

Bowes and Fowler exchanged glances, and drew a little way apart.

'Come, my dear – while any meats and wine remain,' Marie said, taking Mary's arm. 'You are a poppet indeed – an angel, straight from Heaven.'

'Who is Sir Francis, Aunt Marie?' the girl asked quietly, apropos of nothing.

'Eh? Sir Francis? Why, I know no Sir Francis, I think . . . save only, of course, Walsingham. Sir Francis Walsingham, Queen Elizabeth's evil Secretary of State. But he is far from here, thank God! Why, precious?'

'I but wondered.'

'So? There may be someone of that name. But . . . call me Marie, will you, my dear. I . . . I do not relish to feel so venerable.'

They had scarcely reached the now depleted tables when there was a stir, as all heads turned towards the palace once more. The occasion for this was a sound strange to hear these days in Lowland Scotland – the high wailing challenge of the bagpipes. Not a few smiling and carefree faces sobered abruptly at the strains – for little that was good was associated in Protestant and Lowland minds with that barbarous and wholly Highland instrument.

Out from a door of the palace issued first two pipers, clad in kilts and plaids of tartan, blowing lustily. Behind them came two very different-seeming gentlemen; one, large florid, proudly-striding, dressed in an extraordinary admixture of

Highland and Lowland garb, bright orange satin doublet, somewhat stained, tartan trews right down to great silver-buckled brogues, wrapped partially in a vast plaid, hung with dirks, sgian-dubhs and broadsword, sparkling with barbaric jewellery, and on his dead a bonnet with three tall upstanding eagle's feathers; the other, most ordinary-looking, small, stocky and young – Ludovick, Duke of Lennox, Lord High Chamberlain, quietly dressed for riding, and evidently not a little uncomfortable beside his huge and highly colourful companion. Six more to be presumed Highland gentlemen marched behind them, all swords, targes and tartan, and then two more pipers playing approximately the same skirling jigging tune – if that it could be called – as the first pair. Though toes could have danced to that tune, 'The Cock o' the North' as it was called, none of the company there assembled showed sign of any such inclination.

Only King James himself started forward a little, as though to go to meet the noisy newcomers, recollected himself, and stood still, grinning and mumbling.

Mary Gray, much interested, whispered in Marie's ear. 'Who is that? That very strange man with Vicky? I have never seen the like . . . '

'That is my lord of Huntly,' Marie told her. 'A sort of cousin of yours, my dear.'

'Oh! The turkey-cock!' the girl said, smiling delightedly. 'I see why Father called him that.'

George Gordon, sixteenth Chief of his name, Gudeman o' the Bog, Cock o' the North, Lord of Strathbogie, Enzie and Gight, of Badenoch and Aboyne, Lieutenant of the North, fifth Earl of Huntly and principal Catholic of the realm, came stalking down towards his King with every appearance of one monarch joining another, his great purple-red face beaming. Never did Huntly travel without at least this small court of duine-wassails and pipers, never did he make an entry other than this – even when, as now, he was theoretically being brought in ward, for high treason, from nominal imprisonment in Edinburgh Castle. Only when he was within a pace or two of James did he doff his bonnet – headgear never removed for any lesser man, nor even in church, it was said – and produced what was apparently intended as a bow.

'King Jamie! King Jamie!' the Gordon boomed, not awaiting the Chamberlain's official announcement. 'God bless you,
laddie! The saints preserve you! It does my auld heart good
to see you.' Huntly was no more than thirty-three, but looked
and acted as though twice that. He kissed the royal fingers,
and then closed to envelope James in a great bear's-hug,
kissing his face also. 'Man – what ha' you got on you?' he
demanded, in mock alarm. 'Mother o' God – you're puffed
and padded and stuffed so's I can scarce feel the laddie inside!
Dia – it *is* Jamie Stewart, is it no'?' He bellowed great laughter,
while all around fellow earls and lesser nobles, good Protes-
tans all, frowned and muttered.

The King tried to speak, but could by no means outdo the
bagpipes which were still performing vigorously at closest
range. Huntly would certainly not have his personal anthem,
The Cock o' the North, choked off before its due and resounding finish, so perforce all had to await, with varying expressions, until the instruments expired in choking wails.

James, strangely enough, was mildness itself, when he could
make himself heard. 'Man, George,' he protested, ' 'Tis the
latest. The peak o' fashion. Frae France. You wouldna have me
no' in the mode?' He was stroking Huntly's arm. 'Waesucks
– you've been long in coming, Geordie. I hoped I'd see you
ere this. Vicky – I told you to fetch him wi' all expedition, man
– expedition.'

'We were delayed, Sire. By Sir John. By my Lord Chancellor Maitland,' Lennox began. 'He was not for releasing my
lord, here. He said that it was ill advised.'

Huntly interrupted him. 'Precious soul of God! That
snivelling clerk! That jumped-up notary! To seek to hold me –
me, Huntly! Against your royal warrant. By the Mass, I'd ha'
choked him with his own quills if I could ha' won near him
for his guard. *Your* guard, Jamie – your Royal Guard! That
pen-scratching attorney, that . . . that . . . ' The Earl positively
swelled with indignation, like to burst.

The King patted and soothed him as he might have gentled
a favourite horse. 'Och, never heed him, Geordie – never heed
him. He's a sour man, yon. Thrawn. But able, mind. Aye, and
honest. Maitland has his points. Ooh, aye. He shouldna ha'
spoke you ill, mind. And he shouldna ha' questioned my royal

command. I'll speak a word wi' him as to that. But . . . never mind Maitland. It's good to see you, man. The pity that you missed the guizardry. The Master o' Gray's ploy. Och, it was right featly done . . . '

'No doubt, Jamie – no doubt.' Interrupting his monarch was nothing to George Gordon. 'But I *will* mind Maitland! I do mind Maitland, by the Rood! And I'll be heard, whatever! As all yon guard heard his insults! God's Body – he had his men lay hands on me! On me! Your men! The Royal Guard. For that . . . for that I'll hae my recompense! Mother o' God, I swear it . . . !'

'Och, wheesht, wheesht, man. Take it not so. It's no' . . . it's no' . . . ' James was plucking agitatedly at his slack lower lip. 'See you, Geordie – here's it. Here's your recompense, then. I appoint you Captain o' my guard. Aye – that's it. Captain o' the Royal Guard. Is that no' right apt and suitable?'

If the Earl of Huntly took his time to digest this unexpected appointment, his fellow nobles around the King did not. Almost as one man, if with many voices, they protested loudly.

'Your Grace – this is impossible! Insufferable!'

'Sire – you cannot do it! Huntly is tried and condemned for treason!'

'Damnation – this is beyond all! The man's a rebel . . . !'

'He is a Papist, Highness. You cannot put a Papist over your Royal Guard. It's no' to be considered.' That was the Earl of Mar, stepping close. The King's boyhood companion, son of the royal guardian, who had shared to less effect the alarming George Buchanan as tutor, he frequently dared to take even greater liberties with his sovereign than did his peers.

'Aye – but he's no' a Papist. No' any more, Johnnie,' James declared earnestly. 'I have converted him, mysel'. Aye. I have been at pains to bring him to see the blessed light o' the Reformed evangel. Have I no', my lord o' Huntly?'

'Ah . . . just so, Sire. Exactly, as you might say. Amen. H'rr'mmm,' the Gordon concurred, eyes upturned Heavenwards, and stroking a wispy beard.

'God save us all!' somebody requested fervently.

'A pox – here's madness!' a less pious lord declared.

'Huntly converted? Not while Hell's fire burn!' a realist maintained.

'Do not be misled, Your Grace,' Mar urged. 'My lord of Huntly, I think, but cozens you. He would but humour you . . .'

'Not so, Johnnie – not so. My lord wouldna deal so wi' me. We have reasoned well together. Aye, long and well. At Edinburgh Castle. He couldna confute my postulations and argument. Eh, Geordie? I am assured that he will now be as a strong tower o' defence to our godly Protestant religion. Aye.' The King cleared his throat loudly, placed one hand on Huntly's shoulder and the other raised high. He raised his voice likewise. 'Hear ye, my lords. I have fetched my lord o' Huntly here this day to declare to you his devoted adherence to the Reformed faith and to announce to you that I . . . that we are pleased to bestow on him the hand in marriage o' the Lady Henrietta Stuart, our royal ward, daughter to our former well-loved cousin Esmé, Duke o' Lennox, and sister to Duke Ludovick here present. Aye. In marriage.' James came to an abrupt end, coughed, and looked around him.

Into the silence that succeeded this announcement, pregnant and all too certainly disapproving, only one voice was raised, after a few seconds, a voice pleasantly melodious.

'How pleasant to be my lord of Huntly! How greatly to be congratulated.' The Master of Gray had returned, clothed, though with his hair still lacquered in silver. He spoke from just behind Marie and Mary – and probably only the former knew what anger and resentment was masked by those light and silky tones.

Or perhaps, not only Marie. Huntly himself turned around quickly. 'Ha – does that bird still sing?' he jerked. 'I'd ken that tongue anywhere.' He did not sound as though the knowledge gave him any satisfaction.

'The sweeter meeting for so long a parting, Cousin,' Patrick rejoined. It was the first meeting of these two since the Master's disgrace and banishment.

'Come, Patrick man,' James urged. 'Greet well my new Captain o' the Guard . . .' He was caressing the Gordon's hand.

'The King seems very loving towards my Lord Huntly,' Mary said.

'Loving is . . . accurate!' Marie returned dryly.

'Uncle Patrick, I think, was ill-pleased.'

'Ah – you perceived it also! He will be the less gratified.'

The Master of Gray's rearrival on the scene had drawn the Duke of Lennox's glance in their direction. Rather abruptly excusing himself from the King's immediate presence, he came hurrying.

'Mary!' he exclaimed. 'Mary Gray! You, here! I' faith, is it yourself?'

'Your eyes do not deceive you, my lord Duke,' she agreed, curtsying.

'But – here's joy! Here's wonder! When . . . ? How . . . ? I knew naught of this. Are you but new come? To Court? Your father . . . ? He allowed it? 'Fore God, you look beautiful, Mary! You look . . . you look . . . '

'Hush, Vicky!' She indicated the Lady Marie. 'Here's no way to behave, surely?'

'Ah. Your pardon, Mistress of Gray. I . . . your servant.'

'I doubt it, my lord Duke – when you cannot even serve me with a glance! Not that I blame you. You approve of Mary coming to Court? You approve of her looks? You approve of how we have dressed her? Indeed, like us, you approve altogether?'

'Yes,' he agreed, simply but vehemently. He sought to hold Mary's arm, as they stood side by side.

Gently but firmly she removed his hand. She smiled at him, however.

After a brief interval indeed with the King and Huntly, Patrick rejoined them. 'Ah, Vicky,' he said, nodding. 'My congratulations to the so happy bridegroom will scarcely extend to the bride, your unfortunate sister! And you I can scarcely congratulate on your errand to Edinburgh. If I had known . . . ' He shrugged, and took his wife and Mary by their arms. 'Come, my dears – the air further off is the sweeter, I vow!'

The Duke stolidly stuck to Mary's side. He seemed the merest boy in the presence of the other.

'This upraising of Huntly cannot but set back your plans, Patrick?' Marie said. 'As to Dunfermline. I am sorry.'

'It will make my course more difficult,' he admitted. 'James has kept it all devilish secret. He had need to, of course. If the Council had known, it would never have been permitted.

Had Maitland known in advance, Huntly would have been found dead in his quarters in Edinburgh Castle, I have no doubt! But . . . Captain of the Guard! It is a shrewd move. Now Huntly can surround himself with armed men, here in the Lowlands, as he does in the North. Until he is unseated from that position, Maitland cannot reach him.'

'Until . . . ? Who can unseat him, Patrick?'

'The Council can. And no doubt will, in due course. No Papist may hold any office of authority under the Crown save by the Council's permission.'

'But he has professed the Protestant faith. Did you not hear? The King says that he has converted him!'

'That, my dear, can be satisfactorily controverted, I think.' Patrick produced his sweetest smile. 'Matters of religion should not be turned into a jest, should they? Have you not said as much frequently, my love?'

His wife looked at him thoughtfully. Then she inclined her fair head in the direction of Lennox. 'Ought you not to be more discreet, Patrick?' she suggested calmly.

'Vicky? Lord, Vicky's all right. He is no more overjoyed at his sister being given to Huntly than am I, I warrant?'

'I was not asked,' the Duke agreed, frowning. 'James told me only to bring Huntly here.'

'And was the Lady Henrietta asked?' Mary put in.

'I cannot think it likely,' Patrick said.

'I doubt if she has so much as met him,' Lennox added.

'That is wrong, surely,' the girl declared, very decidedly. 'She should refuse such a marriage.'

'Ha!' Patrick smiled. 'There speaks a rebel. It is not hers to refuse, my dear.'

'I would refuse to marry any man save of my own choice,' Mary said quietly.

'So you are served due warning, Patrick!' Marie observed, laughing.

'Indeed? But then, Mary lass, you are neither a duke's sister nor a king's ward.'

'For which I am well pleased.'

'I would make you a . . . a . . . ' Lennox began, and then fell silent, biting his lip.

The Master of Gray looked at him keenly. 'What would

you make of her, Vicky?' he wondered.

'Vicky would forget that he is Duke of Lennox and near heir to the throne,' Mary answered for him. 'And that I am a land-steward's daughter.' That was firmly said. And in a different tone. 'Uncle Patrick – is the King my Lord Huntly's catamite?'

Even the Master of Gray gulped at such frankness. 'Lord, child!' he gasped. 'Here's no question to ask. In especial not at this Court! Sink me, I did not know . . . I would not have believed that you possessed such a word! Knew of such things . . .'

'The Carse of Gowrie is not the Garden of Eden, Uncle Patrick – nor is Dundee the end of the world. As I think you know well.'

'M'mmm.' Patrick glanced sidelong at his wife, who pulled a comic face. They had stopped by the lochside.

'I have heard it said that the King is so inclined,' Mary went on. 'If it is true with my Lord Huntly, then I think it is your plain duty, Vicky, to preserve your sister from him. And you, Uncle Patrick, to aid him.'

'Me . . . ?'

'Yes. Surely such is the duty of all decent men?'

'You see, Patrick,' Marie said. 'As a decent man, your path is now clear. Has anyone ever before flattered you so?'

'A pox!' the Master groaned. 'What sort of a reformer have I brought to this Reformed Court?'

'I will speak with James,' Ludovick said. 'But he is not like to heed me. And . . . Hetty has to marry someone. There are worse than Huntly, I think.'

Almost pityingly she looked from one to the other. 'Poor Henrietta!' she commented.

A herald came hurrying through the throng, seeking Lennox. 'His Grace requests your presence, my lord Duke, forthwith,' he announced.

As the young man moved off, reluctantly, Mr. Bowes, who had been hanging about nearby, came close, obviously desirous of speaking to Patrick without the Duke's presence. For once his smooth brow was distinctly furrowed.

'This of Huntly, Master of Gray, is the very devil!' he declared. 'I can scarce credit it. My princess will take this but ill, sir. Huntly is . . . anathema.'

'I am sorry for that, Mr. Bowes. We can but seek to do what we may in, er, rectification.'

'You must do that indeed. And without delay,' the Englishman said sharply.

'But, of course.'

Mary Gray considered them both, grave-eyed.

Mr. Fowler came, almost running. 'Excellency,' he said to Mr. Bowes, 'the French Ambassador. He is speaking close with the King and the Duke. He has news, I vow – important news. He is most exercised.'

Others apparently had heard the same rumour and were moving in towards the group around the King. Patrick and Mr. Bowes did not linger.

James was looking distinctly upset. Plucking at his lip, he was blinking at the spider-thin but painfully elegant figure of the elderly M. de Menainville, Ambassador of His Most Christian Majesty who, gesticulating vehemently, was pouring out words. Huntly and the other lords, their differences seemingly for the moment forgotten, were gathered close, intent, their expressions various.

Lennox detached himself from the group and came over to Patrick's side, 'It is the King of France,' he announced. 'He is dead. We brought the French courier with us from Edinburgh. With a letter for de Menainville. This was the tidings.'

'Indeed,' the Master of Gray said, inclining his head.

Mr. Bowes was a deal more exclamatory. Tonight, his suavity was being sorely tested. 'Dead? Henri? My God – here's a to-do! He is . . . he was not old . . . '

'In God's gracious providence, it is the way of all flesh!' the Master observed piously.

James was raising his hand for silence. 'My lords, my lords,' he mumbled. 'I . . . we are much afflicted. Sair troubled. Our royal uncle, His Grace o' France, is dead. Aye, dead. Our ain mother's gudebrother. We . . . we much regret it. Aye, deeply. We must mourn him.' Vaguely he looked around him. 'We . . . we'll ha' to see to it, aye.'

M. de Menainville said something very rapidly in French, eyes upturned to the cloudy sky. No one else knew what comment to make – for Henri Third of France had been a weak and treacherous nonentity, wholly under the potent thumb of his late aged tyrant of a mother, Catherine de Medici, and an unlikely subject for grief on King James's part. Yet that the King was distressed was most patent.

The Master of Gray was nowise perplexed or in doubt. 'God save King Henri the Fourth – late of Navarre!' he called out mellifluously. 'Happy France!'

'Ah. U'mmm.' James caught his eye. 'Ooh, aye,' he said.

Hurriedly the French Ambassador demonstrated diplomatic agreement in a torrent of words and gestures.

There was a vibrant silence in that garden, as all eyes turned on the Master. He had had many triumphs in his day, as well as reverses – but this was quite the most unexpected, unheralded and peculiar, and quite undeniable despite its barrenness of all advantage save to his own prestige. If James had taken his advice not so long ago, a mere few months, he would now be betrothed to the sister of the King of France – who moreover had not produced an heir in seventeen years. The cause of their monarch's distress became apparent to all.

Orkney, blunt as always, put the thoughts of many into words. 'It's no' too late to hale back the Marischal frae Denmark, is it?' he suggested.

'Aye, bring him back.'

'Put off the Danish match.'

James was gnawing his knuckles. 'I canna,' he wailed. 'It's no' possible. It's ower later, ower late. I . . . we . . . the Chancellor . . . we sent my lord o' Dingwall to Denmark six days syne. To marry the lassie. By proxy. For me. It was . . . in view o' the delay . . . we deemed it advisable . . . ' The royal voice faded away.

Only a few had been privy to the Lord Dingwall's mission. Patrick himself had learned of it only two days before.

It was Patrick, for all that, who came to the King's rescue. 'It is unfortunate,' he agreed. 'But Your Grace could scarce guess that King Henri Third would thus meet an untimely fate. The Danish precaution was entirely understandable, all must admit.'

Gratefully James looked at him. 'Aye, Patrick – that is so.

We werena to ken. But . . . you were right, man. Waesucks, you were right!'

'It so happened that way, Highness, on this occasion. Another time . . . ' The Master shrugged, and smiled kindly. He had made his point – or had it made for him – for all that mattered in Scotland to perceive. And gained doubly in virtue by his forbearance from saying 'I told you so'. Undoubtedly his credit was well restored – and his position on the Council would be the stronger.

All recognised his triumph – even though not all rejoiced in it. Only Mary Gray expressed her foolish feminine doubts a little later when the company began to move into the palace banqueting hall for the dancing.

'Uncle Patrick,' she asked seriously, at his elbow. 'Are you not glad, really, that the Princess Catherine of Navarre is not to be queen in Scotland? Old and ugly and unchaste as she is?'

He looked down at her, and said nothing.

'And you said, did you not, that the King of France met an untimely fate? I do not understand why you should have said that.'

The man's face for a moment or so went very still, expressionless. Then he raised a hand to touch and pat his lacquered silver hair. 'Did . . . did I say that Mary?' he asked, taut-voiced.

'Yes. I thought it strange, when Vicky and the King only said that he was dead. Also, you were not surprised, I think. You knew already, did you not?'

'No!' he jerked, glancing around swiftly, to ascertain that none overheard them. 'God's eyes – how should I know, girl? And, a pox – what is it to you? Fiend seize you – I'll thank you to mind your own affairs!' When she did not answer or look up, he frowned. 'I am sorry. But . . . Lord, was I a fool to bring you here?' he demanded. 'To Court?'

'You may send me away again, if you will,' she pointed out quietly.

'No doubt. But . . . do you want to go, lass?'

'No, Uncle Patrick.'

'Then' – he mustered a smile again – ' . . . then, my dear, my strange, shrewd and damned dangerous daughter – be

147

assured to remain my friend, on *my* side, will you? For I would not like you as enemy, 'fore God!'

'How could I be that?' she asked simply.

Looking patient but determined, the Duke of Lennox came up to her. 'Mary,' he requested, 'will you dance with me?'

'Why yes, Vicky – in due course. But there is no music, as yet.'

'No. But . . . ' – he waved his hand over towards a group of smirking gallants and lordlings who stood and jostled each other – 'these are speaking of you. They would dance with you. All of them. Say that you will dance with me, Mary.'

'That I will.' She laughed, and patted his hand kindly. 'I will. But not *all* the dances . . . '

Chapter Seven

THE Court moved back to Edinburgh in only a few days. This was a surprise, and much sooner than had been intended – sooner undoubtedly than the King would have wished, for James much preferred residence at Falkland or Stirling or even Linlithgow to adorning his capital city of Edinburgh. Nevertheless it was the King's own sudden decision. The Earl of Huntly was to be married, and as quickly as possible – and Edinburgh, at Holyroodhouse, was unquestionably the right and most suitable venue for a near-royal wedding.

The urgency of Huntly's nuptials was of course by no means occasioned by the usual stress of circumstance, the bride and groom scarcely being acquainted with each other. The need was pressing nevertheless, from the royal point of view. The Gordon's abrupt rise to favour was far from being accepted by the Court in general and the Kirk party in particular – the man's natural arrogance by no means assisting. Despite James's assertions, Huntly's adherence to the Protestant faith was openly scouted. He was shunned, save by sycophants, and termed a Highland barbarian – though in fact he was no true Highlander. Most serious of all, somehow Sir John Maitland got to know of the matter the very next day – which indicated that somebody had despatched a swift courier to Edinburgh that selfsame night – and he sent an immediate and strongly-worded protest to James, declaring that he would resign the chancellorship forthwith were Huntly not at least dismissed from the office of Captain of the Royal Guard.

The King, though much distressed, was stubborn. He confided in the sympathetic Master of Gray that all misunderstood and misjudged him. His elevation of Huntly was not merely out of affection for his well-loved Geordie Gordon, but for the betterment of the realm, the ultimate bringing together of the warring Catholic and Protestant factions, and the furtherance of the true religion. Without Huntly, the other Catholic lords, Errol, Montrose, Crawford and the rest, would be leaderless. It was a serious exercise in statecraft, the mumbling monarch stressed. Patrick declared that he fully understood and concurred, but advised caution, with perhaps some temporising and dissimulation in difficult circumstances. He was even notably civil to Huntly himself. James at least was appreciative. But on one issue he was adamant; the marriage with the Lady Henrietta Stuart must go forward at once. A wedding, by the Reformed rites, with the King's close cousin and personal ward, would establish Huntly's position in the regime more securely than anything else. The Master, as ever, bowed to the inevitable with commendable grace.

So all repaired across the Forth to Edinburgh, and Mary Gray found herself installed in the Earl of Orkney's rag-tag and raffish establishment in the neglected east wing of the palace of Holyroodhouse which had formerly been part of the old Abbey buildings. Patrick, as Master of the Wardrobe, was to have quarters in the more modern part of the palace, but as yet these premises were not ready for him.

My lord of Orkney's household was an unusual one – and as stirring as it was singular. A family man *par excellence*, he liked to be surrounded both by his offspring and his current bedmates – and the latter were apt to be only a little less numerous than the former. This friendly and comprehensive suite demanded a deal of accommodation, for Orkney's reproductive prowess was famous, indeed phenomenal, and the thirteen legitimate progeny were as a mere drop in the bucket compared with his love-children, of whom no final count was ever possible or attempted – and only a percentage of whom could, of course, be conveniently housed in their sire's vicinity. All who could, however, lived together in approximate amity, along with a contemporary selection of lady-friends. To term these last as mistresses would be inaccurate and unsuitable; for one thing, there were too many of them – they could hardly all be mistresses; for another, seldom were any of them old enough aptly to bear such a title; moreover mistress as a designation has overtones of dignity about it, of orderly arrangement – and assuredly there was nothing either dignified or orderly about the high-spirited, boisterous and lusty Orkney household. King James therefore, was thankful to turn over this decaying, rambling and far-out extension of Holyroodhouse to his chronically impoverished uncle, to be quit of him and his entourage – and to hope that the noise of it would not unduly disturb the more respectable quarters. It was noticeable, however, by the observant, that there was a not infrequent drift eastwards by some of the respectable, of an evening, for Robert Stewart was the soul of hospitality and prepared to share all things with practically all comers. How the Lady Marie, eldest of his legitimate brood, serene, fastidious and discreet, could have issued from this nest was a mystery to all who knew her. The Lady Jean, undoubtedly, was more typical.

The Master of Gray kept his own little *ménage* as separate as was possible – and spoke to his father-in-law forcefully and to the point on the subject of Mary Gray, whose youth and loveliness made an immediate impact on the roving eyes not only of Orkney himself but of the regiment of his sons, sons-in-law and less certainly connected male dependents; though so positive and uninhibited a family-circle was not to be held at arm's length very effectively. Not that Patrick need have worried, it seemed – for Mary promptly if unassumingly adopted the entire extraordinary household as her own, apparently taking it and its peculiarities quite for granted. Clad in a sort of unconscious armour of her own, compounded of essential innocence, friendliness, self-possession and inborn authority, she was uncensorious, companionable and happy. If individuals, in the grip of liquor or other foolishness, sought

150

to take liberties, she had learned well in her native Carse of Gowrie how to take care of herself, if in a fashion not usual amongst Court ladies – so that, indeed, only the second day after their arrival, the Master of Orkney, heir to his father, perforce went about with two long red scratches down his smiling face, and moreover enjoyed having them tended and cosseted by the forgiving donor into the bargain.

Huntly and the Lady Henrietta Stuart were wed only a week and a day after the return to Edinburgh, almost in unseemly haste. The bride, a pale quiet girl of sixteen, appeared to be entirely apathetic, and made considerably less impression than did her train of maidenly attendants, gathered together at short notice, including the Lady Jean Stewart and no fewer than four other high-spirited daughters of the King's uncle, these being conveniently to hand, and not fussy about religious allegiance – and all, it was pointed out, by different mothers. Mary Gray was to have been recruited for the bridal retinue, but surprised all by her refusal, polite but firm, unusual an honour as this represented for one in her position. Since she did not think that the marriage was right, she pointed out, it would ill become her to assist at it, even in the most minor capacity. From this peculiar attitude none could budge her, try as Patrick and Ludovick might. The fact that she seemed to be the only person at Court so concerned, including the Lady Hetty herself, made no difference.

Neither the ceremony itself nor the festivities thereafter were just as the King would have wished – whatever Huntly himself felt, who appeared to treat the entire business in a somewhat flippant and casual manner. Lack of time for due preparation was partly responsible, together with the fact that the royal treasury was ever insufficiently full for all the demands upon it – and James's own wedding celebrations, due in a month or so when his bride should have been brought from Denmark, must not be prejudiced. Huntly himself, of course, was rich enough, richer than his monarch undoubtedly, but he was perhaps understandably disinclined to go to any great expense to entertain large numbers of his enemies – which approximately would be the position, for his own friends were in the main far away in the north, and, being Catholics, unlikely to desire to attend any such heretical nuptials anyway. Moreover, the costs of a great marriage were traditionally the responsibility of the bride's family – and the Duke of Lenox lacked wealth. If the entertainment had to be on a modest scale, however, at least there was no embarrassing cold-shouldering of the occasion, no undignified paucity of guests; the King saw to that by the simple expedient of commanding the presence of the entire Court at the ceremony, rather than merely inviting it.

He was less successful over the officiating clergy, unfortunately, for the Kirk was made of stern stuff. Principal Andrew Melville of St. Andrews, the acknowledged leader of the miltant and dominant Calvinist extremists, flatly refused, in the name of his Saviour, to perform the ceremony for such a notorious former enemy of Christ's Kirk and doubtful convert, and his reverend colleagues took their cue from him, so that even Master David Lindsay, the King's favourite divine and royal chaplain, found a convenient illness to excuse him. James had to fall back on Andrew Davidson, Reformed Bishop of St. Boswells and former holy Lord Abbot of Inchaffray – who, incidentally amongst other things was Mariota Gray's father and Mary's other grandfather, completely as he ignored the relationship. This prelatical celebrant was not just what the occasion demanded, admittedly – almost any of the sternly Calvinist divines would have been better – but at least he conducted the union on approximately Protestant lines and spared the restive congregation the usual two-hours sermon thereafter. Also, his rich crimson episcopal robes made a better showing against Huntly's barbaric tartan-hung and bejewelled splendour than would have the plain black gown and stark white bands of Geneva. The King himself gave away the bride, and surprisingly, the Master of Gray appeared as principal groomsman to his far-out cousin.

The banquet thereafter was a comparatively dull and sedate affair, Huntly's unpopularity, the King's role as host, and the inferior quality of the entertainment all combining to inhibit the traditional excesses of the bridal feast. Indeed, carefree horseplay was wholly non-existent, despite one or two gallant attempts by the Orkney faction, and even the public disrobing and ceremonial bedding of the bride and groom, normal highlight of the occasion, was dispensed with – for who would dare lay hands on the fiercely proud and unpredictable Gordon chief surrounded by his Highland caterans armed to the teeth? In consequence the thing degenerated into mere steady eating and drinking, interspersed with uninspired speeches which even the Master of Gray's barbed wit only spasmodically enlivened. So humdrum and disheartening was the cumulative effect of all this that something in the nature of a spontaneous migration eventually developed at the lower end of the hall towards my Lord Orkney's quarters, where no doubt more spirited celebrations were almost bound to develop as antidote and compensation. Soon only the inner and official group around the King and Huntly remained; the women, including the heavy-eyed bride, having been got rid of, these others settled down to an evening's hard drinking, with Highland toasts and pledges innumerable.

When Patrick was able decently to withdraw, the King being noisily asleep and Huntly becoming indiscriminately pugnacious, he strolled over to his own quarters, thankful for the fresh air, to find Orkney's wing in a vastly different state. The entire range of buildings appeared to shake and quiver with life and noise, not a window unlit, the place seemingly all but bursting with active humanity. Shouts, varied music, raucous singing, screams of female laughter, and an almost continuous succession of bangs, thumps and clattering, emanated from the establishment. Patrick had difficulty in even gaining an entrance, two unidentified bodies lying in close and presumably enjoyable union just behind the door, so that he had to squeeze in and step over jumbled clothing and active white limbs even to reach the stair-foot. Thereafter his progress up to his own modest attic chambers on the third floor took on the nature of an obstacle-course, the winding turnpike stairway providing a convenient series of perches, partially screened from each other, for sundry varieties of love-making, physical self-expression, intimate argument and bibulation, up, down and through which screeching girls were being chased by the more agile-minded. Few of the doors were closed, and within, the rooms were littered with wedding garments of many of the royal guests. Giggles, gruntings, and shrieks of not too urgent protest followed him all the way upstairs, and from somewhere indeterminate the great bull-like voice of the Earl and Bishop of Orkney bellowed for wine, wine – to which no one appeared to pay the least attention. The servants, it seemed, were as fully engaged as were their betters.

Patrick found his wife and Mary sitting together alone in one of their three attic rooms – although one of the others at least was patently much occupied. Marie was stitching at a tambour-frame, and the girl rolling hanks of the silken thread into balls. The baby, Andrew, slept undisturbed in his cradle. They made somehow an extraordinary picture in that setting, so entirely normal and respectable did they seem.

The man began to laugh, quietly, with real mirth. 'God save us – virtue triumphant!' he exclaimed. 'Was ever such propriety so improperly enshrined! My sweetings – how do you do it?'

'What would you have us to do, Patrick?' Marie asked.

'Lord knows,' he admitted. 'Just what you are doing, I suppose. But . . . one thing I do know – we must get out of this den if we are to have any peace this night. Your peculiar family is in fullest cry, my love. Gather together some night clothes and blankets, and we shall seek shelter elsewhere for the nonce.'

'Gladly. But where? We cannot go traipsing the streets of the town at this hour. And the palace is full to overflowing.'

'Save for one quiet corner,' her husband pointed out. 'I warrant our unpopular Lord Chancellor Maitland's quarters in the north wing are not overcrowded. They will be a haven of peace, I vow.'

'Maitland!' Marie exclaimed. 'The Chancellor? Your worst enemy . . . ?'

'Whom worthy and righteous folk would say that I should love and cherish . . . would they not?'

She ignored that. 'But the man who worked your downfall? Who clamoured for your blood . . . ?'

'The same, my dear.'

Mary spoke, without interrupting her winding. 'I overheard my lord Earl of Moray say, but yesterday, that he believed that the Master of Gray was privily seeing a deal of the Chancellor.'

'The devil you did!' The smile was wiped off Patrick's face. 'Moray? Say it to whom?'

154

'To Mr. Bowes, it was, Uncle Patrick.'

'A pox! I . . . I . . . ' He paused. 'You have devilish long ears, girl! You overhear too much!'

'Great lords and gentlemen think not to whisper when only such as I am near,' she pointed out, equally as frankly. 'When I do hear your name spoken, Uncle Patrick, would you have me not to listen?'

'M'mmm. Well . . . I suppose not.'

'Is it true, Patrick,' Marie asked, 'that you are secretly seeing much of Maitland?'

'What if it is?' he returned. 'In my present pass, I cannot afford to be at odds with the Chancellor of Scotland.'

'Knowing you, I suppose that I must accept that. Just as you made common cause with Queen Elizabeth, who so shamefully had betrayed you. It is Maitland that I do not understand. What can *you* offer him, I wonder, in exchange for his good offices?'

'Tush, woman – leave statecraft to those who understand it! A truce to talk of this sort.' It was not often that the man spoke thus to her. His glance shot warningly in Mary's direction. 'Gather you together the night gear and wrap up Andrew, and I shall go and apprise Maitland of your coming . . . '

'No, Patrick. You may be prepared to toady to Maitland, but I will not be beholden to the man who sought the execution of my husband . . . and who tortured Davy Gray!'

'Toady . . . ? I mislike your choice of words, Marie – by God I do! And . . . Davy, eh? Perhaps the beating of Davy weighs even heavier against Maitland in your eyes than his impeachment of me?'

'Do you choose to believe so, Patrick?' That was calm, evenly said.

He bit his lip.

'It is none so ill here,' Mary intervened quickly. 'The noise will abate presently, to be sure. Already it is quieter than it was, I think . . . '

'Yes, there is no need to move,' Marie took her up. 'None are doing us hurt here . . . '

'*You* may be well enough,' Patrick rejoined. 'To you, after all, this is nothing new. You were reared in this extraordinary household. But with Mary . . . ! I would not have this squalor even touch the hem of her skirt! What goes on in this house . . . '

'You are become exceeding nice, of a sudden, Patrick? And there are more kinds of squalor than one,' his wife pointed out. 'I make no excuse for my father's habits, for I have ever condemned them. But are there not worse ills for Mary to observe than the mere lusty sins of the flesh? Lies, intrigues, back-biting, dissembling, dishonour, treachery? Statecraft, if you prefer the word!'

The man went very white, dark eyes blazing. 'I'll thank you to be silent!' he jerked.

'Silent, yes. I have been silent for too long, perhaps, Patrick. Silence is a quality much in demand for the wife of the Master of Gray – and I do not come of a notably silent family, as you have observed! There are times when it would serve you but ill to keep silent – and I think that this is one. I know all the signs, Patrick – I have seen them so often ere this. You are about to launch some dark and underhand plot, some scheming subtle venture, in which someone will be direly hurt . . . for the benefit of the Master of Gray! Is it too late to ask that you stay your hand, Patrick? Too much to ask you to renounce it?'

'What nonsense is this? Have you taken leave of your wits, Marie, for God's sake? With an obvious effort, he controlled himself. 'See you, statecraft is none so ill a business. It cuts both ways – works much good for many as well as some small hurt for a few. The realm cannot be served without it. My life it is. I am on the Privy Council again . . . '

'The Council will hear naught of this that you are now plotting, I warrant! Or your meetings with Maitland would not be secret.'

'It is better that way. For the weal of the realm. For the King's peace.'

'The realm! The King! Oh, Patrick – who do you deceive? Not yourself, and not me. Not even Mary here, I think.'

Mary looked from one to the other gravely, hurt in her eyes. 'Do not speak to each other so,' she pleaded. 'Please do not.'

Both reacted to that, and at once. Patrick took a pace towards her, changed his mind, and turning strode to the door and out, without another word. Marie rose from her frame, and came to enfold the younger woman in her arms.

'My heart, my sweet Mary!' she cried. 'Forgive me. That was unkindly done. I was foolishly carried away. I do not know what made me behave so. I am sorry!'

Mary kissed her. 'Do not fret, Lady Marie,' she said. 'All will be well. I know it. Uncle Patrick must scheme and plot. As he says truly, it is his life. And he is very good at it, is he not? He will not stop it, I think. So . . . we must just scheme and plot also. So that whenever he makes a mistake, we may perhaps right it. You and I. Is that not best?'

Marie drew back a little, to stare at the girl, wonderingly. 'Oh, Mary my dear,' she exclaimed. 'Bless you. But . . . you do not know what you say. What you propose. What goes on in Patrick's handsome head.'

'I think that I do. I am very like him, you know – very like him indeed. My father – Davy Gray – says that we come out of the same mould. It may be that the same goes on in my own head. Good and ill, both.' She smiled, warmly. 'Is it not . . . convenient?'

'Lord . . . !' the Lady Marie said, shaking her head.

James was in high good humour. The hunt had found in the boggy ground around Duddingston Loch, a mere mile over the hill from Holyroodhouse; it would have been strange had they not, perhaps, considering the pains taken by the King's foresters to ensure that there were always deer in the royal demesne, however tame and imported – and however many Edinburgh citizens with a taste for venison must hang to discourage poaching. They had killed, after an excellent chase, up on the high ridge near Craigmillar Castle to the south, James himself striking the fatal blow. Moreover, his favourite goshawk, set at a pair of mallard from the loch against Johnny Mar's bird, had flown fast and true, stooped on the drake and brought it down cleanly, whilst Mar's hawk had gone bickering off after a heron to no advantage. So the King smirked and chuckled, railing his former playmate, and declaring that his fine Geordie Gordon should have been there to witness it – for Huntly, who had set out with the rest from the palace, had unfortunately been recalled by a messenger on seemingly urgent business, and had not as yet rejoined them.

It was almost certain that no further quarry would be found, save down in the great swampy area by the loch again, for this was no hunting country in fact, far too populous an area, too near to the city, for deer to lurk save in the marshy, reedy sanctuary west of Duddingston. The head forester, therefore, advised that they return downhill, and suggested that the scrub woodland around Peffermill was the likeliest place to try, with the wind south-westerly and the easten area already disturbed. James thought it would be better further west still, at Priest-field perhaps, but the Master of Gray agreed convincingly with the forester, pointing out the much more free run that they could have from Peffermill, leaving Priestfield for even a pos-sible third attempt. The King's good humour, plus his in-temperance for the sport, allowed him to agree.

It was Mary Gray's first royal hunt, this twenty-second day of August. Only the day before, James had made official announcement that, allowing for all contrary winds and possible delays, his special emissary the Lord Dingwall, acting as his proxy, should have wedded the Princess Anne in Den-mark by now, and that therefore he, James, by the Grace of God, King, could be considered to be a married man, and Scotland to have a queen. That this queen was only the second daughter of the King of small Denmark, and not the sister of the childless King of mighty France, was a pity, but must be accepted philosophically. James therefore concentrated now on the youth – she was barely fifteen – and declared pulchri-tude of his bride, and asserted that he was madly in love. Contemporaneously with the royal announcement had come a proclamation from the Lord Chamberlain, publishing the names of the new queen's household. The Countess of Huntly would be principal Lady-in-Waiting, and amongst others, the Lady Jean Stewart one of the Maids of Honour, and Mary Gray an extra Woman of the Bedchamber. So now Mary held an official position at Court, and should begin to take a fuller part in its activities.

With Jean, she rode between Ludovick of Lennox and Patrick, up near the front of the colourful cavalcade, and even the King, who was apt to be more impressed by male good looks than by female, remarked on her fresh young beauty, and leeringly dug an elbow in the Duke's ribs and mumbled congratulatory jocularities. It was accepted by all, undoubtedly that she was Lennox's mistress.

Down the hill through the fields towards the low-lying marshland between Craigmillar and the great towering bulk of Arthur's Seat they streamed, the head forester and his assistants first, followed by a small detachment of the royal guard, then the King and his falconers. It was in the group of lords and their ladies, immediately behind, that Mary and Jean rode, thanks to the lofty status of their escorts. Further back straggled the field of fully three-score laughing, chattering riders, no great proportion of them vitally absorbed by the hunting, but only there because it was expected of them, it was the thing to do – and since it was their monarch's passion, because those who showed no interest in it might well offend the source of privilege, position and preferment. Some, having put in an appearance, would undoubtedly take the opportunity quietly to fall behind and make their way back to the city, rather than put in some further hours of pounding about the thickets and waterlogged unpleasantness of Duddingston Myres.

From the hamlet of Peffermill a causeway led out into the great green marsh area. The normal procedure would be for the hunt to wait here, while the foresters went in to try to find and rouse a skulking stag amongst the water-meadows, and force him out to hard ground for the sportsmen to chase. But James, timorous and hesitant in almost all else, was a paladin where hunting was concerned, frequently indeed himself doing the work of his foresters. Nothing would serve now, but that he and all others who called themselves men, should plunge into the morass and beat out the place thoroughly. Sighing and shrugging, his younger nobles and some of their more spirited ladies prepared to follow on. This had happened before. The dozen or so members of the bodyguard looked depressed.

As James clattered on to the causeway, past the last of the buildings, the millhouse itself, a stout figure came hurrying out, calling and waving and panting, apron still round a wide middle – no doubt the miller himself. The King frowned impatiently, and gestured a rebuff, for this was no time for petitions and the like. The Master of Gray, however, reined up and over to the man. He exchanged a few words with him before hurrying on after the others.

'Heed nothing, Sire,' he called out. 'Just some complaint of robbers and vagrants. As ever.'

The King waved back in acknowledgment.

Where the causeway forked, perhaps a quarter-of-a-mile in, was the obvious place to spread out. The foresters shouted to that effect, and James was ordering his reluctant guard to fan out left and right, with the group of nobles still a little way behind, when the green leafy place of tall reeds, alder spinneys and drooping willows suddenly seemed to erupt in noise and men. Out from the plentiful cover, as at a given signal, poured scores of unkempt and ragged figures, yelling, brandishing swords and clubs and daggers, some mounted, some on foot. The leaders notably were dressed in tartan and wore Highland-type bonnets.

'A Gordon! A Gordon!' range out on all sides. From somewhere unseen, a single piper skirled the rousing notes of *The Cock o' the North*.

All was immediate chaos amongst the hunting party. The guard was already spread out on either side, dispersed. James all but fell off his handsome black Barbary in alarm, staring wildly about him. This was of all things, indubitably, what he most dreaded, victim already of many abduction attempts. His hoarse cries were almost like those of a trapped animal.

Only a small part of the hunt cavalcade could see what was going on, owing to the windings of the causeway amongst the scrub woodlands, and its narrowness stringing out the company almost indefinitely. Indeed most, having few ambitions to act as bearers in a quagmire, were deliberately hanging back. Most of the lords in the foremost group, however, after a momentary hesitation, spurred on to the aid of their monarch, tugging at their swords. Even the readiest, however, must needs follow Patrick Gray who had his sword drawn almost as soon as the attackers appeared, and dashed forward with ringing cries.

'The King! The King!' he shouted. 'Save His Grace!' And then, 'Guard! Guard! Back here! To the King! Back to the King!'

The men-at-arms who had each more or less been riding at

160

the nearest of the assailants, were somewhat confused by these gallant orders. Some turned back indeed, some hesitated, others pressed on. Those who came back became entangled with the hurriedly oncoming lords – for the level and firm ground of the causeway was narrow, and space for excited horses and riders circumscribed to say the least of it.

Confusion indeed reigned all around, and not only on the side of the defenders. The attackers themselves appeared to be almost as uncertain in their assault, however vigorously brandished their weapons and fierce their cries. If there was a concerted plan of action, it was not evident. Men rushed and darted, wheeled and dodged and sallied, by no means all pressing in on the King himself. The clash of steel, the thudding of blows, the high whinnying of horses, all rose to mingle with the monotonous chant of 'A Gordon! A Gordon!' and to all but drown that turbulent clan's challenging battle-anthem on the bagpipes.

One of the noblemen, at least, did not aid in the confusion. Instead of rushing forward with his elders, the Duke of Lennox reined his mount right round and came plunging back to Mary's side. There he drew sword, and so sat, his pleasant blunt features tense, jaw dourly set.

Mary, flushing, leaned over to grip his arm. 'No, no, Vicky!' she whispered. 'Not here. Up yonder – with the King. You should be with him there.' Uneasily she glanced round at the few other women, clustered together there. It was not often that Mary Gray looked embarrassed. Fear did not seem to have touched her, as yet.

'James is well enough served,' Ludovick returned. 'All run to his aid.'

'But . . .' Mary, noting that set look, did not press him. 'At least, look to these ladies. Not me only,' she urged, low-voiced.

With no very eager or gallant expression, the young man tossed a look at the small group of flustered and alarmed women. He nodded. 'Back,' he told them, gesturing along the causeway. 'Back to the others. Toward the mill.'

Most of them, with only uncertain glances forward toward their menfolk, did as they were bidden. Mary, however, sat her horse, one of the Duke's own, unmoving, gazing ahead with keenest interest rather than apprehension. Jean, after a few moments' hesitation, elected to remain with her. Lennox placed his mount between them and the trouble in front.

It was very difficult to ascertain just what was happening, so congested was the causeway up there. The King, at any rate, seemed to be safe, back amongst a tight group of his nobles, and cowering in a state of near collapse. Fighting of a sort was proceeding at a number of points, so far without any noticeable casualties. The Master of Gray undoubtedly was foremost and most militant amongst the Court party, dashing hither and thither, sword waving, shouting instructions, urgings, threats.

The royal guard, although outnumbered and dispersed, appeared to be gaining the upper hand; at least, the attackers seemed notably averse to coming to grips with them. For that matter, there was a lack of close-quarters engagement all round. The famed Highland dash and ferocity was perhaps only largely vocal, after all.

Three rough-looking individuals, swathed in tartan plaids, came yelling down the line, their very third-rate horses splashing in the reeds and surface-water at the side of the causeway. At the martial gestures of the Earl of Mar and the Lord Yester, they drew away prudently and came on towards Lennox and the girls. The Duke, frowning and a little pale, prepared to take on all three.

More huntsmen were coming up from the rear now, however, bewildered but alerted by the women who had ridden back. The trio of bullyrooks presumably decided in the circumstances that a closer approach would be inadvisable, and contented themselves with standing where they were, shaking fists and weapons and chanting their slogan. Mary, when she perceived that they were not in fact going to attack, was not so frightened as to perceive some other things also; for instance that there was no sign of blood about these warriors, even on their swords; that their voices did not sound in the least Highland; and that under their plaids their clothing seemed to be quite Lowland and ordinary.

The winding of a horn from somewhere out of sight forward sounded high above all the shouting and clash. It had an extraordinary and immediate effect on the entire scene – indeed, not even the rockets of Patrick's pageant of Leda and the Swan were more salutory in their effect. On the part of the assailants, all fighting was broken off forthwith. With a unanimity and discipline that had been somewhat lacking in their advance, the attackers obeyed what was clearly a signal to retire. Men turned about in their tracks and went plunging back into the long reeds and waterlogged thickets of the myre, mounted and foot alike splashing away promptly and wholeheartedly, heading into the cover nearest to them like so many water-rats released near their chosen habitat. If the assault had been a failure, there was no foolish reluctance about conceding the fact.

No single victim was left behind to witness to the fury of the attack.

Patrick Gray made the only gesture at pursuit. He rode a little way after one of the mounted men who elected to flee along the fork of the causeway eastward. He soon came trotting back however, sword still in hand, and actually laughing. Mary, now alerted to such things, noted that his sword was unblooded also.

He found the lords clustered round their trembling sovereign, congratulating him on his escape, inveighing against all traitors, dastards and poltroons, and preening themselves a little on prompt and effective action. Lennox and his two ladies rode forward to rejoin the group.

'All gone, Sire,' the Master of Gray called out, sheathing his sword at last with something of a flourish . . . 'Bolted like coneys for their holes! They will not return, I swear! You are not hurt? They did not reach Your Grace?'

Although James could not yet find words to answer, the others did, volubly. Loud and long were the assertions, questions, demands. Everywhere the name of Huntly was being cursed and reviled.

Patrick appeared to doubt the general assumption. 'I cannot believe that this was my lord of Huntly's work,' he said, when he could make himself heard. 'He would never so move against His Grace's royal person! 'Tis highest treason! After all the King's love for him? No, no. Moreover, Huntly surely, had he planned such wickedness, would have worked it to better effect. These, I vow, were but feeble warriors . . . '

'They were Gordons, man! Did you no' hear them, 'fore

God? Huntly's own ruffians!'

'Who else leads Gordon, but Huntly? That curst tribe!'

'Tartan savages they were! Hieland cut-throats!'

'Aye. And were they any more valiant at Brig o' Dee? They fled then, the arrogant Gordons . . .'

'My lords,' Patrick declared, waving his hand. 'It may be as you say. But let us not judge too hastily. Huntly is not here to answer for himself . . .'

'No, by God – he's no'! Where is he, then? Why turned he back . . . ?'

'Aye – where is the forsworn Papist? He knew well no' to come hunting this day!'

Patrick shrugged elegant shoulders.

The King, unspeaking, was urging his tall horse through the press now, back, southward along the causeway toward Peffermill again, head down, eyes darting. He pushed and prodded his lords, to have them out of his way, all fear, hurt and suspicion. He answered none who addressed him, met no eyes, uttered no words although his thick lips seemed to be forming them. On he urged his mount, regardless of how many he forced off the causeway into the myre. In jostling disorder the strung-out hunt turned itself around and headed whence it had come.

Somehow Patrick Gray managed to draw ahead, and as they emerged on to the firm and open ground near the mill, went cantering towards the millhouse itself, authoritatively demanding wine and sustenance for His Grace the King.

James, still trembling almost uncontrollably, allowed himself to be persuaded to dismount, and shambled into the miller's house, supported by the Master of Gray and the Earl of Mar.

Lennox was about to follow the other great lords inside, when Mary laid a hand on his arm.

'Vicky,' she said quietly. 'Your sister, the Lady Hetty. How greatly do you love her?'

'Eh . . . ? Hetty?' He shrugged, French-style. 'I know her but little. She was reared in France, with my mother, while Patrick brought me here. We are . . . not close.'

'But she *is* your sister. I believed that you owed her a duty – to save her from being wed to my Lord Huntly. But now she is his wife, for better or worse, you owe her another duty, do you not?'

Uncertainly he looked at her.

'She is Countess of Huntly, now. If ill befall her husband in this, she must suffer also.'

'If Huntly is rogue enough to misuse James and attack his King's person, he must needs pay the price, Mary. The price of treason.'

She shook her head. 'Huntly may indeed be a rogue. But this roguery, I think, is not his. Here was no treason, Vicky.' Sitting their horses side by side, she spoke close to the young man's ear. 'Could you not see it? See that it was all a plot? But not of Huntly's making. Those were no true Highland-men, no true Gordons. It was no true attack. No blood was spilt, that I saw. All were too careful for themselves. None pressed close to the King. It was but play-acting, nothing more. I am sure. To bring down Huntly.'

'M'mmm.' Ludovick rubbed his chin. 'You think it, Mary? All that? The fighting, to be sure, was but half-hearted . . . '

'Yes. So the Lady Hetty must be warned, Vicky. And Huntly also. Before . . . before his enemies have their way. Before a great injustice is done.'

'But who . . . ?'

'My Lord Huntly has many enemies. He makes them apace. But that does not merit . . . this.'

Her companion frowned. 'Nor is he any friend of mine,' he pointed out. 'And if I go now, hasten back to the city and leave James, it will be noted. When Huntly is warned, in time to flee, it will be Lennox his new gudebrother who warned him. To the King's declared hurt.'

'That is true. I had not thought of that. Yes, you must stay. I will go. Give me something of yours, Vicky, that I may show to them. Lest Huntly does not believe such as myself. Your signet-ring – that he will recognise . . . '

'Aye – take it, Mary. If you think that is best. God knows if this is wise . . . '

'It is right. Fair. Is that not enough?'

'I do not like you to go alone . . . '

'Why not? It is but a mile or two. If I cannot gain entry

to Huntly, I shall ask the Lady Marie to aid me. All know her. Tell my Uncle Patrick that I felt weary. Upset by the stramash. And went back. Go in now, Vicky – to the King.'

Mary reined her horse round, waved to Jean, and rode off eastwards.

In the crowded millhouse, James sat crouched over a rough table, gulping and spilling small ale from a pewter tankard, pale but apparently recovering. Every now and again he reached out an uncertain hand to pat the arm of the Master of Gray standing close by, whom he evidently looked upon as his saviour. So far, the name of Huntly had not crossed his lips. Those around him, however, made up for his omission. On all hands were demands for the Gordon's immediate arrest, trial, even execution. After all, he was still technically under sentence of death for treason, from the Privy Council, for the Brig o' Dee Catholic rising. The King's personal pardon had never been officially confirmed by the Council, dominated as it was by the Kirk party. Only Patrick Gray raised a voice on Huntly's behalf – which may have been partly responsible for James's obvious gratitude and trust. He was pointing out to all, that he had recognised none of the Gordon lairds in the assault, when Ludovick came in.

'I agree with the Master of Gray,' that young man announced, jerkily. 'It may be that Huntly himself had no hand in this. Only, perhaps, his enemies!'

All eyes turned on him – and none more sharply than Patrick's. A chorus of protest and derision arose from the other lords.

'There speaks a prudent and generous voice,' the Master commended.

'And the Countess o' Huntly's brother!' someone added.

Something of an uproar followed. It faded only as a newcomer pushed his way urgently into the crowded low-ceiled room, clad in the royal livery – indeed, Sir John Home, lieutenant of the King's guard.

'Sire,' he announced. 'Instant tidings from my Lord Chancellor Maitland.' He laid a folded and sealed letter before the King. 'For your immediate eye, Highness.'

James picked up the paper gingerly in shaking fingers, held it away from him as though it might carry the plague, turning it this way and that. Then, the seal still unbroken, he handed it to the Master of Gray, signing for him to open and read it.

Patrick did as indicated. The letter proved to have a second paper within it. He glanced at the contents, and his fine eyebrows rose and his mouth pursed.

James peered up at him, in mute question. As did all present.

'Your Grace,' he said slowly, almost hesitantly for that confident man. 'The Chancellor has . . . has come upon a letter. This letter. Intercepted it. From Huntly. It bears his seal, see you. It is to my lord of Livingstone. At Callendar. Requiring him to muster men and arms. Secretly. To be ready to march. In the service of the Holy Catholic Church and the true and ancient faith . . . '

He got no further before his words were drowned in a flood of furious outcry, passionate, continuous, demanding. Louder and louder grew the din, so that Patrick, shrugging, laid down the papers.

As though moved by a force outside himself, James rose unsteadily to his feet, and so stood for a few moments, ill-shapen features twisted and contorted with emotion, great liquid eyes heavy with sorrow, like some dog ill-used by its master. Then he raised a hand for silence.

'My lords,' he said, 'so be it.' His voice, now that he had found it at last, was stronger, more resolute, than might have been expected. 'Sir John Home, you will take my guard and apprehend and arrest George Gordon, Earl o' Huntly, forthwith. Wherever you shall find him. To be warded secure in the Castle o' Edinburgh. On charge o' conspiracy against the safety o' our realm and royal person, in highest treason. Aye. We . . . we . . . ' The unusually firm voice broke. 'Och, to your ill duty, man – to your duty. And may the good God ha' mercy on me, his silly servant!'

In the succeeding acclaim and fierce plaudits, the King turned to the Master again. 'Take me awa', Patrick – take me awa',' he pleaded. 'I'm no' feeling that well. I'm sick, man – sick to death. I want out o' here. Frae a' these loud men.'

'Assuredly, Your Grace. At once. We shall have you back at Holyroodhouse almost before you know it.'

'Na, na – no' there, man. No' there. Geordie might raise

167

the town against me. There's Catholics aplenty, and other ill bodies, in Edinburgh. He'll maybe try again. I'll need a strong place. A castle. Craigmillar's near – a big, bonny, strong place. I'll to Craigmillar, Patrick – I'll be safe there. In case o' more deviltry. Aye, take me to Craigmillar.'

'As you will, Sire . . .'

It was evening before Patrick Gray returned to his lofty chambers in Orkney's wing of Holyroodhouse. He seemed to be a little bemused, abstracted in his manner, for he quite forgot to kiss, as was his usual, either his wife or Mary or the baby Andrew.

'A busy day you have had, Patrick,' Marie said pleasantly. 'Brave doings, by all accounts – and James much beholden to you, I gather. So your credit stands the higher. My brother Robert tells me that the King has taken refuge at Craigmillar. I wonder that he permits his guardian angel to leave his side thus long to visit us here!'

Thoughtfully the man considered her. 'Do I detect some displeasure here, my dear?' he wondered.

'Why, no. Should it not be pride, rather, in my husband's bold championing of his King? His heroism? All testify to your gallantry, to your . . . preparedness! It seems that, once again, Patrick, your quick wits won the day!'

He stroked his now clean-shaven chin. 'You are too kind, Marie. And you will have heard – that Huntly escaped?'

'So it is said,' she nodded. 'You will have eaten at Craigmillar? Or shall I find you some supper?'

He began to pace the attic room. 'Someone warned him. I would give much to know who it was. Home rode straight from Peffermill to Huntly's lodging here, and found them gone. I have questioned him. They had been gone only minutes. Yet scour the city as he would, he found no trace of them. Some of his Gordon lairds they took – but not Huntly or his wife. Maitland sent men hot-foot along all roads to the north – but without avail. It is believed now that they slipped down to Leith, and took boat to Fife. They will not catch Huntly now, I think.'

'And that will upset your . . . plans?'

'Plans? Is that not a strange word to use? The King's safety

is what signifies. The ship of state upset – not plans of mine.'
He shrugged. 'For myself, it is of little matter whether
Huntly escaped or no. He is forfeit now. The forfeiture papers
are already signed.'

'Indeed? So soon? They were quickly drawn up, were they
not?'

'Maitland, my love, is ever efficient! And prompt. As he
was over my own forfeiture one time!'

'And as he was, it seems, over this letter of Huntly's that
was . . . intercepted. To Livingstone, was it not? Most timely.
Was it a forgery, think you?'

Patrick grimaced. 'Indeed no, Marie. You insult the
Chancellor! Maitland is never clumsy. It bore Huntly's own
seal. I noted, however, that it was undated!'

'Ah! Then . . . then it probably was old? Written some time
ago? Intercepted some time ago? Before Brig o' Dee, perhaps?'

'I commend my wife's intelligence! Let it be a lesson to us
all never to write treasonable correspondence in clear words,
my dear!'

Both were surprised, undoubtedly, by the little gurgle of
amusement from Mary where she sat at the window.

'I see,' Marie said, after a pause. 'So Huntly is forfeit.
But forfeit only. He is still powerful.'

'In the north, Marie – in the north, only. And Dunfermline
is in the south, is it not? Sweet and precious Dunfermline!'

Long the Mistress of Gray looked at her husband from level
grey eyes, and said nothing.

He turned away, to the younger woman. 'My dear, I missed
you after Peffermill,' he mentioned. 'Vicky said that you were
upset. I am sorry, Mary. But there was no need to be so.
None. I esteemed you in no danger.'

'Nor I, Uncle Patrick,' she assured. 'No danger at all.'

His eyes widened a little at that. 'Had I believed there to be
any, I would have looked to you, child.'

'Yes. I know that. You see, *I* looked to the King's head
forester. When I saw that he sat his horse unmoved, in all that
stramash, even with his arms folded, I knew that there was
no danger.'

The man swallowed. 'You watched him? The forester . . . ?'

'Yes. You see, I saw you speaking with him in the stableyard last night, and giving him money. Was I not wise to watch him, then?'

'Wise . . . ?' He drew a long breath. 'Wisdom, God help me, is over rife in this family, I think!' His brows came down. 'Then . . . then what upset you, child? If you were so assured?'

Her pink tongue just tipped her lips. 'I was upset . . . only for foolish woman's reasons. But I am so no longer. I am recovered quite.' Mary rose, and came to him, smiling her warmest. 'I am happy, now. Happy that my lord of Huntly escaped. And the Lady Hetty. Are not you, Uncle Patrick? Really? It is so much better that way. You escaped from Edinburgh to Leith yourself, once, did you not? Just in time, likewise.'

'Ah . . . yes,' he admitted. He blinked quickly.

'I watched you both go – you and Lady Marie. And my lord of Huntly aiding you.'

'H'mm. Yes. But . . . at a price, girl. At a price! It cost me Dunfermline!'

'It cost more than that,' she said. 'It cost my father, Davy Gray more than that. Perhaps you do not know, Uncle Patrick, what it cost him?'

Both of them were now gazing at her strangely, intently.

She looked up at him, smiling again. 'But that is all done with. Dear Uncle Patrick – forget Dunfermline! Forget Huntly! You are high in the King's favour, and all is well. Let us all be happy again!'

He searched the young, eager, lovely face upturned to his, wonderingly. 'A kiss from you, sweeting . . . and I count Huntly well lost! Perhaps Dunfermline, even!' he exclaimed.

'You shall have it.' Flinging her arms around him, she kissed him vigorously, whole-heartedly. Still clutching him, she held out a hand towards the Lady Marie. 'You too,' she pleaded. 'Come. Please do. Now we shall all be happy again, together – shall we not? Come.'

Marie looking from one to the other, bit her lip, hesitating, and then came. Patrick's hand went out to her likewise.

170

Chapter Eight

THE King of Scots walled himself up in Craigmillar Castle, high on its ridge south of the city, seeking security, if not peace of mind, within its outer bailey and inner bailey, its ditch and drawbridge and its massive keep – and would not stir therefrom. All who sought the fountain of honour, authority and government must seek it past three gatehouses, a guardroom and parapets bristling with armed men. Nothing would coax majesty without – not though it was the height of the hunting season, with the stags of the great park of Dalkeith nearby at their best and fattest. Hawks could be flown from Craigmillar's great grass-grown outer court, tennis be played and archery practised – but James was in no mood for such pastimes, and they were followed only by such of his unfortunate Court as found itself immured within the gaunt walls, sombre vaults and frowning towers of the castle.

James himself, after the first fright of the ambush and its implications wore off, and as fear of further repercussions began to fade, not unnaturally perhaps turned his mind more and more to distant vistas far beyond these safe but enclosing walls, and to contemplations more apt for a newly-married young man – even if only wed by proxy. He began to dwell upon the imagined person, parts and prospects of his bride, as a more rewarding thought than the perfidy of Geordie Gordon. Indeed, he shut himself up for most of days on end in a lofty turret chamber, where he could look out over the wind-whipped Firth of Forth estuary, past the rock of Bass and the Isle of May, to the grey North Sea, in the direction of far Denmark. Here, with a portrait of the Princess Anne that had been sent to him, he indulged in a positive orgy of synthetic emotion, an auto-intoxication of purely intellectual adoration for the Viking's princess of his imagination.

No doubt the sad and sudden termination of his pseudo-romantic relationship with Huntly was partly responsible. James, not notably masculine in himself, but brought up to condemn and fear his unfortunate and lovely mother, Mary

171

Queen of Scots, and educated by stern Calvinist divines who frowned on women – at least in theory – had ever sought his emotional satisfactions from his own sex, and all from older men than himself. The succession of favourites, however far they went in their relationship with this unlovely and loveless royal youth, had all proved to have feet of clay; all had used their intimacy with the source of privilege to gain for themselves power and wealth and domination. All had been brought down by jealous nobles. Disappointed, hurt, James, now twenty-two, turned, in at least temporary revulsion, to this new and exciting prospect – a young woman, innocent and fair and already his own, although unknown, who would give him what hitherto his life had lacked.

So, in escape from the reality of the present, he wrote to her innumerable letters which could by no means be delivered, in a strange mixture of passion, dialectics, philosophy, semi-religious ecstasy and gross indecency. He indited poems, large and small, and then decided upon a really major work, which history would rate as one of the literary masterpieces of all time. He studied erotica, consulted much-married men and women – the Master of Gray and his wife, embarrassingly, in especial – physicians, necromancers, herbalists, even mid-wives. He toyed with the idea of having a relay of ladies to bed with, both experienced and virgin, and of various ages and shapes, in order to practise upon – but decided eventually in favour of pristine innocence rather than expertise, for presentation to his sea-king's daughter. He grew pale and languishing and greater-eyed than ever – and kept his Master of the Warbrobe busy indeed in ordering and fitting the most elaborate and fanciful garb ever to be worn by a Scots monarch, for outdoors and indoors, day and night wear, most of it in a taste as bizarre as it was grotesque.

All of which was something of a compensation and source of infinite, if guarded, merriment to the royal entourage in more or less forced confinement within Craigmillar – although one or two of his Court perhaps perceived pathos therein, and discovered in their hearts some sympathy with this strange, complex, shambling creature, born in sorrow and treachery, separated from his mother almost at birth, who had known no true love in all his life, the pawn of arrogant scheming

172

nobles and harsh and dictatorial clerics.

The Gray family was inevitably much at Craigmillar – although its members continued to reside at Holyroodhouse, the distance between being but two or three miles. Patrick was in high personal favour again – although this, unfortunately, owing to James's almost complete temporary withdrawal from affairs of government, was not translated into any real political power, which remained more firmly than ever in the hands of the coldly astute Maitland. The King, in his present preoccupation with womankind, anatomy, and the like, saw a deal of his cousin Marie Stewart, finding in her a quiet sympathy, sensibility and frankness which he had hitherto overlooked. And since Lennox – whose defection at Peffermill did not seem to have been noticed by his royal cousin – was now, as Chamberlain, necessarily domiciled at Craigmillar, he sought to entice Mary Gray there at every opportunity – the Master by no means hindering him. With the new queen expected almost at any time, and her household, of which Mary was now a member, having to be prepared and made ready for her arrival, this proved easy and convenient enough, indeed to be expected – even though Duke Ludovick would perhaps have preferred that Mary did not take her sewing and embroidery duties quite so seriously, as did not the Lady Jean, for instance.

The relationship between Patrick Gray and Ludovick Stuart was interesting and not unimportant. Undoubtedly many about that licentious and idle Court believed it to be illicit and unnatural. They made a strangely ill-assorted pair certainly, the handsome, talented, quick-silver and accomplished man, and the plain, solid, rather awkward and ineloquent youth. But they had been good friends for many years – ever since, at the age of ten, young Vicky had been brought from France by Patrick, at the King's command, to succeed to his late and brilliant father's dukedom. The Master of Gray's part in the downfall and subsequent death of the same father, the usual kind informants had not failed to disclose to the young heir; but Ludovick, who had scarcely known his sire, had clung to Patrick. Indeed his early affection for the Master had grown to an admiration amounting almost to adoration, that nothing then or later could ever wholly upset.

It was a day of unseasonable battering rain and wind in mid-September, that Mary Gray sat stitching at the window of a small room in the main keep of Craigmillar. This chamber was one of three grimly functional apartments, all bare masonry, gun-loops and arrow-slits, set aside for the Master of the Wardrobe, and the unlikely repository of the fripperies and confections of the royal trousseau and plenishings. Shot-holes stuffed with scintillating fragments of cloth-of-gold and brocade, coarse elm tables littered with lustrous and colourful silks and satins, now mocked the severity of those frowning walls where once Mary, the Queen's half-brother Moray, her future husband Bothwell, and her Secretary Lethington, brother to Sir John Maitland, had secretly plotted, urged on the Queen's divorce from King Henry Darnley, James's father, and set alight the train that exploded at Kirk o' Field with Darnley's assassination.

Because outdoor activities today were precluded, and young men for the moment in short supply in the castle, the Lady Jean Stewart, supposedly also applying herself to the new Queen's needlework, but in fact gossiping, gesturing and giggling without cease, kept Mary company. Such was life for this true daughter of Orkney.

It was thus that her distant cousin Ludovick found them. Not infrequently he managed to escape from his duties to this little room. That on this occasion he would have been content for the Lady Jean to be neglecting her needlework elsewhere went without saying, but Lord Chamberlain as he might be, he was not the young man to order her hence. One attempt he did make, however.

'The Commendator of Lindores is at cards down in the Preston Tower. With Ferniehirst, Borthwick and, h'm, others. He might be grateful were you to rescue him, Jean.' That came abruptly, after a silent minute or two.

'If the Commendator prefers his silly cards to . . . to better sport, let him stay!' She shrugged. 'He is losing again, I suppose?'

'Aye, naturally.'

Mary looked out of the streaming window. 'Uncle Patrick plays also?' That was more of a statement than a question.

'Aye.'

Jean hugged her buxom self. 'Then the good Commendator-Abbot's goose is cooked! Serve him right, I vow – for he is plaguey mean. He would have his fairings at the cheapest, would Lindores – including me!'

'I have seen you less than dear, yourself!' Lennox said bluntly.

She did not so much as colour. 'You mistake, Vicky. You would, of course.' She glanced from the man to Mary. 'I am no huckster. I give for nothing – or else I play high. Like Patrick Gray. Lindores does not understand. He has the mind of a tradesman . . . '

'He would wed you, I think,' Mary observed.

'No doubt. But he is old, as well as mean . . . '

'He is less old than Patrick,' Lennox pointed out. 'He is not yet thirty, I think . . . '

'Patrick is different! Patrick will never be old. Patrick is wonderful. At cards as at all else! I dote on him . . . '

'So all the Court knows!' Ludovick grunted. 'As, indeed, do half the women here!'

'No less than yourself, perhaps, Vicky!' That was barbed.

'He is my friend,' the young man declared stiffly.

Jean Stewart skirled high laughter. 'None would deny it . . . !' She stopped, as the door opened. A head peered round, a large somewhat lop-sided head crowned by an absurdly high hat decked with ostrich-plumes.

Hurriedly all three rose to their feet, and the girls curtsied over their needlework, as the King shuffled in, large feet encased in loose slippers.

James ignored them. 'Vicky,' he complained querulously, 'I've been seeking you a' place. Man, you shouldna hide yoursel' away like this. You're the Chamberlain. Here's this wee man – the Provost, it is. Frae Edinburgh. About the reception ceremonies in the town. For Anne. My . . . my wife. The Queen, aye. He says you sent for him. You should be seeing him, Vicky – no' me. I'm busy. I'm in the middle o' a sonnet . . . '

'Your pardon, Sire. I did not know that he was come. You should have sent a page for me, an officer . . . '

'Och, I was for stretching my legs. I was ettling to find Patrick too. He's hiding away somewhere. A' folks hiding

175

away frae me. It's nae better than a rabbit-warren, this castle. I thought on this wee room, wi' your Mistress Mary. Away you down and see the man, Vicky.'

'At once, Your Grace.'

'Aye.' James did not follow Lennox out, but moved over to the window, to peer through. 'It's wild, wild,' he declared. 'Ill weather for the sea. Wind and rain. It's no' right, no' suitable.'

'You could play at the tennis in the Hall, Sire,' Jean said helpfully. 'I have heard that my lord of Moray does so, at Donibristle. Indoors . . .'

'Houts, woman – tennis!' the King cried. 'A pox on tennis! It's no' tennis – it's Anne! Your Princess. My wife. She's on the sea. Coming to me. In these accursed storms. Waesucks – it's no' fair! The lassie – she'll puke. It's an ill thing, the sea – sore on the belly. The great muckle deeps, see you – they're like ravening wolves! Aye, wolves. Opening their slavering jaws for my puir Annie! In this plaguey wind . . .'

'Do not fear, Your Grace,' Mary said earnestly. 'All will be well, I am sure. The Queen will be safe. This is not truly a storm. It may not be blowing out at sea, where the ships are. It is from the west, you see – the other way.'

'D'you think I dinna ken that? So it blaws in her face, lassie – it keeps her frae me! It blew a' yesterday, too. The Devil's in it, for sure. I'll need to have prayers said . . .'

Jean actually giggled.

Furiously James turned on her. 'Quiet, girl! Will you laugh at *me*? God's soul – I'll no' have it! Silence, d'you hear?'

Jean swallowed. 'It was just . . . prayers, Sir! Against a puff of wind . . .'

'A puff! Fiend take you – here's no puff! A' night I lay and listened to it, wowling and soughing round this castle, wheeching and girning. I couldna sleep thinking o' the lassie's boatie. And it's getting worse, I tell you. Aye, and you whicker and snicker! Och, away wi' you, wench! Out o' my sight. I'll no' be whickered at. Begone, you ill hizzy!'

Hastily the Lady Jean, flushing at last, backed out of the room, dropping her embroidery in the process. At the door she turned and fled, forgetting to curtsy. Mary, less precipitately, would have followed her, but Majesty pushed her back into her seat.

'No' you, lassie – no' you,' he told her. 'Och, I canna bide yon Jean! Aye gabbing and caleering! Making sheep's eyes. Sticking out her paps at me! I dinna like it. I'll need to be getting her married off on some man. It's no' decent. She's aye like a bitch in heat. I'll have to think on it.'

'The Lady Jean has no evil in her, Sire,' Mary told him. 'I pray, do not misjudge her. She is but overfull of spirit.' She paused for just a moment. 'Although she would be better married, I truly think.'

'Aye. I'll consider it.' James looked at her sidelong, out of those great liquid eyes. 'And you, lassie? Are you no' the marrying kind, yoursel'?'

She smiled. 'Time enough for that, Your Grace. I am but sixteen years.'

'Ooh, aye. Though, mind you, my ain lass is a year younger. And you're ripe for it – 'sakes aye!' He looked her up and down judicially. Then he tipped forward his extraordinary hat, to scratch at the bulging back of his head. 'But . . . eh, now . . . Vicky. Vicky – the Duke o' Lennox – is young, young. And fair donnart on you, lassie. Mind, I'm no' blaming him that much! You'll be bedding wi' him, belike?'

'I bed with no man, Sire.'

'Eh? No?' The King looked surprised. 'I thought . . . I jaloused . . . ?'

'Then Your Grace jaloused but mistakenly,' she assured, but gently enough. 'Others, I have no doubt, do the same. I am very fond of my lord Duke – but that is all. We have been friends since we both were bairns – good friends. But that is all. I am my own woman, still.'

'Ummm.' James plucked at his sagging lower lip. 'You're . . . you're holding him off, then? For he's hot for you. I've watched him, aye. And, 'sakes, I'm fond o' Vicky, too, lassie.' He began to shuffle about the room, touching things. 'Vicky's near to me, near to the throne, see you. Of the blood-royal, aye. Mind, now, I'm a married man, and like to be making bairns o' my ain, he'll no' be next heir muckle longer. Na, na. But . . . but . . . even so, he's no' just . . . he's a duke. And . . .'

'Sire,' the girl interposed. 'If you are seeking to tell me that the Duke of Lennox is not for such as me to marry – then content yourself, for I know it well. When he weds, it must be to some great noble's daughter. And she must be rich – for Vicky has insufficient wealth. I know it all. Rest assured, Sire, I shall not seek to marry your cousin.'

'Aye, so. Good, good. Proper – maist proper. Nae doubt we shall find a good worthy husband for you. Ooh, aye – some honest decent laird, wi' broad acres belike. Some lordling, even – for you've the Gray blood after a' . . .'

'I thank you, Highness – but I am in little hurry. And when I do seek a husband, it would please me well to choose my own – by Your Grace's leave.'

'Och, well – we'll see, we'll see.' The King began as though to move to the door, but shufflingly, darting looks hither and thither, as though reluctant to go. Suddenly he turned round and came back to the girl, and looks and tone changed quite. 'See, lassie,' he said, almost diffidently. 'You've got a wise-like head on your shoulders, and a decent honest tongue. There's a wheen things you maybe could tell me – things I dinna just ken aright. About lassies . . .' He coughed. 'I ken maist things, mind! – I'm no' just an ignorant loon. But . . . och well, she's about your ain age, and there's things I'll need to do wi' her . . .'

'I understand, Your Grace,' Mary said, soberly. 'Anything that I may decently tell you, I will.'

'Aye, well. I've never had a lassie, you see. Mind, there's some been gey near to it – ooh, aye. Bold brazen hizzies would ha' had the breeks off me if I hadna . . . h'mmm . . .' He paused. 'Will it hurt, d'you ken? I mean, really *hurt*?'

'I take it, Sire, that you mean will it hurt the Queen, and not yourself? For I think, surely, that last is unlikely.' Only a single dimple in her cheek countered her gravity of mien. 'But I am told that so long as you are gentle, any slight hurt for the lady will be swallowed up quite in the satisfaction.'

'Eh, so? Uh-huh. Gentle. Is . . . is that possible. I mean . . . ?'

'I esteem it so, Sire. Firm, but gentle.'

'Aye. Well, maybe. Like . . . like with a new-broken colt?'

'Perhaps. But I would think with rather more of fond affection.'

178

'I've aye been fond o' horses,' the King said simply.

'Yes. I had forgotten.'

'She's young, mind. Anne. And will be a virgin, for sure. A pity it is that you will be a virgin too, lassie? It would ha' been better . . . You'll no' ken so much.'

'I am sorry. But I have good ears, I am told – and have heard not a little. Though, are there not plenty otherwise whom you may ask, Sire?'

'Aye, plenty! Plenty! But . . . God save me, I just canna bring mysel' to ask them, Mistress Mary! Yon Jean, now! She'd ken plenty, yon one! But she'd whinny like a mare at me. Her sister, even – the Mistress o' Gray. She's kind, and she's told me some bits, mind. But . . . you see, she's used wi' Patrick. And . . . and I'm no' Patrick! He's different frae me. We both have the Latin and Greek. We both have the poetry. But . . . we're different other ways. So . . . och, I just canna speak wi' her as I do wi' you.' James looked at her from under heavy drooping eyelids. 'Maybe . . . maybe we could do mair than just *talk*, lassie? Maybe . . . well, maybe you could come ben to my bedchamber, the night? I could arrange it that you bide here, at Craigmillar, the night. It's gey wet for going back to Holyrood. Aye, we'd learn a thing or two, that way . . . ?'

With all seriousness, Mary Gray appeared to consider this suggestion. 'You are gracious, Sire – and I am honoured. But I think, no. No. It would be better, more meet, I think, to await the Princess Anne – the Queen. That you should both learn of these things together. She will esteem you the more, that way, I think. *I* would . . .'

'But she needna ken . . .'

'If she is a woman, then she will ken, Sire.'

'M'mmm. You think it? Ah well . . .' James gave the impression of not knowing whether to be disappointed or relieved. He nibbled at his finger-nail. 'It's right difficult,' he muttered.

'I think, perhaps, you make too much of the difficulties, Highness,' she told him gently. 'After all, it has happened before. Many times.'

'Aye – but no' to me. No' to the King o' Scots. I am the Lord's Anointed, lassie – Christ's Viceroy. I am the father o' my people, see you – the fountain o' the race! It wouldna do . . .

179

it's no fitting, that I shouldna ken the way to handle a lassie in a bed. You see my right predicament? I've heard tell it's no' that easy, whiles, to get your mount to the jump, in time? And I wouldna like to jump my ditch afront my mare! Maybe I'd ha' been better wi' the Navarre woman, after a'. She'd ken the whole cantrip good and well . . . '

'Never that, Sire. You chose aright, I swear. Never heed about that first . . . ditch. There will be many such, after all. And in your own chamber, I cannot think that the Princess Anne will consider you as the Lord's Anointed or Christ's Viceroy – but just as her own new young husband. Be assured, she will not be critical of you, but only of herself.'

'You think it?' That was eager. 'Och, I hope so – I hope so. Maybe . . . maybe if I was to indite a poem about it, for her? Read it to her afore we bedded – maybe that would aid it? I'm good at poems, you see – I ha' the pen o' a ready writer. Aye. Even if I've no' just . . . no' . . . Och, well.'

Mary nodded. 'I understand. I am sure that the Queen will greatly esteem your poetry. But, Sire – I would counsel you to keep the poems out of the bedchamber, nevertheless. At first. Women are but silly shallow folk, you see – and perhaps Her Grace would liefer have just then kisses and fondling. I think that would be my preference.'

'It would? Kisses and fondling.' He sighed. 'Aye, maybe. Mind, it's maybe no' that easy to go about the business with a lassie you havena met wi', till an hour or two before. I'm doubting if it'll just come natural.' The King licked his lips. 'Now, it wouldna be that difficult wi' you, Mistress Mary – now I ken you, you see.' A royal arm slid around the girl's slender waist, and the long and delicate, if ink-stained and not overclean fingers sought for and captured her own.

'The Queen, I feel sure, will not prove difficult, Your Grace. She is young, and by her picture very bonny. And the poems that you have written for her will have greatly moved her, I vow. For few women are so . . . honoured. Your praise of her beauty and grace, your avowal of your great passion – all will move her. If indeed these are what Your Highness has written?' And with the most natural movement in the world, Mary turned to stoop and pick up a fallen hank of silken thread, thereby disengaging herself deftly from her sovereign's clasp.

That hinted question as to the tenor and content of his muse was highly successful, in that James at once reverted to the ardent poet and wordily-confident lover of the past few weeks. He dropped the girl's hand to grope about in an inner pocket of his stained doublet.

'I've two-three sonnets here. By me,' he told her. 'Well-turned and euphonious without being ambiguous – if you ken my meaning, Mistress. Aye. One's notable – right notable. Here it's – this one.' He extracted one of a number of crumpled papers, and smoothed it out. 'Listen you here, lassie. I've no' just decided on its title, mind – but you'll no' deny its quality, I'm thinking.' Striking an attitude, James began to intone – and as he read, his hand came out again to recapture Mary's.

> 'The fever hath infected every part
> My bones are dried, their marrow melts away,
> My sinnews feeble through my smoking smart,
> And all my blood as in a pan doth play.
> I only wish for ease of all my pains,
> That she might wit what sorrow I sustain.'

Finished, eagerly he peered at her, to observe the effect.

Mary cleared her throat. 'Most moving, Sire. As I said. 'Twill move her, to be sure. You did say . . . pan? Blood in a pan . . . ?'

'Aye, pan. Pot wouldna just do. Chamber-pots, you ken. Nor goblet. Cauldron might serve – but och, it wouldna scan, you see. D'you no' like pan, Mary?'

'To be sure, Your Grace – pan let it be. It . . . grows on me, I think.'

'Aye. That's right. That's how I felt mysel', lassie. Now, heed you to this one. It's maybe no' so lofty in sentiment – but it rhymes brawly. Longer too.'

The King was still declaiming, and so engrossed in the business that he did not notice when a knock sounded at the door, nor yet relax his moist clutch of Mary's hand. The door opened, and Patrick Gray stood there, looking in, his scimitar eyebrows rising high. Mary looked over to him, and smiled slowly, tranquilly, with just the tiniest shake of her dark head

181

to advise against interruption.

It was the Master's courteous applause, at the end, that informed the King that they were no longer alone. He flushed hotly, stammered, and dropped the girl's hand as though it had burned him.

'Bravo, Your Grace! Eloquence indeed! A royal Alcaeus . . . with our Mary as Sappho!'

'Eh . . . ? Och, no. No. It's you, Patrick man? You . . . you shouldna do yon. Creep up on me. No, no. And you mistake. I was just . . . just rehearsing a bit sonnet. For Anne, you ken. For the Queen. To hear the way it scanned, just. The lassie here . . . another lassie . . . about the same age, see you . . . listening . . . '

'So I perceived, Sire . . . '

'His Grace was much concerned about the wind and rain, Uncle Patrick – for the Queen's journey.' Mary came to the royal rescue. 'Telling me of his fears for the delay of the ships, he . . . he graciously thought to read over the poems welcoming her to his realm.'

'Ah . . . quite.' Patrick nodded gravely, though his eyes were dancing.

'Aye – the wind, the wind!' James recollected gratefully, turning to the window. 'It's wild – och, a storm it is. And getting worse. Waesucks – ill weather for journeying. And a lassie. It's the powers o' darkness, I swear – Satan himsel' working against me. He'll confound me if he can, I ken fine – for he's dead set against a' Christian monarchs. Ooh, aye. There was Anne's ain faither, King Frederick, met an untimous end no' that long ago. And even my late uncle o' France – cut off in his prime, even though naught but a Papist. By ill cold steel, I'm hearing.' James shivered. 'God rest his soul. Och, it's right dangerous labour being a Viceroy o' Christ – dangerous.'

'I cannot think that the present wind need unduly alarm you, Sire,' Patrick reassured. 'Nor, I esteem, are all crowned heads in hourly danger from His Satanic Highness. For, see you, your right royal cousin Elizabeth of England has well survived his spleen these many years!'

'Spleen!' James spluttered. 'Are you so sure it's spleen, man – in her case? A pox – I'm thinking it's his protection

182

she's had, the auld . . . auld . . . ' He swallowed, and royally sought forbearance. 'Och, well – we maun just pray God will take her in His ain good time. Amen.' One pious thought led to another. 'Aye – prayers. We'll ha' to order prayers in a' churches o' the realm, Patrick. For the abatement o' these ill winds. Aye – forthwith. The Kirk owes it to me, its sure Protector. I'll see Master Lindsay about it, right away. Aye.' With sudden determination, the King shuffled to the door. 'I'll clip Auld Hornie's wings yet, by God!' At the open door itself, he glanced round. 'You needna bow on this occasion,' he announced with regal condescension, and hurried out.

For long moments Patrick and Mary eyed each other, thoughtfully – and seldom had they looked more alike. The man spoke first.

'So I have to congratulate you on another conquest, my dear! A notable one, indeed. It . . . it seems that I am ever underestimating you, Mary! Not, h'm, one of my commoner failings!'

'No,' she told him. 'Here is no cause for such talk, I think. Just a poor, wandering, lonely man in need of a friendly hand.'

'I noticed the hand!' Patrick agreed, laughing. 'Call it what you will, Mary – so long as it is *your* friendship and *your* hand that our Jamie seeks! Properly prosecuted, this may lead to great things. I confess, it had never crossed my mind . . . '

'Nor should it now, Uncle Patrick,' she interposed firmly, seriously. 'I pray you, build nothing out of this. For my sake, if not the King's. He was but carried away by his own rhymings, his own fears and hopes. It seemed that he needed help – and I sought a little to help him.'

'Precisely, sweeting. And let us hope that you will be enabled to help him again, and considerably. For James, you see, has not hitherto looked to women for his help. Dealing with kings, you know, can be to much advantage. But it requires much thought and planning – for they are not as other men. You must take my advice . . . '

'Dealing with kings, Uncle Patrick, it seems may not always be of much advantage – to the kings! It was cold steel that killed King Henri of France, it seems! And you were not surprised by the tidings, that night at Falkland. I wonder why?'

The man's features stilled in the extraordinary fashion that on occasion could change his whole appearance. It was as though a curtain had dropped over those lively laughing eyes. 'What do you mean, girl, by that?' he said softly, almost under his breath.

'Just that, Uncle Patrick, our dealings with kings may often best be kept privy to ourselves – do you not agree?' And when he did not answer, she smiled. 'Do not be angry. Did you win a lot of siller from the Commendator of Lindores? Leave him some, Uncle Patrick, please – for I think that he may well wed the Lady Jean. And she will need siller, too ...'

Without a word he turned and left her there.

Alas for the efficacy of prayer even by royal appointment. The weather that autumn of 1589, whether devil-inspired or otherwise, did not moderate. Indeed it worsened, south-westerly gales blowing almost incessantly throughout the entire months of September and October. They were as bad as those which had dispersed Philip's Armada a year before, and of longer duration. The belated corn harvest was flattened and rotted, haystacks were blown to the winds, all round the coasts fishing-boats failed to return to their havens, and ordinary sober men shook their heads in foreboding.

The state of mind of King James bordered on chronic hysteria, in consequence. He shut himself away even more rigorously in the keep of Craigmillar, and even within the castle itself showed himself to few. He saw the entire climatic disturbance as a personal conspiracy against himself and his unseen beloved, and in a lesser degree and somewhat obscurely, against Christ's Holy Evangel, with which of course he closely identified himself. The Huntly business was all but forgotten; the irresponsible antics of the Earl of Bothwell, who, having won free from Tantallon, was as usual running wild in the Borders, no longer affected his monarch, it seemed; the normal machinations of mutually jealous lords left him apparently unmoved. He filled the long days and nights of waiting, particularly the nights, with alternate bouts of prolonged prayer, increasingly peculiar versifying, even deeper study into the supernatural and the black arts, with necromancers and reputed dabblers in these things sought out and brought to him from all over the land. Not to put too fine a point on it, the sovereign's mind appeared to many to be in process of becoming quite unhinged.

The rule and governance of the realm, in consequence, devolved almost wholly upon the Lord Chancellor, Maitland. This undoubtedly by no means suited many of those at Court; particularly Patrick Gray, who, despite his recent rapprochement with the Chancellor, found his wings considerably clipped – since his influence with that wily if upstart lawyer was inevitably a deal less effective than with the young James. As the weeks wore on, indeed, Patrick became very preoccupied indeed. He spent an ever-increasing proportion of his time in the company of the Duke of Lennox, it was to be noted.

With the continued non-arrival of the ships from Denmark, Mary Gray, for one, watched the King, Patrick and Ludovick, all three, with concern. James himself she did not often see, though when she did he was apt to dart strange, uneasy, almost appealing glances in her direction – glances which, she was well aware, Patrick seldom missed. For his part, the latter saw that Mary was very consistently at the castle; indeed, had not his wife put her foot down firmly, he would have had the girl lodging there. As Master of the Wardrobe he was, with the Chamberlain, the official most responsible for arrangements for the Queen's reception; the Queen's ladies, therefore, he kept under his own appreciative eye.

Ludovick, these long inclement days, tended to be moody and morose. A vigorous and active young man, with no great intellectuality or fondness for indoor pursuits and idle Court dalliance, or for that matter the card-playing which his friend the Master found so profitable, he fretted at the forced immurement within Craigmillar's thick walls. Out of patience with James, ill at ease with most of his fellow courtiers, a fair proportion of the time that he was not with the Master of Gray he tended to spend in the small room in the keep with Mary and her colleagues. There were distinct doubts as to whether Patrick wholly approved now, whatever had been his previous attitude.

On one such occasion, in mid-October, with Lennox watching Mary at her stitchery with more than usual stolid gloom, the girl rallied him smilingly.

'Vicky,' she protested. 'You puff and sigh there like a cow with an overfull udder! Why so dolorous these days? I have not seen you smile in a week, I vow!'

'Eh . . . ? Well . . . in part because I never see you alone, Mary. Always other women are with you. That Jean. And Kate Lindsay. And the Sinclair wench. I do believe that Patrick arranges it so. Always working away at these clothes and trappings.'

'But that is why we are here, Vicky – our duty. You of all men should know it, as Chamberlain. Besides, are we not alone now, and have been these ten minutes? And all you have done is moon and scowl!'

'You are ever sewing and stitching. Never done with this sempstress's work. It's not suitable . . .'

'It is especial work, Vicky – close wear for the Queen's own person. It *is* suitable that her ladies should do it. It is all that we can do for Her Grace, in this pass. Save pray for her safety and speedy arrival.'

'Pray!' The young man all but spat that out. '*Mortdieu* – I've had my bellyfull of that! All this morning we were at it.' He jumped up, and began to pace the small apartment. It was unusual indeed to see Ludovick Stuart thus moved. 'Hours he kept us on our knees. Mine pain me yet! Though, on my soul, it was like no praying I have ever known ere this! He weeps and shouts at his Maker, *parbleu* – when he is not babbling about black arts and wizardry! All over a chit of a girl whom he has never even seen! 'Fore God, I believe – aye, I believe that his mind is going. That we may have to take steps, as Patrick says.'

'I think that is unfair, Vicky. That you are too hard on the King, by far. He is only distraught, surely.' Mary looked up at him thoughtfully, biting a thread with small white teeth. 'And . . . what does Patrick say? What steps are these?'

He frowned heavily. 'It is very secret,' he said, lowering his voice. 'Privy only to ourselves. Perhaps I should not tell – even to you, Mary. He said to keep it close.'

'Even from me, Vicky – who can keep a secret? And I know many of Uncle Patrick's secrets. Did he say not to tell *me*?'

'No. No, but . . . well, if you swear not to tell it to a soul,

186

Mary? Aye. Patrick, you see, fears for James's reason – and *mon Dieu*, he is right, I begin to believe! If the King's mind goes – goes completely, you understand – then it will be necessary to take steps. Great steps, and prompt. For the weal of the realm. He says that a Regency would have to be set up – to rule instead of the King. As a first step. It might be necessary even . . . even to find another king. Later, that is. Should this madness continue.' Lennox was speaking jerkily, and looking almost shocked at his own words. 'But first a Regency.'

Mary did not answer, but only gazed at him great-eyed.

'You see how it is, Mary? You understand? The country cannot be governed by a madman. There have been Regencies before, a-many . . .'

She nodded slowly. 'And who would be this Regent?'

He swallowed. 'Why me, Patrick says. I am next heir, you see. Since it could not be my cousin Arabella Stuart, in England. And . . . and . . .'

'I see.' Steadily she considered him. 'I see. So says Uncle Patrick?'

'Yes.'

Mary looked down at her sewing. 'Not all would welcome this, I think, Vicky. Even those who might be agreeable to turn against King James. Some would say that you are not old enough to be Regent, perhaps. Chancellor Maitland might say as much, I think.'

'Aye. Belike. But Maitland would not be told. He would be the last to be told. He likes me not, that man.'

'But, as Chancellor, first minister, must he not know? And act . . . ?'

'He would no longer be Chancellor,' Lennox told her simply. 'The Regent's first duty would be to appoint a new Chancellor.'

'Uncle Patrick?'

'To be sure. Who else?'

The girl's breath issued in a long sigh. 'Of course,' she said. 'Who else!' After a moment or two she rose to her feet and came over to him, to take his arm. 'Vicky – here are deep matters indeed. I do not wonder that you have been anxious, ill-humoured. But do you perceive how deep? Such talk now

187

is . . . treason! Uncle Patrick at least advised you well in this, that you should not speak of it to anyone. For your head's sake!'

The other's boyish features flushed. 'No, no – not that! Not treason, Mary! Lord – never say it! You do not understand. We must take thought – for the realm. For its safety and governance. We . . . we are high officers of state, members of the Privy Council. You are a woman – you do not understand . . .'

'I understand all too well, I think, Vicky. Men have died for less dangerous words than these. Some might call them betraying your king. Be careful, Vicky – think well. King James is shrewder than you take him for. He is far from mad, I do believe. Promise me that you will say nothing of it to anyone! And that you will tell me should the matter go any further. I do not fear so much for Uncle Patrick – for he has walked dangerously all his days. But, you . . . !'

Unhappily her companion nodded. 'As you will, Mary. I promise. I did not mean . . . perhaps it is too soon to consider these things . . .'

'And it would be better, Vicky, that Patrick does not know that you have told me. Much the best. You see that?'

'Aye. I shall not tell him.'

'Good,' she said. 'Poor Vicky – such anxieties but ill suit you. Statecraft is but little to your nature, I think.'

Heartily he agreed with her. 'You are right, i' faith! Would that I could exchange it all for the good clean air of Methven and the hills of Strathearn! Out of these accursed enclosing walls and crazy humours! And you with me there, Mary . . .'

The girl smiled, but kindly. 'Patience, Vicky,' she said. 'Though, to be sure, I would rather see you Laird of Methven than Regent of Scotland.'

'And you? How would you see yourself?'

'As Mary Gray, just. And your friend. Just that. Always that.'

He sighed, gustily.

During the next three days Mary sought to see the King alone – and found it more than difficult. James did spend most of his time alone – but shut in his own chambers with guards at every door. To have sought audience past these would have made the girl conspicuous and provoked comment inevitably – the last thing that she desired. And no amount of waiting about in likely places, or other like device, was of any avail.

It was on the last day of that week, after mid-day meal taken in the great hall in company with most of the resident courtiers but minus the royal presence, that, climbing the long winding turnpike stair to the Wardrobe rooms again, Mary's glance was caught whilst passing one of the narrow arrow-slit windows. Down below she had glimpsed an unmistakable shambling figure, pacing the flagged parapet walk that surmounted the walling of one of the secondary corner-towers, solitary though every now and again raising a hand in a repetitive gesture.

Only for a moment or two did the girl hesitate. That tower was an inner one, relic of the original smaller fortalice, sheltered from the wind, its top hidden from most of the castle's windows and courtyards – no doubt why James had selected it for privacy. Her Uncle Patrick had recently settled down to a game of cards, she knew, with carefully-chosen and wealthy companions. Ludovick was gone down to Leith, to superintend the repair of decorations erected for the Queen's reception and blown down by the gales. With a brief word to her two colleagues, the Ladies Jean Stewart and Katherine Lindsay, indicating that she had left something behind, Mary turned and ran light-footed down the steps worn hollow by mailed feet.

Darting along the bare labyrinthine mural passages that honeycombed the thick walling, up and down steps, she came to the foot of the little stairway of the tower where the King promenaded. An armed guard stood there. With entire authority she asserted that she was from the Master of the Wardrobe, with word for His Grace. Known by sight to all in Craigmillar, the guard let her past without demur. Another man-at-arms held the caphouse door at the stairhead – but he was no more obstructive; indeed the unexpected sight of a pretty, breathless girl commended itself to him sufficiently for him to whisper confidentially in her ear that His Highness being in a passing strange state, it behoved her to watch her virtue and perhaps close up the front of her gown – a liberty she forebore to rebuke as he opened the door for her.

James was shuffling up and down, up and down, over the counter-placed flagstones at the other side of the rectangular walk that crowned the tower within the crenellated parapet, lips moving, arms gesturing – whether apostrophising his Maker, declaiming poetry, or making incantations, was uncertain. Mary, lifting her skirts a little, went tripping over the stones towards him.

The King halted in mid-pantomime at sight of her, glowering blackly. Then, as she straightened up from her brief curtsy, and he perceived her identity, his features slackened to a grimacing smile.

'Och, it's yoursel' just, Mistress Mary!' he declared, in relief. 'You gave me a right fleg! I was thinking o' Anne, you see – o' the Queen. I wondered if I was beholding her drowned ghost . . . !'

'Oh hush, Sire – how could that be?' she returned. 'Your lady is safe and well, I vow, and no ghost. Moreover, not to be confused with the humble daughter of Davy Gray.'

'Aye. Aye, belike you're right. It was just a sudden notion, you ken.' James scratched at his straggling apology for a beard. 'But . . . what brings you here, lassie? You're alone, just? There's nane hiding behind yon door? I'm no' seeing a'body . . . we are not giving our royal audience to any. We would be private . . . '

'No, Sire – I am quite alone.' The girl hesitated, prettily. 'I . . . I came, Your Grace, to seek a favour.'

'Aye. Ooh, aye. A' folk do that,' the disillusioned monarch agreed, with a sigh. 'What is't you want then, Mary?'

She wrinkled her lovely brow. 'It is difficult. I am overbold, I well know. I should not ask it. But . . . I must needs dare turn to you, Sire, in my trouble. You see, I also am turning my foolish head to poetry. Although that is much too fine a name to give my poor verses. I seek to write an ode to your princess, Sire – a little song of welcome for your young Queen Anne from her most lowly Woman of the Bedchamber. I have got so far, poor as it is – but now I am stuck. Stuck quite, Your Grace, for a rhyme. So . . . so I dared come to you for help . . . '

James of Scotland was quite transformed with delight. Shining-eyed, stammering his pleasure, he turned to her, grasping her arm, her hand again. 'Hech, hech – is that s'so? Y'you are, Mary l'lass? Mercy on us – it's kindly in you, right kindly. Aye. I rejoice to hear it. No' that you're stuck, mind – for I ken what it is to be stuck for a rhyme. Many the time I'm stuck, mysel'. But . . . och, I'd never ha' thought it. And you but a bit lassie . . .'

'That is so, Your Highness. And my, my presumption is the greater in coming to you who are not only the King but so renowned and practised a poet . . .'

'Aye – but who better, who better?' he exclaimed. 'Wae-sucks – do I no' writhe betimes on the same slow fire mysel'?'

'Yes – that is my sole excuse, Sire. Here is my trouble. It is in the third verse. It goes thus:

> My voice I raise, my lyre I tune,
> to thee fair daughter of the seas,
> Thy coming cannot be too soon
> for this poor handmaid of thine ease;
> O end my weary waiting, please
> with solace of thy presence . . . *well* . . . boon.'

'Eh? Boon?' James repeated. 'Boon, you say?'

She bit her lip. 'Boon, yes. That is all that I can think of to end the verse. It is not very good, is it?'

'Boon.' The King scratched his head under the inevitable high hat. 'I canna see how it could be boon, lassie . . . thy presence boon. Na, na – it's no' right, some way.'

'No,' she agreed meekly. 'I know it. That is why I came to you. I cannot think of aught else.'

'Ummm,' he said. 'Oon's no' that easy, to be sure. To do wi' a woman's presence. Moon wouldna do, nor yet swoon. Mind, if you'd done it in the Scots, it would be better, Mary. Then you could ha' said doon or abune or goon. Aye, or her royal croon. Och, it's easier to make words rhyme in the Scots, I find.'

'Perhaps I should have done that, yet.'

'Aye. But maybe it's no' too late to change it a wee thing, here and there. Into the Scots. I ken it's an ill task for a poet having to change the words he's wrung oot o' his heart's blood – but och, whiles it has to be done, lassie. Now . . . wi' solace o' thy presence boon' it was, was it no'? Aye. See you – if you were to change a wheen o' the rest o' the words into Scots, then you could set the last line the other way roond, and say "wi' presence royal my solace croon." '

'Ah – how true, Sire! Splendid!' Mary clapped her hands. 'Why did I not think of it? Not only does it rhyme, but it is better, much better.'

'Aye, I think it so mysel'. But mind, you canna just ha' the one Scots word to it, Mary. You'll need to go through a' the ode and change a bit word here and there to oor ain Scots usage. It'll no' be that difficult. What was the line before it . . . ?'

' "O end my weary waiting, please." '

'I'ph'mmm. I'm no' that rejoiced wi' yon "please", mind. "Waiting, please" is no' just perfect, maybe.'

'Indeed it is not, as I am well aware.'

'Aye. You could mak it "Gladden my weary waesome ees", belike.'

'Waesome ease . . . ?'

'Ees – eyes, you ken. Een would be righter – but, och, it wouldna rhyme. We'll no' mend that. Ees it'll ha' to be.

> "Gladden my weary waesome ees,
> Wi' presence royal my solace croon."

That's nane so ill.'

She moistened her lips. 'Indeed, Sire – it is truly most . . . most apt. So quickly to perceive the need and supply the answer. I am overwhelmed. But . . . I must not keep you further, must not trespass on your precious time, must not intrude more on your own royal muse . . .'

'Och, never heed it, lassie – I like it fine,' James assured. 'I'm right practised at it. Ooh, aye. See you – go you right through your ode frae the beginning, Mary, and I'll gie you a bit hand. Wi' the Scots. For the prentice hand's aye slower than the master's.'

'Oh, but that is too much, Your Grace. You are too kind . . .'

'Na, na. Let's hear it a' . . .'

So, hand in hand and side by side, the teetering unsteady monarch and the dainty girl went tripping round and round that battlemented walk, bobbing up and down over the flagstones gapped for drainage, reciting, inventing, weighing, if scarcely improving the doggerel verses that Mary had so hurriedly concocted, James eager, voluble, authoritative, his companion appreciative and serious, the wind blowing her hair about her face and her skirts about her legs. For anyone in a position to overlook them, undoubtedly they would make a curious picture.

It was only when the King had the pathetic little ode almost transformed to his own peculiar satisfaction, that a thought occurred to him that abruptly halted him in his wambling tracks, his face falling ludicrously.

'Eh . . . but what o' the Master?' he demanded. 'What o' Patrick Gray, your faither? Or your uncle, or what you ca' him? Was it he . . . did he set you to this poetry, girl? He's a right notable poet himsel', I ken. You're . . . you're no cozening me? Seeking to befool me wi' *his* verse . . . ?'

'Sire – my Uncle Patrick knows naught of this. It is my own entirely.'

'But why came you to me when you could go to him, woman? For help and improvement? Eh?'

'Uncle Patrick is much too throng with affairs, Your Grace, to trifle with my poor rhymes. He is much too taken up with other matters to think of poetry, at this time.'

Sidelong he peered at her. 'He is, eh? What takes up our Patrick so?'

'In the main, matters of money, Sire, I think. Siller and gold. In your affairs, and his own.'

'Moneys, eh? Siller and gold? And in *my* affairs, you say? Hech, hecht – what's this?' The muse forgotten, James was all ears. 'Out wi't, lassie. What moneys?'

She hesitated modestly. 'It is not perhaps for such as me to speak of these matters . . .'

'Houts, lassie – ha' done! It's . . . it's our royal will that you tell us o' the business. Aye.'

She bit her lip. 'As you command, Sire. Siller is much in Uncle Patrick's mind, I fear. The cost of the arrangements for the Queen – as Master of your Wardrobe. He and the Duke of Lennox are ever fretting over it. And my Lord Chancellor says that your Treasury is near empty.'

'Ummm,' James said. 'Aye, maybe. Siller's a right rare

193

commodity, to be sure. Aye, and Maitland's close, close, the man.'

'Yes. So Uncle Patrick ever turns his eyes southwards. To Queen Elizabeth. On Your Grace's behalf.'

'Eh . . . ? He does? Elizabeth? Aye – my pension. She doesna pay it, the auld . . . the auld . . .'

'No. But you will recollect, Sire, that Uncle Patrick brought you a thousand gold pieces of it when he returned to Scotland. He believes that he can win more for you – for it appears that he understands this Queen passing well. So he writes letters, many letters, and much presses Mr. Bowes.'

'Aye, he's right close wi' Bowes, I do hear. Ower close, maybe. I dinna like yon man, mysel, wi' his smooth white face . . .'

'Nor, I think, does Uncle Patrick, Your Grace. But as the Queen of England's envoy he must needs work with him on your behalf. For the increase of this pension . . .'

'Increase! Waesucks – if she'd but pay the sum agreed, the woman! Since Patrick agreed it wi' her three years syne, for two thousand pieces each year, she hasna paid a quarter o' it! And she's been right gorged wi' gold and siller since then – maist pecunious. Yon man Drake and his pirates fair load her wi' Spanish gold and plate. Hundreds o' thousands. It's no' right, no' decent. I'm her heir and successor. It'll a' be mine when she dies . . .' The impoverished heir of Gloriana all but brought himself to tears at the contemplation of the gross injustice done to him.

'Yes, Your Grace. Hence Uncle Patrick's efforts. He believes that he can gain you the money. The promised increase. Even more, perhaps. So he writes and writes. But . . . but letters are poor things. If he could but see the Queen. Elizabeth. Speak with her. As before. Assuredly he would be the more successful.'

'Aye. I'ph'mmm. See her.' The King nodded, stumbling onward again. 'Aye. Maybe that is well thought o'. See her. An embassage . . .'

'Yes, Sire. An embassage.'

'Aye. But . . . did Patrick put you up to this, lassie? This embassage? Why did he no' speak o' it to me, himsel'? I had word wi' him but this morning.'

Mary sighed. 'I fear that he but thinks of the embassage as distant. Not immediate. He . . . he has other plans, meantime . . .'

'Other plans? What now – what now?'

'Plans of his own, Sire. I told you, he is much concerned about siller – in his own affairs as well as for Your Grace. Since his forfeiture and banishment he has had but little money, as you will know. My lord of Gray will give him nothing. He has great expenses. He is building again Broughty Castle, his portion. So . . . so he seeks to win back the Abbacy of Dunfermline.'

'No!' For once James Stewart was vehement, decisive. 'No' Dunfermline! I'll no' have it. I told him so lang syne. It's no' to be, no' suitable. If he sent you seeking Dunfermline frae me, Mary . . .'

'Not so, Your Grace. He does not know that I am with you. He would be but ill-pleased, I think, if he knew that I told you of it. But he is powerfuly set upon Dunfermline. He believes that it should be his, yet. That my lord of Huntly should not have it. Like a sickness it is with him, eating away at him. He even plans to take the Earl of Huntly to the Court of Session for it. And for that he needs more money.'

The King wagged his head in agitation. 'No' Dunfermline,' he wailed. 'It's no' like other places, you ken. It's the brawest property in a' the realm. When Patrick was forfeited, he lost it. He got it frae yon ill man Arran, some way. I canna just let him ha' it back. Would he ha' me look a right fool? Maybe I'll see what can be done for him wi' some other place, but no' Dunfermline. Na, na – it's no' to be thought of. Geordie Gordon doesna deserve to keep it, to be sure – but there's plenty wanting it! Johnny Mar. Aye, and the Earl o' Moray. Och, I'm thinking the Chancellor himsel's after it! I canna let Patrick have it. They'd a' be at my throat like a pack o' hound-dogs!'

'I know it, Sire. So, surely, must my uncle. Yet he seems mazed about this matter. Not like himself. Foolishly determined . . .' She paused, as though suddenly an idea had occurred to her. 'Sire – there is a way that this could be resolved, I think. That Uncle Patrick may be turned away from it – and the others likewise. Give Dunfermline to your

195

new Queen, as a marriage gift. Then none can seek it.'

'Lord save us!'

'Yes. Would that not be best, Sire? Uncle Patrick would be weaned from his trouble. He could not sue the Queen, and waste great moneys. Your lady would take it most kindly – and you would have the spending of its revenues.'

Her companion had halted, blinking, licking his lips. 'Precious soul o' God, lassie – here's a notion! A right notable notion!' he exclaimed. 'Aye – Huntley's forfeit now. I can take it. For Anne. But . . . but Patrick? What o' Patrick? When he hears. He'll be fair scunnered at me! He'll plot and scheme against me, the man. He'll no' help me wi' Elizabeth and my pension, I swear . . . !'

'He will be very hot when he hears,' she agreed gravely. 'But . . . he need not hear until too late. If he was not here. If he went on this embassage to England at once. Before your lady arrives. And . . . ' She tipped her red lips with pink tongue prettily. ' . . . if he was to receive some compensation. Some small lands somewhere. And, perhaps, some part, some portion of the moneys that he wins for you from Queen Elizabeth? That would much sweeten him, would it not? Siller that he could use to build Broughty. In exchange for his hopes of Dunfermline. A thousand gold pieces, perhaps – if he could win Your Grace two thousand. Or three. That would be but fair, would it not? And greatly encourage him in his dealings with Queen Elizabeth.'

'Lord ha' mercy on us – who taught you to think this way, girl?' James whispered. 'Who taught you, a lassie, the likes o' this?'

Surprised, she considered that. 'I do not think that anyone taught me, Sire. Save Davy Gray, of course.' And suddenly she trilled a laugh, happily, at some thought of her own. 'Yes – it must have been Davy Gray. Dear Davy Gray!'

Wonderingly the King looked at her, shaking his head. 'Yon dour man . . . ?' he doubted. Then he changed his head-shaking to nodding. 'But you ha' the right o' it, Mary – 'deed aye. The embassage to Elizabeth it shall be – and at once. Aye, forthwith. Before . . . before my Anne comes, belike. We shall see to it. Our special envoy to the Court o' Saint James, the Master o' Gray – *celeriter*!'

196

The girl nodded her head, satisfied. 'I have always wished to see London,' she said. 'And to see Elizabeth the Queen.'

Chapter Nine

THE cavalcade had barely left Berwick Bounds behind it, and crossed into England, before the wind died away and the sun blazed down upon a sodden and battered world. Men and women threw aside their heavy soaking travelling cloaks, sat up in their saddles after long crouching, and positively bloomed and expanded like sun-starved flowers in the genial warmth and brightness, the first that they had known for months on end. It was the second day of October.

'This, I vow, will set King Jamie smiling again,' the Earl of Moray declared, stretching his arms out luxuriously as he rode.

'I hope that you are right, my lord,' Patrick Gray said. He had been laughing gaily, rallying them all, rivalling the new sun's own brilliance this cheerful morning, but fell sober again at the other's words. 'If the sun but shines in Scotland likewise . . . and if His Grace's mind is not itself permanently clouded over and agley.'

Moray looked at him sharply. 'You mean . . . ? You fear, sir, that . . . that . . . ? You are not suggesting that James is affected in his wits?'

'I hope not, God knows. It is my prayer that I may be mistaken,' the Master answered gravely. 'But . . . he has been acting very strangely. For too long. It is a great cause of anxiety. You have not been much at Court of late, my lord. Those of us in daily touch with him cannot fail to be aware of the danger, of the sad but steady deterioration of his powers of judgment, the abdication of his kingly responsibilities . . .'

'He frets excessively for his princess – all Scotland knows it. And always he has been strange in manner, fearful of spirit. But more than that I cannot believe . . .'

Mary Gray, seeking to pay due and respectful attention to

197

the feather-brained chatter of the Countess of Moray at her side, and yet to miss nothing of the conversation of the two men immediately in front, above the clatter of their horses' hooves, bit her lip.

'I do so believe it, my lady,' she said, straining her ears. 'Indeed, yes.'

' . . . for the good governance of the realm,' Patrick was saying. 'I fear – aye, i' faith, I fear for our land. Maitland rules, not James. If His Grace's condition grows the worse, then it behoves us all to take serious thought for the realm's weal, my lord. It will not serve to shut our eyes.'

'God save us!' The Earl's comely and attractive features reflected a simple consternation. 'I have heard naught of this, Master of Gray. No talk of it has reached me. I have been in the north, at Darnaway . . . ' He shook his fair head, at a loss.

Greatly daring, and with a swift apologetic glance at the Countess, Mary leaned forward to speak, and sought to make her voice low but penetrating. 'Hush, Uncle Patrick!' she said. 'If I can hear your words, so may others. And . . . and that is not to be desired, is it?'

Patrick turned in his saddle to stare at her, slender eyebrows raised. 'My dear,' he said evenly, 'what I say to my lord of Moray is for his ears alone, I would remind you.'

'Why, yes – that is why I speak,' the young woman nodded, with a darted look left and right as though to indicate that there were ears all round them – although in fact the nearest squire rode a good ten feet to the flank, and the men-at-arms in front still further away. 'If I overhear, others might. To great ill, perhaps.'

'You have over-long ears, girl – as I have had occasion to remark ere this!'

'Yes, Uncle Patrick – but so I have heard you say has Queen Elizabeth! Ears everywhere.'

'A plague, child! What's this? Would you teach me, *me*, how I should speak?'

'Ah, no. No – but my lord said that no talk of this sort had reached him at Darnaway.' Mary's colour was heightened and her breathing quickened. 'Forgive me – but I would but have you assure yourself that no talk of it reaches London either!

198

For – hear me, please – would not any such talk ruin all? If Queen Elizabeth was to question, even for a moment, whether King James was sound in his mind, to wonder if his wits were disordered, would she indeed cherish him further? Let you have the money for him? Do what you would have her to do, on this embassage? Would she even consider him heir? Heir to her England?'

Patrick had caught his breath. For a long moment he looked at the girl unblinking before, without a word, turning to face the front again.

Moray had gazed behind him also. 'Burn me, but she is right, Gray!' he exclaimed. 'The lassie is right. A knowing chit, eh? A head to her, as well as . . . other parts!' Still considering the girl, he smiled slowly, taking in all her flushed and eager young loveliness, looking at her with new and speculative eyes – eyes that did not once slide over in the direction of his wife at whose side Mary rode. 'Here is matter for thought,' he added, facing forward once more, and still smiling reflectively – for one who was not notably a reflective and thoughtful man.

The Countess of Moray slumped more heavily in her saddle, and fell silent for the first time since the weather had brightened.

James Stewart, Earl of Moray, had been selected personally by his royal namesake to be the second envoy on this embassage to the Court of St. James. It was always the prudent Scottish custom to send two ambassadors on any important diplomatic mission – lest one should perchance be tempted to betray his trust. Moray was a shrewd enough choice, whatever his companion's professed doubts about the King's sanity. Known as the Bonnie Earl, he was both popular and notably good-looking; not so brilliantly handsome and graceful as the Master by any means, but fair to look upon in a lusty, strapping and uncomplicated fashion, tall, broad-shouldered, and of a sort of rampant masculinity – and young. All important qualities where Elizabeth of England was concerned. A favourite of the Kirk party, he could be guaranteed to be suitably suspicious of the Master of Gray, whom few in Scotland believed to be other than Catholic at heart. Moreover he was very rich, in his wife's right rather than his own, and so could comfortably and conveniently pay for the entire embassage – always an important consideration with King Jamie.

Never, surely, was a monarch so well supplied with cousins as was James, thanks to the phenomenal potency of his maternal grandfather James Fifth, whose heart may well indeed have broken at being able to show only the one surviving legitimate offspring, and that a mere girl, the unfortunate Mary Queen of Scots – although unkind gossip had it that his untimely death at the age of thirty was rather the result of being worn out by extra-marital exercises. At any rate, his bastards were legion, and few indeed of the ladies of his Court seem to have eluded his attentions; not that he confined his favours to the aristocratic and highly-born, by any means – for had he not been known as The Poor Man's King? The Reformation and the breaking up of the vast Church lands, at this juncture, had been a godsend indeed, providing properties and commendatorships innumerable for the suitable support of this host. Moray was the son of one of them, another James, titular Abbot of St. Colme, later created Lord Doune. A young man of initiative as well as looks, the son had eight years before managed to obtain the prized wardship of the two daughters of his late uncle, the most important bastard of them all, James Stewart, Earl of Moray and former Regent of Scotland – and the very next day married the elder daughter, Elizabeth, and assumed the earldom. The late Regent, needless to say, had done very well for himself in three years of ruling Scotland in the name of Mary's infant son – and having no son of his own, his heiress brought her husband great lands and riches. In the eight years of their marriage, the new Moray had managed to dispose of much of these responsibilities, but in return had given her five children. Now, at the King's insistence, the Countess accompanied her husband to London, and Mary Gray went as her attendant.

Patrick Gray, after only a brief period of quiet, was soon laughing and gay once more – for he was never the man to sulk or brood. Indeed, as they rode southwards, presently he was singing like a lark, seemingly without a care in the world, to the amusement of Moray, the delight of his wife, and the embarrassment of much of their train – and encouraging Mary to join in, so that apparently he was going to bear no resentment over her intervention. Her clear young voice rose to partner his rich tenor, to while away the long miles. It was noticeable that after fording the swollen River Aln, Moray rode behind, beside Mary, and the Countess in front with the Master of Gray.

That evening, at Morpeth, Moray was markedly more attentive to Mary than he was to his wife.

It was the following night, as the girl was preparing for bed in the country inn just over the Yorkshire border, that he came to her garret room, opening the door without any warning knock. Hastily drawing one of the bed-covers around herself, Mary turned to face him. She did not cry out or otherwise lose her head; indeed she did not even shrink back, but after only a momentary hesitation actually moved towards the man.

'My lord,' she said. 'I think that you have made a mistake.'

Moray's ruddily handsome features were flushed still further by wine. 'Not so, my dear,' he denied thickly. 'Far from it, I vow – as my eyes do assure me!' He grinned at her.

'Nevertheless, sir – you do much mistake. Your wife's room is below.'

'I know it, moppet!' Moray advanced into the room, having to stoop to get through the low doorway, his great frame seeming to fill the little coom-ceiled chamber. He shut the door behind him, with no attempt to do so quietly, furtively. 'Let her be. If mistake I made, it was in delaying so long down there at cards with your . . . your uncle!'

Mary sought to keep her voice even, although the heaving of the coverlet wrapped tightly around her told its own story. 'At cards – and wine, my lord!' she said. 'The wine, I fear, has confused your wits.' She looked very small, standing stiff and upright there before him. 'Else you would not be here.'

'Tush, girl – have done!' he exclaimed, and a hand reached out to her, to grasp the cover and wrench it aside, baring one white shoulder. 'You are good with words, I grant you. Let us see how good you are otherwise, my dear!'

Still she stood, unmoving, her head held high, her dark eyes meeting his steadily. 'It is pleasure that you seek, sir?' she asked, huskily.

'Why yes, Mary – pleasure it is! What else? And pleasure I

shall have, I warrant – for you are passing pleasurable!' He laughed. 'Perhaps, i' faith, you shall win a little pleasure out of it also, lass – for I am none so ill at the business, so others have informed me!' He drew her irresistibly to him, and dragged down the coverlet further, stooping low to bury his face against the swell of her bosom.

She did not struggle, however stiffly she held herself. Her words continued, stiff also, level but emphatic. 'I cannot stop you taking me, my lord – since you are stronger than I am. But I can promise you that you shall have no pleasure in me.'

'Ha – think you so!' Raising his fair head, Moray chuckled in her face. 'Woman – do you not know that a little reluctance, a mite of resistance, but increases the pleasure? Certes, it is so, I promise you. For you also, perhaps. Come now, lass – enough of this foolery. I do not wish to hurt you . . . '

'*Your* hurt it is I fear, my lord. Your grievous hurt.'

'Eh . . . ? A pox – what is this? Here's no way to bed! Am I so ill-looking? And you, I swear, have fire in plenty in this body . . . '

'I would need to have, to warm you . . . when you are bedding with your death, my lord! A cold loving!' Low-voiced she said it.

'Fiend take me – death? What i' God's name mean you, wench?' The man stared at her, actually shook her. 'What fool's talk is this? Are you crazed, girl?'

'I think you do not know the Master of Gray very well – or you would not ask,' she said. 'Nor would you be in this chamber.'

'Gray? I know him well enough to have lost three hundred crowns to him at cards this night, damn him! I will have some return, 'fore God!'

'You will have your death, my lord – nothing surer,' she told him gravely. 'And I would not wish that. You are too proper a man to die so young, for such a cause. And your wife and bairns deserve better, I think.'

Astonished, perplexed, Moray drew back a little, the better to consider her. 'Burn me – never have I heard the like!' he muttered.

'I believe it, sir. But never, I think, have you sought to injure the Master of Gray. My father.'

'Ha!' It was the first time that Mary had publicly claimed the Master as her sire – even though few at Court had any doubts of the fact. The Earl rubbed his chin.

'He is fond of me – otherwise I should not be coming to London with you,' Mary went on, drawing the coverlet over her shoulder again. 'He has other plans for me, I think, than to be your plaything, my lord. And consider well what happened to others who have crossed the Master of Gray! My lord of Morton, the Regent, did so – and died. Ludovick of Lennox's father likewise – and is dead. My lord of Arran, the Chancellor – he fell, and is no more. Even my lord of Gowrie, they do say, his uncle . . .'

'God's curse!' Moray all but whispered, staring at her. 'What are you? Devils both?'

She answered him nothing, but looked him in the eye, unwinking.

He drew himself up to his full and impressive height, mustering a short laugh. 'Do not think that you frighten me, young woman!' he said.

'I think it not. You are a man, and bold. It is I that am frightened,' she answered simply. 'For you. I cannot think that I shall pleasure you, sir.'

The young Earl drew a long breath, opened his mouth to speak, and then shut it again almost with a click. He turned on his heel, strode to the door, threw it wide, and went stamping out.

Mary Gray sank down on her bed, trembling. Dark-eyed she looked through the open doorway. 'Forgive me, Uncle Patrick,' she whispered. 'God forgive me!'

For long she sat thus, motionless, before she rose and closed that door.

The next morning Moray was silent and withdrawn, and rode with his wife. Patrick, in the best of spirits, sought to draw him, and was rebuffed. He turned his attention to the Countess, and soon had that featherhead whinnying high laughter, to her husband's marked offence. Mary, save for being perhaps a little paler than usual, slightly darker about the eyes, was her quietly composed self. But when presently, as they skirted the low rolling Cleveland Hills, so much tamer than their Scottish uplands, Patrick began to sing once more, it was not long before she joined her voice to his. Moray eyed them both askance.

So they pressed steadily southwards. By the time that they reached the flat lands of Lincolnshire, two days later, the Earl was himself again, prepared to chat and even laugh with Mary – as he should have been, for she was at pains to be most kind to him. Now it was Patrick Gray's turn occasionally to eye them both, thoughtfully.

They came to London eleven days after leaving Edinburgh – and smelt the stench of it for miles before they reached its close-packed streets and teeming alleys, Patrick explaining that there being little in the way of hill and sea breezes in this flat inland plain, the cities here must needs stink worse than their windy Scots counterparts. Wait until they reached the oldest and most densely populated area near the river, he warned them.

Mary, for one, although much excited and impressed by the vastness of the sprawling city, the noise and bustle of the narrow thoroughfares and dark field lanes, where every prospect revealed but deeper labyrinths of crazily crowding, soaring, overhanging and toppling tenements, taverns, warehouses, booths and the like, all built of wood unlike Edinburgh's grey stone masonry – Mary was soon all but nauseated by the smell of it, dizzy with the clangour and ceaseless stir of milling humanity, and suffering from a claustrophobia engendered by the endless tall inward-leaning buildings that all but met over their heads to shut out the sky and seeming about to fall in upon them. She did not wonder in the least, and was duly thankful, when Patrick's shouted enquiries elicited the information that Elizabeth – good Queen Bess, as they called her – was not presently occupying her palace of Whitehall, in the midst of all this, but was down the Thames at Greenwich some five more miles to the east, where presumably the air would be at least breathable.

As the now much extended Scots company of about fifty threaded and worked its slow way through the congestion and turned eastwards parallel with the river, Moray demanded of a substantial burgher standing in the doorway of a handsome house with an elaborate hanging sign, what all the church bells were ringing for, in the middle of a week-day afternoon. The man eyed him with astonishment mixed with both scorn and suspicion, and pointed out that no true and loyal citizen need ask such a question. Nettled at his tone, the Earl replied sharply that they were travellers from Scotland, and in the habit of receiving civil answers to civil questions.

'If that's where you are from, cock, then belike you should heed well those bells,' the other returned, spitting at their horses' hooves. 'You'll be heathen of some sort, if not traitorous and bloody Papists, for sure. Those bells, I tell you, ring for the joyful examining and burning of thrice-damned recusants, priests and Jesuits! Aye – and for four days they have rung without cease, by the Queen's command. And Bess, God preserve her, will keep them ringing for four more, I warrant!'

'You mean . . . men are being burned? Now? Catholics? For their faith? Their religion?'

'To be sure they are, simpleton – praise God! Two score but three burned yesterday – and they do say that one lived two hours from his disembowelling. Sweet Jesu, I wish I could ha' seen it!'

'Faugh, man . . . !'

As Mary blenched, Patrick leaned over to jerk her horse's rein and urge the beast forward – but not before she heard their informant declare that if they cared to ride round by the Bridewell they would see a row of Jesuits and Papists hanging by their hands all day in preparation for tomorrow's burnings – which should be most apt warning to all traitors, Scotchies and other enemies of the good Bess.

'Lord!' Moray exclaimed, as they rode on. 'Is this how they treat Catholics here. I' faith, the Kirk has much to learn, it seems!'

With a quick shake of the head Patrick glanced towards Mary. 'They are still afraid of Spain, with Guise and Philip in league, and Spanish soldiers as near as Brittany. There may be profit for Scotland in that same, let us not forget.' He changed the subject, abruptly for that man. 'There is the river, Mary. Down yonder lane. You just may see it. The first time that I came to see Elizabeth Tudor, we met her there. On the water. It was a notable ploy. Perhaps Davy . . . perhaps your father has told you of it?'

Despite the Master's spirited and graphic account of that adventure five years before, the girl hardly heard a word of it. Her ears rang much too full of the jangling of those church bells. It was as though she listened tensely to hear indeed what other sounds those bells hid and covered up. London seemed to be full of clamorous churches that afternoon. Even she sniffed at the tainted air, as though to test what dire elements it carried. Almost she wished that she had never contrived to accompany this embassage.

A mile from Greenwich Park, they were surprised to be met by a brilliant escort of gentlemen sent out to greet the Scots envoys in the name of the Queen. It appeared that Mr. Secretary Walsingham, that grim shadow on England's fair countenance, although reputed to be an ailing man, kept himself and his royal mistress as well informed as ever – so much so that the tall and slender, darkly-handsome man with the haughty manner but flashing smile, who led the party, knew even that he was going to meet the Earl of Moray as well as the Master of Gray. Since of deliberate policy no courier had been sent on ahead to herald their approach, this knowledge was the more remarkable.

'I rejoice to see you again, Patrick,' the spokesman declared, sketching a bow. 'Rejoice too that you are, I perceive, like to dazzle us, as ever! This will be my lord of Moray, of whom we have heard? Your servant, my lord. Her Grace sends you both greetings, and would welcome you to her Court.'

It was noticeable that the speaker's distinctly arrogant glance, whatever his words, slipped quickly away from both Patrick and Moray, quite passed over the Countess and lingered unabashedly on Mary Gray, in keen and speculative scrutiny.

'Her Grace is most kind, Walter. We are sensible of so great an honour – as of your own presence. This, my lord, is Sir Walter Raleigh, whose fame has reached even poor Scotland. And Sir Francis Bacon, if I mistake not? And h'm, others, of no doubt like distinction . . . if that were possible! So much brilliance, I swear, quite overwhelms us humdrum northerners. Gentlemen – the Countess of Moray.'

'Enchanted, your ladyship.'

'Your devoted and humble servitor, madam. And, er, the other, Patrick?'

'A young relative of mine, no more – attendant upon the Countess,' the Master informed briefly.

'Ah!'

'Relative? Precisely. How fortunate is her ladyship! Come, then . . .'

Mary Gray rode towards Greenwich Park surrounded by such a glittering galaxy of male elegance and wit as ought to have quite intoxicated her – had she not still heard through the gay chatter and heaped and extravagant compliments, the echo of those jangling bells.

The travellers were installed, not in Greenwich House itself, which like James's Falkland was small as royal palaces went, but in a goodly house in the town, near the park gates. Here Mary did not have to roost in any remote garret room, but was allotted what seemed to her far too magnificent an apartment on the main floor, intercommunicating in fact with the Master's own. The dandified courtier who conducted them to these quarters clearly took her to be Patrick's mistress – a misconception which nobody troubled to correct.

So commenced a strange interlude for the Scottish party, a period of waiting which was both amusing and galling, flattering and the reverse, superficially active and basically futile and frustrating. They were treated with the utmost cordiality and courtesy. Hospitality was showered upon them, invitations without number. Seldom was there not some lord or gallant calling upon them. Gifts of fruit and comfits and even flowers came to them from the palace daily, many with verbal messages of goodwill and greeting from the Queen herself. Life was an incessant round of festivities, receptions, entertainments, routs and balls. But at none was Elizabeth herself present – although at many she was expected to be just about to come, or had just left – and no actual summons to her presence was forthcoming from the palace. Moray grew restive, however content was his wife to bask in the sun of a social whirl such as she had never even contemplated – for Elizabeth's Court was the most brilliant in the world at this period – and Mary frequently questioned the Master on what all this delay portended. But Patrick himself was unruffled, serene, at his most attractive, all good humour and high spirits, making no hint of complaint. He explained to the girl that this was not untypical of Elizabeth Tudor. Although one of the greatest monarchs in Christendom, with a head as shrewd as any of her counsellers, she loved to demonstrate that she was all woman, to keep everyone about her on tenterhooks, to play the contrary miss even on her glittering throne. None must ever know just where they stood with Elizabeth, even her closest and oldest advisers. Patrick smiled, and added that he thought that perhaps she would particularly apply this contrariness to himself.

'To you?' Mary wondered. 'You mean – yourself? Not just to this embassage?' And at his nod, 'Why to you, Uncle Patrick? Can you be so important to the Queen of England?'

'Why yes, I think so, my dear. Overweening modesty was never my greatest failing!' Laughing, he took her hand.

It was late at night, the eighth night of their sojourn at Greenwich, all but morning indeed, after a great ball and masque at the house of the Earl of Essex, where Sir Francis Bacon had presented Mr. Burbage's players in a notable play by a new young man from the Midlands named William Shakespeare, entitled *Love's Labour's Lost* – vastly entertaining. Mary was sitting up in her great bed, all bright-eyed eager liveliness, with little of sleep about her, and the man sitting on the edge of the bed. Often he came in from his own room, day or night, to talk with her, clearly enjoying her company, frankly admiring her loveliness, caring nothing how tongues might wag. Nor was Mary any more concerned, never experiencing the least fear or embarrassment in his presence – however fearful she was over much that he did.

'This Queen is a cruel and evil woman, I think,' Mary said. 'How you can mean much to her – sufficient for her to play such games with you, to hold you off thus, yet to send these flowers and gifts – I know not. I do not understand it, Uncle Patrick.'

'I believe that you are a little unfair on the great Gloriana, child. I would not call her evil. And I conceive her to be no crueller than the rest of her delightful sex – yourself included, given the occasion, my dear! She is a queen, the reigning prince of this great realm, and statecraft, as I have told you ere this, demands stern measures as well as kindly, cunning as well as noble gestures. For Elizabeth, statecraft is her life. She *is* England, in a fashion that no Scots monarch has ever been Scotland. And . . . I have bested her more than once! Hence her present display of feminine contrariness.'

'You – *you* have bested Queen Elizabeth?'

'Why yes, my pigeon – I think that I have. And hope to again, bless her!'

Intently the girl looked at him. 'Did she not best you? Did she not once best you grievously? Did she not betray you shamefully to Chancellor Maitland? Deliberately. Causing you to be taken and tried for treason? Over the death of our good Queen Mary, whom she murdered? So that you all but lost your life?'

He stroked his chin. 'I suppose that is true, Mary. But . . . statecraft is a ploy in which one must learn to let bygones be bygones. Revenge and vindictiveness are luxuries that may not be afforded in affairs of the realm. Especially towards a reigning prince. I can nowise drag Elizabeth off her throne. Yet because she sits on that throne, I may achieve much of benefit. I would be a fool, would I not, to prefer to remember that it once suited her policy to be rid of me?'

'I see,' Mary considered him gravely. 'She might be so suited again.'

'Aye, she might.' He laughed, fondling her smooth bare arm. 'But enough of such matters – no talk for a girl lacking her beauty-sleep. We shall await Gloriana's pleasure, since we can do no other – and then seek to pit our wits against hers. For all dealing with Elizabeth is such – like swordplay. She has to be approached with a fresh and unprejudiced mind. But, you – you are not wearying, my dear? Finding your time to hang heavily? You, who have half of our ageing Elizabeth's pretty boys running after you, paying *you* court instead of her? I vow she will be sending for us soon, if only in sheerest desperation to be rid of you, my sweet!'

The young woman shook her head. 'I am not wearying, no. I like it very well,' she said frankly. 'But I do not flatter myself that the flattery of these gentlemen is more than that . . . nor their court more than a step towards winning into my bed.'

'H'mmm.' Patrick's stroking of her arm paused for a

moment. 'I' faith, you are . . . plain-spoken, girl,' he said, blinking a little. 'For your years. But . . . I give thanks at least that you are not swept off your dainty little feet by these gentry. Even Raleigh himself, I notice, seems over-eager. You are new and fresh, of course – a freshness that the Court ladies here notably lack. And devilish attractive, although I say it myself . . . !'

'Thank you. Sir Walter, I think, feels it necessary to conquer every new lady,' she said. 'He seeks to do so very spendidly. I would not wish to distress him that he has failed to conquer my heart – so long as that will content him. As I have told him.'

'On my soul, you have! Damme – that could be a dangerous hand to play! You think . . . you think that you can play it, lass? At your age? With such experienced gallants as these?'

'Why yes, Uncle Patrick – I think so. None of these fine gentlemen, you see, are one half so pressing as was Nick the stable-boy at Inchture. Or even the blacksmith's son of Longforgan.'

Swallowing audibly, the Master rose to his feet. 'Is that so?' he said, moistening his lips. 'I . . . ah . . . I perceive that I am but beating the air, my dear. Left far behind you. You must forgive me.' He took a pace or two away, and then came back to the bed. 'Moray,' he said, in a different tone. 'You have no trouble with Moray, I hope, Mary?'

It was the girl's turn to blink a little. 'Why, no,' she answered, after only a moment. 'My lord and I understand each other very well, I think.'

'I am glad of that,' he said. 'You must tell me if it should turn out . . . otherwise.' Patrick stooped to kiss her. 'Goodnight, my dear. Tell me . . . am I getting old, think you?'

Her soft laugh was very warm, as her arms went up to coil round his neck. 'You are younger than I am, I do believe, Uncle Patrick!' she said.

The very next evening they saw Elizabeth. They were all at a great entertainment of dancing and music given by the Earl of Oxford in the Mirror Ballroom of Greenwich House itself – for the Queen preferred her subjects, in especial such as basked in the light of her favour, to provide the festivities for her multitudinous Court out of their pockets rather than her own. An interlude of dancing apes, dressed male and female in the very height of fashion, was just concluding with the females beginning to lewdly discard their clothing, to the uproarious delight of the company, when a curtain of silence fell gradually upon the crowded colourful room. All eyes turned from the grotesquely posturing monkeys towards the far end of the mirror-lined apartment. Only a slightly lesser hush had descended when the apes had been brought in, and at first Mary Gray anticipated only another such diversion, and anyway could see little for the throng. Then, as everywhere women sank low in profound curtsies, and men bowed deeply, and so remained, she could see over them all. She caught her breath, dazzled.

The dazzlement was by no means merely metaphorical. The brilliance of what she saw actually hurt the girl's eyes – so much so that, initially, detail was blurred and lost in the blaze of radiance. Scintillating, flashing in the light of a thousand candles, and duplicated to infinity by the mirrors on every hand, a figure stood just within the doorway – a figure indeed rather than a person. It was only as Mary stared, scarcely believing her own eyes, that she belatedly perceived two facts; one, that there was a pair of very keen and alive pale eyes glittering amidst all this brilliance; and two, that she herself was the only other person standing fully upright in all that assembly, and in consequence that those searching eyes were fixed full upon her. Down the young woman sank.

The tap-tapping of a sharp heel on the floor was the imperious signal that all might resume the upright. Elizabeth Tudor came on into the ballroom on the arm of her host Edward de Vere, Earl of Oxford, with an almost tense and deliberate pacing, as though she held herself in from more rapid motion, and on all sides men and women pressed back to give her clear and ample passage. Even now Mary could scarcely discern the pale thin features of the woman herself, so extraordinary was their framework. The Queen was dressed all in white satin, but in fact little of this material was to be seen, so thick encrusted was it with gems and jewels. Her gown was rigid enough to have stood upright on its own, so closely sewn was it with diamonds, emeralds, rubies, in clusters and galaxies and designs. Her great upstanding ruff, which forced her to hold her head so stiffly, was pointed and threaded with literally hundreds of small pearls and brilliants. Hanging from her neck were at least a dozen long ropes of great pearls. Her once-red hair, now covered with an orange wig, had a myriad of pearls large and small threaded on many of the hairs. Above it a pearl and diamond tiara was perched. Her fingers were so beringed that they could scarcely bend, and her wrists and forearms were sheathed in bracelets of white enamel studded with more gems. All this, coruscating and sparkling in the bright light, was so overwhelming on the eye as to leave the beholder dazed, dizzy. Its absurdity was on such a scale as to benumb the critical faculties.

Woe betide anyone, however, who equated that absurdity with weakness or vapidity of character, took such outward display as indicative of emptiness within. Elizabeth's passion for precious stones was a weakness indubitably, but there was strength enough in other directions to counter-balance many such. None who knew her were ever so foolish as to allow themselves to be deceived.

The Queen paced stiffly round the great and respectful company, throwing a brief word here, a thin smile there, once hooting a coarse laugh at some whispered remark of Oxford's, poking a diamond-studded finger into the padded ribs of my lord of Essex, frowning impatiently at one unfortunate lady who, when curtsying, slipped a heel on the polished dancing floor and thudded down on one knee. It was the respect, awe almost, which so much impressed Mary Gray – so different a reaction to that inspired by King James in his courtiers and subjects. Which the girl found strange indeed, for Elizabeth in her own way was almost an incongruous and ridiculous a figure, on the face of it, as was her distant cousin of Scotland. Fascinated, the girl watched.

Elizabeth moved hither and thither amongst Oxford's guests, but though time and again she came close to the Master of Gray and the Earl of Moray, always she veered off. Almost certainly she was deliberately avoiding them, for it was unthinkable that she did not know well of their presence there; Walsingham and his horde of spies, had for years seen to it that Elizabeth was the best-informed monarch in Christendom. Mary glanced at Patrick sidelong. The man was his smiling assured self – although Moray was much otherwise, flushed and plucking at his pointed golden beard.

The Queen circled back eventually to the little group that stood actually alongside the Scots party – Raleigh, Francis and Anthony Bacon and the Lord Mountjoy. With them abruptly she was a changed woman, vivacious, easy, swift in gesture, rallying the young men, her strange pale golden-green eyes darting. Mary, watching closely, was sure that those eyes flickered more than once over in their own direction, but no move, no hint of acknowledgement of their presence, was vouchsafed.

Elizabeth was now in her fifty-seventh year, and in the girl's youthful eyes, was showing her age, although her clear and absolutely colourless complexion was still extraordinarily free of wrinkles. She was not beautiful, nor had ever been; the long oval of her face, high aquiline nose, faint eyebrows and thin tight lips, precluded it; but when animated, there was an undoubted attractiveness in her features, a magnetism that was not to be denied.

Suddenly, with a ringing laugh, she turned away from the four young men, ordering Oxford to proceed with the evening's entertainment, presenting only her stiffly upright back to the Scots emissaries in the process, and went pacing off towards the head of the room amidst the consequent stir. Seldom could there have seemed a more deliberate snub.

'My God . . . !' Moray growled. 'This is not to be borne!'

It was the Master of Gray's laughter that rang out now, and more melodiously than had the Queen's. 'My lord – you are a notable performer at the glove and the ball, we know. But this is a more delicate sport – and he who holds his hand to the last round may win the game!' He by no means lowered his voice to make this comment, and undoubtedly Raleigh and the rest heard him, possibly even the receding Elizabeth herself.

Oxford gave a signal to the musicians in the gallery, and thereafter Elizabeth led the stately measures of the first dance with her host as partner. Couples were slow to be first to venture out in the Queen's company, and only two or three had in fact been bold enough to make a move when Patrick,

213

bowing to Mary, took her by the arm and swept gracefully out into mid-floor with her. For a few moments, although others were circling on the perimeter, only these two pairs were out in the centre of the room, the target of all eyes. Patrick guided Mary so that they passed very close indeeed to the Queen and Oxford. Darkly smiling eyes met and held narrowed golden-green ones, and then they were past. The Master chuckled in the girl's ear.

'Heigho!' he said. 'Two can play this game. Let Gloriana pretend now that our presence is unknown to her!'

'I think that Her Grace is not greatly going to love me!' Mary murmured.

'Tush, lass – Elizabeth admires best those who stand up to her . . . if so be it she does not chop off their heads! And she can scarce do that to the King of Scots' envoys!'

After only a minute or two more of the dance, the Queen abruptly adandoned it, indeed abandoned the ballroom altogether, stalking off through the doorway by which she had entered, Oxford hurrying in her imperious wake. Few failed to notice the fact, Mary included.

'She has gone,' she told her partner. 'She is set against us, quite.'

'Wait,' Patrick advised. 'She is not gone for good, otherwise the music would have been stopped, and we would be all bowing and scraping. Wait you, moppet.'

They had not long to wait, in fact. The first bars of music for the next dance were just being struck up when Sir Walter Raleigh came to touch the Master on the arm.

'Her Grace commands the presence of my lord of Moray and yourself, with your ladies, in the ante-room,' he said expressionlessly. 'Come.'

'Indeed? We are ever at the Queen's commands, of course. We were about to dance this pavane, however. Perhaps . . . ?'

'I think that would be inadvisable, Patrick.'

'Ah – you think it? Perhaps you are right. You agree, my lord? Lead on then, Walter.'

Elizabeth was seated in a throne-like chair in a smaller chamber beyond the ballroom, Oxford and Essex at her back. As the visitors made the required obeisance, she smiled graciously.

'Welcome to our Court and presence, once more, Master Patrick,' she said pleasantly. 'I see that you appear to be nowise disadvantaged from heretofore. I congratulate you on your . . . resurgence. I think, almost, that you are indestructible!'

'You are kind, Highness – as always. And more adorably beautiful than ever!' Patrick stepped forward, sank on one knee, took the proffered bejewelled hand, and raised it to his lips. 'It is like the summer returned to be put in Your Grace's presence once more.' It was noticeable that he retained a hold of the royal fingers.

The Queen looked down at him quizzically. 'You ever were a talented liar, Patrick!' she observed. She twitched her hand away from his grasp, then, almost flicking his face with the hard diamonds in the process. 'Impudent!' she snapped.

'Say, rather, overwhelmed and beside myself, Lady!' he amended gently, rising.

'I doubt it, sir – God's death, I do! But nor am I overwhelmed, I'd assure you! Be certain of that, my friend. If anyone is beside himself, I conceive it to be my peculiar cousin of Scotland, who can still consider you a worthy emissary!'

'On your own recommendation, Madam, I am grateful to say!' Smiling, Patrick half-turned. 'May I present to Your Grace my prince's other emissary – my lord the Earl of Moray, close kinsman to the King.'

'Aye, I have been noting him! A better-made man than you, Patrick – and more honest, I hope! Welcome, my lord – in ill company as you are!'

Moray, obviously uneasy, uncertain how to take all this, bowed stiffly over Elizabeth's outstretched hand. 'I present my prince's traist greetings and salutations, Your Grace.'

'To be sure, to be sure. No doubt. But not your own – eh, sir?' the Queen rejoined dryly. 'I have heard you named bonnie, my lord – and perhaps with some slight cause. At least you are bonnier than your late good-father and uncle, the previous Moray! For he was as sour-faced a knave as any it has been my lot to meet!' Elizabeth opened her mouth, and then clapped a hand to it in a seemingly impetuous and girlish a gesture as might be imagined. 'Sweet Jesu – a pox on my runaway tongue!' she declared, eyes busy. 'This will be his daughter? You must forgive an old woman's scattered wits, my dear.'

The Countess, flustered and speechless, curtsied, glance darting towards her husband, who seemed all but choking.

'Your Grace . . . !' that man spluttered.

'Yes, my lord?'

When the other found no words, and Patrick seemed about to intervene, smiling still, Elizabeth raised a hand to halt him.

'Tell me, my lord of Moray – how many bastards besides your father and goodfather did the late King James of pious memory produce? On ladies of noble blood, I mean, naturally – since the rest can be ignored. It was always been a question of some doubt with me. Once, I thought that I could count seventeen – but since I had no fewer than five named James amongst that total, I grew confused. Perhaps no proper count was kept?'

The Earl's good-looking ruddy features grew almost purple, but the Queen went on before he could speak.

'And this,' she said, turning to look at Mary now, 'is the wench of whom I have not failed to hear! An interesting face – is it not, Patrick? Even though it need not show its mislike of me so plainly! Your name, child?'

'Mary Gray, Your Grace.'

'Aye. It could scarcely be other! I wonder, Patrick – have I wronged you? Or . . . not wronged you enough?' She was patently comparing the two Gray faces, feature by feature. 'A fascinating problem, I vow! What do you find so amiss in me, child? Come – tell me.'

Mary shook her head gravely. 'I would not dare to find aught amiss with the Queen of England, Madam, in her own palace.'

'Ha! Minx! That is as good as to admit you mislike! What ails you at me? Out with it, I say. Be quiet, Master of Gray! Speak but when you are spoken to!'

The girl chose her words carefully, but with no sign of agitation. 'I but wonder, Your Grace, why so great and powerful a princess should act so. Assuredly there must be a reason.'

Elizabeth's jewelled shoe tapped the floor. 'Act so . . . ?' she repeated. 'You, in your wisdom and experience, chit, conceive it that I act amiss as a princess? On my soul, this

216

intrigues me! And you seek a reason for my actions?'

'Why yes, Highness.'

'And have you thought of one?'

'No, Your Grace. Not yet.'

The Queen barked a brief laugh at that. 'Fore God – you are candid, at least! Like that other you once brought to my Court, Patrick – the natural brother that you miscalled secretary. Was not Davy his name? Aye, Davy Gray. He had the same critical eye, the same damned uncomfortable honesty! Unlike yourself, Patrick! And yet . . . and yet the likeness between you two, otherwise, is not to seek! A strange contradiction, is it not?'

'Not so strange, Highness – since Davy Gray had the upbringing of Mary here,' Patrick told her.

'Ah – so that is it? The upbringing, you say? But not, perhaps, the begetting?' She smiled, looking from one to the other. 'I perceive it all now. A remarkable situation. I see that you deserve my sympathy, child, rather than my just ire. To be such as you are, to have in you such opposing strains – to be Patrick and Davy Gray both! God help you!' The Queen leaned back in her chair. 'But enough of this,' she said, changing her tone. 'Is my young cousin of Scotland in good health? He has sent me no poems, of late. He is not sickening?'

'His Grace is much distressed, Madam, in awaiting his bride. The Princess Anne,' Patrick told her. 'These long continuing contrary winds and storms . . . '

'Ah, yes,' Elizabeth sniffed. 'Had he chosen the Princess of Navarre, as we advised him, he could have spared himself this. You led me to believe, Master of Gray, that you could convince him to that course. And you did not. I do not commend such failures, sir. Navarre is now France, and his sister heir thereto. Here was folly.'

'Admittedly, Highness. Nor have I ceased to point it out. But His Grace had reversed his decision before ever I reached Scotland. Indeed the selfsame day that I arrived there, the Earl Marischal was being sent to Denmark with betrothal gifts.'

'Your prince is advised by fools, I swear! How shall little Denmark serve him? I am much displeased, sir. God help this sweet realm of mine should he and his advisers ever have the ruling of it!'

At her back the two English earls made hurried and fervid protestations that the Queen should even for a moment consider the possibility of such a disaster. Elizabeth, if not immortal, undoubtedly would outlive them all.

Mary shot a troubled glance at the Master, whilst Moray frowned and tugged at his beard.

Patrick seemed nowise upset however. He laughed. 'So far distant an eventuality need scarce trouble us today, Your Grace,' he declared. 'By which time, who knows how much additional wisdom King James will have gained . . . and how much better advisers!' With something of a flourish, he tossed back the tiny scarlet-lined white satin cloak which hung from one shoulder of his padded doublet, to reach into a deep pocket therein. 'At least in this matter, Madam,' he went on, 'I deem that you will consider His Grace well advised – since I myself was consulted! From King James, Your Highness, with his esteem and devotion.'

Elizabeth's eyes narrowed and then widened, as she stared at what the Master held out to her. Too swiftly for dignity her hand reached out to grasp it. 'A-a-ah!' she breathed.

A great diamond, as large almost as a pigeon's egg, set in a coiling snake of amethysts, hung on a golden chain composed of delicately-wrought smaller serpents, each in its tail clutching a pearl.

The Queen, thin lips parted, held the jewellery up to the light, turned it this way and that so that it all flashed and glittered, as did the rest of her sparkling, shimmering display, stroking her finger-tips over the polished surfaces, weighing, assessing, gloating, her breathing heightened, her hands trembling a little.

'Whence . . . came . . . this?' she got out.

'It was one of the late Queen Mary's gifts from her first husband, the Dauphin of France,' Patrick answered easily, without the flicker of an eyelid. 'It was found in one of the houses of the deplorable lord of Morton, but recently.'

'It was . . . hers!'

'Aye. Who more fitting to have it than yourself, in consequence, Madam?'

Elizabeth's eyes met his for a long moment, her lips moving slightly. But no words issued therefrom.

It was Moray who broke the silence. He too delved into a pocket and brought forth a little gold casket, cunningly wrought to represent a beehive which, when its tip was pressed, opened on hinges to reveal a brooch sitting in a velvet nest within, in the lifelike form of a great bee, fashioned wholly in gold and precious stones.

'Also from King James,' he announced, but omitted to proffer with it any message of devotion or regard.

Almost absently the Queen took the casket from him with one hand, whilst in the other she still caressed the diamond and chain. 'I thank you, my lord,' she said, more or less automatically. 'You will thank His Grace for me, for his munificence . . . ' But her glance returned almost at once to the Master's face, to the first gift, and back again.

Moray cleared his throat. 'I shall do so, Highness,' he agreed brusquely. 'Now – as to the subject of our visit, it is our prince's request that you . . . '

'In due course, my lord – in due course,' Elizabeth interrupted. 'Not now.'

The earl blinked. 'But, Madam – we have waited . . . waited . . . '

'A mere day or so, my lord. Is King James in such pressing need that we must discuss his rescue at my good lord of Oxford's entertainment?' Suddenly the Queen was her commanding, assured self again. 'So do not I the state's business, sir. Anon, I say. I shall inform you of a suitable occasion.'

Before Moray could reply, Patrick spoke, quickly. 'We are grateful for this gracious audience, Highness, for your royal acceptance of these toys and of our master's fair wishes. We shall wait your further summonses assured of your kindly goodwill towards our prince . . . and even perhaps towards our humble selves?'

'Do that, Patrick,' Elizabeth agreed, cryptically. 'My thanks for these . . . tokens. I shall consider the quality of your advice to King James.' Her pale eyes flickered over them all – and came to rest on Mary Gray. 'You have given me food for thought,' she added. 'All of you. You have my permission to retire.'

They bowed, and backed out, Raleigh still with them.

219

Although Patrick might have remained to partake of more of Lord Oxford's hospitality, none of the others were so inclined. Moray was seething with ill-suppressed rage, and caring not that Raleigh perceived it.

When they were safely out of Greenwich House, and alone, the Earl burst forth. 'The bitch! The arrogant, grasping, ill-humoured bitch! Fiend seize her! This is not to be borne. To be insulted thus! Mocked at – by that barren harridan! I'll thole no more of it, Gray, I tell you. It's home to Scotland for us – forthwith. I'll not stay to be spat upon by yon Jezebel . . !'

'We must first perform what we came for, my lord . . .'

'How shall we do that, in God's name? She will have none of us, the harridan! She will snatch at your gifts, but give us nothing in return. She is set against us, man. Even you must see it. There is no profit for us or King Jamie here.'

'I think that you misjudge the matter somewhat, my lord,' Patrick declared, soothingly. 'I believe our case is less ill than you imagine. I know Elizabeth . . .'

'Then I do not congratulate you, sir! *You* may swallow her insults and play toady to her – but I will not. Not for King James, or Christ God Himself! I ride for Scotland tomorrow. We have wasted too long here already.'

'As you will, my lord. I cannot stop you. But I think it unwise. I have a card or two yet to play . . .'

'Play them then, sir – but play them without me!'

'I shall, if I must . . .'

Later, in the privacy of her own room, it was Mary's turn to speak. 'Is not my lord of Moray right?' she put to Patrick. 'This Queen will serve you no good. She hates Scotland, I think – or she would not treat its envoys so. She hates our King, her heir though he is. She basely slew his mother. Will it indeed serve any purpose to wait on her longer, Uncle Patrick?'

'Why yes, my dear – I believe that it may. Do not judge Gloriana too sorely. She is not just what she seems, as I have discovered. And recollect that we are the beggars – not Elizabeth. We desire much from her – and she knows it. She needs nothing from Scotland – save only peace . . .'

'And our Queen Mary's jewels!'

'M'mmm. Jewels are her weakness, yes – and thank God

for it! Jewels and young men.'

'She did not greatly esteem my lord of Moray.'

'She might have done – had he played her aright. For he is good to look at. But he was too hasty. I fear he has no gift for statecraft . . .'

'Why did you advise King James to send the Queen that great jewel, Uncle Patrick? Surely that was ill done? The good Queen Mary's, whom this Elizabeth murdered . . .'

'Hush girl – watch your words! In Walsingham's England, even walls have ears! And what you say is foolishness. Queen Mary has no further need of such. They are the King's now. And this was the finest – the most apt to please Elizabeth and bring her to think kindly of our embassage . . .'

'But your embassage is but to gain money from her – this pension. Surely the jewel itself is worth a great sum? To give it to her, when it is worth . . .'

'It is worth a great deal, yes – but only what men will give for it. In money. The King needs money, siller, not jewellery. No lord in all Scotland has sufficient to buy yon toy – even if he wanted it. Scotland is ever short of money, lass. It is the blight of the land.'

'I see. Only one of the blights, I think.' She shrugged slender shoulders. 'So you think that the Queen may be kinder to you hereafter?'

'That is my hope.'

'It may be so,' the girl said slowly, thoughtfully. 'I think that she may have misjudged you – as she said. I think that my presence with you has harmed you with her, Uncle Patrick – and I am sorry. No doubt she was informed that I was close to you. She would believe that I was your doxy, bedding with you – as I think do many. That she would not like, for she is foolish enough to desire that all men around her think only of herself, I do believe. But now – she has seen me, seen us together. She knows the truth of what is between us – for her eyes are sufficiently sharp. I think that she will relent, perhaps, towards you. If that is what caused her to keep us waiting.'

Stroking his chin, the Master looked at her wonderingly.

'You . . . you continue to surprise me, Mary,' he said. 'Where did you get the wits in that pretty head of yours? Heigho – it must have been from myself, I suppose, for your mother, though fair and kind, is scarcely so gifted! Yes – you may well be right. It may be as you say . . '

A knocking at the door of Patrick's adjoining room interrupted him, and drew him through thereto. A servant stood there, and beside him a messenger in the royal livery.

'The Master of Gray?' this functionary enquired. 'The Queen's Grace commands your presence in her private apartments forthwith, sir.'

'Ah! She does? Then . . . then, sir, the Queen's Grace must be obeyed of course. *Instanter.* Give me but a moment . . . '

Chapter Ten

PATRICK was led through a garden and pleasance to a small side door at the extreme east end of the palace where, after a muttered exchange, a guard admitted them. His guide then conducted him, by a maze of passages, to a brightly lit and luxuriously appointed chamber, where instruments of music, embroidery-frames, part-worked tapestries and other signs of feminine occupation were evident, but which at this midnight hour was empty. Beyond was a spacious boudoir, all mirrors, with walls upholstered in quilted satin, in which a single weary elegant paced to and fro. He raised an eyebrow at the Master, sighed, and holding up a minatory finger as though to restrain further progress, turned and opened one of a pair of double doors, knocked gently on the inner one, waited, and then slipped within. When he emerged again it was to beckon the visitor forward, though with no expression of approval. He said no word.

A puff of warm and highly-scented air met Patrick as he passed into the chamber beyond. Just within the doorway he paused and bowed very low – although he could barely distinguish at first what lay beyond, so dim was the lighting. Here was a small room, panelled severely in dark wood, but with a large fire of logs blazing on the hearth – which, apart

222

from only a couple of candles, provided all the illumination. A great bed with canopy and rich hangings occupied much of the apartment, but it was unoccupied. On a couch by the fire, a figure reclined, clad in the loose and very feminine folds of a flowing bed-robe.

'Come, Patrick,' a voice invited, low, companionable, warm as the room. 'This is better, is it not?'

'Immeasurably, Your Grace,' he replied, as easily. 'I rejoice in it.'

'Aye. But rejoice not too soon, my friend, nevertheless,' the Queen warned. 'Do not stand there, man, you were not always so backward! Come, sit here by me – for the night is plaguey cold.' Elizabeth was ever concerned about the temperature.

She did not however move aside on the couch on which she was extended, so that the man, to sit down thereon, must needs perch himself uncomfortably on the edge. He chose carefully to sit approximately half-way down, part-turned to face the Queen.

'Cynthia, Moon Goddess, Queen of the Night!' he murmured.

'And a match for Patrick, Master of . . . Darkness!'

'Match, aye – what a match, Madam, there would be!'

'Bold!' she said, but not harshly.

For a few moments there was silence, save for the splutter and hiss of the burning logs. The Queen drew up her knees a little, so that they pressed into the skin-tight silken hose of the man's thigh. He did not move away – indeed he could not have done so without leaving the couch altogether.

'Your Mary Gray is . . . remarkable, Patrick,' Elizabeth said presently. 'I vow I must congratulate you! My good Moor, Walsingham, misled me, I fear. For once. How old is she?'

'This was her seventeeth summer.'

'Ah! Seventeen? You were an early menace to poor foolish women then, Patrick – as of course you would be!'

'Perhaps. Or else their victim. But here was one indiscretion of youth that I have no cause to regret.'

'No? You are proud of her, then? You would not have brought her here else, of course. Proud . . . but wise? I wonder, Patrick? That one is too like yourself for your comfort, I think.

Take heed for yourself, my friend – for there is a will as strong as your own. And wits as sharp, I'll wager. Your Davy, who so long sought in vain to honest you, may have forged here sweet steel to tame you!'

'I beg leave to doubt it. But I am flattered indeed at Your Grace's interest in my humble person and affairs! It augurs well . . . '

'Tush, man – do not build on it! I am only the more wary.'

'Hence, dear lady, this so privy audience? Such wariness is a delight, indeed . . . !'

Sitting up, she leaned forward, and raising her hand, slapped the man's face – a sharp blow and no playful tap. 'Delight in that also, sir!' she jerked.

Not only did Patrick not draw back, but he did not so much as change expression or tone of voice. 'I do, fair Dian – I do! As I must delight also in what my happy eyes behold!' And coolly, deliberately, he looked downwards.

The Queen's face was very near to his own – for she had not sunk back into her reclining position after her blow. As a consequence of her forward-leaning posture, her bed-robe gaped wide before her, wholly revealing bare breasts, small but firm and shapely for her years, if flattered somewhat by the rosy uncertain flickering firelight. She did not move nor speak, although her lips were parted.

So they sat, close together, considering each other, understanding each other.

At length Elizabeth leaned back again, with a little sigh, and though she raised a slender white arm behind her turbaned head, she made no attempt to close up the front of her robe. Undoubtedly she wore nothing beneath it. Relaxed, she lay thus, a faint smile playing about her thin mouth.

The man reached out and gently took her hand. She allowed him to stroke her long tapering fingers, occasionally to run his own up over her wrist and forearm. Once she shivered slightly, and for a moment his fingers gripped tight before resuming their unhurried stroking once more. Somewhere a clock chimed half-an-hour past midnight.

'Blessed no-words, Patrick,' the Queen murmured, at length. 'I hear ever such a flood, a plague of words. So few may ever keep silent in my presence. Though you – you are eloquent indeed even in silence, my friend!'

He smiled only, and raised her finger-tips, ringless now, to his lips, and kissed each individually before turning her hand over and kissing the narrow palm. His caresses moved on, over wrist and up white forearm, so that it was his turn to lean close indeed. She permitted him to reach the region of her elbow, and therefore to be within an inch or two of her pale bosom, before her other hand reached out gently but firmly to grip his ear, restraining him.

'Linger a little, Patrick,' she murmured huskily. 'The night is young, yet.'

He raised his eyes to hers. 'You are no woman to linger over.'

Elizabeth smiled. 'Impatient!'

'Very, Diana!'

'Then . . . in that case, I have you where I want you, Master of Gray! Pleading! On your knees.'

'Have you not always?' he asked, and slipped down from the couch to kneel beside her. Still she held on to his ear.

'I think not, Patrick. Your mind seldom pleads, I swear. Nor are the knees of your heart apt for bending!'

'They bend to you, fair one.'

She nipped that ear between finger-nails, almost viciously. 'For what does your heart and mind plead, Patrick? Your heart and mind, I say, not . . . other parts?'

'Why is not that evident, indeed, Diana? All my parts are at one in pleading for . . . all of the loveliness before me.' He leaned still closer, against the pain of that ear, so that the warmth of her body actually reached his cheek.

'Liar!' she whispered. 'What did you come for, man?'

'I came because you sent for me, and because of the love I bear you – in hope.'

'Dolt! Not now. Why came you to me, from Scotland?'

Patrick drew a long breath, 'My prince sent me . . . at my own urgent behest,' he said.

'For what purpose?'

'Not the purpose for which I kneel here, Lady.'

'I wonder! Think again, Patrick. You are here for money, are you not? For golden coin, and nothing more! Wait, man –

wait! And if you can come to the money more surely, more swiftly, through my woman's weakness – then so much the better!'

'Your Grace – you wrong me! I vow you do – most sorely.'

'I think not. You use all men – and women, also – for your own ends, Patrick Gray. Always you have done so. But you will not use me, by God! Up off your lying knees, man! If you must kneel, go kneel to my Lord Treasurer!'

Slowly, reluctantly, Patrick rose to his feet. But he did not move away from the side of the couch. Nor yet did his beautiful features show any sign of emotion other than sorrow and a gentle reproach, allied with a hint of wonder.

'You brought me here, to your privy room – only to tell me this?' he asked.

'That – and to test you, sir.'

'Aye – and to tease me, I think,' he added, slowly. 'To torment my manhood. They do say that such makes sport of a sort for some women – half-women. But not, surely not, for the Queen of the Night!' And he sighed.

Elizabeth sat up abruptly, and whipped her bed-robe tight around her. 'How dare you, sir!' she said. But she seemed more put out than angry, searching his face in the flickering firelight.

'I would dare much for your favour, Madam – to banish your suspicions of me.'

'And to win my money, rogue! That damnable pension!'

'The money I seek only for my prince,' he told her. 'For that I would dare but little. Your esteem and regard I seek, for myself – and for that I would indeed dare all.'

'All, Patrick?'

'All.'

'Then dare you to go back to King James empty-handed, my friend. Dare to tell him that he must earn his own gold. Dare to tell him that my heir must be a true man and not a beggar! Dare that, and earn my esteem and love, Patrick Gray!'

'Aye, Lady – that I dare do. I shall do, if it is your wish. And come again. Another day. Happy day. To claim my . . . reward! Joyfully.' He stepped back a single pace.

226

Keenly, warily, the Queen looked at him. 'You would do this? So readily?'

'Why yes, Your Grace. For *I* am no beggar – save of your heart's warmth. Of which I felt the divine breath minutes ago. I agree entirely that pleading for this promised pension but harms the dignity of King James. Mine also, if I were to descend to it. I am glad to be spared that.'

'So-o-o!' He had Elizabeth tapping finger-nails on the edge of her couch now. 'You surprise me, Patrick.'

'Why so, Your Grace?' Almost casually he asked it, and turned to stroll round the back of the couch, so that she must needs turn her head to follow him with her pale eyes. 'Did you deem me happy in mendicancy? Riches have never been a love of mine – and assuredly I cannot prostitute myself for them on behalf of another, even my prince.'

She was silent for a little, but her glance never left his face. 'I still cannot believe that you are so readily dissuaded, Patrick Gray,' she said, at length. 'I think that I know you better than that.'

He sighed. 'My sorrow, that you so judge me, Diana. It is but a woeful end to what might have been the night of nights! A sorry farewell to carry away with me on my long journey.'

'Journey? You would ride, then? Forthwith? Back to Scotland?'

'Why yes, Highness. This very day, since it is now past midnight. Why wait? Such is my lord of Moray's intention, already . . . '

'You are plaguey quick, man, to get away from me!'

'Not so. It will be like plucking the beating heart out of my breast. But better that than teasing and disenchantment here. The sooner that I dare my prince's wrath for you, as you ask, the sooner I may return – I pray, to your favour.'

'You think then that King James will permit you to return, in such case?'

Patrick actually laughed a little. 'Indeed it is next to certain, Lady,' he said.

'Why?'

'He is sore in need of siller, as we name it, for his marriage to the Princess Anne. For her Coronation, likewise. For the

227

strengthening of his Royal Guard, that there be no more threats of abduction by lords who might seek to take him, or his queen, into their power. So, if the King gets it not from Your Grace, he must needs seek it elsewhere.'

Elizabeth snorted. 'And who else will give him so much as a single gold piece, man? Not the King of Denmark, I swear. James will be fortunate if he ever so much as sees his wife's dowry, from there!'

'Not Denmark, no. But it occurs to me that he might well turn to France. To King Henri, formerly Navarre.'

'Faugh, stupid – after rejecting Henri's sister Catherine of Navarre? There will be no French gold for James. Besides – would he send *you* again, Patrick, on such a mission? After returning empty-handed from this?'

'I think that he would, Madam. For only I have the information that he would need for success in it. Valuable information – that would make Protestant Henri look more kindly on my prince. And look askance elsewhere.'

'Eh? What information? What is this, sir?'

Patrick halted in his strolling round that bedchamber. 'Information that I have gleaned, Your Grace,' he said slowly. 'Information that will set Christendom agog! Notable information.'

'Well, man – well?'

'That the Queen of England is proposing to marry Protestant Lady Arabella Stewart, her cousin, to the Catholic Duke of Parma, Spain's Captain-General in the Netherlands, Butcher of the Low Countries!'

'Christ God!' the Queen exclaimed, almost in a croak.

'To be sure,' he nodded, smiling. 'Heigho, Highness – such information is worth . . . a king's ransom, is it not?'

Elizabeth was having difficulty with her breathing and with her words. 'How . . . fiend seize you, where . . . what a pox d'you mean . . . ?'

'I have it, Lady, from a most sure source. Your good Moor, Walsingham, is not the only one with an ear for information!'

'It is a folly! A lie . . . '

'Folly, mayhap – but no lie. Of this I am assured. On excellent . . . authority!'

'Sweet Jesu – when I find who babbled . . . !'

228

'Be not distressed, Your Grace. I would not have Gloriana distressed for . . . for all the gold in Christendom! If this is something that you would keep privy. None need know, other than myself. Have no fears . . . '

Elizabeth's voice grated. 'It is done with. A plan that came to naught. That might have healed the breach with Spain. It is past. A thing of Hatton's . . . '

'But still . . . dangerous, Madam. Still a matter that could greatly concern King Henri. Or other Protestant princes. Arabella is next heir to the Scots throne after Ludovick of Lennox, her cousin. And therefore to your throne also, Lady. Matched with Catholic Parma, the Executioner – who was carried in a litter over the mutilated corpses of thousands of Maestricht's citizens! Here could be gunpowder beneath the chancelleries of Christendom, indeed!'

'Silence! Damnation, man – hold your tongue!' The Queen's slender fists were clenched, and she beat them on her knee. 'How you learned of this – you of all men – I know not. Heads will fall, as a consequence, I promise you! But . . . no word of it must be so much as breathed. You understand? That is my royal command.'

'I understand Your Highness's feelings in the matter, yes. I can be silent, Diana – silent as the grave itself.'

'Aye. As you had better be! And the price of that silence, Master of Gray?'

He drew a long breath. 'Why, fairest one – nothing. Nothing, at all. Or, at least . . . very little!' He moved back to the side of the couch again, and stood looking down at her. 'For love of you, Diana, I would keep silence at the stake itself!'

'See that I do not test you in that, in the Tower or the Bridewell – Papist!' she said. 'What is this very little that you want?'

'First, your smile in place of your frown, fair one,' he asserted. 'That before all.'

'All . . . ?' she repeated.

His little laugh was low-pitched, melodious and purely mirthful, as he sank down on his knees again, where he had knelt before. 'In certain matters, I am greedy indeed, Diana!' he told her, and reached for her hand.

'And I, sir, in those things may well be . . . parsimonious!'

229

she returned. But, after a moment's hesitation, she did not withhold her hand.

'That I will not believe,' he said, shaking his head. 'Let us essay the matter, Your Grace . . . ?'

Although Patrick was very quiet in entering his own chamber later that night, Mary heard him, and jumping out of bed came through to him.

'You have been long,' she said. 'Have you been with the Queen? All this time?'

'Aye,' he nodded. 'You should be asleep, girl.'

'What was this, Uncle Patrick? Why did she send for you? At such an hour. After dismissing us so?'

'Because she is a strange woman, Mary. Strange and cunning. And she thought that she could best me. Test me and best me. The Master of Gray!'

'And did she?'

'She tested me, yes. But I do not think that she bested me.' And he smiled.

She searched his face gravely. 'I would like to hear how that was done?' she said. 'You saw her alone?'

'Oh, yes. But now is not the time for the telling, lass. You should be sleeping. It is only a few hours to dawn – and we have a long day ahead of us. We must by no means sleep late.'

'Tomorrow? Why?'

'Because, my dear, I much respect Sir Francis Walsingham! The sooner that we are on our road back to Scotland, the happier I shall be!'

'Walsingham? Scotland? We are going home? Tomorrow? With my lord of Moray? After all?'

'Aye. Just as soon as I deem the Lord Treasurer to be out of his bed!'

'The Lord Treasurer? And Walsingham? I do not understand.'

'I hold, moppet, a note in the Queen's own hand, ordering the Lord Treasurer to pay me £2,000, being King James's increased pension. I have a notion that Walsingham would by no means approve – and as I say, I have a respect for him and his methods. I prefer to be well on my way back to Scotland before he finds out. And as you know, he is very well informed.'

'So-o-o!' the girl breathed out. 'You have done it! You have the pension – and doubled it! You have succeeded in your mission, after all? I wonder . . . I wonder how you did that, Uncle Patrick?'

'Shall we say that I used the gifts the good God gave me? Now – off to bed again, child, and let me to mine.'

Chapter Eleven

THE unexpectedly successful embassage arrived back in Scotland on the cold bright last day of October 1589, to a singularly surprising situation, notably altered from that they had left – indeed a situation without parallel in the country's history. The King was gone.

At Berwick-upon-Tweed, when the travellers first heard these tidings, they by no means believed them. But resting overnight at Fast Castle, the eagle's-nest stronghold on the Coldinghamshire cliffs of Patrick's freebooting cousin Robert Logan of Restalrig, they learned the truth of it. James had left Scotland eight days before. Word, it seemed, had eventually reached Leith that the Princess Anne's convoy of eleven ships, buffeted, battered and dispersed by contrary gales, after having been no less than three times within sight of the Scottish coast, had finally put back to Norway, abandoning all hope of reaching Scotland that season. James, quite desperate, had decided that there was nothing for a true lover, chivalrous knight and kingly poet to do, in the circumstances, but to set sail himself, go fetch his bride, and challenge the Devil and all his malign works of witchcraft in a heroic royal gesture that in due course would make the most splendid epic of all. Despite the astonishment, disbelief, alarm and unanimous disapproval of his advisers, the King was adamant – and urgent. He had ordered the most suitable ship in the harbour of Leith to be made ready for sea, and had appointed a Council of Regency to govern the realm during his absence, and on the 22nd of

231

October had set sail for Scandinavia, taking Chancellor Maitland with him, his chaplain Master David Lindsay to perform the marriage ceremony, and sundry others. By now, he might well be in Norway.

Even Patrick Gray was quite overcome by this extraordinary news. Eventually, however, he smiled, he chuckled, he began to laugh – and laughed until tears ran down his cheeks. The Earl of Moray was less amused, especially when Logan could by no means recollect his name amongst those nominated for the Council of Regency.

They set off for Edinburgh without delay next morning.

In the capital city they found a most curious state of affairs prevailing. James, in his delegation of authority, had been more astute than might have been expected. He had, with rather remarkable cunning, selected for various offices of government just those nobles who, because of mutual suspicion and rivalry, could be relied upon to counter-balance each others' influence and thus preclude any probable bid for power by a faction. Ludovick, Duke of Lennox, was to be viceroy and President of the Council of Regency; but lest any should seek to use that very young man too ambitiously, as Vice-President was appointed, of all choices, the madcap Francis, Earl of Bothwell, another cousin of James, whose fiery and unpredictable behaviour could be guaranteed to keep everybody on the alert. The chief military power was put in the hands of the Lord Hamilton, no friend of Bothwell's, and another contender for the heirship to the throne. Sir Robert Melville, a rather dull soldier but incorruptible, was appointed Acting Chancellor; but lest he be not sufficiently Protestant, Master Robert Bruce, chief minister of Edinburgh at St. Giles, was added to the Council with especial responsibility for the Kirk. And so on. Despite his hurried exodus, James undoubtedly had given these dispositions much thought. Perhaps he had been contemplating something of the sort for some time.

There were no special appointments for either the Master of Gray nor the Earl of Moray.

The Lady Marie welcomed Patrick and Mary back warmly. The Master of the Wardrobe's own quarters in the north wing of Holyroodhouse had at last become ready and available while they were in England, and Marie had removed there from her father's crowded establishment nearby. Here was space, privacy, comfort, with even a private stairway from the great courtyard, and a room for Mary's own use. After months and years of making do in cramped and inconvenient lodgings, Marie rejoiced in this domestic bliss, and asked no more than that her little household should settle therein quietly and enjoy it, during this unexpected interval of Court inactivity.

But it was not to be. Patrick Gray was not the man for settled and domestic bliss.

'I am sorry, my dear,' he told her. 'But this is no place for us, meantime. With the King gone, I should be but wasting my time in Edinburgh. There is much to be done elsewhere – especially at Broughty Castle. Many decisions await me there . . .'

'Not Broughty, Patrick!' his wife protested. 'Not that great gloomy, draughty pile! To dwell in! Winter is almost upon us . . .'

'It will be less gloomy now, Marie, I promise you. And the draughts somewhat abated, I vow. I love such no more than you do. But it is my house, my inheritance – thrown in my face by my father! I intend that he shall rue the day that he fobbed me off with Broughty!'

'Yes, Patrick – but we need not go to live there. Not yet. In winter. When we have this fine lodging here. You can visit Broughty, yes – to see how the work goes. But that need take only a day or two. We need not all go . . .'

'I fear that we need so, indeed,' he assured her. 'And get there as quickly and secretly as may be. Do you not realise, my heart, that I have here with me two thousand English pounds in gold? A vast fortune indeed. Half the lords in Scotland, not to mention lesser men, would sell their very souls for a tithe of it! That gold, and my life with it, must be protected, must it not? Once it becomes known that I have it – and Moray, I swear, will not fail to let all know that our mission has been successful – men with long knives and empty purses will be after it, and me. Nothing is more certain. So much ready money has scarce been seen in Scotland before. It must be placed in safety – and swiftly. And I can think of few places safer than in Broughty Castle, where only a few

233

men might guard it against an army.'

'But it is the King's money, Patrick. Bestow it in the royal treasury . . . '

'A pox, Marie – that is the last place I would place it! Who has the keys of the royal treasury? My Lord Treasurer, the Master of Glamis, one of the biggest rogues in the land! No, that is not a temptation I mean to put in our friend Thomas Lyon's way! Nor in the way of any in the Council, God save me, with the King far in another land!'

'Ludovick would look after it. He is the King's representative, and honest.'

'Ludovick is young, a mere boy. He is honest, yes – but can be cozened. No – it goes to Broughty, and we go with it. Forthwith. This very night I shall go down to Leith to find a boat that may take us there. Safer, more secretly, than the long journey by land . . . '

'You are sure, Patrick, that you intend that all this gold shall come out of Broughty Castle again, into King James's hands, in due course?'

Patrick frowned. 'If that is a jest, Marie, it is but ill-timed,' he said coldly.

Mary Gray intervened, from the fireside where she had been listening quietly to this exchange. 'It will be good to be back in the Carse again,' she said. 'You will take me with you, Uncle Patrick? I shall go home to my mother and father at Castle Huntly. I am longing to see them again . . . '

A servant knocked at the door to announce the presence of the Duke of Lennox.

Ludovick came in hurriedly, breathlessly, having run up the stairs. His eyes, shining, turned immediately to Mary, before he recollected his duty to the Master of Gray and his wife.

'I was at Dalkeith, when I heard,' he declared, 'that you were returned. I came at once.'

'Ha – the ruler of Scotland in person!' Patrick exclaimed. 'My lord Duke, we are indeed honoured by your condescension in seeking out our humble abode.'

Ludovick's plain freckled features actually flushed a little. 'I came as soon as I heard,' he said, awkwardly. 'I rejoice to see you back. I . . . I have missed you greatly.' Once again his glance slid round to Mary.

The Master came across and put an arm around the younger man's shoulders. 'I will not ask, Vicky, which of us you have missed most!' And he laughed.

'Why, I ... I ... ah ... ummm.'

The girl came to his rescue. She rose, and curtsied to him. 'How good to see you, Vicky,' she said. 'It was kind of you to come, and so quickly.'

'Mary!' he got out, and reached for her hand in a grab rather than in any viceregal gesture. 'You are well? So beautiful! I have wearied for you. It has been so long ...'

'We have only been gone for a month, Vicky.'

'It has seemed more, much more.' Clearly the young woman's absence in England had had a great effect on the Duke, had served to confirm and crystallise his emotion with regard to her. A new urgency had come into his whole attitude.

Patrick did not fail to perceive it, and stroked his chin thoughtfully. 'I am sure that Mary is flattered, Vicky,' he said. 'But ... you must have other matters on your mind, meantime? Matters of state. As President of the Council ...'

'It is damnable,' the young man burst out, 'that James should saddle me with this. Men are at me all the time, to consider this and agree to that. It is papers and parchments and charters, every day – signing, always signing and sealing. Ink and sand and sealing-wax ...!'

'Poor Vicky!' The Lady Marie smiled at him. 'When all that you want is a good horse between your knees, and hounds baying!'

'Aye. And ... and ...' Ludovick looked at the younger woman.

'As well that Mary is going home to Castle Huntly then, perhaps.'

'Eh ...? Going ...? To Castle Huntly? You are not going away, Mary?'

'Why yes, Vicky. Meantime. It is time. I have not been home for three long months. I long to see my father and mother. And Granlord ...'

'But your place is here. At Court. You are one of the Queen's ladies.'

'The Queen will not be needing me for months, to be sure.'

'But ... you should not go. You have been away for too

235

long, as it is. I . . . I . . . ' The Duke drew himself up. 'I could forbid you to go,' he said, thickly. 'I am Viceroy. I rule here, meantime.'

Mary's trill of laughter was spontaneous, mirthful. 'Do not be daft, Vicky!' she told him.

Immediately abashed, shamefaced, he looked down. 'I am sorry,' he mumbled. 'But . . . I do not want you to go.'

'I shall come back, never fear.'

'*I* shall come – come to you, then. To Castle Huntly. Or not to the castle itself, but nearby. You cannot stop me doing that, Mary – none can stop me. I shall leave Bothwell to read the papers and do the signing. He will like it well enough. I shall come to the Carse of Gowrie. Or to Dundee . . . '

'M'mmm – one moment,' Patrick intervened, carefully. 'I think, Vicky, that would be foolish. To hand over the rule to Bothwell. You owe the realm, and James, better than that. Bothwell is quite irresponsible. He might do anything. There would be trouble with Hamilton, for certain. No – you are Duke of Lennox and the King's lieutenant, and must bear the rule.'

The other set his chin obstinately. 'I go to the Carse if Mary goes,' he said.

'Then . . . then come to Broughty Castle with us, and bear the rule from there, Vicky.' Even Patrick Gray could scarcely keep the ring of excitement out of his voice. 'It is but a dozen miles from Castle Huntly.'

Quickly, searchingly, the Lady Marie looked at her husband, and then to Mary. She said nothing.

'That I should like very well,' Ludovick agreed.

'Sir Robert Melville's house in Fife is just across Tay from there. He acts Chancellor, they tell me? Nothing could be more convenient.'

'For whom?' his wife asked, somewhat tensely.

'For the Duke, of course, my dear. For the good governance of the realm. For Scotland,' Patrick answered easily. 'We go at once, Vicky – so soon as I can find a vessel to carry us. Secretly. For I fear for the King's siller that I have brought from Elizabeth. But you – you must come to Broughty later, with no undue haste. And not directly. Calling on sundry lords on the way – calling at your own house of Methven. It will

236

look better so. None must consider your visit to Broughty, your sojourn there, to be aught but casual, innocent . . . '

'Aught but innocent! There we have it!' Marie took him up. 'And if this is not innocent, then – is it guilty, Patrick?'

'Tush!' he exclaimed. 'You have the vapours, my love. You jump at shadows. Come, Vicky – accompany me down to Leith, to enquire of the shipmen. Then, if there is talk of me removing this money, the King's represenative himself will be known to be privy to it. The more reason for him to follow it to Broughty, i' faith!'

Reluctantly, after a longing look at Mary, the Duke followed the Master.

When they were gone, Marie went over to the baby in the crib by the window, and stood gazing down at it. 'I do not like it, Mary,' she said, shaking her fair head. 'I know that look in Patrick's eye. I fear more intrigue, more conspiracy. And therefore trouble. I see Patrick reaching out again for power . . . '

'He was made for power, Lady Marie. There is good in power, as well as ill. You will never stop Uncle Patrick reaching for it, I think. It is for us to be ever near him, to seek where we can that the power works for good. As we have done before.'

'As *you* have done, Mary. Lord, child – I believe that you were made for this power as much as was Patrick! And delight in it but little the less!'

The younger woman considered that gravely for a moment or two, and then shook her head in turn. But that was as far as her denial went.

And so, with scarcely believable ease and minimum of manoeuvre, Patrick Gray slipped quietly and inconspicuously into the rule of Scotland once again. Only a mere five months after the banished felon's uninvited return from exile, he was, temporarily at least, back in the saddle of supreme authority, operative if not titular – for he held the Viceroy of the realm in the hollow of his hand and took the decisions which Lennox promulgated. Scotland, for so long without a strong king or settled central government, swiftly if cynically recognised and accepted the familiar pattern of power, and all men with favours to seek and causes to further, concessions, exemptions, sanctions, positions, must come to seek them at Broughty Castle. In this Patrick was most effectively aided and advantaged by the very virtues of the acting Chancellor; Sir Robert Melville's unimaginative honesty, lack of ambition, and peaceable disposition, played into the Master's skilful hands. He went out of his way to seem to consult and defer to the older man, making many journeys himself and sending couriers daily over the Tay to the Melville house in Fife. He had his reward.

Moreover, despite his wife's fears, the Master of Gray was very good at the business. As had been the case three years before, when for the best part of a prosperous and peaceful year Patrick had largely controlled the destinies of his native land, so now, for those winter and spring months, Scotland was well-managed, discreetly guided, and comparatively tranquil. Admittedly Bothwell rampaged about the Borders, burning and slaying unchecked – but then, that was ever his habit, and neither James nor Maitland had found any method of stopping him. Huntly was feuding with his neighbours in the north, and taking the opportunity to devastate the Keith lands while the Earl of Marischal was still overseas – but that also was chronic, and at least he kept his activities well north of decent settled country. No doubt the far-flung Highlands seethed with strife and endemic clan warfare, but it was to the advantage of all good men that such barbarians should kill each other off as vigorously as possible. For the rest, a moderate calm prevailed, the grosser corruptions were discouraged, some notorious ill-doers were brought to justice, certain judges brought low, and the campaign against witches came almost to a full stop. There were growlings and snarlings from sundry nobles, inevitably, and carpings from the Kirk that Papistical influence was in the ascendant; but such broke no bones. And although tales were rife that a vast sum in English gold for the King was being salted away shamefully in Broughty Castle instead of in the royal treasury, the presence on the premises of the Viceroy himself largely tied the hands of any who might have sought to do more than talk. The Lord Treasurer, the Master of Glamis, at any rate, kept his distance – even though

238

that was not so very far off, in his castle of Aldbar, near Brechin.

Broughty Castle itself, and the little town that lay under its frowning walls, flourished in consequence as never before. Very considerable improvements had been made to the stern and battle-torn fortalice since the previous July, despite dire lack of funds, but now the place blossomed like the May. Suddenly there was no dearth of money – though whence it came was by no means clear. Broughty would never be a palace nor yet a ladies' bower; but at least it was made habitable, even moderately comfortable, timber outbuildings sprang up within the courtyard, whitewashed harling set the massive masonry gleaming, tapestries and hangings graced the bare interior walls – even a painted picture or two. Servants multiplied about the place, and from Dundee came a steady stream of furnishings, fabrics, provender and wines. And above the topmost tower fluttered proudly in the sea breeze no fewer than three standards – the silver lion on scarlet, of Gray; the fess chequery of Stewart quartered with the golden lilies of D'Aubigny and the red roses of Lennox; and the rampant lion of Scotland itself.

By no means could Patrick Gray force his father to come from Castle Huntly to see it all; but at least each day at noon an old cannon, put into commission for the purpose, thundered out a viceregal salute from the battlements, that must have been heard from one end of the Carse to the other and over half of Fife and Angus, proclaiming for all to hear that here on this barren rocky promontory, was authority, jurisdiction, rule.

There was much coming and going between the two castles, of course, even though Patrick would no more darken the door of the one than would his sire the other. Ludovick seldom let a day pass without covering the dozen miles of coastline. The Lady Marie was a frequent visitor at Castle Huntly, ignoring as best she might her father-in-law's jibes and jeers. Davy Gray went often to Broughty, and Mariota occasionally. As for Mary, she was almost as much in the one house as the other, a laughing lightsome figure, apparently reverted wholly to country ways again.

The trouble that Marie feared did not materialise.

The Duke's pursuit of Mary Gray was now frank, determined in a quiet way, and continuous. Though perhaps pursuit is no accurate description; attendance upon and following after would be more apt, for there was nothing of the hunt, nothing of attack and flight about their relationship. The girl remained wholly, if modestly, inconspicuously, in command of the situation, with Lennox the faithful, humble but persistent suppliant. He was quite without pride or self-esteem in the matter, not pressing his cause other than by displaying his devotion and seeking perpetually to be in her company, content to be her squire, her escort, her constant but undemanding companion.

That the young woman did not object to his company and attentions, she made no attempt to hide. She was kind, suitably respectful in public, not at all so in private, but considerate always. That he much preferred to be with her than to concern himself with affairs of state, she accepted – though not infrequently she gently urged him towards his duty, and sought to discuss with him the problems which he tended to avoid or dismiss.

There was talk, of course – much and scandalous talk. That the Duke should require a mistress was only to be expected; but with all the cream of Scotland to choose from, that he should select the ostensible daughter of a mere land-steward, and moon after her as though she were a princess, caused grave offence. That it was all a disgraceful plot of the Master of Gray's, of course, could be taken for granted; he was using this brat to enthrall Lennox and so control the realm.

If such talk worried none of the three principals, the same could not be said of Davy Gray.

One crisp sunny December afternoon, with rime almost as thick as snow upon the ground, my lord of Gray came riding into his courtyard of Castle Huntly, hoof-beats ringing metallically in the sharp frosty air. Davy Gray was crossing from the keep to his own sanctum in the north-west tower. My lord hailed him over peremptorily.

'*You* taught the wench this folly o' skating, Davy – this sliding about on ice. Bairn's play. I said it wasna suitable in a lassie, in a woman. I said she'd break a leg, or the like. But you kenned better – ooh, aye, Davy Gray ay kens better! Well, maybe you'll now change your tune . . .'

'Mary? She is not hurt? Skating? She has not broke . . . ?'

'No' her legs, no – it's mair like her maidenhead's in danger! If it's no' gone already!' the older man returned coarsely. 'She's out there on Sauchie Loch, clutching and hugging her precious duke to her, like any tavern trollop! I wonder we're no' hearing their skirling from here!'

The other eyed his father searchingly. It was not like Lord Gray directly to criticise Mary. 'I think that you are mistaken,' he said evenly. 'Mary behaves not so.'

'You say not? You give me the lie? Then go and look, man. Go to Sauchie Loch. She is sold to yon puppy Lennox. And it is Patrick's doing, God's eternal curse on him! The lassie is ruined, turned into a strumpet. And by yon evil devil in human shape that I had the mischance to beget!'

Davy Gray shook his head wordlessly. There was no profit in arguing.

'Dinna glower and wag your head at me, you ill limmer! It's the truth. I've been to Kinnaird. Going, I went to the smiddy with a loose shoe, and there was the pair o' them sitting by his fire watching yon great dolt o' a cousin o' yours, Don Affleck, fashioning two o' these skating irons for Lennox. God's body, but I gave him better work to do – and a flea in his ear in the by-going! But, coming back, here's them both sliding about the Shauch . . . Sauchie Loch, clasping and nuzzling each other!' My lord was having some difficulty with his enunciation. Abruptly his tone changed, and his flushed, florid and dissipated face fell ludicrously, the heavy, purple jowls seeming almost to quiver. 'Och, it's no' right, it's no' decent, Davy. She used to be my ain lass. She was canny and she was kind – my ain fair bit lassie, my ain troutie. You let her awa' to yon Court, to Patrick. You shouldna ha' done it. I told you. And now . . . now she's nae mair than a toy, any man's toy. Aye, and a broken toy at that, I'll warrant . . . ! A pox on you!' My lord, who had been drinking, was all but in maudlin tears as he stamped off. His son frowned after him.

Yet in only a few minutes that same son was making for the Sauchie Loch. It lay about half-a-mile away, between the castle and the village. It had been ice-bound for days, he knew – all fresh water had been frozen. After the winds and storms of summer and autumn, the winter had so far been one continuous frost, bright and still. King James would have cried witchcraft, indeed.

Sure enough, the man heard laughter ringing in the crisp air long before he reached the loch amongst the birch woods. It sounded clear, uninhibited and innocent enough, certainly.

He halted at the loch shore. They were out in the middle of some five acres of ice. There was some degree of truth in my lord's assertions as to hugging and clutching. The girl was holding the young man round the waist indeed, with both arms. But even as David watched, Ludovick's feet slid from under him and he went down on to the ice with a crash that would have been a deal harder had it not been for those encircling arms. There was much laughter once again, as she aided him to his unsteady feet. It was the Duke's turn to grasp his mentor.

As a turn, largely involuntary, in their erratic but hilarious progress, faced the pair in David's direction, the girl perceived her father standing there and raised a hand to wave. Even such withdrawal of support was enough to upset her pupil's precarious balance, and promptly his skates took the opportunity to slide away in almost opposite directions. Down he went once more, pulling Mary with him.

David was grinning before he recollected the unsuitability of all this, and switched to a frown instead. He paced out on to the ice, but carefully.

'Is not Vicky a fool, father?' Mary called out, as he approached them. 'He will not keep his feet together. I vow the skates should be on his bottom! Then we might do better.'

David did not relax his expression. 'Better still that you should consider my lord Duke's dignity – and your own repute, Mary,' he said sternly. 'Here is no way to behave . . . making a spectacle of yourself! You are not a child now.'

'No, I am not,' she agreed, but still smiling. 'Nor is Vicky.'

'Then remember it. This is unseemly. The realm's ruler should not be seen thus.'

'Is he being seen, Father? By any but you? And how shall it hurt the realm if its ruler laughs a little?'

'My lord saw you. And who knows what others. You can be heard afar off.'

242

'And that displeases you?'

He pursed his lips, for he was an honest man 'I . . . I fear it is unwise,' he said.

The Duke was approximately upright now, but still having to hold on to Mary. 'I thank you, sir, for your concern for my dignity,' he declared jerkily. 'Perhaps I do not esteem it so highly as you do.'

'That may be so, yes. But it is more Mary's name and repute that I think for, my lord Duke. As, I think, should you.'

The younger man, balancing uneasily there, frowned. 'As I do, Master Gray. Indeed . . . ' – he blinked rapidly – ' . . . indeed, I think of little else. She will scarce let me speak of it, but it is ever in my mind. I think so much of her name that, that . . . '

'That he would have me to change it!' Mary laughed. 'And I am very well content with it as it is, thank you! Whatever its repute.'

'Change it . . . ?' David repeated.

'I would change it to mine, sir. I would wed her – if she would have me.'

'God be good!'

'Exactly!' the young woman nodded, quite unabashed. 'So say I. And so would say all . . . '

'But it is I that ask you to wed me, Mary – not all! Not others. I care not what others say.'

'You must care what *I* say, Vicky, must you not?'

'To be sure, yes. But all the time you are thinking of others . . . '

'Myself also, I assure you.'

'See you,' Davy Gray broke in. 'This is madness! You cannot be serious, man – my lord. Such talk is complete folly. You are the Duke of Lennox, second man to the King himself in this land. You cannot wed such as Mary. You are too important a man . . . '

'If I am so important, may I not choose my own wife?'

'No doubt – but not the daughter of Davy Gray! It must be some great lord's daughter . . . '

'I do not desire some great lord's daughter. I have seen aplenty. I want only Mary Gray . . . ' In his emotion, Ludovick gestured with his arm – and it was almost his downfall again.

243

His precarious equilibrium upset, he would have toppled had not Mary tightened her grip and her father grabbed a ducal arm likewise.

The girl's laughter rippled. 'Perhaps Your Excellency should keep your mind on, on matters of immediate moment, sir!'

'Mary . . . !'

'Come,' David said, urging the younger man towards the shore. 'We cannot discuss such matters thus.'

'There is nothing left to discuss,' Mary declared, sighing. 'We have discussed it all overmuch already.' But she helped to steer the Duke towards the bank, nevertheless.

That young man laboured under an obvious handicap in expressing his point of view. 'I will wed none but Mary,' he announced, edging forward between them, with boyish set-jawed obstinacy.

'But . . . cannot you see my lord? It would not be permitted,' David pointed out. 'The King would not allow it.'

'James is not here. I am Viceroy. None could stop me.'

'Not even I, Vicky?'

'The marriage would be annulled when James came back,' David insisted. 'You are not yet of age. King and Council would invoke your lack of years, for certain. Think what it means. You are next heir to the throne. Should James die — should his ship sink in a storm, coming home from Denmark — you would be King, and your wife Queen! Mary Gray, daughter of a bastard of no account!'

'I care not. And if I am old enough to rule as Viceroy . . . '

'But others care, my lord Duke, I do! And Mary is not of age, either. She is under my authority . . . '

'While I am ruler of this realm, my authority is above yours, Master Gray!' the other announced heavily. They had reached the shore now. 'I can do what I will.'

'Vicky — do not be foolish,' Mary said, pleading a little now. 'What father says is true. You might insist on marrying me — but it would be done away with when the King returns.'

'James would heed me. He thinks kindly of me . . . '

'But he would not, could not, have me as good-sister! As good-sister to his new Queen. Wife to his heir. And consider Elizabeth of England. James is her heir, also — but only if she

244

so directs. Think you that she would for one moment agree to accept James if *his* heir was married to a commoner? Guidsakes, Vicky – I might then become Queen of England!'

That gave him pause for a moment.

'Elizabeth would insist on King James having the marriage annulled,' she went on. 'He would do it, for certain. And how would that leave me?'

'Then . . . then I must needs renounce my position. Give up my heirship to the crown. I care naught for it, anyway. That is what I shall do.'

'Dear Vicky – you would so do much, for my sake? You are kind. But . . . it cannot be. We cannot change the state into which we were born – either of us.'

'You are a peer of this realm, my lord – Scotland's only duke,' David said. 'You cannot renounce your blood. None could accept such a renunciation, since at any time you could change it again. I am sorry, lad. A man may not avoid his destiny, I fear.'

'Some would say that a man can *make* his destiny!' Ludovick asserted stubbornly. 'That I mean to do.'

Davy Gray shook his head helplessly. 'I am sorry,' he repeated. 'I cannot command your lordship's actions. But I can command my daughter, forbid her to see you . . .'

'And I can command her presence!' the other returned spiritedly. 'As well as Viceroy, I am Lord Chamberlain. Mary is one of the Queen's ladies, and all such are under my control . . .'

'And I say that she is not! Mary is under age. Until she is of full years, she is in my care . . .'

'Oh, a truce, a truce!' the young woman interrupted. 'If you could but hear yourselves! You are like bairns, both of you. I will not be pulled this way and that, like a bone between two dogs! I cannot marry you, Vicky – that is certain. But neither shall I be forbidden to see you, or . . . or any man! I mean to live my own life. Between you, I declare, you have spoiled a bonny day! I am going home. Alone. I seek my own company, only. If you must squabble thus, you can do it by yourselves.' And tossing her dark head a little, Mary Gray turned and left them there by the frozen lochside. It was seldom indeed that young woman indulged in dramatics of this sort.

The men gazed from her slender back to each other, in sudden silence and discomfort.

It was her father who caught up with her, still some way from Castle Huntly.

'I am sorry, lass,' he said, taking her arm. 'I would not hurt you. That was unseemly, I grant you. Not well done. It is only my concern for you . . .'

'You need not concern yourself,' she told him. 'I can well look after myself.'

'So you think, Mary. But you are young. Too trusting . . .'

'Young? Do years matter so, Father? Can we not be young in some things, and old in others? You are older than Uncle Patrick in some things, but in others you are but a child, I think, compared with him. Myself, I do not believe that I am so very young in all things. Nor so trusting.'

'But in this matter of Lennox . . . ?'

'Vicky is the young one – not I! *He* trusts – not I! Poor Vicky!' She sighed. 'Where has he gone?'

'Back to the smiddy. For his horse. Then he returns to Broughty. Sir Robert Melville is attending him there tonight. With papers.' He looked at her sidelong. 'This is a bad business, Mary. That young man – are you fond of him?'

'I like him very well,' she answered quietly.

'M'mmm.' He frowned.

'He is true. Honest. He seeks little for himself. Save me! Indeed, he is not unlike yourself, Father. And not at all like me!'

Keenly he eyed her, but said nothing.

'Unlike the Grays,' she added, 'Vicky is no schemer.'

David shook his head. 'He has his virtues, no doubt. But better that you should not see him, nevertheless, girl. Further association can only bring you both sorrow.'

'That may be. But think you that *not* seeing him will spare us sorrow? Besides, I must see him. And frequently.'

'Must . . . ? Why?'

'Because . . . why, because of our Gray schemings! Because of Uncle Patrick. He uses Vicky. He would involve him in many things. Not all, I fear, to his advantage. I would not wish to see Vicky hurt, wronged.'

'You mean . . . you think that Patrick intends harm to the Duke?'

'No – for he is fond of him, too. But to Uncle Patrick, schemes, plotting, statecraft as he calls it, is more important than are people. You know that.'

'Aye,' the man agreed heavily. 'I know it.'

'Vicky's position is so important, it is inconceivable that Uncle Patrick would not use him. He has used him much already. I want to know of such things.'

'I see,' David almost groaned. 'This, Mary, is . . . familiar ground! I' faith, it is! What can you do, even knowing?'

'I can perhaps do a little, here and there. Vicky tells me all. He does not see it all, as I do. He does not understand Uncle Patrick as I do. Have I not some responsibility in the matter?'

'Lord knows! But it is not work for such as you, lass. All the dirty, plotting deceit and wickedness of Patrick's statecraft. You are young and fresh and wholesome – a mere girl. I should never have permitted that you go to Court. I blame myself. I should not have allowed you to enter that cesspool of intrigue . . .'

'And yet it suits me very well,' she told him. 'Perhaps I am not as you think me, Father. I do not find it all so ill.'

'Then I am the more afraid for you,' the man declared. 'I had hoped that the Lady Marie would have guided you, warned you.'

'As she does. We are close. Together we seek to aid the good in Uncle Patrick's works, and to hinder the ill.'

'You do?' They walked under the gatehouse arch. 'God of mercy – innocents! On my soul, d'you think that such as you can clip Patrick's wings? Outwit the nimblest wits in this realm?'

'*You* sought to do it for long, did you not, Father? With some little success? And we have certain advantages.'

He paced across the cobblestones, silent.

'You are not displeased? You do not think that we do wrong in this?'

'The Lord knows! Who am I to judge? But what can you do? Have you any notion, girl, of what you essay?'

'Why yes, I think so. We have been learning.'

'Learning . . . ? You mean that you have already been pitting yourselves against Patrick?'

'Not against him. Say rather *for* him. We are his friends.'

247

'As you will. He would scarcely thank you, nevertheless! What have you discovered? Is it plotting, again? What is he scheming now? He is strongly placed once more, God knows. Have you some knowledge of his intentions?'

They stood in the doorway of David's own small flanking-tower. 'He has schemes a-many, you may be sure,' Mary answered. 'Of some we have little knowledge. Some we believe to be good. But three in especial we fear may be dangerous. These we seek to counter, if we can. And it is through Vicky that we may best do so.'

'Dangerous to whom? Patrick? Or others?'

'Both, we think. One concerns Dunfermline.'

'Aye. He is still hot for that place. It is the sheerest folly. He will never regain Dunfermline Abbey. He talks of suing Huntly before the Court of Session, while he is out of favour. But I do not think that he can win the case – however much he may pay the judges. Too many men covert Dunfermline.'

'He cannot win it,' she agreed.

'He is being stupid about Dunfermline. And Patrick is not usually stupid. I think that some hatred of Huntly must be affecting his judgment.'

'And yet he is in close communication with my lord of Huntly.'

'Patrick is?'

'Messengers travel frequently between Broughty Castle and Strathbogie. Secretly. Jesuits. Priests in disguise.'

'Seize me – are you sure? Catholics again!'

'Yes. And Huntly is not the only earl with whom Uncle Patrick is dealing secretly. Messengers come and go to my lord of Bothwell, also.'

'That firebrand! Bothwell, eh? What should this mean?'

'We cannot be sure. But it is very close, secret.'

'And Lennox?'

'He knows naught of it. And I have not told him.'

The man, eyeing her, stroked his chin. 'Tell me, Mary – since clearly you do not miss much that goes on,' he acknowledged, 'have you heard Bothwell's name linked with Dunfermline? Is he also one who desires that well-fleshed bone of contention?'

'I have heard that he has sworn to add it to his earldom.'

'Aye.' Davy Gray's breath came out on a long sigh. 'So that is it, I warrant! Patrick has not changed! I smell treason and treachery once more. And, God help me – how I hate the stink of it! There is to be another Catholic rising. Or at the least, the beginnings of one. Both earls will be implicated. And who knows how many others, who may be in Patrick's way. They need not all be Catholics. Bothwell is not a Catholic – a man of no religion. It matters not. Find out who are seeking to get hands on Dunfermline, and I wager they will be dragged in somehow. Then, when all is ready, the word of it will by some chance come to the King's ear! Or that of the Council, if before the King's return. Patrick will not seem to be the informer, to be sure – but his rivals for Dunfermline will be arraigned. For rebellion. Treason. The ground will be cleared, and the realm grateful!' The man's sigh was part groan. 'It is so familiar . . . '

'Yes.' The young woman's nod was quite brisk, and there was no groaning or sighing. 'That is how we conceived it, also. It must be stopped.'

'Stopped!' he repeated. 'Think you Patrick will effect all this and then stop it, on your plea or mine? He will deny all, and continue . . . '

'If it is as we believe, he will stop it – when he learns that Dunfermline Abbey cannot come to any of them. Or to himself, either.'

'What . . . ? Cannot come . . . ?'

'No. For it is to go to the Princess Anne. To the new Queen. As a wedding-gift.'

David stared at her, seeking ineffectually for words. 'Is . . . is this true?' he got out, at length; and at her nod, 'Patrick . . . ? He does not know it?'

'None knows it, I think. Yet.'

Her father swallowed. 'Save . . . save Mary Gray!'

'That is so. I it was who suggested it to the King. He was taken with the notion.'

'*You* did!'

'Yes. But the King was anxious about Uncle Patrick in the matter. He feared that he would be scunnered at him, he said. And might work harm. So he was to keep it close. Until the

249

Queen is here. But now – now it is time that Uncle Patrick should know.'

'Lord save us!' the other muttered.

A bellow rang out and echoed across the courtyard. From an upper window of the great keep, my lord of Gray leaned out, gesturing down at Mary. 'Come here, lassie!' he shouted. 'Here, I say. To me. Why stand down there? Where's yon gangling loon Lennox? Ha' you got him in there? I'll no' have it – cosseting and nuzzling in my house . . . !'

'He is not here, Granlord. He is gone,' Mary called back.

'As well he has! Then come you up here. You never look near me, Mary. A fine thing, in my ain house . . .'

'I am coming, Granlord. At once . . .'

'He is concerned for you,' David told her, as the older man withdrew his head. 'He fears that Patrick has sold you to Lennox.'

'And does Granlord believe that I could be sold to any man?' she laughed. 'He should know me better. As should you all, I think.'

'Aye.' Heavily David said it. 'I am doubting if I know you at all, girl, and that's truth! What of Patrick, then? And Dunfermaline. Are you to tell him what you have told me? That the Queen is to have it. And would he believe you?'

'I shall not tell him, no. He would be very angry. He would send me away from him. I could then do no more to serve him. And I would not have him hating me. That will not do. Vicky must tell him. Vicky receives letters from Denmark, from the King – long letters. At the next, he must go to Uncle Patrick. Privily. Tell him, as though he had learned it from the letter, that Dunfermline is now the Queen's property. He will believe that. He will be angry – but he cannot change the King's decree. He will halt this plot, it will no longer serve him. So you see, Father – I must not cease to see Vicky. For this, and for other matters. It is important. Besides, I want to see him. Even though I am not sold to him. I shall tell Granlord as much, also.'

Pressing his arm, she ran off, light-foot, across the frosted cobbles.

Davy Gray stood looking after her, long after she had disappeared into the keep of Castle Huntly.

Chapter Twelve

ALL Scotland that counted in the scheme of things flocked down to the Port of Leith that blustery first day of May 1590 – and most of Edinburgh, whether it counted or not. Two days previously a small fast ship had arrived from Denmark, with the information that the King and his bride were belatedly on their way home – and indeed the day before, the fleet itself had been sighted briefly off the mouth of the Forth, but owing to the sudden unseasonable south-westerly gale, had been unable to enter the firth, being blown northwards. Watchers now, however, reported the squadron straggling in distinctly scattered formation, off Aberlady Bay, and plans for the royal reception went into full swing.

The Duke of Lennox was very much to the fore, for in his capacity of Lord Chamberlain he was responsible for the arrangements – although in fact the Master of Gray had organised most of them. Ludovick did not desert Mary Gray, however, and indeed all the functionaries who sought the Viceroy and Chamberlain had to seek him in the cheerful and colourful enclosure below the Council House on the Coalhill, overlooking the harbour, where the Queen's ladies were assembled. He did not seem to be at all depressed about the imminent end to his viceregal powers and privileges.

In the four months that had passed since his spurned suggestion of marriage to Mary, the Duke had not been spared his problems and difficulties as nominal ruler of the land. He had been forced into opposition to his friend Patrick Gray on a number of issues – which had been unpleasant; though nothing like so unpleasant as the occasion when he had had to inform the Master that James had decided to present the Abbey of Dunfermline and all its lands and revenues to the new Queen as a bridal gift. The subsequent outburst of sheer fury and passion, quite unexampled in the younger man's experience, had shaken him to the core, so that for days afterwards he dared hardly look Patrick in the eye, even though that extraordinary man, once the cataclysm of his rage and disappointment was over, seemed to dismiss the entire subject from his mind, and reverted to his sunny normal with scarcely credible rapidity.

There had been some trouble with Bothwell, also. Disgruntled about something more than usually, he had been storming about the Borderland burning, slaying, and raping. This being more or less normal, despite being on a larger scale, would not greatly have mattered, but for some reason he had extended his depredations beyond the Debatable Land and over the Border itself into England – which Patrick Gray obscurely declared was done entirely to spite himself. At any rate, it produced angry representations from Queen Elizabeth, and demands for Bothwell's immediate apprehension and punishment. Which, of course, was quite impracticable, the Earl having more men – and wild moss-troopers at that – at his disposal than had the Crown of Scotland or any other noble in the kingdom save only Huntly. In consequence, Ludovick himself had had to make the humiliating journey to Hermitage Castle in wildest Liddesdale, not in any punitive role but rather with pleas to the devil-may-care Bothwell to be more discreet and to send an apology to Elizabeth – to both of which requests the other had laughed him to scorn. This had not been a pilgrimage on which the Master of Gray had found it convenient to accompany the Viceroy.

Huntly's rumoured new rising had fortunately not materialised; indeed, whether out of a suitable repentance or for some less creditable reason of his own, the Gordon had actually sent south his wife, Ludovick's sister Henrietta, to assist in the royal welcome – she was, of course, officially the Queen's principal Lady-in-Waiting.

The ladies in the roped-off area in front of the Council House built by the King's grandmother, the Queen-Regent Mary of Guise, made a laughing, chattering throng, as eye-catching and ear-catching as an aviary of tropical birds. It was perhaps amusingly appropriate, as certain of the gentlemen did not fail to point out, that this concourse of youth and beauty should be assembled before this especial house, for as it happened, no fewer than fourteen of the seventeen involved were in fact granddaughters of the said Mary of Guise's much respected spouse, King James Fifth – though not of her own.

Save for Mary Gray and two others, all were Stewarts, mainly daughters of illegitimate sons of that puissant prince. Queen Anne at least should not be able to complain about the lowly origins of her maidens, other than one.

The Lady Marie, Mistress of Gray at twenty-seven, was the oldest of them – she was not actually a member of the Queen's household, but was there to keep the others in order, since the limp and apathetic Countess of Huntly certainly would not be able to control all King James's other high-spirited cousins. After Marie, the oldest would be seventeen – and despite their status as Maids of Honour, knowledgeable gentlemen declared that there was not a virgin amongst them. Though, to be sure, there was room for error here, for undoubtedly they included Mary Gray in this category, as Ludovick's mistress, and were mistaken.

Patrick Gray brought to the enclosure a flushed small stout man, Nichol Edward, Lord Provost of Edinburgh, to report to the Duke of Lennox that despite stringent orders the Palace of Holyroodhouse was not ready for the royal couple, workmen having accidentally set fire to the anteroom of the royal bed-chamber. These dire tidings were just being assimilated when a shouting and clattering from up the Tolbooth Wynd turned all heads. Forging down through the narrow crowded street came a mounted cavalcade at the trot, steel jacked and morioned retainers laying about them vigorously with the flats of long swords, careless of who fell and who might be trampled beneath their horses' hooves. In the centre, a great banner streamed in the breeze.

'Sink me!' Patrick said, narrowing his eyes. 'I think that I recognise those colours. All too many quarter the royal arms of Scotland with a bend-sinister – but only one adds to them the white chevron on red of Hepburn!'

'Bothwell!' the Duke gasped. 'That man – here!'

The horsemen came prancing right to the enclosure, only pulling up when their foam-flecked mounts were directly against the rope barrier itself – their leader indeed jerking back his great roan so vigorously to its haunches that it reared pawing forefeet right above the heads of some of the alarmed young women, who pressed back screaming. Its rider laughed mockingly.

'I have been seeking you, my lord Duke,' he cried. 'I find you choose better company than I gave you credit for!' And he ran a scurrilous eye over the shrinking ranks of the ladies.

Lennox glowered at him, uncertainly. 'I . . . I bid you welcome, my lord of Bothwell,' he got out, reluctantly. 'I did not expect you.' Ludovick was little of the diplomat. He looked askance at the large contingent of Hepburn and Home lairds jostling behind the other, all clad for battle it seemed rather than for a royal reception, not to mention the fifty or so shaggy wild-looking moss-troopers who escorted them.

'My lord of Bothwell's known love and esteem for the King's Grace has brought him here hot-foot, Vicky,' Patrick said, easily, at his side. 'It could not be otherwise.'

'Ha, Master of Gray – whose friend are you today?' Bothwell asked coolly. 'On my soul, it will repay a man to know such a thing, any day of the year!'

'Why, my lord – your friend, of course. And the King's And, naturally, my lord Duke's. Indeed, I cannot for the life of me think of any that I would have as unfriend this May day . . . save only, of course, the King's enemies, who must always be mine!'

'Ha?' That was part-question, part-snort, as Bothwell searched Patrick's face. He threw himself down from his horse, tossing the reins to his banner-bearer. He was a tall, powerful young man, not yet thirty, with a high complexion, sandy hair and eyebrows, and vividly blue unquiet eyes – with little or nothing of the Stewart about him, although his father had been one more of James Fifth's bastard brood who had married the sister of the previous and notorious Bothwell, Mary the Queen's third husband. Two half-sisters of his were amongst the Maids of Honour, but he spared them no glance. He was dressed in his habitual steel and leather. 'I saw James's ships from St. Abb's Head, this morning, and came apace. In lieu of other business!' He jerked a laugh. 'I seem to have outpaced the ships!'

'Aye. These winds have been much against them. But they are close now. Your leal fervour, my lord, must be notably hot to bring you thus far so fast!'

The Earl hooted rudely. 'Say that I cannot delay to set eyes on the wench who has cheated me out of Dunfermline Abbey!'

he said, making no attempt to lower his strong, throaty voice.

The Master of Gray could not wholly repress his start. Closely he eyed the other, however suddenly expressionless his handsome features. 'Indeed, my lord? You . . . you know, then?'

'Aye. A letter was writ to me. Unsigned. It was not from you? The courier came from Dundee. I esteemed it from Broughty.'

'Is that so? M'mmm. Many people have been dwelling thereabouts, of late,' the Master said slowly. His glance slid from Lennox to flicker over the company at large.

'The men in the watchtower declare the King's ships just off the harbour-mouth,' a new voice announced. The high buildings that ringed the wharfside made it impossible to see seawards from the inner harbour.

'Lord – my good cousin Moray!' Bothwell exclaimed turning. 'Here's more joy!'

The Earl of Moray eyed him coldly. They were indeed cousins, like so many others present, but there was no love lost between them.

'Have your cannons to fire, then, Master Provost,' Patrick ordered the little stout man. 'Wait no longer.'

'But, sir – my lord,' Edinburgh's representative wailed. 'What o' the palace? What o' Holyroodhouse?' He was wringing plump hands. 'His Grace cannot go there.'

'Then he must needs go somewhere else, man. Lodge him here in Leith, meantime. In the Citadel, in the King's-work. That will suit. It is his own house. Where the Duke was going to lodge some of his new Danish friends. Have men array it suitably for the King and Queen. Bring more tapestries, linen, napery. See you to it . . .'

The Lord Provost hurried away, unhappily, while Moray, who was acting Captain of the King's Guard, perforce changed his arrangements for escorting the royal procession up to Edinburgh.

Bothwell cast his hot eye over the assembled women judiciously, an undoubted expert. It did not take him long to single out Mary Gray, and to inflict upon her a fleeringly comprehensive inspection and summing up, despite the frowns of the Duke of Lennox who moved closer. Mary met his gaze calmly,

255

almost interestedly, making her own assessment. There was a tittering and stirring amongst the throng of young women. Though not handsome like Moray, Bothwell had his own magnetism, sheer blatant and aggressive masculinity, his reputation contributing not a little.

Patrick, his own eyes busy, spoke pleasantly, conversationally. 'My lord, it is devilish crowded along this street and pierhead, is it not? Might I suggest to you to move your, h'm, host some other where?'

'You might not!' the other returned, casually, without so much as raising his glance from Mary Gray.

Patrick's voice did not change its tone. 'Nevertheless, my lord, you would probably find it convenient to do so presently. The pilot will bring his Grace's vessel exactly opposite here, and there is to be some ceremonial and spectacle. Room will be required for it. The provosts and bailies of the city, and the good gentry of the Kirk will be coming . . . '

'Foul fall you – d'you expect me, Bothwell, to stand aside for such rabble?'

'Not so – not *you*, my lord, naturally. I hope that you will remain here to greet their Graces, with the Duke and myself. It is only your, er, line of battle. I fear that there will be no room for . . . '

'There is room for me and mine wherever I choose to stand in this realm, fellow!' the Earl shouted. 'Remember it. I'll not be pushed aside by any simpering, jumped-up wardrobe-master, d'you hear? By God's eyes, I will not!'

Patrick's beautiful face went as still and set as marble, and a sort of glaze came over those lustrous eyes. He did not speak.

A shudder went through Mary Gray as she looked at him, and she bit her lip. Unknown to herself her fingers dug deeply into Ludovick's arm.

Perhaps that young man was urged on thereby. 'Then be so by me, my lord,' he said, into the immediate hush, bluntly. 'I bid you move your bullyrooks.'

'Christ God!' Bothwell ejaculated, fist dropping to his sword-hilt. 'French puppy! Spawn of a boot-licking jacka-napes . . . !'

The rest was drowned in the crash of cannonry, as from the Citadel a few hundred yards away along the waterfront the royal salute thundered out. Bothwell was left mouthing incomprehensibly.

None could have continued the dispute if they would, by any other means than actual blows. Most of the cannon from Edinburgh Castle had been brought down for the occasion, and the concussion in the confined space of Leith's tightly-packed tall tenements, was deafening and continuous. Everywhere men as well as women put their fingers in their ears, grimacing.

The gunfire achieved what Patrick and Ludovick had failed to do. The horses of Bothwell's cavalcade reared and plunged and sidled at the din, some backing almost over the edge of the pier and into the river. As the bombilation maintained with no sign of diminishment, the horsemen, for their own safety's sake, with one accord began to urge and guide their excited mounts away back up the crowded street, to put more distance between themselves and the source of the clangour. Angrily, the Earl looked after them.

Against this ear-shattering racket the final preparations to receive the happy monarch went forward somewhat incoherently. A number of black-robed divines came to take up a prominent position near the colourful band of young women, whom they did not fail to examine with every sign of disapprobation. The bailies and guild representatives of Edinburgh moved self-consciously into their appointed places, the nobility and gentry only grudgingly giving them passage. A small boy dressed, it was calculated, as an angel, was pushed by his red-faced mother into the very forefront of the assembly and there abandoned to the embarrassed care of one of the city halberdiers; his open-mouthed crying fortunately could not be heard for the gunfire, and the more copiously he wept the tighter his dignified guardian gripped him – while appearing not so much as to be aware of his humiliating presence. A garlanded doorway in a timber frame was brought by some workmen, who set it upon the cobbles of the pier – when no sooner were they gone than it blew down in the gusty wind. Everybody eyed it askance, but it seemed to be nobody's business to set it up again – certainly not that of the ministers of Christ's Kirk, nor yet that of the city fathers. Bonfires were lit at strategic points in the vicinity; unfortunately the nearest one, at the harbour head to the west, appeared to be made of notably damp combustibles and produced little of flame, sent down vast clouds of thick smoke on the prevailing wind, to set the entire company coughing and mopping their eyes. As the fumes grew worse rather than abating, Patrick gave orders for the source thereof to be kicked bodily into the harbour.

'It is ever thus with King Jamie,' he shouted in his wife's ear. 'Heaven seldom smiles upon its ally, Christ's Viceregent!'

In the midst of all this, the mast-tops of a tall ship appeared above the lofty buildings seawards, from which the Royal Standard of Scotland streamed in the wind. Unfortunately, however, wait as the company would, the said masts seemed to draw no nearer. Eventually the agitated harbourmaster came hurrying to inform the Duke of Lennox that the King's ship had got as far as the outer harbour but by no means could make further progress against a direct head-wind, with no room to tack, into the inner harbour. Indeed she was dropping an anchor to keep her from being driven against the breakwater to seaward. What should he do? Should he launch small boats and bring off the royal party?

Ludovick looked unhappy. 'That will never do,' he declared. 'With the tide low, like this, it would mean His Grace climbing up a rope ladder to the pier! Twenty feet of it! And the Queen, too! No, no. Lord, that would never do!'

At his ear Patrick actually laughed. 'Is this not a problem for the Lord High Admiral?' he suggested, against the din. And he gestured at Bothwell, who still stood a little way apart.

That indeed was one of Bothwell's many offices – though one titular rather than military, even if productive of considerable revenues. When the situation was explained to him, he glared balefully at all concerned, but proffered no proposals.

'Might I suggest, my lord,' the Master shouted at length, 'that this is where all your horsemen could prove their worth? Ropes from the ship, and towed by teams of horses, would surely bring your liege lord safely into his own land!'

Plucking his small sandy beard, the Earl eyed him doubtfully, wordless.

'I see no other way. Do you, my lord Admiral?'

Cursing, Bothwell stamped off to collect his men.

So, after a prolonged and embarrassing delay, the royal

flagship, sails down, was warped into the inner harbour of
Leith and alongside the pier, at the tails of some two score
horses, a proceeding that set at least the vulgar populace of the
port hooting with hilarity. As the vessel drew jerkily near, James
could be seen standing on the high poop deck, in gorgeous
array of gold and purple, alternatively wringing his hands,
shaking a clenched fist apparently at heaven, and clutching his
very high hat to keep it from being blown off. About him stood
a number of gentlemen, but no ladies.

The cannonade redoubled its fury.

When at length the ship lay safely alongside the pier, and
gangways were run out, the Duke, Sir Robert Melville acting
Chancellor, and the Earl of Moray, were to go aboard to escort
the royal couple ashore. But now all Bothwell's Borderers were
milling about with their horses, disengaging them from their
ropes, laughing uproariously, pushing aside ministers, bailies
and all. The high officers of state seeking to thread their way
through this mêlée, were inevitably delayed. The monarch
himself, however, did not appear to find this awkward, and in
fact came hurrying ashore himself the moment the gangway
from his poop was down, apparently anxious only to get off the
vessel. A few shambling paces on to the pier indeed, and he
sank down clumsily on hands and knees, before thousands of
astounded eyes, apparently to kiss the cobblestones.

Lennox hastened forward to raise him up, Patrick only a few
paces behind. James fell on the Duke's neck, babbling inco-
herencies that were quite lost in the banging of guns. He drew
back a little, to point upwards and vaguely westwards, and to
shake his fist again, and then once more to fall upon his cousin,
stroking his face.

'Och, Vicky, Vicky!' he yelled. 'Out o' the jaws o' death!
Och, it's good to see you. He near had me – aye, he near had
me, I tell you! But I beat him! I beat him, Vicky!'

'Eh . . . ? Yes, Sire,' Lennox said, seeking to disentangle
himself, much embarrassed. 'Who . . . ? Beat who, Sire?'

'Satan, man – Satan. Auld Hornie, himsel'. He's been
clutching at me, all the way.'

'Satan . . . ?'

'Your Grace,' Patrick shouted into the King's other large
ear. 'The Queen?'

259

James started, and whirled round. 'Eh . . . ? What's that? Dinna do that, I tell you! Och, it's you, Patrick man?'

'Yes. The Queen, Your Grace. Er . . . welcome. But – we wait to welcome the new Queen. Your own royal commands . . . '

'Ooh, aye – Anne!' James, in his highly excited state, had obviously completely forgotten his wife. Abruptly he turned, and pushing unceremoniously past certain of his train who were in process of following him ashore, hurried back on board.

A cluster of women were now to be seen standing amidships, with the spare and sombre, well-known figure of Chancellor Maitland in attendance. James grabbed quite the smallest person in the group by a hand, and came back with her, almost at a trot.

Even Patrick was taken aback at the extraordinary appearance of youthfulness of the new consort. Although now fifteen, and only a little more than a year younger than Mary Gray, she looked still a child. Padded and flounced as she was, in the height of fashion, her elaborate toilet only served to emphasise the slim immaturity of the body it covered. Her reddish-brown hair, dressed to stand high above her head, was much blown about by the wind. Nevertheless, as they came off the gangway, she contrived to look considerably more dignified than did her lord.

As the royal couple set foot on the pier, Ludovick, who had rehearsed all this thoroughly, bowed deeply, all the other men following suit, while the women sank low. Musicians were to strike up now – but whether they did or no was impossible to tell, in the continuing contributions of the cannoneers. Moray, as Captain of the Guard, gestured angrily but eloquently at one of his underlings to go and silence these enthusiasts.

James who, despite his written orders on the subject, patently had done no rehearsing himself, was for hurrying on still further, when most evidently his bride restrained him. They stood together on the pier, he fidgeting, she small head held high, while, following the example of the Lord Chamberlain, the great company raised itself slowly erect once more.

Precedence now fell to be strictly observed. As Bothwell came strolling up, Ludovick slipped forward to be presented first the new Queen, by James himself so that he in turn could present others. Bothwell, close behind, ignored his jerky presentation and introduced himself arrogantly, coolly subjecting Anne to something not very different from his normal assessing scrutiny of the other sex, evidently without much satisfaction, James looking on with a strange mixture of pride and apprehension, clutching his hat. There was no occasion for converse.

Moray followed on, and then the great officers of state in turn, followed by many of the King's surviving illegitimate uncles led by Orkney, Marie's father. Then the senior nobility. The Countess of Huntly was the first woman to be presented. In this process, the Master of Gray came low on the list.

Mary Gray, from her position in the enclosure, watched the young Queen. A child, physically, she might be, but there was little else childish about her. She was self-assured, sharp-eyed, with a determined small chin and tight mouth. With no pretensions to beauty, she had a certain prettiness, and she bore herself well.

The Lord Provost was presented, the leaders of the Kirk, a clutch of bishops including Mary's grandfather of St Boswells, and then a long queue of lesser nobility and lairds. In the midst of it all, the cannonade stopped suddenly – to be succeeded by an uncomfortable and bemused silence.

Out of the shuffling, murmurings and whisperings, it was Patrick Gray's musical voice that was upraised. 'God save the Queen!' he called.

Raggedly at first, but steadying and strengthening, the chant was taken up. 'God Save the Queen! God save the Queen!' it rang out, the echoes being thrown back and forth amongst the tall tenements.

James nodded, smirked and rubbed his hands – and then began to pluck his lip and frown, as it continued. Perhaps he felt that an admixture of appeals to the Deity on behalf of the King also would have been seemly. He held up his hand.

Slowly the chanting died away.

'Aye,' he said, wagging his head. 'Just so. I'ph'mmm. Aye – we're glad to be hame. It has been a sair trauchle. The winds! The storms! The waves! Och, Satan opened his ill maw wide, wide to engulf us quite. Aye, he did his worst. But we are delivered out o' his clutches. Like blessed Peter, Galilee didna close ower us . . . '

Unfortunately, even at the best of times, James was no clear and resounding speaker. He was apt to mumble and splutter. In the open air, against three parts of a gale, and much moved about the dangers he had escaped, his eloquence was lost on all but those in his close proximity. Quickly, as a result, murmuring and chatter grew amongst the great company, until not even those nearest could hear a word. James appeared not to notice, until the young woman at his side perked his sleeve sharply, frowning, and his mouthings died away.

Patrick managed to catch the eye of one of the resplendently-clad herald trumpeters attached to the Lord Lyon King of Arms, and gestured to him. That man nudged his companion, and together they blew a shrilling fanfare.

This was the signal for Lennox to make a speech of welcome on behalf of the Privy Council. He had, however, forgotten every word of it, and the phrase or two of Danish, especially memorised, had quite gone.

'We . . . er, bid you welcome, Sire! And Your Grace, Madam. Welcome! To your realm,' he said, haltingly, into the succeeding silence. 'Very welcome.' He stopped, unable to think of anything else to say. The bawling of the small and almost naked boy shivering in the wind as an angel, came to his rescue. 'Provost!' he called. 'My Lord Provost!' He pointed at the infant.

Edinburgh's civic chief strutted forward, took the child from the halberdier who had clutched him manfully all this time, and dragged him towards the royal couple. Nearly there, he drew from beneath his robes of office a golden orb. This he thrust upon the youngster, before pushing him bodily towards the Queen.

The angel, intrigued by the round shining thing, stopped crying and walking both, and began to try to open it, turning it this way and that.

Smilingly Anne stepped forward, hand outstretched. The child shrank back, clutching his prize to him. Prettily the Queen coaxed him, to no effect. James, glowering blackly, pointed a peremptory royal finger, and then stamped his foot hard. The celestial messenger dropped his gift in fright, and burst once more into wailing. The orb burst also, on the cobblestones, spilling out a handsome necklace of wrought gold links inset with pearls and emeralds.

Hurriedly before any of his courtiers could reach the spot, James himself stooped down to pick up the jewellery. Carefully he examined it, peering at the craftsmanship, holding up the stones to the light, assessing its worth – until Anne reached over and quite sharply twitched it out of his hands. She raised it to her young neck, squinting down at it with proprietorial satisfaction, and held it so. A man stepped out from the group of high personages close by, moving in front of Maitland the Chancellor and behind the Queen. He put out his hands to take the ends of the necklace from her fingers, and fastened them together deftly at the back of her slender neck. She turned to him quickly, surprised. It was the handsome Earl of Moray. Anne smiled warmly.

He bowed, but not low.

'So!' Patrick, further back, observed to Marie. 'Here is both an allegory and a lesson to be learned, I think!'

Before there could be any more unseemly and unprofitable time-wasting, the Kirk took charge. It had, indeed, been very patient. Andrew Melville, Principal of Glasgow University and fiery pillar of godly reform, a massive sombre figure with voluminous black Geneva gown and white bands flapping about him, stepped forth to announce in a rasping but powerful voice that had no difficulty in competing with wind or chatter, that Christ's true Kirk, recognising well the sins and follies that so readily beset those in high place – particularly women – greeted Christ's humble vassal James and the woman Anne whom he had brought back from a land where the truth was perhaps less firmly established than in this realm of Scotland, and prayed God that both might be delivered from the temptations to which they were all too vulnerably exposed, in fleshly lusts, carnal concupiscence, heretical doctrine, Popish idolatry, worldly converse and the curse of evil company. At this last, Master Melville glared round him at practically everyone present, especially the bishops. In token of which, he went on, he would now, in the Kirk's name, deliver an address of welcome.

Tugging at a forked beard, and fixing Anne with a fierce eye, he raised his voice to a higher pitch. Forceful, clear, vigorous, his sonorous periods rang out, cleaving the rushing air, throbbing in all ears. There could be no more doubting of the eloquence than the clarity – only, unfortunately for some, the said periods were entirely in Latin. Excellent Latin, needless to say, if delivered in a harsh Fife accent – all two hundred stanzas of it, a feast, a banquet of worth, edification and warning.

James paid due, indeed, appreciative attention to it all. Anne, whose education, is to be feared, had been neglected, did the epic performance less than justice, her sharp little eyes fairly soon beginning to wander. The Kirk did not fail to note, especially when more than once she yawned.

A right and proper atmosphere having thus been introduced, Andrew Melville launched into prayer. This was powerful stuff which could not fail to have a marked effect on his Maker, however incomprehensible it might be to most of the visitors. The real kernel and pith of the matter was still to come, however. With a wave of his hand, Melville summoned forward Master Patrick Galloway to preach the sermon.

Master Galloway, a noted divine, excelled himself, rising to the occasion untrammelled by notes or hour-glass, in an ever-mounting crescendo. His theme was the necessity of the obedience of wives to their husbands, and obedience of husband's to Christ's Kirk. After half-an-hour of it, Bothwell, who had been carrying on a loud-voiced conversation with some of his henchmen, abandoned the struggle, and with hooted laughter marched from the scene, followed by most of his party – and, sad to relate, not a few others who suddenly found pressing business elsewhere and took this opportunity to attend to it. After an hour, much of the crowd had melted away. Mary Gray, noting how pale the Queen looked, slipped under the rope-barrier, picked up a small drum that one of the city drummers had set down, and moved forward with it, braving the frowns of nearby clerics, to the group of wilting notables nearest the royal couple. There she handed it to Moray, whispering in his ear. The Earl, nodding, took it and carrying it over to Anne, threw his short velvet cloak over it, and motioned for her to sit. Thankfully the Queen sank down on it, eyed sidelong by her husband, who pulled at his ear, uncertain it seemed whether to be envious or scandalised.

Master Galloway thundered on.

At last it was over. There was to have been an elevating ceremony of Faith, Hope and Charity beckoning the King and Queen through the garlanded doorway to receive the keys of the city from the Lord Provost, but by unspoken consent – and since they would not in fact be going to Edinburgh today, after all – this was dropped meantime. With most of those who had been unable to escape hitherto rushing off incontinent for relief and refreshment to Leith's numerous taverns, it seemed that the royal welcome was completed. It but remained for the Master of the Wardrobe to acquaint the King of the unfortunate fire at Holyroodhouse and the consequence that the royal quarters would not be ready for Their Graces for a day or two. The King's-work, here in Leith, however, was prepared . . .

James threw up his hands. 'Fire!' he cried. 'Flames! Here, too! Even here he rages against me! In my own realm, my own house! He's aye clawing at me, clutching . . . '

'It was but some careless workmen, Sire . . . '

'It was Satan! It's aye Satan, I tell you. Reaching out for me. But he'll no' have me – God Almighty is my ally. The powers o' darkness winna triumph ower the Lord's Anointed!'

'Er . . . quite. Exactly, Your Grace. But, the Queen – she must be very tired. Her ladies await her, at the King's-work. Next to the Citadel. Just along the waterfront. Refreshment is there, Sire . . . '

'Aye, refreshment. Refreshment for the battle!' James muttered. 'Come, Annie – come you.'

But already the Queen had started out, on the arm of the Earl of Moray.

Chapter Thirteen

IT did not take Scotland long to discover that her new-married monarch had something on his mind more pressing than the cosy joys of matrimony. He had been in a strangely distraught state before ever he set sail for Denmark; he returned, with his bride, even more preoccupied – though no longer distraught. Whether it was marriage that had done it, the months of absence from his own land, or discussions with curious foreign authorities, is not to be known – but he came back a man with a mission. He was going to get to grips with Satan, without delay.

Always James had been interested in and much aware of the supernatural. His lonely parentless childhood had been beset by devils, ogres and apparitions, all malevolent – many of them in the guise of steel-clad, hard-faced grasping lords. George Buchanan, his stern tutor and taskmaster, had been a student of demonology. The ministers of the Kirk who had borne heavily upon him all his days, were much concerned with the dark powers of evil. Now was the reckoning.

Despite all the other matters which clamoured for his attention, the King was much closeted in small dusty rooms, first in Leith and then in his own quarters at Holyroodhouse, with books, parchments, folios, on abstruse and difficult subjects such as necromancy, sorcery, Black Magic, wizardry, astrology and the like. No longer did he ink his fingers with much writing of poetry; now he was inditing more serious stuff. It was difficult for his officers and ministers to get in at him in these locked sanctums – and there was so much to be done; the innumerable matters of state that had had to be held over, awaiting the monarch's return; deputations to be received from all over the land; the due entertainment of the great company of distinguished foreigners, Danes in especial, who had come over with Anne; most important of all, the Queen's Coronation. James expended only grudging attention on all these.

The very night before the Coronation, indeed, with many of the details still to be arranged, Patrick Gray, responsible as Master of the Wardrobe for much of the ceremonial, prevailed on the Duke of Lennox to gain him the King's presence, somehow. Ludovick was in fact almost the only person for whom James would open his locked doors.

After much knocking and a certain amount of shouted re-assurance, the King was persuaded to draw the bolts of his study in the south-west drum-tower of the palace, and peer round.

'What's to do now, Vicky?' he demanded querulously. 'Can you no' see I'm busy? And who's yon you've got there wi' you, man?'

'It is the Master of Gray, Sire. He has urgent matters for your attention. Regarding tomorrow's crowning.'

'Och, him! Patrick's aye at something . . .'

'Aye, Sire – but since he found the money to pay for this Coronation, he should be heard, should he not?'

'Humph! I'ph'mmm. Well . . .' Grumbling, James let them in, and quickly shot the bolts again. 'He got a third part o' the gold himsel', did he no'? A thousand pounds! Bonnie payment for a' he did . . .'

'Was that not in lieu of his claim for Dunfermline Abbey?' the younger man asked bluntly.

'Tut, man . . .'

'Your Grace's generosity was notable,' Patrick intervened smoothly. 'I have no complaints. The difficulties now are otherwise. The most serious is the problem of the Queen's anointing. The Kirk is proving . . . obdurate.'

'There's nae problem in it, Patrick,' James answered testily. 'I have given my royal commands. The Kirk has but to carry them out in a seemly fashion. Waesucks – must I do their work for them? I hae other work o' my ain, 'fore God! That only I, the Lord's Anointed, can accomplish.' He pointed a stained finger at the tables littered with parchments and books. 'Have I no' plenty on my hands, man?'

Lennox looked askance at the disarray of papers. 'Inky work, Sire, it would seem! Is such not for clerks . . . ?'

'Clerks!' James all but squeaked in indignation. 'Could clerks wrestle wi' the Devil? Could clerks bind Satan in his ain coils?'

'Lord, James – are you drowning Satan in ink? Choking him with dust . . . ?'

'Dinna scoff, Vicky Stuart – dinna scoff! I'll no' be scoffed at, d'you hear? Belike he'll turn his assault on you, man, as well as me. I am binding Satan wi' words, see you – potent and mighty words. In the beginning was the word, mind. I, James, by the Grace o' God, am writing a book!'

His visitors stared from the King to each other and back again.

Apparently encouraged by the impression he had made, James nodded vigorously. 'A book. A great and notable work. On the wicked wiles o' Satan and his black kingdom. A book to undermine his ill powers and reveal his evil ways.'

'You . . . ?' Lennox swallowed. 'How may you do that, James? What even the Pope of Rome cannot do.'

'H'rr'mm,' Patrick coughed warningly.

'The Pope!' That was a snort. 'The Pope's ower near allied to the Devil himsel' to do any such thing! Forby, he hasna my advantages, as the Lord's Anointed. I am Satan's especial foe, see you – and his ways are revealed to me.'

'But . . . '

'You learned this in Denmark, Sire?' Patrick asked.

'I jaloused it before I ever went, man. You'll mind a' the storms that prevented my Annie frae coming to me? Yon was Satan's work. He wouldna hae me married and my royal line strengthened against him. A' the way yonder my ships were sore assailed. I was near the gates o' Hell. But I won ower. In yon Denmark, the winds dropped and the storms died. He couldna reach me there. A' winter there was scarce a breeze. But when I set sail again, the hounds o' Hell were quick after me, God kens! That very day the storms rose. Day and night the seas clawed at me. The deep opened its maw to engulf me. We were sucked in and spewed out again. Like yon Jonah. But I wrestled. I wrestled wi' Satan in person – aye, and wi' God too, in prayer. Notable prayer. And so we won back to this my realm. As an ill grudge, he set his flames to this house o' mine, but . . . but . . . ' Panting with his vehemence, the King paused for very breath.

Embarrassed, Ludovick looked at the floor. Patrick stroked his chin.

'And if you are convinced, Sire, that these unseasonable storms are the Devil's work, raised expressly against your person,' he said, 'how do you seek to bind him by writing a book?'

'Och, Patrick – where are your wits? You, of a' men, should see it. The Devil thrives in darkness, ignorance. He canna abide the light. The word is light. Do the Scriptures no' say so? The Good Book is the light that lightens the world. *My* book shall lighten Satan's ain world, Hell itsel'. To his undoing.'

'H'mmm. A lofty ambition, Your Grace. A Homeric task, indeed.'

'Do I not ken it, man? That is why I labour at it, day and night, thus – why I shouldna be disturbed wi' lesser things. I must mysel' read a' that's written. And I must test what I read. Try it. Aye, there will need to be a deal o' testing. I shall require your aid, belike . . . '

'Testing, Sire? What mean you by testing?'

'Ha – wait, Patrick man! Wait! You shall see. In good time. Aye, a' my realm shall see Satan tested. But no' yet. I'm no' ready yet. There's that much to do.'

'But . . . can you reach the Devil, to test him?'

'Satan works through men, Patrick. And women. As well as in winds and storms. Them I can reach.' James rubbed his inky hands, and actually chuckled. 'Ooh, aye – I can reach them.'

The Master of Gray searched his monarch's face intently, and said nothing.

'There is much to do at the Coronation also, Sire,' Lennox reminded. 'And on the morrow. This matter of the anointing. As Chamberlain, I must know . . . '

'Tcha! I told you – I have given my commands.'

'Unfortunately, Your Grace, the Kirk has other views,' Patrick pointed out.

'It canna. It canna. I am the head o' Christ's Kirk.'

'Yet the Kirk says that anointing with oil is a Popish practice. An idolatrous vanity. Master Robert Bruce says that he will not be a party to it.'

James gulped and giggled. 'He'll no' . . . ? He'll no' . . . ? Vanity? Idolatrous – the royal anointing! Guidsakes – is it no' what makes the monarch different frae other men? I am the Lord's viceregent – His Anointed. No subject will deny the anointing oil to my Queen!'

'Master Bruce says that he will, Sire.'

'Then Master Bruce is acting for Satan, no' Christ. Aye, that's it. Satan again, it is! He'd deny my Annie her royal due, and so hae my seed less than kingly. For his ain ends. Och, I ken him. He's but using Bruce. Tell you Master Bruce that he will anoint my Queen wi' oil, or I'll hae one o' the bishops to do it! That will scunner him! Or I could do it mysel'. Who is mair fitted to transmit the blessed unction than I who am already anointed? Tell me that.' James was trembling with emotion.

'Very well, Sire. It shall be as you say. Then there is the matter of where the bishops shall stand. And in what precedence. The Kirk would not have them in the ceremony, at all. It would put them after the last of the presbyters . . .'

'Soul o' God!' the King cried. 'Away wi' you! Hae them where you will. I'll no' be embroiled, d'you hear? Let them fight it out for themsel's. I hae God's work to see to – no' man's pride and folly. Away, now. Out wi' you both. I'll hae no more o' it. This audience is closed. Aye, closed.'

Patrick and Ludovick bowed themselves to the door, being all but pushed through it in the process. The latter eyed his companion ruefully.

'Heaven save us – do you think he's parted from his wits entirely?' he demanded.

Patrick took a little while to answer, as they went down the winding stairs. He was looking very thoughtful. 'I do not know, Vicky,' he said. 'It may be so – but the situation is not as it was, mind. He is married. Has been for six months. The Queen may well be with child even now – child herself as she is. She may soon produce an undoubted heir to the throne. So what we had in mind before will no longer serve . . .'

'What *you* had in mind,' the Duke pointed out.

The Master ignored him. 'It is . . . interesting. It behoves us to think carefully. Most carefully.'

'To what end?'

'Why – to the weal and benefit of the realm, Vicky. And us all. What else?' The other smiled his sweetest. 'You heard him. Testing, he said – trying. He would need our aid, he said. Know you any of the Devil's spawn to test and try, Vicky?'

Mary Gray, with Jean Stewart and Katherine Lindsay, stood or knelt around the thin white naked figure of Queen Anne, sponging and wiping and dabbing. Still in their fine gowns that they had worn for the Coronation ceremony, Mary's borrowed from the royal wardrobe, they busied themselves amongst the steam from the cauldrons of hot water, exclaiming, twittering consolations to their mistress.

Anne stood stiffly, on a pile of cloths and towelling, in the circular tower-room off the royal bedchamber which she was

270

calling her boudoir – the room indeed directly below the King's study in the drum-tower. Pale, her lips tight, she was breathing hard – but even so her tiny budding bosom scarcely stirred. From most aspects, naked, she might have been a boy, so unformed in womanliness was her slender body. But her expression was neither childish nor lacking in definition. Her cold anger was remarkable in its still intensity. She answered nothing to her ladies' commiserations.

Mary reached for a new cloth, and hotter water. The oil was very hard to lift. It seemed to impregnate the very skin, as it had done the clothing. It seemed, also, to be of a singularly sticky and viscous consistency, and of a penetrating and unlovely smell.

It would be hard to say who had won the battle of the anointing oil. Master Robert Bruce, of Edinburgh's High Kirk of St. Giles, faced with the King's furious commands and threats, and with bishops only too anxious to do the work for him, had at length consented, at the climax of the Coronation ceremony in the Abbey, to anoint with oil. But when the Countess of Mar, James's sour old foster-mother, had somewhat opened the neck of the Queen's gown for the application, Bruce had roughly jerked the opening wide, to bare her pathetic padded bosom, and therein emptied the entire ampulla of oil. Thus, soaked and humiliated, Anne had had to wait through a further two hours of ceremonial, including another sermon, with the oil running down her body to her very feet, and ruining the splendid jewel-sewn dress and all below it.

A loud and impatient knocking sounded at the locked door on the other side of the bedchamber. Alarmed, the three young women looked from their naked mistress to each other. Anne gave no sign, made no move. Lady Jean giggled.

'The door, Your Grace . . . ?' she began. She was interrupted by renewed banging.

'Open!' the King's well-known thick voice cried. 'Annie – it is I. James. Your Jamie. Open, I say.'

The Queen shrugged thin shoulders. 'Let him in,' she said, in her stilted foreign accent.

Uncertainly the Lady Katherine went to open the further

271

door, flushing, whilst Mary reached for a robe to put round her mistress.

Impatiently Anne shook it off. 'Finish your work,' she directed shortly.

Jamie came pushing in, a paper in his hand. At sight of his unclothed wife amidst the steam, he halted, peered sidelong, and leered. 'Hech, hech,' he chuckled. 'Are you no' right bonnie that way! Aye, bonnie. I . . . I dinna like fat women.' He glanced over at his voluptuous cousin Jean, who sniggered.

'I care not how you like,' Anne said sharply. 'I am insulted. I am made a fool before all. In my country that man would die! He must be punished.'

'Houts, lass – wheesht you! Here's no way to take it. You mustna speak that way about ministers o' the Kirk. It was a mishap, just . . . '

'It was no mishap. The man Bruce looked at me, as he did it. He must be punished. And before all.'

'Na, na, Annie – it canna be. You hae it wrong. It was a victory, see you. The Kirk anointed you wi' oil, when it didna want to. What's a wee drappie ower much oil? Better than nane, lassie – better than nane. A victory for the Lord ower Satan. Christ's Kirk brought in . . . '

'I like not your Kirk, James.'

'Wheesht, girl – dinna say it! The Kirk's strong, powerful . . . '

'More powerful than the King?'

'Na, na. But it doesna do to flyte it.'

'As it has flyted me! I think my lord of Moray to be right. He says that it is the Kirk that rules in Scotland, not the King!'

'Waesucks – Moray shouldna hae said that! It's no' right. The King o' Scots is head o' the Kirk. But it's a gowk that smites his ain left hand. The Chancellor and Council is my right hand, see you – but the Kirk is my left. My lord o' Moray should watch his words. Aye, and his ways! I'd thank you to see less o' him, Annie.'

The Queen's sniff, though eloquent, more aptly matched her childish appearance. She looked down. 'Are you finished? Is it all gone?'

'I think it,' Mary told her. 'I see no more.'

'Save on Your Grace's feet,' Jean pointed out. 'There is some even down between your toes!' That was a further cause for giggles.

'That can wait. My clothes.'

'Look, lassie – forget the oil for the nonce. See – I hae a letter here that tells me that a coven o' witches meets at North Berwick. A score o' miles, just down the coast. A right convenient place, eh? For raising storms against me. We passed it in the ship – you'll mind where yon great muckle rock rises frae the sea. The Bass. Ooh, aye – this could be maist significant.'

Anne did not so much as glance at his letter. 'I care naught for your witches,' she exclaimed. 'Is this time for such foolishness? I much more mislike your Kirk.'

'Och, hold your tongue anent the Kirk, Annie, I tell you! I need the Kirk to fight Auld Hornie. These witches and warlocks are belike his earthly instruments. And so his weakness. Satan's soft side, see you. It wouldna do to neglect this.'

But the Queen was not listening. With only her shift on she pushed aside the other clothes being held out for her, and hurried into the main bedchamber adjoining. The Ladies Jean and Katherine, after a glance at the King, followed her. Mary was left to clear up the towels and the steaming pots.

James tut-utted. 'Och, she doesna understand,' he said. 'She's ower young, belike. Mind, she's wiselike too, in some matters. Ooh, aye – she's no fool. But she's no' acquaint yet wi' the powers o' darkness, Mistress Mary. Och, it's no' to be expected.'

'No, Sire. It is not.' Mary looked up. 'Does Your Grace not fear this world of witches and warlocks is an invention? Of idle men? Or mischievous!'

'Guidsakes no, lassie! Witchcraft is a right serious matter. The Devil is never lacking his minions. And he's no' backward in this Scotland o' mine, I warrant! I hae been reading about witchcraft and the like. Plenty – aye, plenty. A' the signs are there. I must root them out.'

Mary bit her lip. 'Witches, I think – true witches – will not be easily found.'

'Hech, but you're wrong Mistress Mary. There's aplenty o' them – and I'll soon hae my hands on them, never fear. There's a worthy bailie o' Tranent laid godly hands on one.' The King glanced at the paper. 'Seton, his name. He's put her to the question, maist properly, and she's given the names o' plenty mair. Waesucks – I'll hae her here and see what *my* questioners can do! Aye, I'll uncover the Devil's work, I promise you.'

She was silent.

'I'll get your . . . I'll get Master Patrick to help me. He has the kind o' wits to pit against Auld Hornie. They hae much in common, eh?' James whinnied a laugh. 'Nae offence, mind, Mistress Mary. Where shall I find the man? He's no' in his quarters.'

'I do not know, Your Grace . . .'

'This new folly of the King's?' the Lady Marie charged her husband. 'All this of witches and spells. Might not this cause much evil? Much cruel wrong?'

'Tell me anything that a king might do that could not?' Patrick answered.

'But this in especial. Anyone may cry witch. Proving innocence may be less easy.'

'No doubt. But that may have its advantages also, I think.'

'For whom, Patrick?'

'For those who would preserve the King's peace, my dear.'

'Preserve . . . ? You do not believe such nonsense? Such bairn's chatter about spells and incantations brewing unchancy storms?'

'The longer I live, my heart, the less I would declare what I believe and what I do not!'

'You do not speak plain, Patrick – so that I mislike it all the more!'

'You are a hard, hard wife to have, Marie Stewart!'

Mary joined in. 'This of North Berwick, Uncle Patrick? Can there be anything of truth in such a tale?'

'There could be. I have heard strange things of North Berwick ere this. That is what we must find out.'

'We . . . ?' his wife echoed.

'Why, yes. His Grace seeks some help in the matter. You would not have me deny my King?'

Marie sighed, and shook her fair head. 'I know you when you are this way, Patrick. There is nothing of worth to be had from you. But this I do know – if you are for aiding James in this foolishness, it is for your own advantage.'

'Say to *our* advantage, my soul's treasure. For are we not one? Doubly one, if such a thing were possible, since we were wed by both Catholic and Reformed rites! And, to be sure, for the advantage of many others also. That is the great comfort of statecraft. I find. Whatever is done must of necessity advantage almost as many as it injures!'

'I desire no advantage at the cost of others' suffering and sorrow, Patrick.'

'Think before you speak, my heart. All that you do, all that you are, all the food you eat, the very threads that you work in your frame there – all come of the sorrow, pain and toil of others. So our Maker made us. It is all a matter of degree. All acts of man have more consequences than one. There is black and white to every picture, to every man. I but seek to choose the lesser evil. The compromise between black and white.' He laughed aloud. 'Not for nothing am I named the Master of Gray!'

'I have heard your philosophy before, Patrick – and have seen where it has brought you.'

'It has brought me back to the King's right hand,' he told her lightly. 'Which minds me – whither I must now go . . . with your permission, ladies.' Bowing deeply, and throwing them a kiss each, he strolled out.

'God help me – why must I so dote on that man!' the Lady Marie exclaimed. 'When he is the most part knave, reprobate, as I know full well.'

'Because he is . . . Patrick Gray,' Mary answered her, gently, briefly, but sufficiently.

Chapter Fourteen

IT was not really dark enough to suit the King. But truly dark nights are rare in Scotland in July. It requires heavy cloud, storm perhaps – the sort of weather with which Satan had plagued James heretofore. Now, of course, night after night, there were clear pale skies and never a breath of wind. Satan's adversary was not surprised.

The royal party was congregated in a deep hollow of the sand-dunes at the west side of the great sandy bay of North Berwick. It was exactly half-past eleven, and the King was much agitated lest they be too late – for these affairs, he asserted, always started at midnight, the witching hour. But Patrick was adamant that they would spoil all by being too soon. The church was on what amounted to an island, a bare peninsula of rock jutting into the sea, offering only the one covered approach. To arrive there before all the coven had assembled would almost certainly end in their discovery, the abandonment of the meeting, and therefore the ruin of their plans.

'There is time yet, Sire,' he pointed out. 'We can cross this bay in but a few minutes. Let them be started.'

'Satan will see us coming, belike, and warn them.'

'If that be so, he could have warned them any time since we left Edinburgh, Your Grace.'

There were five of them in the royal party besides James; Lennox, Sir James Melville of Halhill who was Sir Robert's brother, Master David Lindsay the King's chaplain, and, much overawed by the company he was keeping, Bailie David Seton of Tranent. In a nearby and larger hollow was a score of the royal bodyguard, standing by their horses.

James was actually trembling with excitement. The great round timepiece which he carried shook as he consulted it, unhappily raising it to his ear in case it had stopped.

'Guidsakes, it's an unchancy business this!' he exclaimed, not for the first time. 'I pray the Lord God will see us right! It's His work, see you. Master David – will you gie us another bit prayer, man?'

Nothing loth, the divine obliged, his stern voice a little less confident perhaps than usual. Patrick nudged Ludovick in the ribs, and grimaced.

Their due devotion occupied them until midnight, the Kirk being equally strong on volume as it was on intensity. James was in major agitation, on the horns of the dilemma of offending God or being too late for the Devil, when Lindsay finally panted to a close.

Leaving the escort and horses, with strict instructions as to what to do on seeing certain signals and flares, the six men emerged from their hiding-place. They did not head straight across the open beach, but crept round the side in the shadow of the dunes. It was not dark enough wholly to hide them, but undoubtedly at any distance they would not be noticed. Patrick led the way.

Very soon he had to slow down. James, never very good on his feet, was stumbling and puffing. Melville and Lindsay were both middle-aged and found the soft sand heavy going. The bailie was a lean and hungry-looking character of a sour and sanctimonious expression, but nimble enough.

It was nearer the half than the quarter-past midnight when they reached the rocks wherein nestled the harbour of North Berwick and on which stood its ancient whitewashed kirk. High above the tide it crouched, amongst scattered graves that were scooped out wherever there was sufficient soil in pockets amongst the rocks. The place was silent, seemingly closed up – but from its windows a faint flicker of peculiar light glimmered.

'Up to the east end,' Patrick, who had prospected the site two days previously, whispered. 'Behind the altar.' He coughed, apologetically glancing at Master Lindsay. 'Behind the Communion Table. The windows are low. To see in. Keep away from the door, at the other end.'

They crept up over the rocks and between the hummocks of the graves. They began to hear faint sounds of music coming from the church.

Crouching under the easternmost windows, they gradually raised their heads, to peer inside.

The King's croaking gasp of alarm ought surely to have been heard within. Whatever any of them had been expecting, indeed, the sight that met their gaze was sufficient to catch their breathing – even Patrick Gray's. The church was almost full – fuller no doubt than the minister was accustomed to seeing it on a Sabbath. It was not a large church admittedly; there might however have been one hundred and fifty persons present. Of them all, fully nine out of ten were women. This was entirely obvious, for though otherwise fully clothed, indeed seemingly dressed in their best, their bosoms were wholly bare. It made a quite extraordinary sight, all those breasts, large and small, young and old – a scene most aggressively, intimidatingly female. The few men, in fact, seemed quite pathetically humdrum and feeble, looking painfully normal save that they all wore hats in the pews, and highly self-conscious expressions.

Patrick had the temerity to hush his monarch, who was babbling something incoherent and disgusted about cattle; James never had been much of an admirer of the opposite sex.

The church was lit with a ghostly light, by candles – ghostly in that they burned with a blue flame, the candles themselves being black, not white. Four burned on the Communion Table, where a cross stood upside-down amongst a litter of flagons, obviously empty.

But it was towards the pulpit that all eyes were turned. There, flanked by two more of the black candles, stood an extraordinary apparition. Tall, commanding, clad wholly in black, with a cloak over tight trunks, a black mask over his features, a close-fitting hood over his head out of which rose two small curving horns, this individual was clearly reading aloud from a great book, by the light of the blue flames, although the watchers outside could only hear the murmur of his voice, deep-toned, sepulchral enough to be one of the luminaries of the Kirk.

The King chittered and mouthed. Master Lindsay groaned deep within him, and Lennox crossed himself. Patrick Gray was less affected.

'A pity that we cannot hear,' he mentioned.

However, the reading stopped almost at once, and the congregation rose and proceeded to turn round and round before the speaker, all in their own place, widdershins – that is, contrary to the movement of the sun – in a slow and stately fashion, the women six times, and the men nine, most peculiar. Then a young creature with fair hair, notably well-developed, came forward to the pulpit steps and producing a tiny instrument known as a Jew's-harp, proceeded to thrum and twang a strange and haunting melody with a catchy and mischievous lift at the end of each verse. The entire company sang to this in hymn-like fashion, solemn and dignified – save that at the end of each stanza the women all lifted their skirts high and executed a skittish dancing-step and shook their breasts. The effect was quite original.

Although the chanting was slow and in unison, it was difficult outside to follow the actual words. That it was a travesty of some sacred cantata, however, was apparent. Repetitions of the strange phrase:

> *'Cumer go ye before, cummer go ye,*
> *Gif ye will not go before, cummer let me.'*

kept recurring. It was a pity that no sense could be made of this.

When this was over, the masked individual in the pulpit descended to the floor of the kirk, and moved forward to the table. There, with some ceremony, he removed his tight-fitting black trunks and hose before the assembly. And, lo – his flesh beneath shone as black as the rest of him. He thereupon hoisted himself up on to the table itself, clearing away up-ended cross and bottles to do so, and sat so that his sooty posterior projected a little way over the far or eastern edge, not a dozen feet from the wide eyes of the hidden watchers. Then he waved imperiously towards the congregation.

'Christ God save us!' James gasped. 'See his . . . see his . . . !'

'No tail, you'll note,' Patrick observed, more prosaically, to Ludovick.

Led by the young woman with the Jew's-harp, the company now formed itself into a long and orderly queue, and moved forward in single file.

The plump girl, rosy-cheeked and comely, came up to the table, turned widdershins six times once more before it, and then moving round to the rear, bowed low and kissed the outthrust black bottom. One by one the entire assembly filed up and followed suit.

Master Lindsay began to pray again, with muted fervour.

This lengthy proceeding over, and everybody back in their seats, the satanic Master of ceremonies pulled on his trunks again, and returned to the pulpit. He raised his left hand, made

279

the sign of the crooked cross, and loudly announced the curious text:

'*Many comes to the fair, and buys not all wares.*'

This could even be heard by the watchers without. It was Patrick's turn to groan. He had never been an appreciator of sermons, and obviously one was now to follow.

However, this sermon was mercifully brief, though not loud enough to be intelligible outside. From the deliverer's manner and gesticulations it seemed to be a rousing affair, with perhaps even a certain amount of humour about it. It ended very abruptly, with the preacher suddenly producing a black toad from under his gown, and pointing thereafter towards the door, clearly urging some action upon the company.

His commands were obeyed with alacrity – so much so that the watchers had to go scrambling downhill amongst the rocks in undignified haste in order to avoid being discovered as the congregation came flocking out of the church, the King yelping his fright. Fortunately the crowd did not make for this eastern end of the precincts. Nor did they stream off landwards, however. Splitting up into groups, they went, laughing and joking, towards various parts of the rocky peninsula, spades and mattocks being picked up as they went. Two parties, all women, came uncomfortably near to where the King's party hid, and removing any remaining clothing which might have encumbered their upper parts, set about digging at a couple of graves quite close together amongst the rocks – which, by the darker soil rather than green turf which outlined their oblong mounds, were evidently of recent construction. The women took turns with the spades, and went about their task with vigour and gusto.

It was not long before something long and pale began to appear from the nearest of the graves – obviously a corpse in its white winding-sheet. Amidst skirling laughter and cackles, this trophy was unrolled, no attempt being made to lower voices or smother hilarity – the noise of the waves, of course, would cover the sound at any distance. In only a moment or two the stink had penetrated even the two-score yards to the watchers, that warm summer night.

The stench had no ill effects on the women however. With cries of delight and satisfaction they stretched out the body of what appeared to have been a youngish man not very long buried. Knives materialised from under skirts, and with these, certain of the party set upon the remains, encouraged by the others rapturously. Two went to work at the groin, and others at each of the hands and feet. Whether or not these were practised butchers it was impossible to tell, but before long they were holding up grisly objects in triumph, presumably toes and fingers as well as less public members. Roughly bundling up the ravaged cadaver, the others returned it to the grave, covered it over, and stamped down the soil.

The group at the next lair were equally busy; it was impossible, from the watchers' stance, to see what they had achieved, however.

Lennox licked dry lips, muttering his horror and disgust. 'Foul harpies! I could vomit!'

'Spare yourself,' Patrick advised him. 'They are not finished yet.'

'We have plumbed the depths of hell this night!' Melville averred.

'Wait you, Sir James!'

'*Deus avertat!*' James said. '*Quieta non movere!*'

Presently the twanging of the Jew's-harp sounded as a signal, and all the congregation began to wind up their activities and stream back to the church. It took some time for them all to finish their various tasks however, and an impatient shout, presumably from their sable leader, hastened the stragglers. At last all were inside again, and the door was shut.

Without delay the six men hurried back to their former vantage point.

Now a most fantastic scene was being enacted. The horned master of ceremonies had taken up his stance behind the Communion Table. In front of it an aged crone was extracting from a sack, held open by other women, a clawing and frightened black cat, oblivious apparently to the bites and scratches she received.

The unfortunate animal was placed on the table, and held down there. Strangely enough it lay almost completely still, gripped by the old woman presumably in such a way as to render it nerveless. Then, from a horrible and gruesome pile of objects on the table beside it, certain choice items from the dead bodies were selected by the masked individual, and tied by the woman to the corresponding parts of the cat – finger-joints to the forepaws, toes to the rear legs, an ear round its neck, genitals round its middle.

Thus bedecked, the animal was returned to his sack, and the remaining trophies shared out amongst the congregation. This indeed was the only undisciplined incident of the entire performance so far, as the women fought and clawed at each other to obtain these most unattractive mementoes. What they would do with them beggared the imagination.

Thereafter there was a caricature of a benediction, with the master of ceremonies making rude signs with his raised fingers, and the assembly turned widdershins, chanting some sort of antiphon. This time the watchers had due warning, and were safely hidden before the company emerged into the open. Even so there was some alarm when, led by the tall black figure and the Jew's-harper, the crowd came surging in an easterly direction. However, they kept to the highest part of the rock, and were clearly not in the least concerned with searching for possible spectators. Seemingly they were heading for the ultimate point of the peninsula. Letting them get well past, the royal party followed on discreetly.

At the extremity of the headland the people clustered, while their leader made another of his orations, gesturing towards sea and sky. Unfortunately, since he faced in that direction, his words remained unintelligible from a distance behind. Never long-winded, however, he was soon done. Then the old woman with the cat descended alone to the tide's edge, and stepping gingerly on to something low, small and dark tethered there, sat down.

'Hech, hech – the sieve!' James exclaimed. 'Yon'll be her sieve, Seton man.'

'Nae doot, Your Majesty,' the bailie agreed. His unfortunate maid-servant Geilis Duncan, under severe pressure, had informed her determined questioners that the witches of North Berwick habitually sailed in sieves.

'It could be only a raft,' Lennox pointed out, reasonably.

'Houts, Vicky – wheesht!' the King decried. 'Dinna mock.'

To further chanting from the company, the crone and her cat were pushed out from the rocks, and whether by supernatural means or merely by the action of the outgoing tide, the strange craft proceeded seawards, unpropelled by oars or sail. It was not long before it faded from their sight, in the gloom. Soon after, there was an unearthly screech, from out on the water, high-pitched, penetrating, and then silence.

'Christ preserve us!' James prayed. 'Was yon the cat or the auld wife?'

'Here they come again,' Patrick warned.

Their business at the sea evidently completed, the crowd came trooping back. Once again the watchers had to hide. Now a distinctly different attitude seemed to prevail amongst the coven. The solemnity was gone. All was jollity and capering. Back at the kirkyard, the buxom harpist mounted up on to the back and wide shoulders of her horned master, and from this lofty perch, white thighs gleaming on either side of his dusky masked features, strummed her strange music while her cavalier jigged beneath her with an astonishingly light and graceful step, and all around the graves the company skipped and danced.

'See the wicked strength o' him!' the King whispered. 'Carrying yon big heifer like she was a bit birdie!'

'A notable physique,' Patrick agreed. 'Tall. Broad of shoulder. But with no great flesh to him. And a deep voice. H'mmm. Also, did I detect a slight lisp?'

Lennox looked at him sharply. 'I did not note it,' he said.

'No? Perhaps your ears are less sharp than mine, Vicky?'

The dancing continued, growing ever wilder.

A council developed around the King. Melville proposed that one or more of them should get down into some hidden corner, facing westwards, and light the signal flare which they had with them, to summon the Royal Guard hotfoot. To catch the entire coven before it could disperse.

'This will be the end of it,' he foretold. 'They will work themselves into a frenzy, and afterwards go home.'

'Think you . . . ? Think you . . . ?' James peered doubtfully, biting his nails. 'Is it no' ower dangerous? There's that many o' them. Our royal person . . . ?'

'We must smite them hip and thigh, Sire!' Master Lindsay

283

urged. 'As Samson smote the Philistines. It is no less than our duty.'

'Unfortunately we are unprovided with asses' jawbones,' Patrick mentioned. 'His Grace's safety must be our first consideration.'

Even Ludovick looked surprised; such caution was scarcely in character for the Master of Gray.

'You would not let them all go free?' Melville wondered.

'Why, no. I propose to wait here, and follow one or more of these beauties back to their lairs. Alone. Unseen. It should not be difficult. Then when we know who they are, where they live, the rest will be simple. And all with no danger to His Grace.' He paused, for a moment. 'No *further* danger.'

'Eh . . . ? Danger, Patrick? Mair danger . . . ?'

'That cat, Sire. We must believe that this curious proceeding of the cat was done for some purpose. And since it seems that Your Grace is Satan's immediate target, the purpose is against your own royal person, perhaps. I would counsel a speedy return to Edinburgh and the safety of the palace.'

'Against my person!' James stammered. 'You think it, man?' He gripped Patrick's arm. 'Another storm, belike? I didna like yon o' the cat. Aye, you're right, Patrick – you're right. It's a gey long ride back to Emburgh. Let's awa', let's awa'.'

'But, Your Grace, we cannot be sure that the Master of Gray will be successful in following these evil folk,' Melville pointed out. 'If he loses them, then all our vigil is fruitless.'

'Na, na – no' fruitless, Sir James. We ken a deal that we didna ken before. Certes, we do! Patrick has the wiselike head in these matters. And you'd no' hae me further endangered, man?'

'No, Sire. But . . .'

'Come, then. Sufficient unto the day is the evil thereof. Mind that. We mustna' waste mair time. Back to the horses. Will I send you some o' the Guard, Patrick?'

'No. I am better alone.'

'I shall come with you,' Lennox said.

'No Vicky – your place is with His Grace. One man will more easily follow these others unseen than will two.'

'You're no' feared, Patrick?' the King asked.

'It is not me that Satan seeks to overwhelm is it, Highness?'

'Waesucks – no! That's right. It's me. Aye – let's awa' frae here. Quick, now.'

'I shall report to you in the morning, Sire,' the Master assured. 'I trust that no storms develop on your road home . . .'

Mary Gray sat on the grass and played with a daisy, as Ludovick paced up and down on the turf before her, high on the green flank of Arthur's Seat that towered above the grey palace of Holyroodhouse and all the jumbled roofs of the burgh of Canongate. She watched him thoughtfully.

'You believe it – and yet you disbelieve?' she said. 'It was evil – but you could not quite credit it?'

'Some of it,' he nodded. 'Something did not ring true. I do not know. But I felt it . . .'

'You felt perhaps that they were not true witches, Vicky?'

'How can I tell? *Are* there true witches? Do they indeed exist? These women were shameful, disgusting. All that they did was ill. Devil's work it may have been. But . . .'

'But it was not the Devil who directed it?'

'I think not. Certainly the black man with the horns but played the part.'

'Yet the King believes that it was Satan himself?'

'To be sure. James went expecting to see Satan – and saw him. As did, I think, Melville and Lindsay.'

'But not Uncle Patrick, I warrant!'

'Patrick was strange. In many ways. It was almost as though he himself was play-acting.'

'Yes. I can believe that. Tell me, Vicky, what he did. What he said.'

'It was scarcely what he said and did. It was his manner, Mary. As though he knew what was to happen. Almost as though he was privy to it all.'

'He went to North Berwick two days before, to spy out the land.'

'It was more than that. He knew much more. He told us when there was more to come. Worse things to be seen. He seemed to be surprised by nothing. The evil of it scarcely seemed to touch him.'

'Perhaps because it *was* play-acting? Perhaps because he had arranged it so, for the King?'

'But why?'

'That I do not know. You said that the King was expecting to see the Devil. Uncle Patrick perhaps produced the Devil. For some purpose of his own. Always he has a purpose of his own. You say that he did not return with you?'

'No. That also I did not understand. When the others would have signalled for the Guard, he would have none of it. He held that there was danger for James. Until then he had not seemed to think it. All must hasten away – save himself. He would watch on, and follow some of these people to their homes. To discover who they were. I would have gone with him, but he would not have it. I found it strange.'

'Yet did not the Lady Marie say that Uncle Patrick was home before the King?'

'Aye, we were much delayed. By a sea-mist. Near the Salt-pans of Preston. Thick mist in which we could scarce see our horses' ears. James swears that it was the cat's doing – that Satan sent it instead of a storm. So that he should perchance ride over a cliff, like King Alexander of old. Patrick got none of it. He followed a man home to Kilmurdié, a place near to Dirleton, helped himself to one of the man's horses, and rode back to Edinburgh bareback. He took the inland road, by the Gled's Muir, and saw no mist, he says.'

'This man that he followed – he was not the one who played Satan?'

'No. That one had a horse waiting. Not far from the kirk. And a groom, Patrick said. So that he might not follow him.'

'He was of the gentry, then – if he had horses and groom. Did you not learn anything of him? Who he might be? Even masked as he was.'

Ludovick shook his head. 'It was not possible. Besides the mask, he was all over blackened. And the light was but dim. All that we could see was that he was a tall man, well made but not fleshy. And of much strength, for he danced with a young woman on his shoulders. He had a deep voice, And . . . ah, yes – Patrick said that he spoke with something of a lisp. Although myself I did not hear that.'

'Do you think, then, that Uncle Patrick knew this man? If it was play-acting, and he was the leader . . . ?'

'Who can tell? But I do not believe it play-acting in the true sense, Mary. These people were practising evil, denying God, insulting Christ. And they were well versed in it. They had done it many times, to be sure. It may, as you say, have been arranged last night especially for James. But it was no mummery. It was a coven practising its wickedness – that I'll swear. It was most vile.'

The girl scanned his face. It was not often that Ludovick Stuart was moved to this extent. 'What will the King do now, think you, Vicky?' she asked, presently.

'Why, send for this man Hepburn, no doubt. To put him to the question. To see what he may tell. Of the others . . .'

'Hepburn . . . ?'

'Aye. The one that Patrick followed. To Kilmurdie. He is Hepburn of Kilmurdie – a small lairdship near to North Berwick.'

'Hepburn – that is my lord of Bothwell's clan.' Suddenly Mary Gray sat up straight. 'And . . . and Bothwell speaks with a slight lisp, Vicky! A lisp! And his castle of Hailes is but a few miles from North Berwick!'

They stared at each other.

'Bothwell is tall and strong and wide of shoulder,' she went on.

'Aye, and deep of voice, too, by God! Could it be? Could it? Always he was crazed, wild . . .'

Mary was silent.

'Bothwell!' Ludovick repeated, almost breathlessly. 'One of the greatest in the land. The King's cousin, also. Who could think it . . . ?'

'Perhaps only the Master of Gray!' she said, slowly.

'What do you mean?'

'I mean, Vicky, that the Earl of Bothwell insulted Uncle Patrick yon day at Leith, when the Queen came. That was a dangerous thing to do!'

Askance he eyed her from under down-drawn brows.

'He called him a jumped-up wardrobe-master, before all. I feared for him, even as I listened. Now, I fear the more!'

'But, if it be the truth . . . ?'

Mary got to her feet and set off downhill without another word.

Chapter Fifteen

QUEEN Anne, very small in the great four-poster bed with purple hangings, pointed imperiously. 'The comfits, Mary – give them here. Then you may go. And bring the candles nearer.'

'Yes, Your Grace,' Mary did as she was bidden. 'There is nothing else . . . ?'

From under the pillows embroidered with the crown and royal monogram, Anne drew a sealed letter. 'See that this reaches the lodging of my lord of Moray. Forthwith. And . . . not by one of His Grace's pages, nor yet my own. You understand, Mary?'

The girl inclined her dark head.

'Also, see that the Lady Jean is in her room, and abed, as you go. The last night that it was her duty to attend me she was not there when I rang the bell. She was gone, for long. Off like a bitch in heat after some man. And not to the Abbot of Lindores, I vow! I know her. See to it, girl!'

'Yes, Your Grace. And a goodnight,' Curtsying, Mary slipped out of the royal bedchamber.

The Lady Jean Stewart was not, in fact, in the room across the stairway occupied by the lady-in-waiting on duty. Mary went into the larger anteroom on the same level. Jean was not there either. Two of the King's pages were present, one sprawled asleep across a table, the other, a pretty boy with painted lips and rouged cheeks, lounged in a chair, a goblet in his hands, a lute at his feet.

'Master Ramsey,' she said 'know you where the Lady Jean may be?'

The youth yawned. 'Know I do not – nor care. But I might hazard a guess, Mistress!'

'Then go, if you please, where you guess, and request that her ladyship come back here.'

'Not I, wench. I have more to do than run sniffing after such game!'

'No? I think that you have not!' Mary considered him comprehensively, calmly. 'Besides, it is the Queen's express command. And I will thank you to mind your words, Master Ramsay. Where is His Grace?'

Ramsay grimaced and pouted, pointing a finger upwards. 'Where but, as ever, amongst his papers and books? A pox on all such dusty foolery!' Grumbling, he strolled off on his errand.

Mary followed him down the winding stone stairs, past the sleepy, yawning guards. She crossed the inner courtyard of the palace to another corner-tower, and mounting to the first floor, entered a room, spartan-bare and untidy, where a young man was in the act of removing his doublet.

'Your pardon, Peter,' she smiled. 'At this late hour. Is my lord Duke here?'

'Abed and asleep, Mistress Mary. We rode from Linlithgow.' The other's face had lighted up at the sight of her. 'But it is never too late to see *you*. Come – a glass of wine? Shall I wake the Duke?' Without saying so, he implied that that might be a pity.

'No – thank you, no, Peter. It is just a letter. To go to the Earl of Moray's lodging in the Canongate.'

Peter Hay raised his eyebrows at the folded paper. 'The King's seal – but not the King's hand o' write, I vow!' he commented. 'Blows the wind so?'

'I perceive no such wind, Peter. Will you carry this letter, please?'

'Must it go to my lord tonight, then?'

'I fear so. Forthwith, was the command.'

Lennox's page sighed, and reached for his boots.

When he had gone, Mary went to the inner door and quietly opened it. In the dim light of a single guttering candle, Ludovick lay naked on the top of his bed, on his back, arms thrown wide, while all around him his fine clothes lay crumpled as they had been cast down, littered anywhere. Lips slightly parted, curling hair disarrayed, breathing with little puffs, he looked more boyish than ever. One hand lay open, but in the other a yellow velvet ribbon was entwined round his fingers. Mary recognised it at once. It was one that she had used sometimes to tie up her hair, and had unaccountably lost a week or two before.

For a little while she watched him there, a faint smile playing round the corners of her mouth. Then quietly she tip-toed into the room, picked up all the scattered clothing, folded it neatly and placed it on a bench near the bed – having to displace a riding-boot, a crossbow-bolt, a pistol and an entanglement of fishing-line, in the process. This completed, she stood over the bed for a moment or two before, with a little quiver of sigh, she snuffed out the candle and slipped away, closing the door behind her.

Mary did not go to her own chamber in the Master of the Wardrobe's quarters, but returned across the courtyard to the tower that housed the royal private apartments. Climbing the corkscrew stairs again, she looked in at the ladies-in-waiting chamber, but Jean was still amissing. A further flight she mounted, to pause outside a shut door. Softly she knocked – and knocked again.

'What now, what now?' The King's voice sounded irascible.

'It is Mary Gray, Highness,' she said, as quietly as she might.

'Eh? Eh? Speak up. Who's there? What's to do?'

'Mary Gray, Sire. To speak with you.'

'Och, awa' wi' you, lassie. Tell the Queen I'll no' be long. Tell her to go to sleep. I'm occupied, see you – much occupied. Wi' important matters.'

'Yes, Sire. But this is important also. The Queen has not sent me. I crave word with you. Concerning this matter of witches.'

That ensured her admittance, albeit with much royal muttering. Carefully locking the door behind them, James, untidier even than usual, peered at the girl in the candle-lit confusion of parchments, books and papers.

'Well, lassie – well? he demanded testily. 'You shouldna be here, you ken. It's no' suitable. I'm no' sure that Annie would like it . . . '

'That I have considered, Sire. But I believe it to be important.'

'You said it was anent the witches? Has Patrick found out mair . . . ?'

'No. The Master of Gray has not sent me. I have heard that

290

the Earl of Bothwell is shut up in Edinburgh Castle, Sire. On charge of witchcraft?'

'Aye, the ill limmer! He is so, God be praised! I believe him to be Satan's lieutenant in this realm o' Scotland. A man sold to the Devil.'

'But, Sire, how can . . . ?'

'No buts, Mistress! I saw him at his wickedness. Wi' my ain two eyes. In the kirk o' North Berwick. A right terrible sight.'

'Yes. But did you not declare to the Queen, Your Grace, and to others, that it was the Devil himself that you saw there? How could it then be my lord of Bothwell?'

'Eh . . . ? Och, well.' James plucked at his loose lower lip. 'Belike it was Bothwell acting for the Devil.'

'Did you not tell the Queen that he had horns and claws and cloven hooves? How could that have been Bothwell?'

'M'mmm. Aye. But I saw his shape, girl. I heard his voice.'

'Yet you did not think that it was Bothwell then, Sire? You thought it was the Devil.'

'No. But . . . och, dinna harry me, this way. You canna talk so to the King, woman. It's no' respectful.'

'I would never show disrespect for Your Grace,' Mary assured him earnestly. 'I am but your humble and honest servant. I but seek your Highness's weal and honour.' That might have been Patrick Gray himself.

'As is right and proper,' James nodded sternly. 'Mind it, then.'

'Yes.' Then directly she put it to him. 'Do you believe that my lord of Bothwell *is* the Devil, Sire?'

'Houts, lassie – houts! Na, na – I wouldna just say that.' James was wary. 'No' just Auld Hornie himsel', maybe.'

'Then, Highness – if it was one or other that you saw at North Berwick, I can assure you that it was not Bothwell. For he was in Edinburgh all that night. In bed in the house of the Commendator of Lindores.'

'Nae doubt that is what he *says*, Mistress.'

'He did not say it to me. I learned it otherwise. Perhaps the lady will speak for him.'

'Lady . . . ? His wife, mean you? Would she no' say aught to advantage him?'

291

'Not his wife, Sire. The lady with whom he spent the night at the Commendator's house in the Lawnmarket.'

'Guidsakes!' The King shambled round the table, touching papers here and there. 'Who was she – this woman?'

'I would prefer not to tell her name, Sire.'

'It's no' what you'd prefer or no' prefer, i' faith! I'm asking you, woman!'

'I believe that Your Grace also would prefer not to hear it.'

'Eh . . . ? How might that be?'

'She is the wife to another. To one close to your Highness. Notably close, it is said. Who complains that she is being neglected by her husband. In her wifely rights. Since coming to Court.'

'Oh! Ah . . . ummm. Ooh, aye. D'you tell me that, Mistress?' Eyes rolling in alarm, the King moved further away. 'Here's a right pickle! How d'you ken a' this, Mistress Mary? About Bothwell,' he added hurriedly.

'I made it my business to find out, Sire.'

'Aye – through that Jean Stewart, nae doubt. She beds wi' Patrick o' Lindores. But why, lassie? What interests you that much in Francis o' Bothwell? You're no' taken up wi' the rascal your ain sel'?'

'Far from it, Sire. Indeed I like him but little. But I would not have Your Grace's fame spoiled by the hurt of an innocent man.'

'Aye. I'ph'mmm. Would you no' . . . ? Well, well – we'll see. This requires thinking upon. Much thought.' James edged towards the door.

'Sire,' the girl said, a little breathlessly for her, 'do you not write any more poetry? It is a great wonder to have a king who is a poet. Your renown goes forth . . .'

'Och, I havena time for yon,' James interrupted. 'I'm ower busy dealing wi' this o' the Devil.'

'Could that not be what the Devil wishes you to do, Your Grace? That you serve him best by fighting him at his own game, with his own weapons? Perhaps by poetry and other things – kindly arts reaching to the hearts of men – you may do better. Injure his kingdom more.'

'Och, Mary lass – dinna haver! I'll no' beat Satan wi'

292

poetry. He needs harder knocks than that. Forby, I'm writing a book. To open men's eyes to his wiles and deceits. Na, na – I've no time for rhyming.'

Mary sighed. 'I am sorry. I had hoped that Your Grace might have helped me again. With my own poor verses. You were so good before. So clever. A true poet, you guided my faltering lines . . .'

'You are writing mair verses, Mary? To the Queen? Annie's no' that taken wi' poetry, I've found.'

'No. To . . . to another. I am finding it difficult. But with your help . . .'

'Na, na. Go you to Patrick Gray, lassie – to your uncle. No' to me. He's a poet, and he's far mair time, forby. He hasna this realm to rule and Satan to fight. Off wi' you now, and let me to my work. Begone, girl.'

Sighing again, Mary curtsied. 'I beg Your Grace's pardon,' she said, and moved to the locked door.

Patrick Gray paced back and forth across the stone-flagged floor, behind the table – the only man so to do. Which was unlike that self-possessed individual. Indeed, he was probably the man least himself in that sombre wood-panelled chamber of Edinburgh Castle. His companions sat or lounged around three sides of the great table, interested, concerned, bored or lethargic – or plain drunk. One or two goblets were already overturned, with the wine spilled and dripping on the floor.

In his high chair at the top, the King sat forward absorbed, eager, avid almost. Seldom had any of those present seen that strange young man so much alive, so keenly intent. A large sheet of paper lay before him, with ink-pot and sand, and in his hand he held a newly-sharpened quill, with others, used and unused, lying by. The paper was one-third written upon in James's spidery hand. Clerks sitting at another smaller table clutched their pens much less earnestly.

'Sit you doon, sit you doon, Master o' Gray,' James said, licking thick lips. 'Dinna be so impatient, man. We'll win to the truth yet.'

'I doubt it, Your Grace – mightily I doubt it. By this road,' Patrick returned without pronounced respect. 'If I am impatient, it is at this waste of your royal time. Of all our time. Here is no way to . . . '

He stopped, both his speaking and his pacing, as a high-pitched screaming came through to them from some chamber beyond, bubbling, half-strangled. Broken and crazed it rose, three times, before sinking in a whimpering that presently failed to reach them.

The King rubbed his hands. 'Hear you that?' he charged them. 'We'll no' be long now, I warrant!'

'May the Devil so screech eternally in his hell, and all who favour and abet him!' Master Lindsay observed, piously.

'Amen, amen!' James agreed wholeheartedly. Hastily some others of the company added their assent.

'Christ's cause will triumph!' added the Chancellor, newly created Lord Maitland of Thirlstane by a grateful monarch. 'God's will be done.'

Patrick swung on him. 'How can you listen to that, my lord, and call it God's work or Christ's cause?' he demanded. 'I am a sad sinner, as none knows better – but I would not saddle the sweet Christ with such as this!'

'Tush, sir . . . '

'The Lord Christ scourged the wrong-doers out of the temple, Master of Gray,' Lindsay reminded him sternly. 'All evil must be scourged and beaten out of wicked men. Only so shall Christ's kingdom come. The punishment of evil-doing is God's work.'

'Punishment, sir? This then is punishment? For sins committed? I understood that this was a court of law. Duly instituted by the King. To try. To enquire into. No verdict has yet been pronounced. No decision reached. No sentence given. Is it not early for punishment . . . ?'

'Och, Patrick man,' James interrupted, 'you ken very well we must needs put them to the question. Likewise that Satan keeps their lips tight closed lest they tell his black secrets. Ooh, aye. Only by sic-like pains can we overcome his ill hold on them. It's full necessary, man. Forby, they're a' guilty as hell itsel'. You ken that fine. We saw it wi' our ain eyes. Waesucks – their punishment is well earned! We but require the evidence established according to the law. Is that not so, Sir William?'

Sir William Elphinstone, Senator of the College of Justice,

one of the three Lords of Session present, roused himself, peered, and hiccuped. 'Undoubtedly, Your Grace,' he said.

'Aye. We but seek the truth, Patrick. The truth we must have. You'll no' deny that? Guidsakes, man – it was yoursel' that uncovered for us this nest o' infamy and . . .'

An animal squealing interrupted even the monarch, a sound grotesque and repetitive that seemed impossible to have come from human lips.

One of the more somnolent judges sat up, eyes open, suddenly interested. 'Fiend seize me – is yon the auld one or the young one?' he demanded. 'I'll wager you a crown it's the auld one, Dod.' Then recollecting the King's presence, he choked and stammered. 'Your . . . Your Grace's pardon!'

James was not listening – at least, not to this. He was craning his head forward, a little to one side, staring directly at the blank wall of panelling, as though he would project himself entirely into what went on in that next chamber.

Patrick came directly up to the King's chair. 'Your Grace,' he urged, 'I pray you halt this, this savagery. No evidence gained thus is worth a packman's whistle. They will say anything.'

'Wheesht, man – wheesht!' With an almost physical effort, James brought himself back to present company. 'You err, Patrick. These toils are necessary and proper. The creatures will no' speak, otherwise. That we ken. Even at my royal command.'

'They will speak, Sire – have spoken. Only not what you would have them to say . . .'

James straightened up in his chair. 'Houts, sir – that's no way to speak to me! I'll thank you to watch your words in our presence.'

'I think that you forgot yourself, Master of Gray,' Maitland said coldly from across the table. 'Recollect that you are not in your Wardrobe now!'

Patrick ignored him. 'Sire – these methods smack of Queen Elizabeth's Walsingham rather than of the King of Scots,' he charged – a shrewd stroke, for of all men James loathed and feared Mr. Secretary Walsingham, the greatest spy-master and inquisitor outside Spain.

Visibly the King drew back. 'Eh . . . ? Walsingham!' he

muttered. 'No' that . . . you'd no' say . . . '

The door of the adjoining chamber opened, turning all heads. A continuous chittering moaning sound was at once evident; as well as a most unpleasant smell. With these, in through the doorway, came a moon-faced fat man, bald, indeed hairless, as a baby, and as pink-and-white. In shirt and breeches, with sleeves uprolled, he came forward, bobbing a series of jerky bows at the King, sweat streaming from his cherubic features and soaking his shirt. Red blood too splattered the latter.

'Well, Master Broun – well?' James demanded. 'Ha' you been successful? Ha' you displaced the Devil and let in the fear o' God?'

'Aye, Majesty – mair or less,' the other answered. He had a high squeaking voice to match his face. 'But I'm thinking she'll no' tak mair, the noo. It's weak flesh, weak. It fails me, for a' my craft and cunning. Mair, at the present, and you'll get nae sense oot o' her, I fear – just mowlings and mewings nae better than a cat. Twice she swooned awa', Majesty. But I'm right nimble at fetching them back. I ken the ways o' their bodies. I'm skilled at searching oot their . . . '

'Enough of yourself, man!' the Lord Chancellor broke in. 'His Grace is not interested in your fell trade. Is the woman yet in her senses?'

'Aye, my lord. It's been a sair trauchle to keep her so. But she has her wits yet, in a manner o' speaking . . . '

'Then fetch her in, Master Broun,' the King ordered, 'fetch her in.'

The fat man backed out, and presently returned with two brawny guards half-carrying between them an extraordinary and distasteful apparition, a sagging and untidy bundle of trailing hair, limbs, and torn and soiled clothing. This twitching, sprawling spectacle they brought forward to the table – until, wrinkling his nose in disgust, the Chancellor waved them away.

'Further back, for a mercy!' he ordered. 'Further back, fools! A pox – how she stinks!'

'Ha – see you, Dod!' the Lord of Session Graham chuckled. 'I said it was the auld one . . . '

'Yon's no' the auld one, Johnnie,' Sir William Elphinstone

296

reproved. 'See her paps. The auld gammer couldna show the likes o' yon, I'll warrant! It's the young quean. Use your eyes, man.'

'Your Grace – this . . . this is beyond all bearing!' Patrick Gray exclaimed. 'You cannot countenance such barbarity!'

'Then stand you back, Master of Gray – if your stomach is over-nice!' Sir James Balfour observed dryly. 'I would scarce have believed one of your, h'm, experience to be so delicate!'

The King did not seem to hear any of them; nor did he appear to be ill-affected by either sight or smell. He had half-risen to his feet involuntarily, as though indeed he would have moved closer to the sorry creature that had been brought in to them, but he slowly resumed his seat, contenting himself with leaning forward over the table, slack lips working.

'Aye, aye,' he got out at length. 'So is ill pride fallen! Here's the end o' black shame and whoring wi' Satan!' He actually wagged a minatory finger at the unsavoury scarecrow. 'You're nane so vaunty now, Mistress! Changed days since you rode the Devil at North Berwick! Siclike are the wages o' sin, woman.'

Certainly the broken and repulsive eyesore before them was hardly to be accepted as the same comely and voluptuous young female who had played the Jew's-harp at North Berwick kirk and led the dance on the shoulders of the horned preacher. The worthy Lord of Session was scarcely to be blamed for mistaking her for the old hag whom they had interrogated with her, previously; hollow-eyed, her flesh turned grey where it was not discoloured with bruising, her tawny hair ragged, sweat-stained and matted with blood as a result of the twisting of a rope around her head – a favourite method of extracting the truth from witches – she looked as she had sounded, scarcely human.

'Can she speak, Master Broun?' the Chancellor demanded, doubtfully.

'Oh, aye. Fine, my lord. Naught wrang wi' her tongue. You should ha' heard her back there . . . '

'Quite, man – quite.' Maitland raised his voice, as though to bring the prisoner to her senses. 'Woman,' he said sternly. 'Hear me. You will now give answer to our questions. Honestly and respectfully. We will have no more lies and evasions . . . '

'Bide a wee, bide a wee, my lord,' James intervened, frowning. 'Wi' your permission *I* will question the creature.' He signed to the man Broun. 'Cover her up. She's no' decent. An offence, just!' Primly he tutted. 'Now, Mistress Cairncross – your attention, if you please. We maun hae an answer to these several points. *Imprimis* – do you admit that you are a sworn servant o' the Devil and the enemy o' the Lord God and His Kirk? *Secundum* – that the true and veritable reason for yon ill conventicle at North Berwick was the sore hurt and harm o' me, James Stewart, your liege lord, King o' this realm o' Scotland, and Christ's viceregent? *Tertium* – that you and your coven hae held the like wicked and abominable conventicles and practices at times previous, and in especial when I was aship at sea, wi' the object o' effecting storms and great waves to swallow me up. Aye, and mists too. Yon mist. And other siclike calamitous hurts. *Quartum* – was your captain, precentor and leader in all such abominations the Devil himsel', or a man in his dark service? A man, just? Aye, and *Quintum* – if a man, was he no' Francis Stewart, calling himsel' Hepburn, Earl o' Bothwell?' James scanned his paper, to make sure that he had missed no point. Then he jabbed his pen at the wreck of a young woman. 'Now, Mistress – that's clear enough, is it no'? We'll hae the first. You admit that you are a sworn servant o' the Devil? Eh?'

The faint mumbling and moaning that came from the prisoner slumped between the two guards was no different from what she had been emitting since being brought into the council-chamber.

'Tut, woman – speak up!' the King urged. 'I canna hear you.'

'Sire – she is in no state to speak to any effect. Your butcher has seen to that . . . !'

'Master o' Gray, I'll thank you to hold your tongue!'

'A mouthful of wine, Highness,' Melville suggested. 'To loosen *her* tongue.'

'Aye, gie her that, Broun man. A bit sup.'

While wine from a goblet on the table was being forced into the woman's slack mouth, Patrick brought the chair that he should have been seated upon, set it behind her and eased her down into it. Even so, the guards had to hold her up or she

298

would have slipped to the floor.

'You are exceeding tender towards an idolatrous hellicat, Master of Gray,' the Chancellor observed.

'She is still a woman,' the other answered simply.

'So, sir, was His Grace's royal mother the late Queen Mary – was she not?'

'God's passion, Maitland . . . !' Patrick swung upon the Chancellor.

King James banged his hand on the table. 'A truce, a truce!' he squeaked. 'Hold your tongues, both o' you. Guidsakes – I'll no' have it! This is a court o' law, I'd mind you. Doing God's business. Aye, Now you, Mistress Cairncross – answer me. Admit to me that you are sold to the Devil.'

Wild bloodshot eyes flickered over the company, and returned shrinking, not to the King but to the baby-faced man beside her. A thick and unintelligible sound issued from her swollen lips – but she nodded her head, helplessly, hopelessly.

'Ha! And so we have it.' James beamed on her, on them all. Then he bent, to scratch his pen over the paper. 'The panel admits the prime complaint. Why couldna you have tell't us that before, woman – and saved a deal o' time. Now, *secundum*. Wasna yon ploy at North Berwick aimed against my ain royal sel'? Directed at me, the King?'

Again the mouthing and nodding.

'See you, my lords and gentlemen,' James looked round them, squaring his normally drooping shoulders, heavy head for once held high. 'It is as I said. Me, it is – me!' He beat on his padded chest. 'Me, James Stewart, that the Devil is fell set against. Me he fears. I ken it, fine.'

Heads bowed in due acknowledgment.

'Aye.' He consulted his papers. 'Well, then. Mistress Cairncross – the third point leads on frae the second. You'll no' deny previous conventicles o' sin? And nae doubt they'd be for the same ill purpose? The storms when I was on the sea? And when the Queen couldna win to me? These too were your detestable work? Your foul coven brewed these ills for me likewise, did they no'?'

The woman was nodding and gabbling before ever he had finished.

Triumphantly James turned to the Master of Gray. 'Did I no' tell you, Patrick? We win to the truth at last. Master Broun has well furthered the Lord's work.' He wagged his admonitory finger. 'You erred, Patrick – you greatly erred.'

Patrick Gray shook his head. 'What have we learned, Sire, that we did not know before? What does it advantage us to hear it again, wrung from a foolish country wench by torture?'

'It is evidence, man.'

'Evidence of what? Evidence of the frailty of human flesh against the rope and the screw? Naught else, I swear. The evidence that we need is from my lord of Bothwell. Question *him*, Your Grace . . .'

James nibbled at his pen. 'We canna do that, Patrick,' he interrupted. 'You ken it. Bothwell is a peer o' Scotland. Forby a member o' my Council, and a cousin o' my ain. We canna put him to the question like, like . . .'

'Like less fortunate of Your Grace's subjects!'

'A peer of this realm and member of His Grace's Privy Council may only be tried by that Council,' Chancellor Maitland intervened stiffly. The period of co-operation between these two had been only brief; now their mutual antipathy was as pronounced as formerly. 'As well you know, Master of Gray – who were in the same position not that long syne!'

'I have not forgotten, my lord. Nor what went before that peculiar trial – and the questioning of my half-brother, Davy Gray! And who performed that questioning. Davy was only a peer's bastard, of course – which no doubt makes a deal of difference. But I am not here talking about my lord of Bothwell's trial. I referred but to his questioning.'

'He has been questioned – and admitted nothing. You know it.'

'But not questioned as this wretched woman has been questioned.'

'Would you, *you*, have a noble of Scotland, and one of the highest in the land, thus mishandled, sir?'

'For so fresh-minted a noble as yourself, my lord, you are touchingly considerate for your new kind!' Although Gray's lip curled, he eyed the Chancellor keenly, thoughtfully. Maitland had never loved Bothwell, indeed had suffered at that madcap's hands. If now he was taking Bothwell's part, then it must be for good and sufficient reason. This would obviously require watching.

That Bothwell appeared to have another unexpected friend present now became apparent. The Earl of Moray had hitherto taken no evident interest in the proceedings. Now he spoke up.

'Is it not the case, Sire, that Bothwell is known to have spent yon night you were at North Berwick, in Leslie of Lindores' house in the Lawnmarket? And there's a certain lady can prove it!'

Nervously, the King peered at him from under down-drawn brows. 'Eh . . . ? Say you so? Well, now. A tale, nae doubt – a tale. Did he tell you it himsel', my lord?'

'No, Sire. It was a lady who told me. But not *the* lady, mark you!'

All members of the court were now sitting up, with interest introduced into the occasion. Patrick's eyes were busy.

'This lady . . . ?' he began.

Elphinstone was leaning forward. 'Aye, the lady's name, my lord?' he demanded.

The King banged his hand on the table. 'Enough o' idle tattle and gossip!' he ordered squeakily. 'You, my Lord o' Session, should ken better. Aye, better. This is a court o' law.' He coughed. 'To proceed. Woman!'

The unfortunate prisoner had sunk into a partial coma during this exchange. Now she was roused roughly by the man Broun, into gasping attention.

'My fourth question, Mistress, if you please.' James pointed the pen at her. 'It is fell important, see you. Was yon limmer in the pulpit at North Berwick – aye, whose black arse you so shamefully kissed – was yon the Devil or man?'

Gnawing swollen lip, the young woman gazed around her like a trapped animal. This was not a question to which she could merely nod her head.

'Come, Mistress – out wi' it,' James urged irritably. 'You must ken – you who lewdly bestrode his wicked shoulders.'

Still she did not answer.

'What's wrong wi' you, woman?'

'She does not know what you would wish her to say – that's

301

what is wrong with her,' Moray shrewdly asserted. 'In your other questions, she knew.'

'It was a man, was it not?' Patrick put in swiftly. 'A man, acting for the Devil?'

Almost eagerly the prisoner nodded. 'Yes,' she said. 'Yes.'

'Now we have it. Aye, now we come to it,' the King said.

'Belike the wretched creature would have said as much for the Devil,' Moray observed. 'Put it this way. Tell me, woman. This man – it was the Devil in the guise of a man, was it not? A man in form, but the Devil in person?'

For a moment or two she hesitated. Then she nodded. 'Aye,' she whispered.

'You see, Sire!'

James frowned and tutted. 'I'll thank you, my Lord o'Moray, to leave the questioning to me. Aye – all o' you. D'you hear? To me. You but hae the woman confused. Mistress – see here. This man in the Devil's guise – was it my lord o' Bothwell, or was it no'?'

Desperately the unhappy creature looked from one to another of them. 'I . . . I canna say,' she got out.

'Waesucks, you can! And you shall. You are a right obdurate woman. Aye, obdurate. I'm right displeased wi' you. Was it Bothwell or was it no'? Answer me.'

'Sink me!' Moray exclaimed. 'So there's your evidence!'

'Aye, Bothwell has naught to fear here,' Chancellor Maitland agreed.

'It is as I said, Your Grace.' Patrick smoothly altered his stance. 'Such evidence is of no value to us. None of it. This last but means that Bothwell, if it be he, does not use his own name at such affairs. And who would expect him to?'

But James was not satisfied. 'I say she lies,' he declared. 'She kens the creature well enough, wi' his breeks on an' wi' them off! She kens him as carnally as he kens her, I warrant! Dinna tell me that she never asked his name. Woman – what is the man's name?'

She shook her head.

'Answer me, witch – answer me!'

'We . . . we but ken him as Jamie. Jamie, sir – the same as yoursel'.'

'Guidsakes, do you so!' The King was indignant. 'Jamie,

is it? Jamie what? What's the rest o' it?'

'Just Jamie, sir.'

'Havers, woman! Dinna tell me that you never spiered mair about the man whose arse you kissed. And who's had you times aplenty, I'll be bound! How d'you name him, eh?'

Dumbly she shook her head.

Exasperatedly the King wagged his pen at her. 'Master Broun – to your trade! See if perchance *you* can bring back her memory!'

The fat man grasped a handful of her hair, close to the head, and twisted it, and the already wrung and tortured scalp beneath. Half-rising in her chair to the agony of it, the woman emitted an ear-piercing shriek that rang the very rafters, and swooned away unconscious, dragging down even the expert questioner. Disgustedly he threw the inert body to the floor.

'Fiend tak her!' he exclaimed. 'She's failed me, at the last.'

'Is it not yourself that has failed *us*, fellow!' one of the professional judges complained. 'That's the end o' her, for a wager. We'll get no more out o' her. We're wasting our time.'

'Not quite the end o' her, my friend,' James corrected. 'That is still to come. Nor have we entirely wasted our time, I think. We've this ill woman's confession, added to the testimony o' our ain eyes, that she has committed the vile sin o' witchcraft – which is a burning matter. Aye, and that she and others contrived it against my ain royal person – which is highest treason, forby. You a' heard her. In consequence, this being a court o' justice duly constituted, we needna spend mair time on her. I pronounce her black guilty o' these maist abominable crimes and offences, and do hereby sentence her to just and lawful punishment.' He paused, licking thick lips. 'Aye. She shall be taken out the morn to the forecourt o' this my castle o' Edinburgh, and the good burghers o' this town and city summoned by tuck o' drum to witness. And before them a' she shall be worried to the half-deid, and thereafter burned wholly wi' fire. As is just, right and proper, according to the law o' this realm and the precepts o' Christ's Kirk. *Ex auctoritate mihi commisâ.*'

'Amen!' the Church, in the person of Master Lindsay agreed fervently.

'Correct, meet and due,' the law acceded, by the lips of one of the senators.

' 'Fore God – has she not suffered enough?' the Master of Gray demanded.

'Thou shalt not suffer a witch to live!' the King intoned. 'Would you deny Holy Writ, man Patrick?'

'I can recollect other Scripture, I think, less savage . . . '

'Tush, man – dinna bandy words. You're no' in a proper and seemly state o' mind this night, Master o' Gray – you are not. You've no' helped the assize. You've but hindered the course o' justice. Aye. But enough o' this. Our royal word is said, and sentence passed. Awa' wi' her, Master Broun. And then we will hear the other. Fetch in the auld wife.'

'In that case, Your Grace – have I your permission to retire?' Patrick asked. 'Since my presence is of no help . . . and my stomach will scarce stand more of this!'

'Aye – go then, Patrick. You may leave us. But I'm right disappointed in you – I am so. A weak vessel, you prove. Tried, I find you wanting, man – wanting.'

'I had believed that it was to be the Earl of Bothwell who was tried – not myself, Sire. Seemingly I was wrong. Your Grace . . . my lords . . . gentlemen – I bid you a good night. If that is possible after . . . this!'

Chapter Sixteen

LUDOVICK STUART came long-striding up the steep grassy hillside, breathing deeply. Mary Gray waved to him as he approached, from where she sat on a green ledge amongst the yellow crowsfoot and the purple thyme. But she did not smile.

'I thought . . . that I might . . . find you here,' he panted. 'I searched all the . . . palace for you. None had seen you. Jean said . . . Jean said that you would be with my page, Peter Hay. But I did not believe her.'

'The Lady Jean is of that way of thinking, Vicky. So works her mind.'

'Yet you are a deal away from the palace these days, Mary.'
He stood before her, hands on padded hips, his Court finery
as usual looking somehow out-of-place and alien to his sturdy
stocky figure. 'Is it ever here you come? All this way?'

'Not always. But often, yes.'

'And alone?'

'Alone, yes. Although sometimes the Lady Marie comes with
me. And little Andrew. To escape . . . to get away, for a
little, from, from . . . ' It was not often that that young woman
left her sentences unfinished or lacked due words – save
perhaps when she had occasion to play the part of an innocent
girl.

Involuntary both of them turned to look out across the
deep trough where acres and acres of jumbled roofs and spires
and turrets, part-hidden in the swirling smoke of a thousand
chimneys, climbed the crowded mile from the grey palace of
Holyroodhouse up to the great frowning fortress of Edinburgh
Castle on its lofty rock. If they did not actually see more and
different smoke drifting down from that grim citadel's forecourt, they did not fail to sense it, smoke tainted with a smell
other than that of wood or coals.

'Aye,' the young Duke said heavily. 'I also. Often I could
choke with it. The palace, the whole town, stinks of death.
Aye, and fear. I would be out of it all, Mary – away . . . '

'Yes,' she said. 'I knew that smell in London. Elizabeth's
fires at the Bridewell. I had not thought to smell it here in
Scotland. Madness, it is – cruel madness . . . ' She paused.
'Once I feared that it might be the Spanish Inquisition's fires
that would burn on the Castle-hill of Edinburgh! Now . . . !'

For three weeks the fires had blazed on the windy plateau
before the gates and drawbridge of Edinburgh Castle. For
three weeks the screams of the condemned had rung through
the crowded vennels and tall stone tenements of the capital.
For three weeks the citizens had daily been gorged with the
spectacle of justice most evidently being done, of strings of the
Devil's disciples being led in chains through the streets to the
wide and crowded castle forecourt, there to be part-strangled
publicly by teams of lusty acolytes and then tied to stakes to
burn, for the confounding of evil and the greater glory of God.
Day in, day out, and far into the night, the work went on, King

James himself personally supervising much of it, especially the examining, determined, indefatigable, confounding his arch-enemy Satan. There was no lack of material for his cleansing fervour; sufficiently questioned, almost all suspects could be brought to the point, not only of confession to the most curious activities, such as sailing the Forth in sieves, and turning themselves into hares, hedgehogs and the like, but also of denouncing large numbers of their acquaintances as equally guilty of these disgraceful practices. These, apprehended and similarly questioned in turn, could be brought to implicate ever greater numbers more. It was extraordinary how, once the rope was sufficiently twisted round their heads, names would come tumbling from their lips. The process was cumulative, the good work ever widening its scope and ramifications, growing like a snowball – to the notable enlargement and improvement of the King's monumental book on demonology. Seldom indeed had an author been so blest with the supply of excellent research material.

The citizens had long lost count of the numbers of culprits, after it had run into hundreds – mostly women, but with a fair sprinkling of men, and even children. Clearly the abominable cult and practice of witchcraft and warlockry was infinitely more widespread than anyone had dreamed. North Berwick and that part of Lothian had soon ceased to be the centre and hub of activities; the net was spreading far and wide over Scotland. To cope with the alarming situation, King James hit on the ingenious expedient of granting Royal Commissions throughout the land, with power 'to justify witches to the death' without further formality – stipulating only that all interesting occult revelations should be passed on to himself. Fourteen such Commissions had indeed been granted in a single day. There seemed no reason to suppose that the momentum would not further increase and the harvest expand.

The Earl of Bothwell meantime remained warded in the fortress, still not brought to trial – but warded as befitted his rank and standing, with his own suite of rooms and his own servants.

'Madness indeed,' Lennox agreed, thickly. 'I fear that Patrick may have been right, yon time. That James is indeed mad. Either mad or a monster. And yet, if he be so, so many others are likewise. James leads, yes – but he has no lack of followers.'

Mary shook her head. 'I do not believe that he is mad. Nor yet a monster. I think that he is a man frightened. Fearful of so many things. Unsure. His head so full of strange learning that he cannot comprehend. If he is working a great wickedness, it is because he is what men's wickedness has made him. And he is so very lonely.'

A little askance the Duke looked at her. This sort of talk was beyond him.

'All kings are lonely,' the girl went on. 'But James is the most lonely of all. He has never known mother or father, brothers or sisters. Always he has been alone, close to none – but watched by all. Trusting none, and for good reason. Yet greatly needing others close to him. More than do many.'

'He has a wife now, Mary.'

'I cannot think that the Queen is the wife that he needed. She has a hardness, a sharpness. She will not pretend for him, as he needs – pretend that he is a fine gallant, a notable poet, a strong monarch.'

'And she has the rights of it – for he is none of them!' the young man said bluntly.

'No. But a wife could aid him to be more of them. A wife should aid her husband,' Mary averred. 'And James needs aid greatly. You, Vicky, are closer to him than is the Queen, I think.'

'Not I. I will be close to no man who delights in blood and torture and burnings.'

'But if you could help to wean him away from these evil things, Vicky? The Queen will not do it. She cares not, it seems. But he still thinks well of you.'

'Think you that I have not tried? He will not heed me, Mary. He treats me like a child – he who is but five years older than I. I am near eighteen years, see you . . .'

She smiled. 'But nearer seventeen! Do not forget that we are almost of an age, Vicky.'

'What of it? I am a man. Man enough to be Chamberlain of Scotland and Commendator of St. Andrews. To have been President of the Council. Man enough to marry . . . ' His expression changed. 'Mary,' he said urgently, 'enough of all

307

this of James. He will not change for me. And I cannot breathe at Court, these days – or in this Edinburgh itself. Nor can you, it is clear. Let us away, then – together. You and me. Marry me, Mary – and let us leave all this. Forthwith. Marry me.'

Troubled she searched his face. 'Vicky – why do you hurt us both? You know that I cannot marry you. You know that it is impossible. I am not for such as you. A great lady you must marry, with name and lands and fortune.'

'I wish only to marry you. How many times have I told you so? Come away with me, Mary – away from this Court, from cruelty and fear and the smell of death. From plotting and lies and intrigue. Come to my castle of Methven, on the skirts of the Highland hills, where we can be free and live our own lives. Together. I can find a priest to marry us – a minister. Tonight, if need be. Then it will be too late for James to say no. Too late for others to arrange my life for me!' That was eloquence indeed for Ludovick Stuart.

She reached up to touch his arm, her fingers slipping down to catch and hold his own. But she shook her head. 'You are kind, Vicky – most kind. I thank you for it. But it is not to be – however much we could wish it. We are born into very different degrees, different places in the world – and nothing that we may do will alter it. Besides, I cannot leave the Court. Not just now . . .'

'Why not? What keeps you here? You hate it. The Queen will do very well without you, I swear.'

'It is not that . . .'

'It is Patrick again, I suppose? Always it is Patrick Gray! This world turns round that man!' Ludovick ground his heel into the turf.

'Yes, it is he. While I can serve him, I must, Vicky.'

'Serve him! Think you that he needs *your* service? Or any? Think you that Patrick Gray requires any but himself? That he cares for any but himself? The Master of Gray is sufficient unto himself, now and ever. Damn him!'

Mary stared, and her hand slipped out of his. Never had she heard Lennox speak so; about anyone, but especially about Patrick. 'You are wrong, Vicky,' she protested. 'Grievously wrong. He needs friends also – much, he needs them. Against himself, most of all. He needs his wife. I think that he needs even me. And you. Yes, you. Are you not his friend? Always you have been that.'

'Always I have been, yes,' the other repeated bitterly. 'But has he been mine? Is he any man's friend, the Master of Gray – save his own? How say you – is he?' Almost the young man was fierce.

Mary looked away and away, and did not answer.

'I will tell you how much he is my friend,' the Duke went on, hotly. 'The King has commanded me to marry the Lady Sophia Ruthven! Aye, marry. And it is on the advice of the Master of Gray.'

The young woman sat up straight, now, stiffly, eyes wide. For a long moment she did not speak. Then her breath came out in a quivering sigh. 'So-o-o!' she said.

'Aye, so. His cousin. His uncle Gowrie's daughter. His mother's brother, Gowrie, the Treasurer, who was executed. Patrick has gained the wardship of her and her sister Beatrix. Did you know that? Profitable wardship. Beatrix is to be lady to the Queen, in place of Jean Stewart, whom Anne will have no more of. Jean is to marry Leslie of Lindores forthwith . . . and I am to marry Sophia Ruthven.'

'I see,' Mary Gray said, quietly.

'Do you see? All of it? *I* see, likewise! The Earl of Gowrie, you'll mind, lost his head and his lands, for treason. Six years ago. There are plenty say that the Master of Gray had a hand in that. His lands were forfeit. But he had lent much money to the Crown. Private money, expended by him as Treasurer – through the Master of Gray. A dangerous practice. They say that the Crown owed him £80,000! Though how much got past Patrick Gray's hands is another matter! It was when Patrick was acting Chancellor. So . . . Gowrie died. And now I am to marry his daughter.'

'Who has been telling you all this?'

'Who but his son, the young Gowrie. He is still not of age, and still has not the use of his father's estates. Or what is left of them. Gowrie was one of the richest lords in the kingdom.'

'I see,' she said again. For that young woman her voice was flat, level, but still calm. 'Sophia Ruthven. Why, if you must marry, my lord Duke, it might as well be the Lady Sophia. She is gentle and, and guileless . . . as well as rich.'

'She is sickly and plain, and scant of wits! But do you not see? I am but to be made use of! Married to me, Patrick and the King think to control her wealth. I, her husband, will be no trouble to them! Until her brother Gowrie is of age, they will have their hands on all the Ruthven wealth. The bills for £80,000 are not like to be claimed! It is but a covetous plot – with me the fool, the clot-pate!'

'You are sure that this is Uncle Patrick's work?'

'Young Gowrie says that it is. He is but fifteen years, but he should know. Patrick has been dealing with him. He is to be sent away to Padua. To the University there. For study. By the King's kindly command. But by Patrick's arranging, who was there but a year or so ago, in his exile. Has it not all every sign of the Master's hand behind it?'

'It may be so,' she admitted. 'But he could be acting your friend still, Vicky. Thinking for you, also. And for her, perhaps. After all, many a great lord would be happy to wed the Lady Sophia. So rich, and of so powerful and ancient a family. Knowing that you, Scotland's only duke, must needs marry some such, it may be that he seeks to serve you well by recommending Sophia Ruthven. She is his cousin. And his ward, you say – though that is new . . . '

'If it was a kindness to me, might he not have consulted me? *Me*. If I am to marry her!'

'He knows . . . ' She hesitated. 'He knows that . . . '

'Aye – he knows that I would only marry *you*. Which does not suit his plans.'

She sighed. 'He knows, as do all others save only you, Vicky, that that is impossible. Surely you must see it?'

'I see, rather, a man selling his friend. As some say he sold my father. Selling me to the King. Or, better, buying himself back into James's favour, through this marriage project. All know that James has been cool towards him since these witch trials began. Somehow his plot to bring down Bothwell has failed. Something has gone amiss. I know not what. And James frowned on him.'

'I think that I know,' Mary said evenly. 'Uncle Patrick has many faults, no doubt – but he has many virtues also. He is a plotter, but there is no savagery in him. He is not cruel. He could not stand by and see women tortured, I think that he never actually believed in the witchcraft himself. He but sought to make use of the King's fear of it, for what he calls statecraft. He sought to bring Bothwell down, yes. But when he saw what hurt and evil was being visited upon these unhappy women, he would have none of it. He is sorry now, I believe, that he ever took a hand in the business . . . '

'It may be so. But that does not explain how Bothwell has escaped. What went amiss with the plot. There is more here than that Patrick mislikes these questionings and burnings. Bothwell must have more potent friends than was believed, arrogant and unfriendly as he is. James, it seems, is afraid to bring him to trial. Why? It is said that my lord of Moray spoke strongly for him. Had some information which saved him. Moray, who was Patrick's friend. And yours.' Ludovick looked at her directly. 'You have become very friendly with Moray, Mary, have you not? I have seen you much in his company, of late. I do not like the way that he looks at you.'

'Moray looks at any woman that way.'

'But you see over much of him.'

'He is much about the Queen. And I am the Queen's servant.'

He sighed. 'Well . . . know you what is at the bottom of it all? Why he turned against Patrick?'

'Perhaps he but seeks to save Uncle Patrick from a, a foolishness? The act of a friend indeed.' She changed the subject. 'When must you marry the Lady Sophia?'

'When? Why, never – if you will but come away with me. Marry me first. Once I am married to you, Mary, I can laugh at James's royal commands. And Patrick must needs think of a new plot to control the Ruthven siller!'

She shook her head. 'Do not cozen yourself, Vicky. It would not serve. The King, and the Kirk, would annul your marriage. Nothing would be easier. We are both under age. Nothing would be resolved.'

'Let them, then. Let them annul our marriage, if they can. But what matters it if we are beyond their reach? We shall go, not to Methven, but to the far Highlands. Clanranald is my friend. We could go to his far country, where James could never reach us. Better even, we could flee to France. I am a noble of France as well as of Scotland – the Seigneur D'Aubigny. I have lands and houses there.'

'You could give up all this for me, Vicky. All your high position and esteem, here in Scotland? Your dukedom, your Priory of St. Andrews, your castle of Methven, the office and revenues of Lord Chamberlain? All – for Mary Gray, the bastard?'

'Aye, would I! And more. All that I am and have. Did I not promise you, long ago, that I would give up life itself for you – swore it on my sword hilt. I meant it then, and I mean it now. You only, I have wanted, always. None other and naught else. You, my true love – the truest, fairest, most kind, most gentle woman in this land. Or any land . . .'

'Hush, Vicky – hush!' The girl's voice actually broke as she stopped him, and she turned her face away so that he would not see how it worked and grimaced. 'You are wrong, so wrong!' she exclaimed. 'I am not what you think, Vicky – believe me, I am not! I am far from so true, so gentle, so kind. I am two-faced and a deceiver. A dissembler. I am Patrick Gray's daughter indeed, and like him in much. I also am a plotter, an intriguer – so much less honest than you are. In some ways the life of this Court that you hate suits me very well. Here I can pit my wits against others, intrigue with the best. You are deceived in me, Vicky. You must not esteem me as other than I am.'

He craned his neck, to look at her curiously. 'I am not deceived,' he declared. 'I have known you too long for that. You are much that I am not, yes – clever, quick of wits. But true. Unlike Patrick, true. But . . . why do you tell me all this?'

'Because I would not have you believe that in not having me you were in aught the loser.' That was level again, flat.

'Loser? Not having you? Then . . . you will not come away with me? You will not marry me? Whatever I say? Whatever I do? Wherever I go?'

'No, Vicky, I fear not.' She swallowed. 'Go you and marry Sophia Ruthven. You could do a deal worse, I think. Keep the King's regard and your high place in the realm. You need not play Uncle Patrick's game thereafter.'

There was a silence.

'And that is your last word?' he said, at length.

'It is, yes. I . . . I am sorry, Vicky.'

'Then I am wasting my time.' He straightened up, then suddenly turned back to her. 'It is not . . . it is not Peter Hay? My page?' he demanded.

'No, Vicky. It is not. Nor any man.'

'Aye. Well . . . so be it. I bid you good-day, Mary.' Stiffly, awkwardly, ridiculously, he bowed to her on her grassy ledge, and swung away abruptly to go striding back down the steep green side of Arthur's Seat, whence he had come.

Mary Gray sat looking after him steadily, dry-eyed, tight-lipped, motionless. Motionless but for her hands, that is; her fingers plucked at and tore to shreds stalk after stalk of the tough coarse grasses that grew there, methodically, one after another, strong and sore on her skin as they were. Long she sat there, long after the tiny foreshortened figure of the Duke of Lennox had disappeared into the busy precincts of Holyroodhouse, before sighing, she rose and went slowly downhill in her turn.

Chapter Seventeen

LUDOVICK OF LENNOX did not flee to France – nor even to the distant Highlands. He remained at Court, although in no very courtly frame of mind, and in a few days the announcement was made from the palace that King James had been graciously pleased to bestow on his well-beloved cousin in marriage the hand of the Lady Sophia Ruthven, sister to the Earl of Gowrie and ward of the Master of Gray. The wedding would be celebrated shortly.

This was not to say that the young man was reconciled to his fate, however. According to Peter Hay, his page, he spent a large part of each night pacing up and down the confines of his bedchamber, unapproachable, disconsolate. Nor by day did his attitude typify the eager bridegroom. He spent an inordinate proportion of his time riding, tiring out horseflesh and himself by furious and otherwise purposeless galloping about the countryside, apparently with no other object than working off pent-up feelings and spleen – a notable change in one so normally level-headed and straightforward. He was barely civil to any with whom he came in contact – although he avoided as many as he could – including his monarch and cousin. The Master of Gray he sought to ignore completely. To the Lady Marie, whom still he appeared to trust, he confided that he was only remaining because he could not drag himself away from the vicinity of Mary Gray.

In Mary's company, however, he was only a little more civil than in others. Without being actually rude, he was aloof, abrupt, jerky, most obviously ill at ease, seeking her presence yet rebuffing her when he had gained it. She, for her part, sought to be no different from before with him, even kinder perhaps – but found this to be impossible. He would have none of it. Frequently she would catch him gazing at her with reproachful eyes, but when she made a move towards him he shied off like an unbroken colt.

That behaviour such as this on the part of so prominent an individual as the Duke of Lennox did not arouse more stir and comment than it did, might be accounted for by the fact that there was so much else to occupy the attention of the Scottish Court that summer of 1590. The witch trials went on, and had reached new heights of sensation with the naming, arrest and putting to the question of two ladies of some quality, Barbara Napier, sister-in-law of the Laird of Carschoggil, and Euphame MacCalzean, daughter of former Lord of Session Cliftonhall. That such as these should be implicated, sent a tremor of new and more personal excitement through all. At this rate, who was safe? Could any, save the most highly placed, be sure that the accusing finger might not next point at themselves? What had been a mere subject for gossip, speculation and some entertainment at Court, became suddenly a matter for serious thought, for discreet precautions, for assessing one's neighbours and acquaintance – even one's friends. Clearly the King's new obsession was becoming more than a joke.

Then there was the intriguing business of the Earl of Moray and the Master of Gray. These two seemed to be beginning to clash at all points – no one quite knew why. They had been esteemed as friends after the London embassage, but that obviousy no longer applied. Some said that the rift dated from Moray's unexpected support of Bothwell – who still lingered in ward, though comfortably enough; but the more popular theory was that it was over rivalry for influence with Queen Anne. The King's preoccupation with witchcraft, the black arts and book-writing, left Anne with much time on her young hands, and she was apparently of a nature to interest herself in sundry affairs of state – which by no means suited Chancellor Maitland. Those who deplored Maitland's power and influence, therefore tended to encourage the Queen in this, and something of a Queen's party gradually developed. In this, two men, Moray and Patrick Gray, were from the first pre-eminent. To both Anne turned for guidance, support, company. But it was noted by those particularly interested in such things that whereas in matters of statecraft, appointments and suchlike, she was apt to lean more heavily, naturally, on the experienced Master of Gray, in matters personal she seemed to delight rather more evidently in the younger Earl of Moray. After all, at thirty-two Patrick was twice her age, whereas Moray was nine years younger. Which, according to these acute observers, was a situation not to be borne by the handsomest man in all Europe, for whom women in general were to be expected to swoon and prostrate themselves. Another suggestion was that Moray, while dancing attendance on the young Queen, was interesting himself quite notably at the same time in her much more delectable tire-woman, Mary Gray – to the Master's disapproval.

Whatever the truth or otherwise of these intriguing theories, there could be no doubt that these two ornaments of the Court, the quite beautiful Master of Gray and the so bonny Earl of Moray, were no longer on the best of terms. They displayed this in very different ways, needless to say, the Master being exceedingly polite with only occasional viciously barbed remarks open to various interpretations, while Moray could be frankly scurrilous.

Then there was the Queen's supposed pregnancy to add spice to the situation. The Court was fairly evenly divided in opinion as to whether or not she was indeed with child. She showed no physical signs of it – but acted as though she was. King James himself, too, was for ever making knowing references about an imminent heir, winking towards his wife, and somewhat crudely playing the expectant father. Certain close to the royal couple, however, asserted that it was all pretence – notably Jean Stewart, formerly Lady-in-Waiting, although she might indeed have been prejudiced.

There was much speculation, also, about Bothwell and his probable fate. He had been warded now for months without trial. It seemed to many that the King was in fact afraid to bring him to trial. Yet determined and persistent questioning brought to bear on others, had produced evidence quite sufficient to incriminate him – as indeed was scarcely to be wondered at – including two especially valuable testimonies, from a matronly dame named Agnes Sampson, known as the Wise Wife of Keith, renowned for good works, and from Doctor Fian, the schoolmaster of Tranent. Both these had testified, after due persuasion, that Bothwell had approached each of them with requests for the means whereby he might encompass the death of King James by witchcraft. Mistress Sampson said that she had produced the well-tried method of making a wax image of the monarch, which was passed round the coven, each saying in turn 'This is King James the Sixth, ordained to be consumed at the instance of a noble man, Francis Earl of Bothwell,' and thereafter melted in fire. Doctor Fian had aspired somewhat higher, and roasted alive a black toad in place of the King – much to his sovereign's subsequent indignation.

All this may have seemed a trifle elementary for someone so notably close to Satan himself – and moreover, markedly unsuccessful. But at least it was testimony to high treason, and many had died for a deal less – including, needless to say, the two informants. That, even so, Bothwell remained untried could only mean that he had friends sufficiently powerful to prevent the King from forcing the issue.

Mary Gray came to this conclusion rather sooner than did most, perhaps. Frequently she pondered the matter, and wondered how Patrick saw it all and how he might react. He had not taken her into his confidence, on matters of any import, for many a month.

It was Patrick himself however who brought up the subject with her on a notable occasion – or at least on the day thereof. It was indeed the day of Ludovick's marriage, in the Abbey church of Holyrood, beside the palace. Mary, for perhaps one of the few times in her life, shirked an issue, and pleaded a woman's sickness as excuse for not attending in the Queen's retinue at the wedding, remaining in her own room when all others flocked to the ceremony. Few, probably, wondered at this, for she was generally esteemed to have been Lennox's mistress, and so might tactfully have absented herself; but Patrick Gray at least was surprised, knowing her quality. He was concerned enough to leave the marriage festivities early, and come back to the Master of the Wardrobe's quarters of the palace, where he found Mary on hands and knees on the floor of her own room, playing a game with young Andrew, now a lusty boy of eighteen months.

'Ha! So I need not have concerned myself for your health, my dear!' he commented, smiling down at her. 'You make a pretty picture, the pair of you, I vow – and far from sickly!'

'And you, Uncle Patrick, a most splendid one!' she returned, unabashed. 'I like you in black velvet and silver. And to see you smile again. You have smiled at me but little, of late.'

'M'mmm.' He eyed her thoughtfully, as she rose to her feet. 'You have not done a deal of smiling yourself, Mary, I think.'

She shrugged. 'Perhaps not. They have not been smiling times. But – the wedding? Did all go well? You are back betimes. There were no . . . hitches?'

'None – save that the bridegroom might have been at his own funeral, and the bride a ghost!' he told her. 'The feast now proceeding lacks something of joy and gaiety in consequence. I have seen wakes more rousing!'

'Poor Vicky,' she murmured. 'Poor Lady Sophia, also.'

Patrick stroked his chin. 'Do not waste your compassion on Vicky, my dear,' he advised. 'He is none so unfortunate. Amongst such as might marry the Duke of Lennox, Sophia Ruthven stands high. She has more to commend her than most. And as husbands go, Vicky I have no doubt, will serve her well enough.'

'No doubt,' she agreed, a little wearily. 'So all do assure me.'

He reached out to run a hand lightly over her dark hair.

'Mary, lass – you are not hurt, in this? It is not like you to avoid the wedding to feign sickness. I know well that you are fond of Vicky. You have been friends always – since that first day I gave him into your young hands at Castle Huntly. But you have always known, also, that this must happen, that he must marry. That he was . . . '

'That Vicky was not for such as me,' she completed for him, evenly. 'Yes, I have always known it. Do not fear, it is not for myself that I grieve. It is for Vicky. He is unhappy.'

'He will get over it – nothing more sure. He is very young – little more than a boy, indeed. Young even for his years. He has a deal to learn. High rank, high office, demands much . . . '

'All that I know well,' she interposed. 'I but preferred not to watch a marriage in which there was no fondness. You will mind that I did not attend his sister's to my lord of Huntly, either. Tell me – did Master Bruce preach a sermon? Did the King make a speech?'

'Both, woe is me! And belike we shall have to sit through it all tomorrow when Jean weds Leslie of Lindores.' He groaned. 'Ah, me – the folly of it! This flood of words that poor old Scotland drowns in! I heard Johnny Mar bewailing that he was not shut up safely in ward like Bothwell, so as to be spared further attendance at such!' He stopped, as though the name of Bothwell had given him pause, and took a pace or two across the room. 'I wonder, now . . . ?' he said slowly, looking out of the window.

Mary followed him with her eyes. 'You wonder about Bothwell – or my lord of Mar?' she asked.

'About both,' he answered. 'The way that slipped out, from Mar. I would say that he does not therefore esteem Bothwell to be in great danger. A small thing, but . . . '

'And do you so think, Uncle Patrick?'

'Why no. Not now – not any more.' He turned back to her. 'Why? Are you interested in Bothwell, moppet?'

'I have wondered much about him. He has been held so long imprisoned in the Castle, and not brought to trial. Despite the wicked deaths of so many others. Does the King no longer seek his life?'

'The King would have his head tomorrow, if he dared!' Patrick told her.

'That means, then, that my lord has powerful friends. As I thought.'

'The most powerful, it seems!' the man agreed grimly.

'The Chancellor? My lord of Moray? They were not formerly his friends.'

'More powerful than these.'

'More . . . ? But, are there such? The Kirk? Surely not the Kirk? Bothwell has been no friend to the Kirk.'

'More powerful even than the Kirk.'

'Then there is only . . . only . . . ?'

'Aye – only Elizabeth! Only the Queen of England. That good lady chooses to interest herself in Bothwell's fate.'

'But why? Did she not ever speak only ill of him? Call him a brigand? Write that he treated her borders like his own backyard?'

He shrugged. 'All true, my dear. But she is a woman, and may change her mind. She must have some reason – but I have not fathomed it. I have seen a letter from her to the King, urging clemency, saying that he is but a young man misled, that there is no real ill in him. She offers no reason for this change of face – but needs none. James dare not controvert her – if only for his pension's sake! That is why my Lord Chancellor has turned Bothwell's friend. Although I cannot think that it is Moray's reason.'

'So he will not die?'

'Not, at least, on this occasion, I fear!'

'How long then, will he stay in ward?'

'As for that I neither know nor care,' the Master said, with a snap of slim fingers. 'Until he rots, if need be! Not,' he added sardonically, 'that he is in any present danger of rotting, I believe.'

'No,' she agreed. 'I hear that he is very . . . comfortable.' Mary came over to take his arm. 'Uncle Patrick,' she said. 'Do you not think that you might serve yourself better, over my lord of Bothwell?'

'Eh? Better? How do you mean better, girl?'

'Better than now. Better than by leaving him there, to rot. You brought him low, did you not, for your own purposes? Now, raise him up again, also for your own purposes.'

He gazed at her, scimitar brows raised. '*I* brought him low . . . ?' he repeated.

'Yes. Over the North Berwick witchcraft plot,' she answered factually, calmly. 'Now you say that the King will not dare to try him. So that you can gain nothing more with him. Can you? In ward. Because of his powerful friends. But if his friends are so strong, why fight them? Become one of them, rather. Aid Bothwell now, Uncle Patrick. Once you told me that it was a fool who fought a losing battle. And also that in statecraft a man could not afford to keep up private enmities.'

Still-faced the man considered her, silent.

'Aid Bothwell now,' she repeated. 'He has paid sufficiently for what he said at Leith, yon time – has he not? And gain much credit with his powerful friends.'

Patrick was actually smiling again. 'It warms my heart to see you so!' he declared. 'To hear you. I' faith, it does.'

'Perhaps . . . but laugh at me at your peril!' she warned. 'For I am very serious. Does what I say not make good sense? By your own measure, Uncle Patrick?'

'I do not know – yet. It will require thought. But, on my soul, if you are for teaching me my business, child, will you not spare me this uncling? Uncle Patrick! Uncle Patrick! Will you uncle me all my days? Can you not call me but Patrick, as others do?'

'Why, yes, Patrick – I shall,' she agreed. 'If you will spare me the child. You scarce consider me a child, yet, do you?'

'By God, I do not! You are right, young woman. It is a bargain! No childing, and no uncling!' He folded his arms. 'Now Mistress Mary Gray – what would you have me do with Bothwell?'

'You could seek to have him released. Do better than these so powerful friends of his.'

'And lose more favour with the King? That I cannot afford, my dear.'

'Then . . . could you not aid his escape from ward? From the Castle. Others have won out of Edinburgh Castle ere this, have they not? With assistance. Secretly. Might it not be arranged?'

He tipped his lips with his tongue. 'You are . . . quite a little devil, are you not, Mary my pet?'

320

'You are not jealous?' she wondered seriously.

He laughed musically. 'Perhaps I should be! Instead, damme, of being . . . well, just a little proud!'

'Of me? Then, you think well of my suggestion?'

'Say that I see possibilities in it – no more,' he told her lightly. 'Possibilities, sweeting.'

'Yes,' she nodded, satisfied. 'That is what I thought. Now – go you back to the wedding-feast, Patrick. Or your absence will be noted . . . and the unkind will say that you are plotting some ill! Which would be very unfair, would it not?'

He took her chin in his hand, and considered her quizzically. 'Witch!' he accused. 'If our King Jamie seeks true witches, he has not far to look for one!'

Her lovely face clouded at his words, and she turned away. 'How can you jest about so terrible an evil?' she demanded.

'Why, girl, sometimes I jest that I may not weep.'

'Yes. I am sorry. Go then, Patrick – and thank you for your coming. It was kindly. Will you tell Vicky that I wish him very well?'

'Aye, if you say so.' He grinned. 'That should much aid his bridal night! A kiss, now, moppet . . .'

The officer unlocked the great door at the foot of the turn-pike stair, and raised his lantern to point down the further steep flight of stairs.

'Yonder is the room, sir,' he said, handing Patrick a key, and also the lantern. 'My lord may be abed by this. His man has left him for the night, and sleeps in the guard-room above, with my fellows. You will find me there when you are finished.'

'My thanks, Captain. I may be some little time.'

Patrick went down the remaining steps to the door at their end. Some perhaps misplaced courtesy made him knock thereon before fitting the key to the lock. The door opened to a darkened chamber which the lantern revealed to be vaulted, fair-sized, and though walled and floored in bare stone, to be furnished in reasonable comfort. On a bed in one corner a man lay, in shirt and breeches, blinking and frowning at the light.

'A God's name, Wattie – what ails you?' he snarled. 'What do you want at this hour?'

'Here is no Wattie, my lord,' Patrick answered pleasantly, 'But another, more . . . effective.'

'Eh . . . ?' Bothwell sat up. 'What is this? Who, i' the fiend's name, are you?'

'I wonder that you are still so free with the Fiend's name, at this late date, my lord!' Patrick observed, laughing. 'I would have reckoned that you might have had your bellyful of him!'

'I know that voice,' the other cried. 'It's Gray, is it not? That ill-conceived and treacherous scoundrel, the Master of Gray?'

'Your tongue would seem to lack both accuracy and charity – but there is nothing wrong with your ears! Gray it is.' Patrick held the lamp high. 'I see that they have given you a better chamber than they gave me three years agone!'

Bothwell rose to his full height. If captivity had weakened his frame or blanched his cheek, it did not show in the lantern's light. Tall, muscular, hot-eyed, angry, he stood there, swaying slightly.

'Curse you!' he spluttered. 'You it is that I have to thank that I am here, they tell me!'

'How mistaken you are, my lord. That is wholly the King's doing, in his diligent assault on witchery and warlockry. Poor James – he is much upset . . .'

'Liar!'

Patrick shrugged. 'Have it your own way, my friend. But I would urge that you do not make my mission here tonight of no avail.'

'Aye, what are you here for – reprobate!'

'Your release, my lord – what else?'

That brought the other up short. 'Release . . . ?'

'Release, yes. Or, more exactly perhaps, your escape. At any rate, your abstraction from these present toils.'

Bothwell was staring at him. 'Mockery becomes you no better than does lying!' he said, but with less of conviction.

'I no more mock than lie. But perhaps you do not choose to leave the security of these four stout walls, my lord?'

'Fool!' the other jerked. 'Come – say what you came to say, and be gone!'

Patrick sighed. 'For one so ill-placed as yourself, I confess that I find you much lacking in civility. You are a hard man to be friends with, it seems! I am almost minded to leave you to your fate.'

'Out with it, man – out with it.'

'Very well. I am prepared to aid your escape out of this place. It can be done.'

'A trick, I vow!'

'No trick. What would it serve me to trick you in this?'

'I do not know. But I know that I do not trust you one inch, Gray.'

'Then remain here and die, my lord.'

'I will not die, I think. But why should *you* seek to aid me?'

'Why, that one day you may aid me in return, my friend.'

This frankness may have commended itself somewhat to Bothwell, for he considered his visitor with at least more attention. 'What do you want?' he asked.

'Let us leave that, for the moment. Say that I feel sure that you can be of more benefit to me out of ward than in it, my lord. Now – to get you out of here, I believe, three items only are required. A rasp, a rope, and a bold courage. The first two can be supplied. The third you must contribute for yourself.'

'My courage, sir, has never been called in question. A rope, you say . . . ?' Bothwell's eyes swung towards the two small barred windows.

'Aye.' Dryly the Master glanced in the same direction. 'It is a long drop, my lord. Some forty or fifty feet of walling, and then a couple of hundred feet of good Scottish rock. But a knotted rope of ample length, a clear head and a stout heart – and helping hands to aid you on the rock – and heigho, it will be your own Borderland for you again!'

The Earl said nothing.

Patrick strolled over, and raised his lantern to look more closely at the window bars. 'Aye – nothing here that a stout rasp will not cut through in an hour or so. Nor is the space so small that you could not win through. There should be no difficulty, my lord.'

'Save getting the file and the rope to me, here! The rope

323

in especial. How are you to get that past the guard, man? Enough rope . . . ?'

'It must needs be a very slender cord, I fear – but sufficiently strong, for it would be a pity if it broke, would it not?' The visitor's eyes gleamed in the lamplight. 'I fear that you must just trust the jumped-up wardrobe-master for that, my lord! Slender enough to be wound around a man's person many times, under his clothing as an officer of the King's Guard. He will bear also a rasp, of course – and a letter for you with the King's seal. Also an order to see you, bearing the signature of my lord of Moray, Captain of the Royal Guard!'

'But . . . a pox! Moray would never do that! Put his own head in a noose! For me?'

'I did not say that he would – did I?' The Master smiled. 'Just have a little faith in your treacherous scoundrel, my Lord Bothwell. I have achieved much more difficult tasks than this. Give me a few days – a week – for I would not wish this my visit to you to be linked with the business. That would serve neither you nor me, you will agree?'

Bothwell remained silent, suspicious.

'That is all, then, I think. Wait you for a week. Do not disclose to any, even to your man, that you think to be leaving these quarters. The letter will tell you when to assay the escape. Also where men will be waiting for you, with horses, below the rock. All will be dealt with, never fear.' Patrick laughed. 'And the rope will be long enough and strong enough, I promise you!'

'And the price, Master of Gray? Your price for this service?' Bothwell got out at last.

'That can wait. Let us not haggle and chaffer like hucksters. We neither of us are merchants, my lord – both men of the world. Say that I may seek *your* aid at some later date – and hope not to be rejected!'

Still the other did not commit himself. 'We shall see,' he said, cryptically.

'Undoubtedly. I give you goodnight, my doubting friend. When next we meet you will be a free man.' He sighed. 'Or a dead one!'

The King was all but in tears. 'It must ha' been Moray, I

tell you!' he cried, thumping his hand on the table. 'Here is the warrant, signed in his ain hand, to admit the bearer to visit the Earl o' Bothwell on the King's business. On *my* business, waesucks! It's treason, I tell you – blackest treason!'

The hastily-assembled members of the Council, such as could be gathered together at short notice thus early in the day, eyed their dishevelled monarch and each other with various expressions of unease, resentment and blank sleepiness. Most had barely got over the last night's potations, and were in no fit state to deal with high treason before breakfast. James himself was only part-dressed; after long studies later into the night than usual owing to the Queen's absence, on witchcraft and the writing of his book, he was blear-eyed and unbeautiful. Never apt for early rising save when hunting, today he had been awakened with the dire news of Bothwell's escape from Edinburgh Castle, and nothing would serve but an immediate meeting of his Council, assured that his royal person was in imminent danger.

'I cannot believe that my lord of Moray would be a party to this escape, Sire,' Sir James Melville declared. 'He is not a man for such ploys. He does not concern himself with affairs of the state. His interests are, h'm, otherwhere! He is no dabbler in plots and treasons. He spoke for my lord of Bothwell yon time, yes – but he was never Bothwell's friend.'

'Aye,' his brother Sir Robert agreed, and yawned.

'They are full cousins,' Chancellor Maitland observed briefly.

'Aye, but so are they both cousins o' my ain!' James took him up. 'God's curse – I've ower many cousins!' He flapped the paper with Moray's signature. 'This bears his name. None could ha' gained Bothwell's escape but through this officer o' my Guard he sent yesterday – the traitorous carle!'

'Who was the officer, Sire?' his uncle Orkney asked shortly. 'Have him in. We'll soon ha' the truth out o' him.'

'But nobody kens who it was, man!' James wailed. 'It wasna one of my usual officers. But dressed in my royal colours, mind. An imposter, just, I swear. Wi' this letter frae Moray. And Moray is Captain o' my Royal Guard!'

'An appointment, Sire, of which I never approved,' the Chancellor reminded, sourly. 'I ever say that such beautiful men are seldom honest!' And he shot a baleful glance at the Master of Gray sitting far down the table.

'At least he was a more honest beauty than the last Captain of the Guard – my lord of Huntly!' the Earl of Mar snorted.

James flushed. 'Is there no man I can trust?' he asked, broken-voiced.

Patrick spoke. 'Your Grace – might I see the pass-letter?' When the paper was passed down to him, he scrutinised it closely. 'It is certainly like my lord of Moray's hand o' write. Such is familiar to me – after our embassage to London. But . . . it could be a forgery, Sire.'

'Eh . . . ? How should it be a forgery, man?'

'There are not a few expert forgers in this town, I think – even in this Court! At my own trial, of unhappy memory, forgeries were produced to damn me – most admirable likenesses of my own writings. Were they not, my Lord Chancellor?'

'Sire – this is intolerable! The Master of Gray was condemned by his own writings, and the sure testimonies of others. Including Queen Elizabeth. Not by forgeries. Just as, I swear, this is no forgery. Why should it be a forgery?'

'Have him in, then. Ask him.' Orkney said impatiently. 'Where is Moray?'

'He's no' here,' James declared. 'He's awa' to Fife.'

'He is escorting the Queen to Dunfermline, my lord,' Patrick informed his father-in-law easily. 'To inspect the progress of her new house at the Abbey there. The house I myself started to build, one time!' He smiled. 'They left yesterday. Her Grace was very concerned to see the house. And my lord of Moray is entirely attentive to Her Grace's wishes, is he not? His Highness being . . . otherwise occupied.'

The King peered at the Master in new alarm. 'You're . . . you're no' saying . . . ? You dinna mean, Patrick, that she . . . that my Annie . . . ? That Moray . . . ?'

'No, so, Sire – of course not! Never think such a thing. The Queen is entirely safe with my lord of Moray, I vow. His love for her is most fervent, as we all know.'

James swallowed, and achieved only a croak.

Orkney hooted rudely.

'Moreover, have they not his Countess with them, Sire. Have no fears.'

'Yon addlepate . . . !' the King muttered.

'Sire – is not this profitless talk?' Mar interjected. 'Moray can wait. He will deny this signature, anyway. Is it not more needful to be considering Bothwell? What *he* will do. He will be an angry man – and he is crazed enough when he is not! I wager he will now be a man beside himself. And only Huntly can field more men-at-arms.'

'Aye – I ken, I ken!' James quavered. 'Is that no' why I called this Council? He'll be rampaging the Borders, now. Raising the Marches against me!'

'Or nearer – at Hailes Castle, raising Lothian and the Merse.'

'Or nearer still, at Crichton, ready to descend on this Edinburgh!'

'My lords – Your Grace!' Patrick protested. 'Bothwell only made his escape last night. He can raise many men, yes – but they are scattered. It will take him time. He is hot-headed – but despite some of the testimony we have listened to, he is but human! He cannot descend upon His Grace, whether from the Borders or Hailes or Crichton, today or tomorrow – if such is his intention. Men take time to assemble – as most of us know from experience. *We* have time, therefore – a week, at least.'

'Aye, maybe,' James conceded. 'But time for what, man Patrick? I canna trust my Royal Guard, after this. Can I assemble men as quick as can Bothwell? And whose men . . . ?'

'Have I not ever urged, Sire, that you should seek to enroll many more men? Not merely to increase the Royal Guard, but to have a force always ready. Your own men, for the sure defence of your realm. Other monarchs have such, and do not depend only on the levies of their lords . . . '

'But the siller, man – the siller! Where's it to come frae? To pay them. Elizabeth's that mean . . . '

'There is siller, Sire in your own Scotland – not a little. And there are means of winning it. But now is not the time for that . . . '

'I rejoice to hear the Master of Gray admit that, at least!' Maitland remarked.

Patrick ignored him. 'Increase your Guard, yes. Appoint a new Captain. Have the Provost call out the City Bands.'

'I misdoubt if I can trust them!'

'They hate Bothwell, Sire. He has ridden roughshod down their High Street too often . . .'

The Lord Chancellor intervened again. 'Highness – all this will be done, without the Master of Gray's advising. You may entrust your safety to my hands.'

'Ooh, aye,' James acknowledged doubtfully.

'Heigho – then all is settled securely!' Patrick laughed, pushing back his chair. 'All will now be well. We have the Lord Chancellor's word for it! Surely we need no longer delay our breakfasts, gentlemen?'

Uncertainly they all looked at each other.

'Na, na,' the King objected. 'What's been decided? I dinna ken what's been decided?'

Orkney guffawed. 'Why – that we adjourn. Maitland, here – a pox! I forgot. My Lord Maitland o' Thirlestane. My lord will attend to all. He kens our mind. To breakfast, then – before our bellies deafen us!'

The Privy Council broke up forthwith, however uncertain the monarch or frosty the Chancellor. As the members streamed out, Patrick stooped to the crouching King's ear.

'Sire,' he said quietly, 'the stags are fat and free of velvet in Falkland woods. You have been neglecting them! Overmuch study, overmuch witchcraft, overmuch work, is serving you but ill. Move the Court to Falkland, Your Grace, and chase the deer again, instead of warlocks. You are further from Bothwell there. The Queen then can watch her house abuilding at Dunfermline, without bedding away from your side. And my lord of Moray, at Donibristle, is under your eye. To Falkland, Sire! Leave this Edinburgh to my Lord Chancellor.'

James Stewart looked up, and almost eagerly he nodded his heavy head.

Chapter Eighteen

MARY GRAY pulled up her sweating, foaming mount, and peered from under hand-shaded eyes into the already declining October sun. This *ought* to be the valley, surely? She had forded the River Earn fully five miles back, at Aberdalgie, and the land was obviously falling away, in front, to the next strath, that of the Almond she had been told, with the Highland hills rising beyond. Methven was this south side of the Almond, all agreed. Where then was the castle? This green land of wide grassy slopes and identical rounded knolls was confusing.

Stroking the mare's soaking quivering neck, she urged the tired beast on. She herself was tired, but this was no time to acknowledge it. For almost five hours she had been in the saddle – for foolishly, she had got lost amongst the Glenfarg foothills.

Rounding one more of the grassy knolls a mile or so further, she heaved a sigh of relief. Ahead, the hillocks seemed to draw back to leave a broad open basin of fair meadowland, cattle-dotted, and gently rising pasture, wide to the south but hemmed in and guarded on the north by the frowning ramparts of the blue heather hills. And on a tree-scattered terrace between meadows and upland, bathed in the golden rays of the slanting autumn sunlight, stood a large and gracious house, its red stonework glowing like old rose.

At first sight of it, Mary found a lump risen in her throat. Often she had visualised Methven Castle, Vicky's home, the place that he had besought her so often to come and rule as mistress. In her mind's eye she had seen it as little different from all those other castles which she knew so well, Castle Huntly where she had been born, Broughty, Foulis, Craigmillar, tall frowning battlemented towers of rude stone, small-windowed, picked out with gunloops and arrow-slits, stern, proud, aggressive. But this was quite other, a smiling place of pleasing symmetry, of slender turrets and many large windows reflecting the sun. A sort of royal dower-house for generations, and never a grasping lord's stronghold, James had given Methven to Ludovick in a fit of eager generosity on his first coming to Scotland from France, as an eight-year-old boy. Like a magnet it beckoned to the lone rider now.

Nevertheless, as Mary rode into the fine paved courtyard on the north side of the castle, enclosed by wings of domestic buildings, she gained no sense of welcome, no feeling of reception of any sort. The house itself was nowise unfriendly, quietly detached, serene, rather; but of human reaction there was none. No grooms came churrying to her horse's head, no men-at-arms lounged about the yard, no faces looked out from the ranks of the windows. The great front door stood wide open, certainly, and white pigeons strutted and fluttered and cooed about the courtyard, but otherwise the place might have been deserted. Autumn leaves had drifted in heaps in many corners, and no single plume of smoke rose above any of the numerous chimneys.

Mary's heart sank, as she dismounted stiffly

Leaving her mare to stand in steaming weariness, she moved over to the open doorway. After a moment or two of hesitation, she raised her voice in a long clear halloo. Other than the echoes, and the sudden alarm of the pigeons, there was no response.

She stepped in over the threshold, into a wide vestibule. It was lighter, brighter, in here than in any of the houses that she knew, with their thick walls and small windows. At either end of it a broad turnpike stairway arose – two stairs, an unimagined luxury. Yet even in here dead leaves had blown. The great house was entirely silent; only the soft murmuration of the pigeons broke the quiet.

Somehow Mary could not bring herself to shout out again, inside that hushed place. Biting her lip, she was moving over to one of the stairways when she perceived a cloak thrown carelessly over a chair in a corner, most of it trailing on the floor. Her heart lifted at the sight. She recognised it as one of Vicky's cloaks, and certainly it was thrown down in his typical fashion. The familiarity of it, so simple a thing as it was, warmed her strangely. Kilting up her riding-habit, she ran light-footed up the winding stair.

From the wide first floor landing long corridors stretched

right and left, lit in patches by the yellow beams of westering sunlight slanting in from sundry open doors. The first such that she peered in at showed a fine panelled room, with a splendid painted coved ceiling in timber, depicting heraldry and strange beasts. The grey ashes of a dead fire littered the handsome carved stone fireplace, and the rugs of skin on the floor were scattered haphazard. At one end of a great table were the remains of an unambitious meal.

The next room was even larger, but was only partly furnished and gave no impression of habitation. The next door again was locked.

Frowning, Mary was for moving over to the other corridor, when she stopped. Faintly she heard a dog barking – or rather, the high baying of a hound.

Hurrying through the first room to its south-facing window, she peered out. Away to the south-west, across the water-meadows, a single horseman rode, flanked by two loping long-legged wolf-hounds. He rode at the gallop, high in his stirrups, hatless, towards the house, scattering the grazing cattle left and right. Mary knew that stance, that figure. Thoughtfully she considered it, before she went tripping downstairs.

Ludovick of Lennox came clattering into the courtyard, still at a canter. His glance lighted on the drooping mare, still standing there, and swung at once to the front doorway. At sight of the young woman waiting therein, his eyes widened, and he reined up his mount so abruptly that its shod hooves scraped long scratches on the paving-stones, showering sparks. Before the beast, haunches down, could come to a halt, he had thrown himself from the saddle and came running.

'Mary! Mary!' he cried, amidst the agitated flapping of pigeons and the excited yelping of his hounds.

The girl herself started forward, hands outstretched – and then halted. But no such discretion could halt the young man. Upon her he rushed, arms wide, to enfold her, to hug her to him, to lift her completely off her feet. His lips found hers, and clung thereto, as together they staggered back against the door jamb.

Mary did not struggle or protest in his arms. But when, panting for breath, he lifted his head for a moment to gaze into her dark eyes, before seeking her mouth again, she raised a

331

hand between their lips, so that it was her fingers that he must needs kiss. She did not trust herself to words.

'Mary, my dear! My dear!' he exclaimed. 'How come you here? From where? Are you alone? How good it is to see you. Oh, my dear – how good!'

'And you, Vicky – and you!' she whispered.

'It has been so long. An eternity!'

'Silly – a bare month. No more.'

'An eternity,' he insisted. 'Each hour a day, a month . . . '

Gently she disengaged herself from his closest grip. 'Here . . . here is no talk for a wedded husband, Vicky!'

He snorted a mirthless laugh. 'Whatever else I am, that I am not!' he declared.

'Hush, Vicky . . . !'

'It is the truth. But . . . how are you here, Mary? And alone? But one horse . . . ?' He still held her arms.

'Yes. Alone. I have ridden from Falkland. To see you.'

'Falkland! That is thirty miles. Forty . . . '

'More – as I rode it! Foolishly, I lost myself. In the hills beyond Glenfarg.'

'You should not have done it, Mary! A woman, alone . . . '

'Tush – I am not one of your fine Court ladies. I can look after myself. I had to come, Vicky. Matters go but ill.'

'When did they do other?' he asked, a bitter note in his voice, new to that uncomplicated young man. 'And why from Falkland?'

'The Court has moved there. Did you not know? After Bothwell's escape.'

'I heard that Bothwell had escaped from ward, yes. All the land knows that. But . . . come inside, Mary. You must be weary, hungry. What do I dream of, keeping you standing here! I will tie the horses for the nonce – and bait them later.'

'*You* will bait them . . . ?'

'Why, yes. I am alone here.'

She stared at him. 'Alone . . . ?' she echoed.

'I prefer it that way. I sent the servants back to the village. It is but a mile off. And Peter Hay has ridden to Edinburgh for me, two days agone. He carried a letter. For you . . . '

'But . . . ' She searched his face. 'The Duchess?'

'Sophia? She is not here.'

'But, Vicky – why? Where is she?'

'I sent her home. To Ruthven Castle. It is not far. Near to St. John's Town of Perth. It is better that way.'

Mary bit her lip. 'Oh, Vicky – I did not believe that you could be so cruel.'

'Is it cruelty, Mary? I think not. Sophia Ruthven has no more joy in this marriage than have I. And she is sick, very sick. She coughs. She is never done coughing. She coughs blood. She is better with her mother at Ruthven.'

The young woman was silent for a little. 'I did not know,' she whispered, at length. 'Did not know of her sickness. Poor lassie.'

'Nor did I. But Patrick knew. And the King knew, I swear. And yet . . . !' Scowling, he left the rest unsaid.

Unhappily Mary eyed him. 'I am sorry,' she said. 'So very sorry. But . . . does she not merit the more kindness? Need you have sent her away . . . so soon?'

'I deemed it kinder that she should go. She wished to go. She wanted nothing that I could give her. We did not once sleep together.'

'How much did you . . . offer her, Vicky?'

'God – would you have had me force her? You?'

She shook her head. 'Never that. Only a little of kindness, of patience, Vicky. You are man and wife. You took vows, in the sight of God . . . '

'Is that how you name what was done to us in yon Abbey of Holyrood?'

She drew a long breath. 'No. Perhaps not. Vicky – do not let us talk to each other thus. It is . . . not for us. Forgive me.'

'And me. This is folly. You are tired, Mary – and I keep you standing here. Come you inside.'

'We shall see to the horses together, first. I am none so tired. Not now.'

'What brought you here then, Mary?' he asked as they entered the great stables, empty save for two other horses. 'You said that matters went ill?'

'Yes. I need your help, Vicky. That is why I came. I am not so clever as I thought myself, I fear. I . . . I am frightened.'

So little in character was this for Mary Gray that Lennox

paused in his unsaddling, to stare at her. 'You?' he said. '*You* are frightened?'

'Yes. For what I have done. For what may happen because of what I have done. Because of my presumption. This time. I fear that I have been too clever, and a great evil may follow.'

'Patrick again?' he asked.

She nodded. 'I led him to effect Bothwell's escape. Yes, it was my doing. Thinking at least to aid one man, to undo one wrong. Perhaps even to help bring these evil witch-trials to an end. Hoping that with Bothwell free, the King might relent, might even be afraid to go on, to fear what Bothwell might do if he continued.' She looked away. 'Patrick said, did I think to teach him his business? God forgive me, I think that perhaps I did! If it is so, then I have my reward. For Patrick but used my conceit to bring down another. My lord of Moray.'

'Moray? And Bothwell? How comes Moray into this?'

'He is Captain of the King's Guard. Or was. Bothwell was the King's prisoner. He could be held responsible. But, worse – the escape was gained through a man dressed as an officer of the Royal Guard, and bearing an order supposedly signed by Moray, as Captain, to gain him admittance to Bothwell on the King's business. A forgery, of course. But ample for the occasion. Ample to poison the King's mind. Moray's denials count for little.'

'Who was this man? This officer of the Guard?'

'Nobody knows . . . or will tell. But he was dressed in the royal colours and livery. And only one close to the Guard could have gained him that. Or close to the Wordrobe!'

'I see. So Patrick cries down Moray, now? Why?'

'Not so. He is loud in Moray's defence. Too loud. Making excuse for him in this. But also in the matter of the Queen. It is for this last that I am frightened, Vicky. This of the Queen.'

'You fear for the Queen, Mary? Surely not that? Not even Patrick could . . . '

'The Queen, yes. Although not so much as for Moray. I fear for them both. Together. Patrick is very attentive to the Queen. But she has Dunfermline, that hateful place that he had set his heart on. He will never have it now – and I think that he will never forgive her. And, sorrow – that was my doing also. It was I who urged the King to dower her with Dunfermline Abbey. To prevent Patrick from ruining himself to get it. I was clever again, you see – so very clever. So I bear responsibility for both, for Moray and the Queen, Vicky . . . '

'I think that you blame yourself overmuch, Mary.' He frowned. 'But . . . I do not understand. How comes the Queen into this matter? Of Moray and Bothwell? What do you fear for her, in it?'

'It is not that. It is that the Queen is seeing overmuch of Moray. From the first she has liked him well, as you know. But it becomes too much. In especial since coming to Falkland. And Patrick is effecting it so, I am sure. Falkland is not far from both Dunfermline and Donibristle, Moray's house in Fife. The Queen is ever going to Dunfermline, to see to her house building there, while the King is hunting or at his books and papers. Moray is in disgrace, and banned the Court meantime – but he is much at Dunfermline, and the Queen at Donibristle.'

'You think that they are lovers?'

'No. Not that. Not yet. But Moray is . . . Moray. And very handsome. And the Queen is lonely, and very young. And Patrick, I think, would have the King come to believe it. To Moray's ruin.' She sighed. 'I have spoken to him, of course. He but laughs at me, denying it. But as one of the Queen's women I see much. I see how he ever entices the Queen to Dunfermline, with new notions for her house, new plans for the pleasance she is making, for the water-garden, for new plenishings that workmen he has found for her are making. When she would have the King go with her, I have seen how Patrick works on him to do otherwise – a deputation to receive, a visit to Cupar or St. Andrews or Newburgh, new papers to study, or some notable stag spied on Lomond Hill. He is always with the King, closer than he has ever been. With Moray and Bothwell and Huntly banished the Court, the Chancellor still in Edinburgh, and many of the lords at their justice-eyres – aye, and you away here, Vicky – thus there are few close to the King to cross Patrick's influence. Only Mar, who is stupid. And Atholl, who is drunken.' She paused, almost for breath. 'I fear greatly for Moray and the Queen,' she ended flatly. 'And I must blame myself.'

'You blame yourself for too much, Mary. This is Patrick's doing, not yours.'

'But I – I thought to outplay Patrick at his own game. That there is no denying.'

He carried an armful of sweet-smelling hay to the manger. 'Patrick is nearer to the Devil than ever was Bothwell!' he said.

Her lovely face crumpled as with a spasm of pain. 'Do not say that, Vicky!' she pleaded. 'Never say it.'

'It is the truth,' he declared bluntly. 'The man is evil.'

'No! Not evil. Not truly evil. My father – Davy Gray – said that he had a devil. I did not believe him. Yet he loved him – loves him still. Perhaps he is right – perhaps he has a devil. Perhaps he is two men – one ill and one good. There is much good in him, Vicky – as you know, who are his friend.'

'*Was* his friend,' Lennox corrected briefly.

'Was and are, Vicky. You must be. True friendship remains true. Even in such case.'

'May a man remain friends with evil, and still not sin?'

'I think he may, yes. Is it sin for me to love Patrick still, as I do. Not the evil in him, but Patrick himself.'

'He is your father . . .'

'I do not love him because he sired me. Davy I love as my father. I love Patrick . . . because he is Patrick.'

'Aye.' Ludovick sighed. 'So do we all, God help us! Come – into the house with us.'

'Then – you will come back with me, Vicky? To Falkland? To help me? To try to save Moray. And the Queen. And Patrick from himself. I know that you hate the Court, Vicky – but come.'

'Lord!' Almost he smiled. 'All that! So many to save! I will come, Mary – but cannot think to achieve so much. I am no worker of miracles, as you know well. Or you would be my wife here in Methven. But come I will – since you ask it. As you knew I would – or you would not have come, I think.'

'As I knew you would,' she agreed, gravely. 'Thank you, Vicky.'

Later, with a well-doing fire of birch-logs blazing and spurting on the heaped ash of the open hearth, filling the handsome room with the aromatic fragrance and flickering on the shadowy panelled walls, Mary sat, legs tucked beneath her skirt, on a deerskin rug on the floor, and gazed deep into the red heart of the fire, silent. It was indeed very silent in that chamber, in all the great house, in the night that pressed in on them from the vast and empty foothill country. The only sounds were the noises of the fire, the faint sigh of evening wind in the chimney, the occasional call of a night-bird, and the soft regular tread and creak of floorboards as Ludovick paced slowly to and fro behind her. They had not spoken for perhaps ten minutes, since she had cleared away the meal that she had made for them, and he had lit the fire against the night's chill.

The young man's voice, when it came, was quiet also, less jerky and self-conscious than was his usual. 'This . . . this is what I have always dreamed of, Mary. You, sitting before my fire, in my house. Alone. And the night falling.'

She neither stirred nor made answer to that. His steady but unhurried pacing continued at her back, without pause.

'You are so very small,' he mentioned again, presently, out of the shadows. 'So slight a creature to be so important. So small, there before the fire – so slightly made, yet so perfect, so beautiful. And so strong. So strong.' That last was on a sigh.

'I am not strong, Vicky,' she answered him, after a long moment, calmly, as out of due consideration. 'No, I am not strong.'

'Yes, you are,' he insisted. 'You are the strongest person that I know. Stronger than all the blustering lords or the frowning churchmen. Stronger than all who think that they are strong – the doctors and professors and judges. Aye, stronger even than Patrick Gray, I swear.' He had halted directly behind her.

She shook her head, the firelight glinting on her hair, but said nothing. Nor did she look round or up.

'Why should the woman that I want, and need, be so strong?' he demanded, his voice rising a little. 'When *I* am not strong? Why should it have been you . . . and me? In all this realm?'

'I do not know, Vicky,' she told him. 'But this I do know

. . . that I do not feel strong this night.'

'You mean . . . ?' Looking down on her, he opened his mouth to say more, and then forbore, frowning. When she did not amplify that statement, made so factually, he resumed his pacing.

An owl had the silence to itself for a space.

'All men want you,' he said, at length. 'I watch them. See how they look at you. Even some of the ministers of the Kirk. Even James, who is fonder of men than of women. All would have you, if they could. Yet you look to care for none of them. You smile kindly on all. On many that deserve no smile – ill, lecherous men. But yourself, you need none of them?' That last was a question.

'You think that?'

'I know not what to think. I wonder – always I wonder. You keep your inmost heart . . . so close.'

'You make me sound hard, unfeeling, Vicky. Am I that?'

'No. Not that. But sufficient unto yourself, perhaps. Not drawn to men. Yet drawing men to yourself.'

'I mislike the picture that you paint of me. Is it true, then?'

'It cannot be – for I would paint you as the loveliest picture in all this world, if I could, Mary – if I but knew how.'

'Dear Vicky.'

'Mary.' Abruptly he was standing directly above her again, his knees all but touching her back. 'Have you – have you ever given yourself to a man? So many must have tried to have you. Have you let any take you?' That was breathlessly asked.

'Why no, Vicky. I have not.'

He swallowed, and was silent.

She turned now, to look up at him. 'Why do you ask? Do you fear that I am cold? Unnatural? That I find no pleasure in men, perhaps? And think that this may prove it?'

'No, no – never that, Mary. I am glad. Glad. I hoped . . . ' He paused. 'You see, neither have I ever had a woman.'

Slowly she smiled. 'No?'

'No.' Something, perhaps her faint smile, made him add, hurriedly, almost roughly, 'I could have had, Mary. Many a time. Many would have . . . that Jean Stewart . . . '

She nodded. 'I know it, Vicky. The Duke of Lennox need never lie lonely of a night.'

'But I do, Mary – I do!' he cried. 'There's the nub of it! And it is your doing.'

'I am sorry,' she said flatly.

The silence resumed, and Ludovick's pacing with it.

Presently, and very quietly, the girl began to sing, as though to herself, an age-old crooning song with a haunting lilt to it, as old as Scotland itself. Softly, unhurriedly, deliberately, almost as if she picked out the notes on a lute, she sang, eyes on the fire, swaying her body just a little to the repeated rhythmic melody. The song had no beginning and no end.

Gradually the young man's pacing eased and slowed, until he was halted, listening, watching her. Then, after a minute or two, he came to sink down on his knees on the deerskin beside her. His hands went out to her.

'Mary!' he said. 'Mary!'

Turning her head, she nodded slowly, and smiled at him, through her singing. She raised a finger gently to bar his lips. Her strange song continued, uninterrupted. The two wolf-hounds, that had sat far back in the shadows, crept forward on their bellies into the circle of the firelight, until they lay, long heads flat on outstretched forepaws, on either side of the man and woman.

A quiet tide of calm flowed into and over that chamber of the empty house, and filled it.

Her singing, in time, did not so much stop as sink, diminish to a husky whisper, and eventually fade away. Neither of them spoke. Ludovick's arms were around her now, his face buried in her hair. Presently his lips found her neck below her hair. In time a hand slipped up to cup one of her breasts.

She did not stir, nor rebuke him.

More than once words seemed to rise to his exploring lips, but something in the girl's stillness, the positive calm of her, restrained him. He held her close, while time stood still.

It was the sinking of the fire, the need to replenish it with logs, that changed the tempo. Lennox, after throwing on more wood, became imbued with a new urgency. His lips grew more daring, his hands roved wider. At last Mary stirred, sighing.

'Vicky,' she said, 'this way lies sorrow, hurt. For us both. You must know it.'

'Why, Mary? Why should it? We shall not hurt each other,

you and I. And we are not children.'

'Not children, no. But you have a wife, Vicky. I cannot forget it.'

He frowned. 'In name only. I have told you. And many men have wives . . . and others.'

'Yes, my lord Duke,' she said. 'And others!'

'Lord – I am sorry, Mary! I did not mean it that way.'

'No. But that way the world would see it, Vicky. Not that I greatly care what the world thinks of me. But I care what I think of myself. And of you. Moreover, I will not further hurt your Lady Sophia. In this house, where she should be.'

He shook his head, wordless.

'We must not think only for the moment,' she added.

'Moment!' he jerked. 'This marriage of mine is not for any moment. It may be for years – a lifetime! I cannot wait for that. I have warmer blood than that!'

'And you think that I have not?'

'I do not know. I only know that you are strong. So much stronger than I am.'

'Do not talk so much of strength,' she said, low-voiced. 'If I was so strong, I would not be here in this great empty castle with you now. I would have gone back, forthwith, late as it was. When I found you alone. Not to Falkland but at least to St. John's Town. Or even to the inn in your village here. If I had been so strong.'

Uncertainly he eyed her, surprised at her sudden vehemence.

'I have told you before, Vicky – I would not have you think me other than I am.'

'Will I ever know you?' he demanded. 'Know you as you are?'

It was her turn not to answer.

'Are you unhappy, Mary? Here. Alone in this house, with me?'

'No.'

'You are not frightened? Not of me, Mary? Never of me!'

'No, Vicky. I do not think that I could ever be frightened of you. Only of myself, perhaps.' She paused. 'So . . . so you will help me, will you?'

He stared at her, swallowed, and could find no words. But after a few moments his arms came out again to encircle her –

but protectively this time, and so remained, firm, strong.

Her little sigh might have been relief, relaxation, or even just possibly, regret.

Presently she settled herself more comfortably on the deerskin, leaned her head against his shoulder, and closed her eyes.

She did not sleep. But after a while Ludovick did, his weight against her becoming heavier. Long she crouched thus, supporting him, growing cramped, sore, although with no discontent thereat showing in her features. Indeed frequently a tiny smile came and went at the corners of her mouth. Sleep overcame her, at length.

Sometime during the night she awakened, stiff, chilled. Ludovick lay relaxed, arm outflung, but shivering slightly every so often in his sleep. The fire had sunk to a dull glow, and the hounds had crept close about them for warmth. Smiling again a little at the thought of forty empty beds in that great house, Mary carefully reached over to draw up another of the deerskin rugs that littered the floor. Settling herself as best she could, she pulled it over them, man, hounds and all.

Chapter Nineteen

AT first light they rode away from Methven Castle. They went first to the village nearby, where Ludovick knocked up his steward and left sundry instructions, and then turned eastwards for the Earn and Fife, going by unfrequented ways and avoiding Perth. They parted company some miles outside Falkland, so that Mary could enter the town alone and without arousing special comment. The Lady Marie knew of her errand anyway, and she had chosen an occasion when Patrick had gone on one of his many brief visits to Broughty Castle, to examine progress of his works of improvement.

Lennox's return to Court that evening, even without his new wife, evoked no great stir. James was glad to see him, in an absent-minded way. Patrick also professed himself to be overjoyed, when he got back from Broughty next day. Otherwise there was little interest, for the Duke had as few friends as he had enemies.

Thereafter began a strange and unacknowledged tug-of-war over the activities and influences and persons of James Stewart, Earl of Moray, and Anne of Denmark, Queen-Consort. Undoubtedly none of the principals knew anything of it. Nor did the King, though the effects were not lost on him, perceive the tugging, the stresses and strains of the warfare, the gains and losses sustained. Even Patrick Gray himself probably did not fully recognise the positive and consistent nature of the opposition to his plans. He could be amusedly sure that his daughter, wife and Lennox would disapprove of any obvious moves against Moray; but then, the Master's moves were seldom obvious. That Mary Gray was, in fact, little more obvious than himself, had not yet fully dawned upon him.

Moray was still banished the Court, but was living less than a score of miles off at his own house of Donibristle. Dunfermline was only five miles away, and Anne was as often there as at Falkland. Mary, as was to be expected, was usually with her – and so now was Ludovick Lennox who had never previously shown any notable interest in the young Queen. He was seldom far from her side, indeed – which did not escape the notice of the Court, and did not endear him to Moray any more than to Patrick, whatever Anne thought of it. James would remark, waggishly, that his good Coz Vicky seemed a deal fonder of the Queen than of his own Duchess – but few doubted that the stiff and unforthcoming Lennox was in fact more interested in the Queen's tire-woman than in Anne herself, Mary being sufficiently kind to him in public to give some substance to this assumption.

The Queen, therefore, although she saw much of Moray, seldom saw him alone. Lennox was as good as a watch-dog – and notably well-informed as to Anne's every move. Probably she believed that James had arranged it, and even Patrick may have assumed the same. As a situation, it verged on the comic.

Patrick sought continually to arrange matters so that the Queen should be thrown in Moray's way, and that the King might find them together in some incriminating circumstance.

Mary, Marie and Lennox, from their positions of strategic vantage close to the King, Queen and Patrick himself, sought to make sure that this did not happen. It could not have been achieved without Lennox, and him devoting almost his full time to the business. Patrick, in due course, came to realise this, even though attributing much of it to the King's instigation – and the rift between these two former close friends widened. And, in time, however successful the countermeasures, that rift began to worry Mary Gray almost as much as the fate of Moray. Thwarting the Master of Gray, however secretly, was a chancy activity, and like trying to damp down a volcano; there was no saying where one might cause another irruption to break out, in consequence, with who knew what hurt to others.

When, one day, Lennox came to her in the Commendator's House of Dunfermline Abbey, Mary saw the writing on the wall. Actually in this instance the writing was Bothwell's, in the form a letter just delivered to Ludovick, and of which that young man could make neither head nor tail. It was written from Hailes Castle in Lothian, and after professing the keenest regard for the Duke and asking after his health, declared that the writer understood that he, Lennox, was interested in the better running of the realm and the reform of certain notable tyrannies at present afflicting it, in especial the witch-trials which had become no more than a means for bringing down one's unfriends. Bothwell urged Lennox to band himself together with him and sundry other similarly well-intentioned lords, with a view to ending this reign of terror, and assured him that the time was almost ripe. He prayed that he might have an affirmative reply – as it was indeed the plain duty of all honest men in the kingdom to act in this matter.

'I cannot understand it, Mary,' Ludovick declared. 'This, from Bothwell. Why write this to me? I am no friend of his. I am against all bonds and plots. I have not great tail of men to help form an army. I am against this folly of the witches, yes. But I cannot see that Bothwell is the man to reform the government of this realm. And he has ever scorned me. Why should he approach me now? What can I answer him? I do not see the meaning of this letter . . .'

Mary looked out into the wet street. 'I fear that I do, Vicky,' she told him. 'And you should nowise answer it. This letter – do you not see? It is a trap. Burn it, Vicky – in case any other see it but ourselves. And pray that there are no more from whence it came! This may be Bothwell's writing – but I fear that it is Patrick's hand behind it!'

'Patrick's? Surely not!'

'Yes, Patrick's. Do you not see it? Answer this, show but the least interest in what Bothwell says, and you could be deep in trouble. Any communication with Bothwell, the King would take amiss. This, a bond with others, and against his precious witch-trials, he would name treason without a doubt. Aimed at himself . . . '

'James knows that I would never commit treason. That I would never league myself against him.'

'Are you so sure, Vicky? Remember that once you talked of deposing him, with yourself as Regent. Because you feared him mad. If he was to hear word of that . . . !'

'That was Patrick's project.'

'Yes. And there is the danger. Vicky – you have put yourself in Patrick's way. Because I besought you. But – whoever does that is in danger. I should have realised this before I sought your help. I have begun to fear something of the sort, these last days. Patrick's hand is behind this, I am sure. This way he could have you removed, out of the way. He may intend no more than that – but it could lead to worse things.'

'I cannot believe that this is Patrick's doing, Mary. How could he have Bothwell write to me?'

'Easily. Remember, he now can act Bothwell's friend and counsellor. Bothwell owes him his freedom. No doubt Bothwell *is* planning all kinds of treasons – he is ever at it. What more simple than for Patrick to have him include you in his crazy plans? One day a letter will come into the King's hands, from you to Bothwell, or from him to you, and you will be no longer dear Cousin Vicky but a treasonable plotter! This is a warning.' Mary stepped over to the fire, and thrust the letter into its heart.

'Suppose that I told James that it was Patrick who aided Bothwell to escape from Edinburgh Castle?' Ludovick said slowly.

344

'Would you? And think you he would believe you? Patrick would deny it – and you have no proof. Only my word. None would accept that. Even . . . even if I would agree to testify against him!' Her voice faltered just a little as she said that.

Helplessly he shook his head. 'What are we to do, then?'

'What we should have done ere this.' She quickly was her calm self again. 'I spoke of it before, with the Lady Marie, but we believed that it could wait. Have the King send Moray north, Vicky. He has great lands there – his own earldom of Moray. Convince the King that he is seeing overmuch of Queen Anne, here in Fife. Abet Patrick in this, at least! It should not be difficult. Have him banish Moray to his castle of Darnaway. Work on Mar and some of the other lords to support you in this. I do not see how Patrick can object. But do it secretly, so that the Queen does not come to hear of it, or she may prevail on the King not to do it. Then . . . you will be no more in Patrick's way in this matter.'

'Lord, Mary!' Brows furrowed, he stared at her. 'How do you do it? How do you think of these things. On my soul, it is a marvel! And yet so simple. So simple that I would never have thought of it. Where do you get such wits?'

'You know where I get them,' she answered him, her voice strangely flat. 'I heired them. They are my inheritance. Sometimes I wish to God that they were not!'

Long he considered her. 'I think that I do, also,' he said, at last.

'Yes.' She turned away. 'But you will do this? Speak with the King. Secretly. Plague him, if need be. He will do it, if only for the sake of peace. His mind is wholly on his book and his witchcraft. It is the best course. Better Moray banished to the north, but free, than languishing in a pit of Edinburgh Castle. Which is where Patrick, I think, would have him.'

'Aye. But why is it, Mary? Why does Patrick so hate Moray? He did not, formerly.'

'I do not believe that he hates him. Indeed, I do not believe that Patrick hates any man. It is never hatred, I think, which makes him act so, but something quite other. You may laugh at me – but I believe that the greatest evils that Patrick has done were done with no malice to any. Not to the persons he injures. Can you understand that, Vicky?'

His blank face was eloquent enough answer.

'It is so hard to explain. But I think that I have come to understand him. By looking deep into my own mind, perhaps. Patrick is not interested in *hurting* people. In especial he would not seek to injure poor people, ordinary folk – although many innocent folk may come to be hurt in the working out of his plots. He is a better husband than most, a good master, and one of the ablest rulers this realm has ever known. But he sees statecraft as a game, a sport. And all that influences the rule of the state, in power, position, even religion, as but pawns in that game. He is a gamester, in more than cards and horse-racing. His greatest sport is this – the game of power. As Moray excels at the glove and the ball, so Patrick excels in this greater sport. He knows that he is better at it than is any other. Any that cross his path in this, he must remove. It is a challenge that must be met, and overcome. It is not the man that he fights, or the woman, but the challenge. Do you not see it?' Urgently she put it to the young man, so urgently that she gripped his arm, all but shook it. 'Do you not see it?'

Doubtfully he eyed her. 'It is difficult, Mary. I see a little, perhaps. Patrick is not as other men, I do perceive. But this bringing down of others, so many, to their ruin, even their deaths – that is evil, surely? Only evil.'

'I know! I know!' she cried. It was seldom indeed that Mary Gray raised her voice thus. 'I do not say that it is not evil. But Patrick does not see it so. You asked me why he hates Moray. I do not believe that he does. But Moray has crossed his path, with the Queen. Moray's folly with the Queen could harm the realm. So Moray must fall. There may be more than that – I do not know. But that is enough, for Patrick.'

He shook his head. 'You are too deep for me,' he said. 'Too clever – you and Patrick both.'

Strangely enough that remark seemed to strike home at her. 'So clever,' she repeated, dully. 'Yes – too clever. I could be too clever. I was, before. I hope, I pray, that I am not being too clever. This time. But . . . we must do something, Vicky. We must do *something*.'

He nodded. 'That we must. And this appears the wise course. What you now propose. I shall see to it. Never fear.' He kicked at the floor with his toe. 'I am sorry, Mary. I did not mean . . . that you thought yourself too clever. Never that.'

'I know it, Vicky. But it is true, nevertheless.'

'The Queen?' he asked, changing the subject abruptly. 'How is it with her?'

'All is well. Mistress Cunningham is curling her hair. Moray is there – but so are Lady Kate and your good-sister, the Lady Beatrix. All is well, for the moment.'

He sighed. 'I wish, Mary . . . !'

She completed that for him. 'Methven Castle will wait for you, Vicky,' she assured.

Although in the past King James had cared nothing for weather, so long as the hunting was good, this season his heart was not in hunting, and the November rain drove him back to Edinburgh. Bothwell seemed to have lain suitably low since his escape from ward, and it was to be hoped that he had learned his lesson at last. Even the Master of Gray seemed to consider that it would be safe enough to return to the capital. There was some talk of going back to Craigmillar Castle for security, or even to Edinburgh Castle itself; but none of the Council seemed to think that this was necessary, not even the cautious Maitland. Since Moray had been packed off to his northern fastnesses at Darnaway, a certain aura of peace had descended upon the Court. There was no denying it. The Queen was less upset than might have been expected. After only a day or two of sulks, she consoled herself readily enough with the Duke of Lennox and the Master of Gray – which allowed her husband to get on with the all-important issue of his book and his warfare with the Devil.

In this connection there was a grave, a shameful matter to put right. One of his special courts for trying the witches had actually acquitted the woman Barbara Napier – after he had forfeited her lands of Cliftonhall and bestowed them upon young Sir James Sandilands of Slamannan, his latest page, who was an extremely talented youth in certain ways, even if the ladies did not like him. In righteous wrath James had had the entire jury responsible arrested, brought to Falkland, and themselves thereupon tried on a charge of bringing in a false verdict, in manifest and wilful error, the King himself presiding. Faced with a fate exactly similar to that they should have

347

imposed upon the high-born Mistress Napier of Cliftonhall, the jury sensibly and humbly confessed their fault, and clearly would not so err again. James was magnanimously pleased to pardon them. But others might do likewise, and it seemed clear that Christ's vice-regent should return to the centre of affairs forthwith – for it demanded eternal vigilance sucessfully to counter the Devil. The Justice-Clerk was instructed peremptorily to have the woman Napier re-tried and condemned, without further delay.

So to Holyroodhouse they all returned. The Queen, in lieu of the fascinations of house building and plenishing, fell back upon the cosy winter-time delights of possible pregnancy, and set her ladies to much making of baby-clothes.

Satan was not backwards in seeking to overturn King James's godly campaign. By a most unhappy coincidence, the same young James Sandilands, in an excess of youthful spirits, had the misfortune to shoot and kill a Lord of Session, Lord Hallyards, in the street soon after the return to Edinburgh. This greatly upset many of the judicial fraternity, some of whom even went so far as to demand that James should have his new page tried and punished. The King's indignant refusal undoubtedly had a deleterious effect on the witch-trials, which he had ordered to have precedence over all other matters juridical. He came to believe that the entire legal profession began to drag its feet in this vital issue – indubitably to Satan's glee.

As if this was not enough, there came a complaint from, of all people, George Gordon, Earl of Huntly. Although banished to his own countryside, he was still Lieutenant of the North – since there was nobody else up there powerful enough to control that barbarous land – and while besieging the Laird of Grant in Castle Grant, for some reason or another, had been attacked by the Earls of Moray and Atholl, coming to Grant's aid. No doubt only the fact that Moray was the King's cousin had produced this petition of protest from Huntly in place of a much more drastic and typical reaction. James was annoyed, justifiably. A plague on them all!

Mary no sooner heard of this than she imagined Patrick's hand behind it somewhere, pursuing Moray even two hundred miles into the Northland. He was in constant secret touch with Huntly, she knew. Atholl, a weak and unstable character, was married to the Lady Mary Ruthven – the same who was suspected of playing Leda to Patrick's swan at Falkland, and his full cousin as well as the elder sister of Ludovick's new wife. Patrick had used Atholl as his tool before this. Or it might have been a trumped-up clash arranged through Huntly himself . . .

In deep trouble, Mary Gray looked within himself. To such a state of suspicion, of irrational fears and dark imaginings, had she come. She saw Patrick's shadow everywhere, suspected his every action, sensed mockery behind every smile, tainting her love. It could not go on, thus. Either they must come to terms, or one must yield and go. And she did not see the Master of Gray conceding the game, the game that was his very life, to his unacknowledged daughter.

Chapter Twenty

ONLY five days before Christmas, with Queen Anne planning Yuletide revels on a Danish pattern and scale, something new and therefore suspect in Scotland, Patrick Gray surprised his wife and Mary by announcing that it would be suitable and fitting that he and his family should celebrate Yule in their own house of Broughty, not in this rabbit-warren of a palace. To Marie's protests that it was late in the day to think of this, that the journey at this season of the year would be most trying, and that Broughty Castle was indeed the last place that she would choose for festivity, her husband made laughing reply that she was obviously getting old and stodgy, and needed shaking up a mite; that the weather was excellent for the season; and that Broughty Castle was somewhat improved since last she had seen it. Moreover, would she not see her beloved Davy Gray?

He was in the best of spirits, anything but harsh, but adamant in this sudden whim. They would travel first thing the next morning. Mary was included in this arrangement.

While they would be sorry to miss her company, she could spend her Christmas at Castle Huntly if she preferred it. Evidently there was no question of her being left at Holyroodhouse, Queen or no Queen.

Sudden as seemed this decision, Ludovick would have accompanied them – but Patrick demurred. It might look somewhat blatant, he suggested, for so newly a married man. Moreover, Anne might well be sufficiently concerned over losing her Maid-in-Waiting for her Yuletide antics, without sacrificing her most faithful admirer and constant attendant into the bargain. The Duke of Lennox was not as lesser men, and must bear the responsibilities of his high calling.

They took two easy days to the journey, stopping overnight at Falkland. Mary was escorted to the gatehouse of Castle Huntly, but neither the heir thereto nor his wife and son crossed the threshold. My lord's shadow lay too heavily athwart it.

Mary was joyfully received, the unexpectedness of her arrival nowise detracting. My lord, three parts drunk, welcomed her like the prodigal returned. Mariota wept in her happiness. The young brother and sister shouted. It was left to Davy Gray to remark concernedly that she was looking pale, great-eyed, strained – not the same cool and serenely lovely young creature that she had been, although almost more beautiful.

Mary, for her part, was more glad to be home than she could say, more in need of its settled normalcy and security than she had realised – and especially her father's strong, reliable presence. Undoubtedly prolonged association with Patrick Gray enhanced an appreciation of David, his illegitimate half-brother.

The day after Christmas, in sunny open weather, Mary rode pillion behind her father the dozen miles to Broughty. Even at a distance, Patrick's hand was notably visible. After the French fashion he had harled the bare stone wall outer walls and colour-washed all but the actual battlements and parapets in a deep yellow, so that the fortress on its rocky promontory soared above the sparkling, blue and white of the sea like a golden castle, gleaming in the sun. The place was larger too, new building towering above the high curtain-walling that faithfully followed the outline of the small headland; the restricted site precluded any lateral extensions, so Patrick had built upwards, and again in the French style, with corner-turrets, rounded stair-towers, overhanging bartizans and conical roofs. Over all no fewer than six great banners fluttered in the breeze, proud, challenging.

'Patrick has done as he vowed,' David said, over his shoulder, pointing. 'Broughty is no rickle of stones, any more. It is a finer place than Castle Huntly now – finer than any castle that I have seen north of Tay. But the cost! He has poured out siller like water. Where does he get the money, Mary?'

She shook her head. 'A thousand pounds of Elizabeth's pension to the King he got – for fetching it, and as solace for Dunfermline . . . '

'That is as nothing to what has been spent here. You have not yet seen the inside. I cannot think where he has gained it.'

'He wins much at cards. And it may be that he has his hands on some of the Ruthven money already, with the wardship of the daughters. And he still has dealings with Queen Elizabeth.'

'Aye, then. To pay so well, what does he sell her?'

When they reached the castle, the reason for David's wonderings was amply clear. The place was transformed. From a bare echoing shell, it had become a palace. Tapestries and hangings clothed every wall, and not skins but carpets on every floor, brought from the East. Great windows had been opened in the thick walls to let in the light, fireplaces blazed with logs in every chamber, and candles in handsome candelabra turned night into day. Furnishings, bedding, silverware, pictures – nothing was stinted, nothing less than the best. Nothing in Holyroodhouse could compare with this. If Patrick Gray knew how to find money, he knew how to spend it also.

Questions and doubts, however, had to give way to greetings, admiration and festivity. Patrick was at his dazzling best, all laughter, wit and brilliance, like quick-silver. Even to Davy he was all affection, gaiety, frank brotherliness. As for Marie, with all she loved most gathered around her, she accepted this day as snatched from care, not to be spoiled. The others found themselves of a like mind.

It was evening when this pleasant interval of accord was

interrupted. A sudden great hullabaloo and outcry from outside, from the direction of the gatehouse and drawbridge, sent David striding to the nearest window. Quite a large company of horsemen were milling about just beyond the artificial ditch spanned by the drawbridge, which separated the promontory from the mainland, many of them with blazing torches held high, while two of their shadowy number held a shouted exchange with the porters on the gatehouse parapet.

'Ah – company!' Patrick's voice sounded softly at his brother's shoulder. 'A pity, perhaps, that they could not wait until morning. We were so . . . well content.' He turned back into the great vaulted hall. 'You will excuse me, my dears? It seems that I must go play host.'

'Who is it, Patrick?' Marie asked, tension coming back into her voice. 'At this hour? What can it be?'

'That remains to be seen,' he told her easily. 'Nothing for you to distress yourself over, at least. And there is victual enough here to feed a host.' He closed the door behind him.

Marie looked from Mary to David. 'So short a time,' she sighed. 'It is not . . . your father?'

'No,' David perked. 'It is a large company. But whoever it is, my lord it is not! He will never darken this door, I fear. Patrick has fulfilled the rest of his vow, yes – that he would make this rickle of stones a palace that the King might envy. But he will never bring his father here to his gate, begging admittance, as he swore. Some tasks are beyond even Patrick.'

'I would not be so sure,' Marie said, shaking her head. 'Do not underestimate him, Davy. But a few days ago he won from the King the appointment of Sheriff of Forfar – in place of his father. So that he is now justiciar of all this region. Why? Why should he saddle himself with all this duty and responsibility? It is not like Patrick to take on such tasks. He will require to pay a deputy, since I swear he has no intention of dwelling always here in the sheriffdom. So that he will make little out of it.'

David whistled soundlessly. 'My lord was much hurt at being dismissed the office. He has held it long – and is moreover an Extra Lord of Session. But . . . he does not know that it is Patrick who succeeds him. That will be the sorer blow.'

'Yes. But that is the least of it, Davy. Do you not see? What it means? He is now the law in this sheriffdom, the voice of the King. If any transgress that law, or the King's will, Patrick can summon the same to him. Here, to Broughty. To judgment. And they must come, or suffer outlawry, banishment. Including my lord of Gray – should some transgression be suggested!'

'God's mercy! This is . . . this is . . .'

'This is Patrick! He has not told me that this is his purpose. But I think that I know his mind.'

Mary spoke. 'If we could but bring them together. In love, not in hurt.' Her dark eyes were pools of trouble. 'Deep in his heart I believe that Granlord aches for his son. And Patrick does not hate his father – only what he stands for, I think. He must beat all who oppose him.'

'Perhaps,' David sighed. 'Think you that I have not tried? All my life I have tried. There is that between them neither will yield . . .'

He stopped. Plain for all to hear came the thin wailing of bagpipes.

They stared at each other.

'Dear Lord!' David exclaimed. 'I know only one man who so loves that sound that he must have it even here and now! Huntly!'

'Huntly – here!' Marie looked startled. 'But, why? What could bring him here? So far from Strathbogie. That man . . . !'

'I do not know. But this I do know – that wherever that turkey-cock gobbles there is trouble.'

'This . . . this could be construed as treason! Harbouring Huntly, who is banished to his own North . . . ' Marie faltered.

'This may be why we are here, nevertheless,' Mary suggested quietly. 'We came here to Broughty. So that Patrick might meet Huntly. Secretly.'

'I thought of it,' Marie admitted. 'But why bring *us*, then? Better without us, surely?'

'Patrick knew that he was coming,' Mary insisted. 'Or that someone would come.'

In doubt they eyed each other.

A moment or two later the door was flung open, and on a gale of sound Huntly strode in, a moving mountain of flesh, tartans, armour, jewellery and eagles' feathers, with Patrick behind him. He had not doffed his bonnet. Even Marie rose to her feet.

'Greetings, my lord of Huntly, to this house,' she said, somewhat thickly. 'In this season of goodwill and peace. We . . . we wish you well. You have not brought your lady wife?'

'Wife . . . ? God – no! I do not travel the passes in winter on women's work, Lady!' Huntly boomed. 'A blessing on your house.' His choleric eye lighted on David Gray, and he looked as though he might retract that benediction. 'You!' he barked.

'Aye, my lord,' that man gave back evenly. 'It is a far cry from Strathbogie.'

'My lord of Huntly has come south on important business,' Patrick interposed, pleasantly. 'On the King's business, indeed. He heard in Dundee that we were at Broughty, and came, assured of a welcome in any house of mine.'

'Young Jamie Stewart needs my services,' the Earl amplified, chuckling. 'He'll no' long manage this realm without Gordon!'

'But . . . only north of Dee, is it not, my lord?' Marie said. 'Coming south, thus, do you not endanger yourself? And . . . and others?'

'Wait you!' the other advised her shortly, cryptically. 'You will see.'

Marie inclined her fair head. 'No doubt.' She swallowed. 'Now, my lord – you will be weary, and hungered. If you will come with me, I shall see to your comfort. And your people also. How many . . . ?'

'There is no need, my dear,' the Master mentioned. 'I have already given orders. All is in train. If you will come with *me*, my lord . . . ?'

When the door closed behind her visitor again, Marie sat down abruptly. 'There is villainy here!' she exclaimed. 'I smell it. I hate and fear that man.'

'And yet, if such there is, then it would be Patrick who conceived it, not the Earl of Huntly.'

Surprised, the other two looked at Mary. It had always been the girl's part to uphold Patrick, to speak for him, to find excuse. This was a notable change.

'That is true,' David nodded. 'Huntly is a vain and stupid man, with not a tithe of Patrick's wits. If he is here, it is because Patrick moved him to come.'

354

'Yes. So that, if there is danger in it, hurt, Huntly himself is in more danger than are any of us whom Patrick loves,' Mary pointed out. 'We should, perhaps, be sorry for my lord.'

Marie suddenly buried her face in her hands.

Both of them went to her, Mary to kneel beside her chair, David to stand behind her, his hand on her bowed shoulder.

'Do not be downcast, lassie,' he said thickly. 'Naught may come of it – naught of harm. You have faced much worse than this – and smiled through it.'

'Oh, Davy! Davy!' she mumbled brokenly, reaching out to clutch his arm. But she kept her head down.

'My dear,' he said.

Mary looked from one to the other, but said nothing.

'I am foolish, Davy – oh, I know that I am foolish,' Marie declared. 'But I am tired, weary of it all. Weary of struggling, of fighting against shadows, of fearing what each day may bring, of living a lie . . .'

'*You* never lived or thought or told a lie, all your days, woman!' the man declared, deep-voiced, set-faced. 'I know you.'

'Do you, Davy? Do you? Even so?' She looked up at him, now, urgently. 'Oh, I wish that it was true! You do not know that even now I am living a lie – and to you. To you both. And endangering you, it may be, because of it. For there was danger, treason itself perhaps, in this house before Huntly came to it – and I did not tell you. There are Jesuits living here secretly – priests, emissaries, spies from France and Spain, sheltered here by Patrick . . .'

'Jesuits! Here?' David looked startled.

'Yes. It seems that they have been here for months. Coming and going. They use this house as a centre for their journeys and missions. They are thought of here as but foreign artists and craftsmen, employed by Patrick in the building and plenishing of this castle, working in paint and plaster and glass and tapestry. Some indeed do so. They can come and go secretly by boat, at night. None can observe them, on this sea-girt headland. They could scarce have it better arranged.'

'Aye, that I see,' David sighed. 'So Patrick still paddles in that mire! I had thought that in this, at least, he would have learned his lesson. What does it mean? That still he hopes to restore the Catholics to power in Scotland? Is that why Huntly is here – the greatest Catholic of the realm? Is Patrick truly a Catholic himself, at heart, Marie?'

'God knows – for I do not!' she cried. 'Patrick's heart lies well buried. I know not what he is, or what he believes, deep down. Or where his heart lies. Even after these years . . . '

'Save that he loves *you*, Lady Marie,' Mary put in quietly. 'That you know.'

Slowly, steadily, the older woman turned to look at the younger. 'Do I so, Mary?' she asked, at length. 'Do I know that, if driven to it, he would not sacrifice me also, to his scheming? Use me, like all others, as but a pawn in his game. Has he not done so, indeed?'

Mary shook her head. 'Not to your hurt. Not of intention. He loves you. Indeed he loves all three here. Each differently. That we do know, if naught else.'

'He has used me full often, for his gain and my risk,' her father jerked. 'And you also, girl, I think. Let us not cozen ourselves. Enough to have Patrick ever cozening us . . . '

More shouting from the gatehouse stopped him. There was no such outcry as formerly, but clearly some new visitor was demanding admittance this busy Yuletide night, against the gate-porters' doubts. David stepped over to the window again.

'But the one man, I think,' he reported, peering out into the dark. 'It is hard to see. Only the gatehouse torches to light him. Some messenger for Patrick, no doubt. Aye – there clank the drawbridge chains. They are letting him in.'

'Wherever Patrick may be, messengers come day and night,' Marie said, shrugging. 'At least, this one comes openly at the gate, and does not slip in at a secret postern, from the sea.'

It was a little time before voices sounded from the echoing stone-vaulted passage without, one of them urgent, excited. The door opened to reveal a travel-stained, mud-spattered and dishevelled young man, blinking in the light, with Patrick behind him.

'Vicky!' Mary exclaimed, and started forward, before she recollected herself.

Lennox came to her without hesitation or ceremony, and undoubtedly would have embraced her before them all had she not drawn back. Only perfunctorily, then, at her warning gesture, did he pay his respects to his hostess and nod to David.

'Vicky has strange tidings. From Edinburgh,' Patrick mentioned easily. 'Most . . . interesting.'

'I' faith, I'd call it more than that!' the young man burst out. 'It was treason. Rebellion! Only by a mercy was the King saved.'

'Precisely,' Patrick nodded. 'As I said – distressing.'

'The King? Rebellion? Not . . . not Huntly?' Marie gasped.

'Huntly . . . ? No. How should it be? It was Bothwell. He struck yesterday. On Christmas Day. At Holyroodhouse. With many men. They came at darkening. Wild mosstroopers and broken men. How many I do not know – but they swarmed like rats over the palace. We were all at the Queen's revels, in the banqueting hall. Save James. And Maitland. James had gone back to his books and papers, tiring of the Danish play. The Guard was keeping Yule in my lord of Orkney's quarters. Mar, the new Captain, was with the Queen. As was I. We found ourselves to be locked in the banqueting hall, with Bothwell's bullyrooks guarding the doors. I won out through a window, to reach the Guard. But they were for the most part drunken, or . . . or . . .'

'Aye – we know how it would be!' That was Davy, briefly, as the other paused, partly for breath. 'What of the King?'

'Aye – what of the King, Vicky?'

'He was locked in his room. In his own tower. The guards on the stairs had the wit to lock the great double doors at the foot of the tower, when they heard the din and clash. They shouted to the guard on Maitland's tower, across the court, to do the same. Bothwell had not considered that – or else his men were slow. No doubt he thought to find James with the Queen and the rest at the revels in the hall. The great doors held. One is a yett of iron. So they could not get at James. So little a thing saved the King.'

'Saved the King . . . ?' Marie echoed, appalled. 'But, what would Bothwell have done, Vicky? What was his purpose? You do not think that he would have harmed the King? Done him a hurt?'

'I do not know. Some said that he would have slain him. In revenge for imprisoning him, and naming him devil-possessed. All know that Bothwell is half-crazed . . . !'

'Nonsense!' Patrick intervened. 'Whoever so said is equally crazed. How would it serve Bothwell to kill the King? He would turn all against him. It is but the old game. He who holds the King holds the power.'

'He may have thought to make himself king in James's place,' Ludovick claimed. 'He is of the royal house. Closer than am I, save for the illegitimacy . . . '

'But that is all-important. And others are closer still, but with the same taint. Marie's father. Moray. No, no – he would but hold the King. Get rid of Maitland and the others. Be assured of that.'

'James feared for his life, nevertheless. Still does.'

'James always does that! Bothwell is not so great a fool. He would have all against him if he slew the King. Including Elizabeth, who presently aids him. But . . . how stands the position now, Vicky? How do they, now?'

'James is in Edinburgh Castle, safe. Bothwell's Borderers could not gain entry to his tower. I roused such of the Guard as I might. There was much fighting.' Ludovick flushed slightly, stumbling over his words. 'I . . . I killed a man! It was him or me. He had a whinger. Swording. He near had me. I could not get my sword out of him. It was fast held. He had a black beard. Blood running down it . . . ' His voice tailed away.

'Vicky!' Mary came to his side, to hold his arm. 'Dear Vicky – I am sorry!'

With an obvious effort the young man recovered himself. 'They were too many. We could not hold them,' he went on, jerkily. 'We were driven back. I got away. Took one of their horses. I won past their picquets. Into the town. I went to the Tolbooth. Roused them there. Had the bells rung – to summon the lieges. To bring out the Blue Blanket. Turned out the Town Guard. We had the church bells ringing. The burghers took long about it – but the apprentices rallied quickly. With them, and the Town Guard, I went back to the palace. And with some lords lodging in the town. Four score of us, perhaps – or a hundred. At first we could do little, against Bothwell's men who held the gates. But when the burghers and the crafts came, with their Blue Blanket, to save the King – then they could not hold us. They came in thousands – half the town. Shouting for the King. We forced the gates. The mosstroopers could not stand against so many. They fled. But I heard Bothwell shouting that he would be back. That he would burn the city, and hang the provost and bailies. So the provost hanged eight of the Borderers that they had caught. In front of the palace. As a warning . . . '

Panting, the Duke took the glass of wine that Mary was holding out to him, and gulped it down unsteadily. His features, under the grime of long and hard riding, were lined with weariness.

'You would seem, Vicky, to have been most . . . adequate,' Patrick murmured. 'Quite the paladin! And Bothwell notably ineffective. A bungler. So the town mob saved James, did it? I had scarce thought that he was so popular! Or is it just that they mislike Bothwell more?'

Lennox raised his brows. 'They but did their duty to their liege lord, as leal citizens, did they not?'

'Ah, yes. Of course, bless them!' The Master, though he spoke lightly, was clearly somewhat preoccupied, his mind not wholly on this exchange. 'And now the position is . . . ?'

'The townsfolk carried James up to the Castle. He was in great alarm. He could scarce speak. I saw him safe bedded there. Then I took horse forthwith. To ride here. To tell you.'

'Vicky! You did not sleep first? You have not rested, since that evil fighting? You rode through the night? And all day . . . ?' Mary was shocked.

'It was necessary. It is a long ride. I have worn out three horses. I had to come, Mary. All is confusion at Court. Bothwell is not far away. Only at Crichton, they say. Gathering more men. He can raise thousands, from the Border valleys and Lothian and the Merse. He said that he would be back. None knows what to do. James is safe for the nonce – but all the realm is endangered. I could think only of coming here, to you . . . '

'What of the Chancellor? My lord Maitland? Is not all in his capable hands?' Patrick wondered.

'He is a clerk, no more! As you know. He blames all, but does nothing. Save pray! He is at the Castle likewise, but helpless. None need him, anyway. Mar talks loud enough, but knows not what to do. You, Patrick, I thought . . . you always know what to do . . . '

'I am flattered by your faith and confidence, Vicky. We must see what can be done, yes.' The Master laughed. 'Heigho – is it not most fortunate, most convenient, that we have here at Broughty, by purest chance, the one man in this peculiar realm who can out-man Bothwell! In the circumstances, my lord of Huntly might be described as a God-send, might he not?'

'Huntly? He is . . . he is not here? At Broughty? Huntly himself . . . ?' Ludovick stared.

'Huntly, yes – your own potent good-brother! He is indeed. He arrived but an hour ago. Did you not see his troop's horses thronging the courtyard? Huntly has honoured us at an auspicious moment, it seems.'

'But he is banished! In disgrace!'

'Whom the King has banished, he can unbanish! Especially if the disgraced one can produce five thousand armed men to counter Bothwell's mosstroopers and rievers!' Patrick smiled, and patted the younger man's shoulder. 'Tomorrow I shall ride for Edinburgh – though in not quite such haste as you have ridden here, Vicky. I shall acquaint our liege lord of his great good fortune! All shall be well, for the best, never fear. I warrant that Jamie Stewart will fall upon my undeserving neck – and summon Huntly back to favour and the Court *instanter*!'

Mary Gray was considering Patrick long and thoughtfully. So much that had been unexplained now fitted neatly into place. She turned her head, to catch the grey eye of Lady Marie. Then she found David looking from one to the other of them. None spoke, nor required to speak.

Lennox, bewildered, ran a hand over his brow. 'I do not understand,' he faltered. 'This of Huntly . . . ?'

'Never heed it, Vicky,' Mary advised. 'You are done – tired, hungry. Come with me.' She took him by the hand.

He nodded, and went like a child.

Chapter Twenty-one

On 29th December 1591, King James signed a decree ending the banishment of his trusty and well-beloved councillor and Lieutenant of the North, George Gordon, Earl of Huntly, Lord of Strathbogie, Enzie, Badenoch and Aboyne, and summoned him to Court at the Castle of Edinburgh with all haste, duly accoutred and equipped for the sure defence of his sovereign lord and fast friend, James R. And on the first day of January 1592, the Cock o' the North rode in through the West Port of the city, with a mere token tail of two hundred Gordon swordsmen at his back, and the hearty assurance that there were plenty more where these came from, and indeed on the way. The citizens looked on askance, silent; the Kirk groaned in spirit; Mr. Bowes, the English envoy dispatched an urgent courier to Walsingham. But the Catholics rejoiced, and the sentinels up on the grim walls and turrets of Edinburgh Castle relaxed a little their anxious southwards vigil. Bothwell, reading the signs aright, turned and retired to his castle of Hermitage, deep in the Border fastnesses.

So Huntly strutted the stage again, and Edinburgh resounded to bagpipe squeals, strange Gaelic oaths, and the skirls of women outraged or prepared to be. The Court, after an interval, moved back thankfully to Holyroodhouse, and Catholic lords unseen for years, like Erroll, Crawford, Montrose and Seton appeared thereat. Bishops and prelates crept out from their holes and corners; Chancellor Maitland sank back like a snail into its shell; the witch trials came to an abrupt halt. Patrick Gray stood, debonair and smiling, close to the King's ear – none closer.

The delicate scales of Scottish politics teetered to a precarious balance, once more. None anticipated that they would do so for long, however assured seemed the urban Master of Gray. Men watched and waited.

James, temporarily lacking witches to justify, was at something of a loose end. He had ever been rather more fond of horseflesh than the human variety, and the death of his Master

361

Stabler, one John Shaw, and the loss of some of his favourite mounts in the Bothwell raid, caused him great concern and presently a return to poetry. He wrote a sonnet to commemorate the Stabler's gallant end, the first gesture towards the Muse in a full year, and roused himself to such heights of indignation and passion in the process that nothing short of some sort of demonstration and physical action against the perpetrator of the outrage would relieve his emotions. After consultation with the Master of Gray he first held a ceremony to divest Bothwell of his great office of state, that of Lord High Admiral, and promptly bestowed it upon the reluctant and embarrassed Duke of Lennox who so gallantly had brought the citizens of Edinburgh to the royal rescue. And secondly he mounted an expedition to the Borderland, January though it was, to display to that unruly and disobedient area who ruled in this realm of Scotland. With a mixed but strongly armed force consisting of the Royal Guard, Gordons, city levies and retainers of various lords, James in person made a hurried excursion southwards. Admittedly he confined his attentions to the East March, whilst Bothwell was known to be at Hermitage in the west, and after burning a few peel-towers and hanging some rievers and mosstroopers who were always the better for such firm treatment, hastened back to Edinburgh before Bothwell could do anything substantial about it – much to the disappointment of Huntly who was congenitally in favour of such entertainment, of Johnny Mar who enjoyed being Captain of the Guard, and even of Ludovick, who felt that a demonstration of the royal authority was overdue, whatever the risks. But James was adamant. A four-day expedition was quite adequate; moreover he had fallen into the Tyne in crossing that rain-swollen river of the Debatable Land, and was in dire alarm at catching cold in consequence.

Patrick Gray had excused himself from this martial adventure, on grounds of pressure of work. Nevertheless, the King's company was not half-a-day on its way when he took horse, with his hard-riding cousin Logan of Restalrig as companion, and headed southwards into the hills himself, although in a rather more westerly direction. He was back two days later, tired but good-humoured, only a day before his sneezing monarch.

James, despite aches and shivers, was much uplifted in spirit by this warrior-like gesture, and from his foot-baths and doctorings issued strong and manly pronouncements on the stern duties of kings and their subjects and the inescapable punishment and doom of all malefactors, especially those in high places. In some glee he sent a long letter to his royal cousin of England, acquainting her of his escape from enemies unfortunately supported by those who should know better, and of his strong measures against Bothwell on their mutual frontier, at which he was sure she would rejoice – mentioning, in passing, that his long promised English dukedom had still not materialised and would not this be a most suitable occasion for its bestowal? Patrick Gray enclosed a more cryptic covering-note of his own.

In this uplifted and magnanimous mood, the King was pleased to reconsider a petition to which he had hitherto been determinedly opposed, despite Patrick's generous and disinterested pleas. The Countess of Moray had unfortunately died, back in November, of some unspecified female ailment, and Moray had requested royal permission to come south to Donibristle to bury her – for in her sickness she had not accompanied her husband to the north and his banishment. Now, on Patrick's representations that it would please the Kirk, which was becoming ever more restive under increasing Catholic advancement – for Moray had ever been a favourite in that quarter – and moreover might help to keep Huntly from becoming so arrogant as to be unbearable, James relented. Moray might return to Donibristle, but no further; he must not cross the Forth or come to Court. The Queen, although she listened to their conversation, made no pleas of her own.

Mary, back at her duties in the Queen's household, watched and wondered.

On the last day of January, she overheard Patrick telling Anne that the new tapestries in the Flemish style that he was having woven for her were finished and it only required Her Grace's own decision as to which rooms of her house at Dunfermline each would best enhance. A short visit to Fife, perhaps . . . ? Mary's heart sank within her. She might have known. Was there to be no end to it? Were they back where they had been, so soon? Patrick was inexorable, to be diverted by nothing and nobody. Or was she but imagining evil, treachery? Seeing menace in the most innocent of actions? Had she reached the stage of suspecting Patrick's every move, however much she claimed to understand him? If so, how much was her vaunted love worth? She was weary, weary of it all; she could shut her eyes to that no longer. There it was, then; she was weary, but Patrick was not. The day that Patrick Gray wearied of his sport, his game with men, he would be dead. She knew it now.

Weary, imagining things, or not, she went to Ludovick forthwith and told him what she had heard and what she feared. If the Queen decided to go to Dunfermline would he be sure to go with her, scarce leave her side, she demanded.

'Again?' he sighed. 'I had thought to have finished with that. I find her passing dull, Mary. And all will say that I but follow you, who will be in Anne's train. That it is you that I follow, not her.'

'Let them say it. Better that they should. Indeed, I could entice you to do so. Before others. Before the King if need be. Persuade you. So that your coming will seem the less strange.'

'And have yourself named courtesan!' he exclaimed, frowning.

'Why not? I am so named already, I have no doubt. I care not, so long as *I* know what I am. And you do, likewise. If that I am to be called, let the name have its uses.'

'Its uses,' he repeated. 'As have I!' That was just a little bitter.

She touched his arm. 'Poor Vicky,' she said. 'I am sorry . . .'

The good burghers of the grey town of Dunfermline scarcely glanced at the young man who cantered a tired horse through their narrow streets. They had seen many much finer fish than this, of late, since the young Queen had come to lodge in the Abbot's House – even this very afternoon. Only the fact that the horse was a fine one and was tired, obviously having been ridden hard, attracted any attention; a courier with tidings for the Queen, no doubt.

The young man brought tidings, certainly – but not for Queen Anne.

Reining up in the stableyard of the Abbot's House, beside

which the Queen's fine new lodging stood all but completed, Ludovick of Lennox gazed about him urgently. A few other horses stood therein, hitched to rings and posts; but not what he had looked for – no large troop, nothing hard-ridden like his own beast. Frowning and biting his lip, he jumped down and ran indoors, shouting for Mary Gray and not the Queen.

He found her lighting lamps from a long taper in the former library of the Lord Abbot, for already the short February afternoon was dying towards dusk.

'Vicky!' she exclaimed, surprised but welcoming. 'How good! You are back. So soon!' It was the 7th of February, and he had only been gone from Dunfermline for three days, summoned back to Holyroodhouse expressly by the King at, they had suspected, Patrick's instigation.

'No. I am not.' He came to her, but anxiously rather than with his usual impetuous eagerness. 'Mary – is Huntly here?'

'Huntly? No. He was. But he is gone.'

'When?'

'An hour ago. More. Why, Vicky?'

'Did he ask for Moray?'

'No. He called merely to pay his respects to the Queen, he said. As he passed through Dunfermline.'

'Going where?'

'I do not know. He may have told Her Grace. Ask her, Vicky. Is it . . . bad news?'

'And Moray? He is not here, then?' This curt questioning was unlike Lennox.

'He was here yesterday. And the day before. But not today, no. You think that Huntly is looking for Moray?'

'I know it. He carries a decree from the King for Moray's arrest. For high treason.'

The girl drew a long breath. 'So – it has come to that!' she said. 'After all.'

'I would to God that was all!' he jerked. 'Mary – will Moray be at Donibristle? Now?'

'I would think it, yes. I do not know – but it is likely. His house . . .'

'Did Huntly take that road, then? The sea road, for Fordel and Aberdour?'

'I did not watch his going, Vicky.'

'No. The stable-boys may know. But . . . why ask? Whatever road he took, he will have gone to Donibristle. Nothing surer. As therefore must I. At once. Pray God I may be in time.' Already he was making for the door.

'In time, Vicky? For what? To warn Moray? It will be much too late, I fear. And what else can you do?'

'I do not know. But if I am there, it may be that Huntly will hold back. From his worst intent.' He was striding out now, down the long corridor towards the courtyard, Mary having almost to run to keep up with him. 'I may yet save Moray's life.'

'His *life*!' the girl gasped. 'What do you mean?'

'I believe that Huntly means to slay Moray, not arrest him!'

'Slay? Oh, no! No!' That was a wail.

'Yes. I cannot wait, Mary. To tell you all, now. But I believe it is so. And that James knows it, God forgive him. Aye, and Patrick also.'

'Never! Not that. You must be mistaken, Vicky . . . '

'Would that I was. But I heard the King's parting words to Huntly. Saw his look. Patrick's also. We were hunting. This morning. At Barnbougle. It was to be secret. Huntly rode direct from the hunt. I wondered at it. Then Peter Hay told me that he had heard one of Huntly's lairds saying to another that Moray would not live to see another day. He said Huntly had sworn it.'

'But . . . but . . . ' Helplessly, Mary shook her head. 'Why? Why, Vicky?'

'Reasons a-plenty – of a sort.' They had reached Ludovick's horse, now, where it stood steaming. 'Huntly has a blood-feud with Moray. From the days of his father, brought low by Moray's uncle, the Regent. Half the earldom was Huntly land once. And James becomes ever more jealous of Anne. Patrick has worked on him all too well. Now that Moray's wife is dead, he fears still worse things. That his wife may be stolen from him. Even his heir, possibly. And so the realm. You know James. It is crazy – but no crazier than the witches and Bothwell.' The young man hoisted himself up into the saddle. 'I must be gone.'

She laid a hand on his knee, as though she would restrain him. 'Moray may not need your warning, Vicky. He has men of his own. Huntly had but two or three gentlemen with him.'

'Aye – when he called here! As when he left the hunt. But at the Queen's Ferry I learned that forty men-at-arms had awaited him there. So all was arranged beforehand. If he did not bring all these here, he must have left them somewhere in the town. Hidden. And at the Ferry, Huntly had given orders, in the King's name, that no ferry-boat, or other craft, was to sail across to Fife today. After him.' Ludovick snorted a mirthless laugh. 'It required siller, and my fine new authority as Lord High Admiral, to get across myself! Think you now that Moray is in no danger?'

The young woman shook her head. 'I know not what to think. Save . . . save that there is danger for you also in this, Vicky. Must you go? What can you do? One man . . . ?'

'You know that I must, Mary. I can do no less. Huntly is married to my sister. You would not have me fail to do what I can?'

She sighed. 'No. No. But . . . take care, Vicky. Oh, take care.'

Lennox bent to pat her hand, then dug spurred heels into his beast's flanks.

Ludovick smelt the tang of smoke on the chill east wind before ever he saw the fitful glow of fire. The evil taint of it caught at more than his nostrils and throat. He flogged his weary mount the harder.

He saw the dark loom of the sea, and the red glare of flames at the same moment, as he breasted a low ridge, the one against the other. The house of Donibristle stood on a pleasant grassy headland of the Forth estuary midway between the burghs of Inverkeithing and Aberdour, six miles from Dunfermline. A tall narrow tower-house, rather than any castle, Moray's father had built it here instead of on the island itself, a couple of miles off-shore, when his royal sire had granted him the abbacy of St. Colm's Abbey; it was a deal more convenient than being marooned out there on Inch Colm amongst the seals and guillemots. Moray's widowed mother, the Lady Doune, still made it her home. But would not, it seemed, after this night.

Appalled, Lennox stared. There was no doubt that the flames came from the house; he could just glimpse the lofty outline of it intermittently against the glare, though the smoke and the dusk confused sight. This was worse than he had feared.

He spurred headlong down to the lower ground, through copse and farmland. He passed groups of cottars gazing, horror-struck. Soon, above the drumming of his horse's hooves, he heard on the wind the hoarse shouts of men. Then a woman's thin screaming.

At a gateway to the demesne itself, two mounted guards came rearing out of the shadows of trees to bar his progress, Gordons with broadswords drawn.

'Back! Back! Halt, you!' Highland-sounding voices cried. 'In Gordon's name – halt!'

'Aside, fools!' the younger man flung at them. 'I am Lennox. The Duke. Stand aside.'

His authoritative tone seemed to impress one of the sentries, but not the other. With a flood of Gaelic this individual blocked his way, sword point flickering wickedly in the ruddy uncertain light of fire. Ludovick had to pull back his mount to its haunches, and drag its head round.

'Knave! Idiot!' he shouted. 'Out of my way! I am from the King,' he lied. 'Do you not know me – your lord's good-brother, the Duke of Lennox?'

That last appeared to penetrate, and they let him past, if doubtfully.

With those flames as beacon, he rode on, down to the little headland. With a measure of relief he perceived as he drew close that it was not exactly the house itself that was burning – although it probably would be, very shortly. It was brushwood heaped high all around its stone walls that was blazing, and busy figures, black and devilish against the red, were running to and fro, adding fuel to the conflagration – pine-tree branches, hay from the nearby farm-steading, implements and furnishings from the farm itself, anything which would burn and smoke. The smoke, without a doubt, was as important as the flame. Moray was in process of being smoked out.

These stone towers, with iron-grilled outer doors, stone vaulted basements, and lower windows too small to admit a man, were all but impregnable, save to artillery. But smoke, skilfully applied, could render them untenable. The glass of lower windows, and especially of stairway arrow-slits, smashed, and fire applied judiciously, with fierce heat to cause a great updraught of air, and the tower became little less than a tall chimney for sucking up billowing clouds of smoke. None within would be able to endure it for long. Huntly no doubt was an expert on the subject.

Nevertheless, Ludovick knew some relief. At least, since they were still piling on fuel, Moray was presumably still untaken and safe, however uncomfortable. There might yet be time.

Above the crackling of the fire, Lennox began to distinguish the louder reports of spasmodic shooting. Then, against the glare, he perceived occasional brighter flashes from the topmost windows of the house, especially from the watch-chamber that surmounted the stair-tower. Moray was fighting back, then – no doubt trying to pick off the hurrying figures that were feeding the flames. Shots, too, came from various dark groups on the ground, scattered around the house, firing arquebuses, hackbuts and dags at the upper windows.

Throwing himself off his horse, Lennox hurried to the first of these groups. Somewhere nearby a woman was sobbing hysterically.

'Where is Huntly?' he demanded. 'My lord of Huntly – where is he?'

Only one man so much as deigned to glance at him. 'Who asks, cock-sparrow?'

'I am Lennox. The Duke. Chamberlain of this realm. I ask in the King's name.'

The other cleared his throat. 'Och, well. I'ph'mm. Yonder's himself, my lord. By the horses. There, at yonder tree . . . '

Ludovick ran forward. To windward of the blaze he could distinguish Huntly's tall and ponderous figure now, steel half-armour on top of the tartans which he had worn for hunting. He stood with some others just back from gunshot range of the house.

'George!' Lennox cried, panting a little. 'What . . . what folly is this? Have you taken leave of your wits?'

'Precious soul of Christ!' The big man whirled round. 'Vicky Lennox! How a God's name came *you* here?'

'Following you. From Barnbougle. In haste. Praying that I would be in time.'

'Eh . . . ? Aye, you are in time, a plague on it! The fox is still holed up in his cairn! But we'll have him out soon, never fear. A curse on him!'

'No!' the younger man cried. 'Not that, George. You must stop it . . .'

'Stop it? Are you crazy, Vicky? Who says so?'

'I do. Listen to me, George. You cannot do this. This evil thing . . .'

'Sink me – what brought you yapping at my heels, boy?' Huntly demanded frowning blackly. 'Has our Jamie changed his mind, then? So soon?'

'Yes! Yes – that is it.' Ludovick clutched at any straw. 'I have come from him. From the hunt. No harm is to come to Moray. No harm, d'you hear?'

'I hear pap-sucking and belly-wind!' the other snorted. 'Think you that I am a bairn like yourself? If James Stewart cannot remain of one mind for two minutes on end, Gordon can! Gordon will do what Gordon came to do!'

'No, George – you shall not! You are not in your North now. The King's rule runs here – not Gordon's!'

'Faugh!' Huntly hooted his opinion of the King's rule. 'Besides, I have your King's decree to take Moray. Here in my pouch. Signed with his own hand.'

'To take. Not to harm. Not to burn, to shoot . . .'

'Think you not so?' The other grinned.

'No, I tell you! The King at least has come to his senses in this. You are not to do it.'

'If the fool resists the King's orders, he must take the consequences.'

'Not this. Not burning, slaying. Not murder. Moray is of the blood-royal. You cannot do it.'

'No? You watch me then, boy. Watch Gordon!'

'I say no! In the King's name. I am Chamberlain and High Admiral of this realm. I command that you call off your men. Douse those fires.' Ludovick's voice cracked a little as it rose.

'And I am Gordon – and no man commands in my presence! Nor do puppies bark! Out o' my way, loon – this is man's work, not laddie's!'

'I warn you, George – if harm befalls Moray . . . '

'Hold your fool tongue, boy!' the other snarled, and turned away.

Donibristle House seemed now to be a roaring inferno. How any survived, even in the topmost storey, was a mystery, for clouds of smoke were belching out of all the broken upper windows. Yet shots continued to be fired from some of the same windows.

An outbreak of shouting from round at the west side of the house, where the smoke was thickest, attracted attention. Soon one of his Highland swordsmen came running, to inform Huntly that two of the defenders had bolted from the tower by leaping out of a third-floor window on the roof of a range of outbuildings and so to the ground, under cover of the smoke blown to that side on the east wind. Both had been caught, however, and were now suitably dead. Apparently they were mere craven Lowland hirelings.

Huntly reacted swiftly. If two had done this, others might also. Moray himself, perhaps. They would scarce win out any other way, now. The place would repay watching. The Earl led his group of lairds thither. Lennox, ignored, followed on.

In the lee of the building, the heat and smoke was highly unpleasant. Soon they were all coughing, with eyes smarting and running, complaining that they could see little or nothing.

In the event it was their ears which warned them. The shooting from the tower seemed to have stopped. That could mean either that the remaining defenders had been overcome by the fumes, or that they might be seeking to make their escape.

'Watch you, now!' Huntly shouted to his minions. 'We'll have the tod out now, I vow!' He drew his broadsword with a grim flourish.

'George – put back that sword!' Lennox exclaimed tensely. 'For Henrietta's sake, if naught else.'

'Glenderry!' Huntly commanded. 'Keep you an eye on my lord Duke. I hold you responsible for him. I will have no interferences – you understand? Use what force you must, should he be foolish. See you to it.'

'I' faith, if your bullies lay hands on me, George, they shall suffer! And you also. I swear it!' Ludovick cried. 'I swear likewise, that if you harm Moray, in capturing him, you will pay a dear price . . . '

'Quiet, fool! Enough of your babe's puling. See to it, Glenderry . . . '

A volley of shouts interrupted him. Fingers, weapons, were pointing. Dimly to be distinguished in the swirling smoke, men had appeared on the outhouse roof. This was itself now ablaze. Even as they stared, part of it fell in with a crash and a shower of sparks – and one of the men with it. His screams shrilled high – and then ceased abruptly. There were still three left, four, crouching desperate figures, crawling on the steep flame-spouting roof.

From as near-by as they dared approach, watchers mocked them and skirled, swords ready.

In a window higher in the tower, a man appeared framed, a fearsome spectacle, ablaze from head to foot. Arms flailing wildly, he leapt out and down, for the roof a dozen feet below. Blinded, no doubt, by smoke and pain, he misjudged, struck only the edge of the guttering, and plunged another twenty feet to the ground, there to lie still. The impact extinguished some of his fire, but not all.

Huntly hooted. 'This is better than Patrick Gray's fireworks!' he chuckled. 'The pity he is not here to see it.'

'Christ God – save these men!' Lennox shouted. He would have rushed forward, but strong arms held him on either side.

The men on the roof were jumping now – a long jump. Broadswords, dirks, flickered redly in the lurid light, to receive them should they survive. Taunts, challenges, rang out.

Then a kilted warrior came running round the south front of the house, calling for Huntly. Two men had won out of a window on the east side, he reported breathlessly. By a rope of sorts. Proper men, richly dressed. Buckie thought that one could be Moray himself.

Huntly delayed not a moment. For his bulk he was extraordinarily nimble on his feet. Bellowing for men to follow him, he rushed off round the house, cursing furiously.

His minions streamed after him. Ludovick, sensing that the men who were holding him were straining to do likewise, dragged forward also. They all went, running.

A single swordsman awaited them at the other end of the

372

house. He pointed southwards, seawards.

Strung out, stumbling in the darkness, tripping over stones and obstructions, they raced on, armour clanking. The house stood a mere couple of hundred yards back from the shore. The beach was narrow, stony.

Panting hugely, Huntly came to the edge of the sea-grass, where a group of men stood, dark against the faint luminosity of the sea.

'Fiend seize me – where are they?' he demanded, spluttering. 'Buckie – why in God's name are you standing there?'

Gordon of Buckie, a dark hatchet-faced man, broadsword in one hand, dirk in the other, grinned. 'Never fear, my lord,' he answered, and pointed. 'See you there. I but waited for you.'

All stared whence he gestured. Over there, a little way to the east, amongst the rocks and reefs of the shore, something glowed dully red.

'By the Rood!' Huntly gasped. 'You mean . . . you mean . . . ?'

'Aye – yonder he is. My bonnie lord o' Moray. Singed a mite – but all fowl are better so to pluck and truss, are they not? He conceives himself to be hidden . . . '

'You are certain that he it is, man?'

'To be sure, yes. He was well illuminated as he ran, my lord!' Buckie chuckled. 'His hair burned but indifferently – but the plume of his helm flared like a torch. As good as a beacon. Yon is the stump of it you see, I wager. Wiser he would have been to throw it into the sea.'

'He is not alone, your man said?'

'No. Another is with him, there. Him they call Dunbar, the Sheriff of Moray, I think. Sore hurt, I believe. Else Moray might have fared better, for he is an agile carle. He was aiding him . . . '

'Aye. Come, then. Let us finish the matter.'

'George Gordon!' Lennox cried, from the rear. 'Moray is to suffer no hurt. No further hurt. I charge you, in the King's name. Before all these. Heed well . . . '

'Mother o' God! Does that cockerel still crow?' Huntly threw back over his plaided and corseleted shoulder. 'Quiet, loon!'

Down they streamed towards the tell-tale glow of smouldering stump of proud horse-hair helmet-plume. Too late its owner realised that his position was discovered. Springing up, and by his height and splendid stature revealing himself to be Moray indeed, the fugitive looked as though he might seek to bolt still further along that rock-bound shore. Then glancing down, presumably at his wounded companion amongst the weed-hung boulders, he straightened wide shoulders, shrugged, and raised his voice.

'I am the Earl of Moray,' he called. 'I yield me.' And he threw his sword from him, towards them. It fell amongst the stones with a ringing clatter.

The chorus of shouts that greeted his gesture might have come from a pack of wolves, Huntly's own fierce vituperation high amongst them.

Down upon the unarmed man the yelling crew rushed. Moray stood waiting. Above the shadows of the rocks his upper half was clearly illuminated in the glare of the burning house. He wore no armour, other than the helmet. His fine clothing was blackened and soiled. His long fair hair, that normally fell to his shoulders, was burned away unevenly almost to the edges of the helmet.

Too late he perceived that his surrender meant nothing to his attackers; that there was no mercy for him here. He turned, and started to run towards a black crevice amongst great rocks – no cave, but perhaps some shelter and shield from flanking blows; but Gordon of Buckie, fleet of foot, headed him off. Leaping boulders like any deer, his broadsword lifted, and he brought it slashing down upon the Earl's shoulder and back.

With a choking cry, Moray whirled round, his fine frame bent, twisted to one side, to lean against a rock, gasping. He thrust out both hands, empty – although one drooped limply.

Buckie drew back his sword, laughed aloud, and lunged forward again with his full force, to run the other right through the belly.

Coughing, vomiting, groaning, Moray sank to the stones, the steel still transfixing him.

Yelling, the others came surging round the prostrate Earl. But as they stared down at the convulsive figure, their cries died away. Even Huntly was silent.

Not so Gordon of Buckie. 'There is your tod, Huntly!' he cried out. 'Your fox out of its cairn. Is it Huntly's fox – or only Buckie's? Where's your steel, my lord? Your steel?'

His chief drew a deep breath, clenched his teeth, and raising his sword, hacked it down, right across the dying man's upturned face.

The moaning shudder which followed that ghastly blow was not only Moray's.

Ludovick's shocked cry of horror died away as a thick uncouth sound came from the riven mouth itself, that spouted blood blackly over the stones. Out of the jumble, words came with infinite difficulty, slowly, one by one.

' . . . Huntly . . . you Hieland . . . stot! You ha' . . . spoiled . . . a better . . . face . . . than . . . your own! May . . . God . . . '

A great spate of blood came gushing, and the voice choked and gurgled, not to silence, but to incoherence.

As of one accord the company fell upon the twitching, writhing body, flailing, slashing, stabbing, with dirk and broadsword and whinger.

Lennox was violently sick on the shingle of the beach.

Chapter Twenty-two

SCOTLAND seethed like a cauldron on the boil. The bonnie Earl of Moray was dead, slain foully by Huntly, by the King, by the Master of Gray, by the Catholics. Moray was of the kirk's persuasion, if less than zealously. From every pulpit in the land thundered furious denunciation, protest, demands for retribution, fierce attacks on the King. Moray, the idol of the faithful, must be avenged. The Papists must be crushed. Huntly must die. Parliament must assemble and express the people's horror and detestation.

Moray, of course, had been a notable performer with the football, the boxing-glove, the tennis-racquet and the golf-club. Even Mary the Queen's death at the hands of Elizabeth, five years before, had not aroused such a clamour.

James dared not appear in the streets of Edinburgh for fear of being hooted and jeered at, even having refuse pelted at him. Moray's hacked and battered corpse was brought to the family burial ground at Leith for public display in the kirkyard there, by his mother, displaying her own singed grey hair and refusing burial for her son until she was granted vengeance. A Campbell, daughter of MacCailean Mhor himself, Earl of Argyll, she was not one to be content with half measures.

On Patrick Gray's advice James persuaded Huntly to ward himself in the West Lothian fortress of Blackness Castle, meantime. It was not truly a warding, of course, for Huntly swaggered there in style with all his men, indeed kept up almost princely state within its extensive walls and went out hunting in the adjoining woodlands, inviting James as his guest. But it did enable the King to declare that he was taking steps, and that justice would be done. He also announced that he had evidence linking Moray with Bothwell's treasonable attempts, and that was why Huntly had been sent to arrest him. This scarcely satisfied many, needless to say, but it made a gesture towards public opinion. More effective, again on Patrick's advice, was James's announcement that he had sent Lennox hot-foot after Huntly as soon as he had heard rumours that the Gordons might carry out the arrest over-vigorously. Unfortunately, the Duke had arrived too late. Moray had resisted lawful arrest, fired on Huntly from his tower, and largely ordained his own fate.

Since there was nothing to be gained by bringing the King into lower public estimation than he enjoyed already, Ludovick kept quiet. He did not leave James, or Patrick Gray either, in any private doubt however as to his opinions and feelings. The rift between them widened.

Lennox had gone back to Dunfermline that dire night, eventually. On hearing his news, Queen Anne had taken to her bed, and had there remained for almost an entire week. She ate little or nothing, permitted only her closest women near her, and received no single visitor — save, strangely enough, at the end of the week, Patrick Gray. He came to comfort her, and to urge a prompt return to her husband's side, pointing out that this separation did not look well in view of the popular slanders anent herself and the late lamented Moray. All who had the privilege to know Her Grace realised how baseless was such talk, how true and leal was her devotion to her royal and loving spouse; nevertheless, undoubtedly monarch and consort being parted at this difficult time was arousing comment and speculation. Also it would much please her devoted admirers, Patrick Gray in especial, if Her Highness would restore to them the sun of her presence at Holyroodhouse.

Anne agreed to consider the matter.

It was as Patrick left the royal bedchamber that Mary Gray awaited him.

'Can you spare me a moment, Patrick?' she asked, even-voiced.

'Why, my dear – need you ask? Always I can do that, and more. It is my pleasure.'

Without answering, she showed him into an anteroom, and closed the door behind them.

Ruefully he eyed her. 'Do I sense, moppet, that in some way I have transgressed? Displeased you? Of what am I to be convicted, now?'

She turned to face him. 'Any displeasure of mine matters nothing,' she said. 'If your conscience does not convict you, how shall I?'

'Conscience?' he repeated. 'Ah, me – a chancy and unreliable witness! What is conscience, my heart? An irrational sense of guilt, largely affected by what one ate for supper the night before? Regret for aspects of failure? One is seldom conscience-stricken, I find, over successes! Fear of consequences? I am suspicious of too active a conscience, Mary.'

'Words, Patrick,' she gave back, levelly. 'Easy and fine words. Always you have them in plenty. But words will not serve to bring back my lord of Moray to life. Words will not undo what has been done.'

'Why no, lass. But should not you address your homily to Huntly? He it was, I understand, who unfortunately made an end of the so popular Moray. Not your erring sire.'

'Was it? she asked flatly.

He raised slender brows at her. 'That was my impression.'

'But not mine, I fear. Would that it was. Nor Vicky's. Huntly's was only the hand that struck the blow, I think.

377

Your's was the mind that planned it so, was it not?'

His beautiful features, that so nearly mirrored her own, went completely expressionless. '*I* think that you go too fast, my dear,' he said softly. 'Too fast and far.'

She shook her head. 'I have watched you working for months to pull Moray down. As you have pulled down so many. You conceived him as in your way. Now he is dead. Whether you ordained his killing or no, I think that you knew that Huntly intended his death. And did naught to stay him. I see blood on your hands, therefore.'

'You see phantoms! Vain imaginings, girl,' he returned, more sharply now. 'You, in your wisdom, think this and think that! How can you tell what I know or plan or intend? How could I know that Huntly intended the death of Moray — if he did?'

'Vicky saw his parting from you. At the hunt. He heard the King's instructions. You were at the King's side. Vicky said . . . '

'Aye – Vicky! Always it is Vicky! That young man that I cherished is, I fear, become a viper in my bosom! It seems that I shall have to deal with Vicky.'

'No!' she cried, alarm widening her eyes. 'Not that! Never Vicky . . . '

'Then tell him to keep his fingers out of my affairs, Mary.' Patrick recovered his smile. 'With all suitable parental diffidence, my dear, I would suggest that you might even do the same! For your own sweet sake, if not mine!'

'You . . . you are warning me, Patrick?' she put to him. 'Warning me off?'

'Why, not so, my heart. I would do nothing so unseemly. I but plead with you not to meddle in affairs beyond you, lest you burn your pretty little fingers. Which I would not like to see. You cannot label that a warning, I vow!'

'No? Then let me offer you a similar plea, Patrick,' she said, calm again. 'Do not seek to bring any more men low. Cast down no others. You used Huntly to bring down Moray. Now, brute-beast as Huntly is, I fear for him. As I fear for Bothwell still. Sometimes, I even fear for the King himself!'

Their eyes met, and held. He did not speak.

'Oh, Patrick,' she exclaimed, in a different voice. 'Will

378

you not stop it? Make an end of it. For Marie's sake. For little Andrew's. And Davy's. And mine. Who love you. Will you not?'

He drew a long breath. 'You dream, girl,' he said. 'You deceive yourself.'

'No. For I know you, you see.'

'How do you know?'

'I know you, because I know myself. We are none so different, perhaps, you and I. So, I beg you, I entreat you, I urge you – hold your hand. Lest . . . lest . . .'

'Aye,' he said, eyes narrowing. 'Lest what?'

'Lest I forget that I am your daughter. And do . . . do what I conceive to be right. My duty, Patrick.'

Long he looked at her, searching her lovely elphin face, staring deep into her dark eyes, as though to probe to the very core of her being. Then abruptly, without another word, he swung about and left her there, striding to the door and out.

She stood alone, trembling a little, gazing blindly at the open door.

Anne returned to Holyroodhouse two days later, and Mary with her. James made a great show of welcoming her, riding out with half his Court as far as the Queen's Ferry, to escort her to the city and the palace. To emphasise their happy conjugal bliss a touching ceremony was organised at the West Port, where carefully selected representaives of the citizenry presented the allegedly pregnant young Queen with items of baby-wear, and James made a speech in Latin, with droll obscenities in Greek and Hebrew, intimating the joys and privileges of fatherhood, and the realm's felicity in anticipating the arrival of an heir to the throne. He even patted his wife's stomach, in an excess of enthusiasm – although it had to be admitted that Anne, pale and drawn and unsmiling, had never looked slimmer.

Unfortunately the cosily domestic atmosphere engendered by this scene was rather spoiled by the appearance in the crowd of some rude fellows leading a horse on which was displayed a man-size picture of the Earl of Moray. It was no ordinary picture this, for the Lady Doune had had it painted of her son lying outstretched on the ground, naked save for a loin-cloth, and most obviously and unpleasantly dead, his body hacked, slashed and punctured with major realism. Queen Anne all but swooned away at the sight of it – indeed she would have fallen from the saddle had not Patrick Gray ridden alongside to catch and support her bodily. From immediately behind, Mary Gray spurred her mount forward at the same time, and across the Queen's swaying person man's and girl's eyes met for an instant, tensely.

James, ever affected drastically by the sight of blood, even painted blood apparently, gobbled in horror, dug spurs into his horse's flanks, and slapping high hat hard down, went galloping off down towards the Grassmarket, scattering the crowd right and left, and leaving wife and entourage behind.

The royal procession took a deal of reorganising thereafter.

The ball which had been hastily arranged for that night at Holyroodhouse, was as hastily cancelled on account of the Queen's indisposition.

In the weeks that followed, the bonnie Earl of Moray continued to make a greater impact on the affairs of the realm in death than ever he had done in life. Various determined folk saw to that. The Kirk promoted him to the status of Protestant martyr, and inspired true believers to make pilgrimage to the kirkyard at Leith, where his unburied body still was on gruesome display, with an armed guard of the faithful on duty day and night to ensure that the King's men did not spirit it away or unsuitably inter it. Parallel with this beatification of the martyr of Donibristle, came a steady series of demands to the King and Privy Council that rigorous steps should be taken against Huntly; Catholicism should be proscribed and made a penal office; and Parliament called to enact laws to make Presbyterianism the official church government for all time coming, and to remove all bishops, abbots and commendators from the seats they held in Parliament.

The Lady Doune was tireless in keeping her son's memory not so much green as red. She paraded the streets, not only with her painting, but with Moray's rent and blood-stained shirt as banner, picqueting the Holyroodhouse gates day after day. She involved her brother Argyll and much of Clan Campbell in the business. It was said that she kept re-singeing her own and her daughter's hair, to counteract the healing effects of time.

As well as oratory, art and pageantry, poetry and literature also seemed to gain new life out of the death of Scotland's posthumous hero. The country was flooded with printed verses, songs, lampoons and pamphlets on the subject, extolling the virtues and beauties of the deceased, his royal blood, proclaiming that he was the Queen's true love, and hinting that in the circumstances the hand behind Huntly's was not far to seek. Since printing was a new and expensive process, the quantity and distribution of these compositions held its own significance.

Mary Gray, watching the Master these days like any hawk, came to the conclusion that for once he had made a grievous miscalculation in his statecraft, had quite failed to estimate public reaction to Moray's death. Until, that is, one day the Lady Marie showed her a scrap of paper which she had found in the pocket of one of Patrick's doublets, given to her for cleaning. It was in his own handwriting, and consisted of a couple of verses of a typical – if better composed than usual – panegyric on Moray, insinuations of the King's guilt, and demand for vengeance. Certain words had been scored out here and there and improved upon, in the same hand. And Maitland's name was included amongst those who were to be held responsible for the tragedy.

Obviously here was much much food for thought.

James was forced, in varying degrees, to bow to pressure. A judicial enquiry was at last ordered into the allegations against Huntly – and in due course and not unnaturally, found that nobleman innocent of any greater offence than over-zealousness in discharge of his appointed duty. With Gordons innumerable parading Edinburgh streets, hands on dirks, such a verdict was entirely realistic. The Cock o' the North emerged from Blackness Castle vindicated, and after a single high-spirited demonstration in Edinburgh, sensibly set out for his own North, where Protestant lords like Atholl, Forbes, the Marischal and Grant had been at play while the cat was away.

The Lowlands heaved a premature sigh of relief.

Lord Chancellor Maitland, who had been keeping much in the background of late anyway, came to the conclusion that overwork was affecting his health, and with the King's permission retired to his house of Thirlestane in the Borderland for a vacation of unstipulated duration. No acting-chancellor was appointed but the Master of Gray, with all his wide experience, was at the realm's disposal at all times.

A Parliament was called for June, to consider the Kirk's demands on church government, bishops and the like, and other weighty matters. One of these, curiously enough was a claim put forward by the Master of Gray against the royal treasury; a notably large claim amounting to the peculiar sum of no less than £19,983 – pounds Scots, of course, since there was nothing like that sum in gold or English pounds in all the land. This claim, it transpired, was reimbursement and interest allegedly due to the Master for private monies expended on the nation's business during his previous period of acting-chancellor six years before. The King had signified his assent to this substantial requisition – indeed there were rumours that he was much more deeply involved, and that the whole thing was merely a plot on the part of Patrick and himself to lay hands on a deal of ready money that had recently accrued to the treasury through a spate of fines and forfeitures, to share it between them. Be that as it might, the Lord Treasurer, the unco-operative Master of Glamis, had his reservations, and the matter was to go before the Parliament.

Embalmed now, the corpse of the Earl of Moray remained unburied at Leith, a symbol and a challenge.

With Huntly safely out of the way and fully occupied in the North, Bothwell re-emerged from the wilds of Liddesdale, and took up his threat against the King more or less where he had left off. He was said to be at Crichton, at Hailes, in the Merse with the Homes, at Fast Castle with Logan of Restalrig. True or false, peaceable folk groaned in spirit.

It was only a day or two before the Parliament that Lennox came seeking Mary Gray in the Queen's quarters of the palace. Without ceremony he extracted her from the company of her colleagues, and taking her by the arm led her into the privacy of a tiny turret chamber.

'Sakes, my lord Duke!' she exclaimed. 'You are exceedingly ducal today! Should I be honoured? I so seldom see you now. You are so ducally busy. Closeted with my lord of Mar, with Master Andrew Melville, consulting with the Earl of Atholl, and, they say, with Chancellor Maitland away at Thirlestane.

Even, whisper it, while you are down in those parts, with Bothwell himself . . . !'

'Who said that?' he jerked. 'Patrick?'

'Why, no. Patrick no longer honours me with his confidences. I had it from the Master of Orkney, the Lady Marie's brother. He hears most of what goes on at Court, I have found.'

'I'd liefer you discussed my affairs with others than that lecherous clown, Mary,' he said stiffly.

Surprised, the girl eyed him. 'Vicky – this is strange, from you. He was but idly gossiping. About all and sundry . . . '

'What else did he gossip to you? About me?'

'So! There is something in it all then, Vicky? I did not believe it . . . '

'Well?'

'He said that you were set on being named second man in the kingdom. By this Parliament. Next heir to the throne. I could not credit that. It did not sound like you, Vicky. Do not tell me that it is true?'

'Aye,' the young man said heavily. 'It is true. In some measure. Not that I care anything for such, myself. As you well know. It is but to forestall the Lord Hamilton. He is known to be going to claim that position. His great-grandmother was a daughter of King James the Second. Why he is making the claim, I know not. But it is feared that he has ill designs. I am closer to the Throne than he, so this has been projected. That Parliament should name me as next heir, lacking issue of the King. Lest Hamilton and his friends make trouble . . . '

Mary all but moaned. 'More of it!' she whispered. 'This . . . this sounds like Patrick again, Vicky. Is it? Is he behind this intrigue? I vow it was never the King's doing. It smells of Patrick!'

'No. He has no hand in it. He has few dealings with me, now. He may be behind Hamilton's claim – I know not. But not this of mine. It is Atholl who led me to it. And Master Melville. The Kirk party do not trust Hamilton. It appears that they trust me. They believe that they can carry sufficient votes in this Parliament . . . '

'Yet Patrick is seeing a deal of my lord of Atholl, these days.

And he dined with Master Melville but two nights ago. Oh, Vicky – have naught to do with it! I suspect it. I do so . . . '

'It is but for the good of the realm, Mary. It is only a gesture. To give Hamilton pause. Anne will have a child – even if she is not pregnant yet. Besides, it is gone too far for me to withdraw now. And it but states the truth. That I am the next heir if James lacks children – as we have always known.'

'It is dangerous,' she insisted. 'I feel it, I sense it. Do not lend yourself to plots and intrigues, Vicky – whosoever concocts them. They are not for you.'

'I am Chamberlain and Admiral of this realm, Mary. I have been Viceroy. I cannot shut my eyes to what concerns its weal . . . ' Abruptly he abandoned the lofty and dignified tone that came so unnaturally to him, and was at once his normal, urgent and unaffected self again. 'Mary,' he declared, 'heed none of all this. Not now. It is not important. For us. It is not what I came to tell you. I . . . I . . . Mary – Sophia is dead!'

'Sophia Ruthven! Your . . . your wife! She is dead? Oh, Vicky!'

'I have just had word. Her mother, the Lady Gowrie, is new come from Ruthven. She was buried four days back. Of a flux of blood. A consumption.'

'I am sorry, sorry. She was so young. So unhappy. To die alone! You had not even seen her? Her mother did not send for you?'

'No. She did not want me. Her mother says it, and I know it. We meant nothing to each other. You know it, also. I am sorry for her, Mary – sorry that she suffered so. But she was ill when we were wed. She should never have been married. Now she is gone. I cannot mourn her – else I make myself a hypocrite. I think her better dead, indeed, than as last I saw her – coughing in her pain, weeping in her misery . . . '

The young woman nodded, sighing. 'I know, Vicky. I am sorry – for you both. It was a hard thing for both of you. But worse for her. Always it is worse for the woman. A bad marriage, a marriage without affection and trust, is for a woman utter woe and disaster.'

'Is that what *you* fear, Mary?' He took her shoulder, and turned her to face him. 'Do you fear a bad marriage? To me?'

384

'To you, Vicky? No – no, not that. That is not what I fear. How can I fear the impossible? *We* cannot marry . . . '

'But we can. I am free, now. To marry again. To marry you, Mary.'

Unhappily the young woman shook her head. 'You are not, Vicky – you are not! Nothing has changed. You must see it. Do not shut your eyes. Do not be blind to what all others can see. We can never marry, you and I. A moment ago you were reminding me of who and what you were. Great Chamberlain of Scotland. Lord High Admiral. Next heir to the throne. How can you be all these, and marry the daughter of Davy Gray, the land-steward?'

'All know that you are in fact the Master of Gray's daughter. His mother was Gowrie's sister. So you are indeed cousin to Sophia, once removed.'

'Removed by a great gulf. Not legitimate. Either I am the steward's daughter, and honest. Or I am illegitimate. Neither will make a wife for the Duke of Lennox. That is certain. The realm, whose weal you would serve, would not allow it. Ever.' Her voice quivered. 'Accept it, Vicky. As I do. I thank you for your . . . your devotion. Your love. And for asking. But do not ask it again, I beseech you. Never again. For, for I cannot bear it!'

It was Mary Gray's turn to cut short an interview. She turned in a swirl of skirts, and ran from that little chamber, blindly enough to collide with the door-post as she went.

Chapter Twenty-three

THE Countess of Atholl was vastly unlike her recently deceased sister Sophia Ruthven. Much the eldest of Lady Gowrie's children, she was a bold piece in more ways than one. That she it was who probably played the part of Leda to Patrick's swan at the Falkland pageant, was doubted by none on the score of boldness at least. This early summer morning, however, she was playing a part still bolder than in any pageant. An extra

Lady-in-Waiting to the Queen, who yet lodged, not in the palace of Holyroodhouse itself, but in her mother's house in the Abbey Strand close by, she was one of the very few persons who held a key enabling her to use the small postern gate which led in through the old Abbey precincts to the palace itself. This morning she brought in by this her usual route two servitors wearing the Atholl colours and bearing large baskets filled with delicacies for the Queen's Grace. One of the bearers, although he stooped notably, could be seen to be an exceptionally tall man.

Such guards as were on duty at that hour yawningly saluted the Countess and betrayed no interest in her servants. Most of the palace's occupants still slept deep, only two or three hours abed indeed after a great ball and masque held therein to mark the penultimate day of the momentous sitting of the Estates of Parliament; this had been a brilliant function in the organisation of which the Master of the Wardrobe had excelled himself, despite the stresses and tensions of the moment. If Lady Atholl looked a little less challenging-eyed and provocative than usual, she had her excuse, for she had, as ever, taken a major part in the procedings and had not been to bed since.

Life seemed to be stirring only in the kitchens and domestic quarters of the great rambling establishment, and the trio made their way, without meeting others, towards the drum tower from which were reached the royal apartments. At the great doors in the tower's foot, a double guard of four men was even reinforced by a fifth – no less a person than the Captain of the Royal Guard himself, John, Earl of Mar. The Countess found a brief smile for him. With only an inclination of his head, he turned and led the way upstairs, the guard remaining at their posts.

Halfway up the winding turnpike stair, the couple paused, by mutual consent, to glance through the window overlooking the main forecourt of the palace. Down there a large addition to the guard was in process of being posted at the gates and along the flanking walls, many men, fully armed. Two figures, conspicuous as not being in the livery of the Royal Guard, stood out, recognisable as the Earl of Atholl and the Duke of Lennox. Both kept glancing up and back towards the drum-tower windows. Mar and the Countess moved closer to the glass so that they might be seen. They raised their hands.

There were brief nods from the two noblemen below, as they turned away.

The first floor landing opened on to two apartments, the royal pages' room and that of the ladies-in-waiting. In the first, two young men slept, one on a bed, the other, fully clad, sprawled over a table; this latter was Thomas Erskine, a cadet of Mar's own family. Quietly the Earl closed the door and turned the key in the lock.

The Countess listened at the second door. This was locked on the inside, as well it might be with the royal pages so close; but the duty Lady-in-Waiting who slept beyond it was her own youngest sister, the Lady Beatrix Ruthven.

Exchanging nods, Mar and Lady Atholl proceeded quietly up the second stairway, the two servitors still following.

The same arrangement of two doors prevailed on the second landing. These each admitted to anterooms, and off these opened the King's and the Queen's bedchambers. These were by no means the finest and most convenient bedrooms in the palace, but James, not without reason, was much concerned with security, and had selected these carefully with that in view. Although Anne's boudoir had still another anteroom beyond, which communicated with a further corridor of the palace, the King's own apartment was only reachable by this one door. None therefore could approach him save past the guard at the stair-foot and his pages on the first floor. Above was only his study in the top of the tower.

The Countess carefully opened the door of the Queen's anteroom. It was in a state of untidiness from the night's festivities. The door to the bedchamber beyond was closed. Quietly she abstracted the key from the inside of the anteroom door, transferred it to the outside, closed the door and locked it. Then she dipped in a mocking curtsy, first to Mar and then to the taller of her two attendants, and with a whisper of skirts slipped away downstairs without a word said.

The tall man straightened up. He cast off the voluminous but somewhat tattered cloak and hood of the Atholl colours which had masked both figure and features, and stood revealed, in splendid half-armour, as Francis Hepburn Stewart, Earl of

Bothwell. From the basket, beneath the sweetmeats, he drew out and buckled on his sword.

Mar beckoned, and cautiously opened the door of the King's anteroom. Peering within, he signed the others forward.

They moved inside, the third man revealing himself to be Mr. John Colville, a professional diplomat and one of the original Ruthven raiders, high in the Kirk party despite being an associate of Patrick Gray's.

Tip-toeing to the royal bedroom door, Mar listened thereat. He shook his head. With the utmost care, he tried the handle. It was locked, as anticipated, from the inside. James was unlikely ever to forget such a precaution.

The three men drew back. Mar took up a position close to the window, where he could watch the forecourt below. The other two examined the arras which hung against the stone walls, in case it should be necessary to slip behind it for cover from view. They waited, silent.

They were not long inactive. Quite soon there were sounds of stirring from the next room. Then a bout of spluttering coughing. The trio exchanged glances at the unmistakable sound of a chamber-pot being filled. Then, after some more movement, there was a loud thumping on the floor-boards beyond the door. This was the monarch's method of summoning his pages from the room directly below.

Motionless the three men stood, watching the door.

After some more thumping, the King's voice was raised in querulous shouting. 'Tam! Tam Erskine, you ill loon! Here! To me. A plague on you, you lazy limmer! Here wi' you!'

A pause. Then they heard cursing from within, and the turning of the key in the lock. The door of the royal bedroom was flung open.

James came shambling out, to halt suddenly as though transfixed, as Bothwell stepped forward into the middle of the anteroom. The King made an extraordinary figure. He was naked from his bed, apart from a dressing-robe thrown hurriedly over his sloping shoulders, and his hose which sagged down to his ankles. In one hand he clutched certain of his underwear. Never an impressive figure, he showed now to

388

less advantage than almost ever before. A wail escaped from his slack lips.

'Eh . . . ! Eh . . . ! Christ God – Bothwell!' he gasped. 'Fran . . . Francis Bothwell!'

The Earl removed his hand from his sword-hilt to sweep off his bonnet in a deep bow, smiling but unspeaking.

The King's great liquid eyes rolled and darted. Panting, he took a single step, almost involuntarily, towards the window.

Mar moved back a pace or two, so that his broad person filled the narrow embrasure. At the same time, Colville hurried from his stance by the inner wall, and slipped past the King and into the bedchamber. It was essential for their purpose that James did not reach either of the windows, to shout to or otherwise alarm the guard in the forecourt below.

James stared from Mar to Bothwell, and back. 'Johnnie!' he choked. 'You, Johnnie! Johnnie Mar.' Then his voice rose in a bubbling yell. 'Treason!' he cried. 'Treason!'

A shade anxiously Mar glanced out and down, to see whether this dread shout had reached the massed ranks of the guard confronting the palace gates. There was no sign of alarm below, however. He raised a hand to Lennox and Atholl, who still stood there, waiting to calm and reassure the soldiers, if necessary.

Bothwell spoke, the first word of any of the conspirators. 'Not treason, Your Grace. Far from it. We but seek your good. And the good of your realm . . .'

'Liar! Traitor! Devil! 'Tis treason! You seek my life. I ken it – fine I ken it, Francis Stewart!' Wildly the King glanced behind him, to find Colville standing there within the bedroom doorway. 'Waesucks – I am betrayed! Betrayed!' he all but sobbed.

'Not so, Highness,' Mar declared urgently. 'Would *I* betray you? This is but a necessary step. To ensure your royal safety. There may be trouble. Fighting. The Papists are stirring, assembling. This Parliament has been sore on them. It is even bruited that Huntly is returning. I have the guard protecting the palace. But who knows who are your enemies within, Sire? The Hamiltons. Morton. Crawford. *We* are all good Protestants, but . . .'

'False! False!' James exclaimed. But it was at Bothwell

that he gazed, as though fascinated by those piercing, vividly blue eyes under sandy brows. Seeking to cover his nakedness in some degree, he backed against the wall. 'Satan's tool! Satan's right hand . . . !'

Bothwell grinned. 'Scarce that, Sire — or I could have arranged this a deal more conveniently by witchcraft! I come but to seek your pardon, indeed, for breaking my ward. To stand trial before my peers on the witchcraft charge, if so be that is your royal wish. And to protect Your Grace from the evil that threatens from the Papists and those who would endanger your throne.' All this, the Earl announced with an expression of mockery quite at variance with his words. 'Your Grace has cause to thank me, not to fear me.'

James gnawed at his lip, in an agony of doubt.

'It is the truth, Sire,' Mar assured. 'Fear nothing . . . '

There was a diversion. Footsteps sounded on the stairs and the landing outside, and the door opened to admit a party of gentlemen. The royal eyes widened at the sound and sight of them, and he started forward in sudden hope, forgetting his precarious modesty and all but leaving his bed-robe behind him. He faltered, stopped, one trembling hand out appealingly, the other seeking to draw together his robe and cover at least his loins with the clutched underwear.

Ludovick of Lennox came first, followed by the Earl of Atholl, the Lords Ochiltree and Innermeath, the Master of Orkney, Sir James Stewart of Eday and Sir Robert Stewart of Middleton. They all bowed to their unclothed monarch, but kept their distance at the other side of the room.

James's expression underwent a series of swift alterations, as sudden relief was banished by uncertainty, perception, renewed fear and alarm, almost despair. He recognised that every man who had come in was a Stewart, of his own house. But they had none of them come to his side. All stood ranged behind Bothwell, even Lennox. Almost, it might have seemed, they left a gap amongst them for their dead kinsman Moray.

The King tried to speak, his thick lips working. 'Vicky . . . !' he got out, at length.

That young man inclined his head slightly, but said no word.

James looked from one to the other, and back to Bothwell,

and a new gleam of hope dawned in those tell-tale eyes. He had his own intelligence, and perceived, panic-stricken as he was, that Bothwell could not have assembled all these fellow Stewarts in order to murder their royal relative before their eyes. Out of a strong sense of self-preservation, and no little cunning, he summoned an excess of courage of a sort, deliberately changing his whole attitude and bearing. He addressed Bothwell only, in as loud and declamatory a voice as he could muster, dropping his underwear and drawing himself up, to hold wide his robe, so that his nakedness should be displayed, not hidden.

'Do your worst then, my lord,' he declared strongly, even though the words trembled. 'I am wholly in your power. Take your King's life. You, nor your master the Devil, shall have his soul!'

Bothwell was scarcely to be blamed if he stared, so unlike James Stewart was this.

'Strike, man!' the King went on, warming to his part. 'I am ready to die. Better to die with honour than to live in captivity and shame. Aye, better. Stay . . . stay not your steel, Francis.'

That this was sheerest play-acting all knew well, for James's horror of cold steel was common knowledge.

But the performer had met as keen a play-actor as himself. Bothwell, recovering from his surprise, glanced round at his supporters. Then he drew his sword with a dramatic flourish, and as James involuntarily cowered back at the sight of it, he threw himself forward. But somehow he had his sword whipped round now, and he sank to his knees before the other, presenting the hilt to his monarch.

'Here is my sword, Sire,' he cried, to the shrinking King. 'Take it and use it on me, if you truly believe me traitor! See – I bare my neck.' He bent his head and pushed up his sandy hair with his left hand. 'Strike shrewd and fair, Your Grace, if you deem me ever to have harboured a thought against your royal person.'

James gobbled and blinked and wagged his head, hoist with his own petard. He could no more have used sword on Bothwell, or on any man, than he could have flown in the air. On the other hand, to do nothing, to indicate that Bothwell did not deserve death, was to condone all, besides displaying the greatest weakness. He temporised.

'False!' he mumbled. 'Nay, kneel not, man – and add hypocrisy to treason. You ha' plotted my death. I . . . I call upon you now to execute your purpose. Aye, your purpose. For I'll no' live a prisoner and dishonoured.' That was declared with rather less conviction than before.

'Nor will I, Highness,' Bothwell assured, straightening up a little. He kissed the hilt of his sword theatrically, and thrust it almost into the King's hand once more. 'Here shall be the end of your distrust of Francis Stewart! Us it now – or trust me hereafter.'

'Waesucks! I . . . I . . . ' In his predicament, James looked appealingly at the others, especially at Lennox.

That young man, in some measure, answered the appeal. Nodding, he spoke, if stiffly. 'Your Grace, I counsel you to raise up my lord of Bothwell. We are convinced that he intends no treason. If his manner of entry here offends you, how else could he have gained your face? He can serve you well in this pass, we are assured. Heed him, Sire.'

Something like a growl of agreement came from the assembled Stewarts.

James, thankful no longer to have to look at the kneeling Earl and his outstretched sword, released a flood of disjointed eloquence. 'It's no' right. It's no' suitable. This violent repair to me. To our royal presence. Is it no' dishonourable to me? Aye, and disgraceful to my servants who allowed it? It was ill done. Am I no' your anointed King? I am twenty-seven years of age, mind. I am no' a laddie any mair, when every faction could think to make me their ain property. You hear me? It is ill done.'

All eyed him steadily. None spoke. Bothwell had risen to his feet again. He returned his sword to its scabbard, with a noticeable screak and click. Play-acting was over.

The King did not fail to perceive it, and drooped puny shoulders, drawing his robe around him again. 'What . . . what would you have, my lords?' he muttered, almost whispered.

'Your goodwill and trust, Sire – what else?' Bothwell declared, briskly now. 'Your realm is in poor state. We shall order it better for you. These are true and leal men, of your own house. Trust them, if you still do not trust me.'

'Aye,' James sighed.

'Much must be done, and swiftly. Now. Before this Parliament breaks. That it may show the consent of the realm. And of the Kirk.' Bothwell paused, and waved a hand to Colville. 'But we can consider this while Your Grace dresses. Tom Erskine shall attend you forthwith. I would advise that you attend the morning session in person, Sire. To announce certain concessions. And decrees. We shall support you.'

'This morning? Aye.' There was a hint of eagerness in that. James darted a glance towards the window. 'Aye. This morning.'

Bothwell read his thoughts. 'Your Highness will be entirely secure, rest assured,' he said, with a thin smile. 'I have five score horsemen to escort you thither. And a thousand men in the city. All will be well.'

The King all but groaned.

Mar led the way into the royal bedchamber, taking care however to resume his stance at the window. James looked from him to Lennox.

'Vicky . . . ?' he began. 'Och man, Vicky!'

Ludovick inclined his head, but kept his boyish features stern, unrelenting.

'Where . . . where is Patrick? Where is the Master o' Gray, my lords?'

'In his bed no doubt, Sire,' Ludovick answered. 'We have not concerned him in this matter.'

Once more Bothwell smiled, briefly. But he made no comment.

Thus, simply, quietly, without a drop of blood shed, the fearsome, devil-possessed and unpredictable Earl of Bothwell took major if temporary control of the realm of Scotland, after more spectacular attempts innumerable. There was no clash, no active opposition. A deputation of the citizens of Edinburgh, hearing rumours from the palace, did present themselves at the gates, and by the mouth of Provost Home asked if the King required their aid, perchance? James, only too vividly able to imagine his fate during the period of waiting for any such succour, sadly dismissed them. Thereafter, he rode in the

393

midst of a strong escort of mosstroopers, Bothwell on one side, and happily the Master of Gray on the other, to the Parliament Hall, where he made a short and largely unintelligible speech conceding practically all that the Kirk party demanded, removing episcopal and prelatical seats from the legislature, and promising compensation for Moray's family, preferment for his young son and heir, and vengeance on his killers. More ringing and heartfelt cheering than he had ever known followed the monarch out into the High Street, with Bothwell doffing his bonnet right and left, and Patrick Gray singing gently beneath his breath.

A special court of the Privy Council, consisting of Bothwell's peers, the Earls of Atholl, Argyll, Mar, Orkney, Glencairn, and the Marischal, considered formally whether he could be said to be guilty of treason or conspiracy. The accused tactfully absented himself from the proceedings, but his men surrounded the court in serried ranks. After a fairly brief deliberation their lordships acquitted Francis Hepburn Stewart on both counts, and commended him to the King's grace and assured benevolence. The next day, therefore Bothwell's peace was proclaimed by the heralds at the Cross of Edinburgh, amidst much jollification and free liquor for the citizenry. The matter of the witchcraft charges, which came into a different legal category altogether, were sensibly postponed until some suitable future date.

The Earl of Bothwell invented a new title for himself – Lord Lieutenant of Scotland – with Patrick's acclaim, though Lennox and others tended to look askance at it. The Kirk set up a Committee of Security to assist in the governance of the realm. Along with a number of others, Sir Robert Cockburn of Clerkington, the Secretary of State and Chancellor Maitland's son-in-law, was summarily dismissed. Patrick Gray, with typical sense of duty, made himself responsible for his office, meantime – this despite the fact that an ungrateful Parliament had not wholly accepted his claim for the £20,000 Scots, but had feebly passed it on to a special committee to consider.

On the subject of titles and offices, the Duke of Lennox found himself relieved of that of Lord High Admiral, in favour of its previous holder. He was allowed to remain Chamberlain, however.

The Earl of Moray remained unburied. His mother, as well as being a Campbell, was a woman of distinctly sceptical and disbelieving character.

Scotland watched and waited, as it had done so often before.

Chapter Twenty-four

PETER HAY, Lennox's page, came up the winding stairway of the King's tower two steps at a time, his spurred riding-boots stamping and jingling, his sword clanking – despite the edict that no swords were to be carried within the palace. Mary Gray and the Lady Beatrix Ruthven were descending, the former carrying a tambour-frame and the latter a box of threads, for the Queen's embroidery. They met at the first floor landing.

'Mistress Mary! Here's well met,' the young man exclaimed, somewhat breathless. 'I was looking to see you.' Recollecting, he doffed his distinctly battered bonnet. 'Your ladyship,' he acknowledged perfunctorily to the other and still younger girl. 'I'd hoped I'd find you, Mistress Mary . . . '

'Why, Peter – what's the haste?' Mary asked, smiling. 'What's to do? I thought that you were at Hailes, with the others? And you are all muddy. You . . . ' Her eyes widened, and the smile left her lovely face. 'Peter – there is blood on your hands! What is it? What has happened? Is something . . . wrong?'

'Well . . . no. No, naught is wrong.' He said that without conviction, however. 'A mishap, that is all.' His glance flickered towards the interested Lady Beatrix. 'I bear a message for the Queen. From his Grace. From Hailes Castle. He sent me, for young Ramsay is sick and Erskine gone to my lord of Angus, at Tantallon. I am to escort the Queen to Hailes Castle. Forthwith. The King is to stay there long. Hunting. For some days. But . . . but I wanted to see you first, Mistress Mary . . . '

'You are not hurt, Peter? That blood . . . ? Nor, nor any other?'

'No. It is nothing. Not *my* blood.' He looked again towards Beatrix Ruthven. 'Can I have a word with you, Mistress Mary? Before I see the Queen?'

The younger girl laughed. 'Give me the frame, Mary. I will tell the Queen that you will be with her presently. And shall not mention Master Hay! Her Grace is in the Orangery,' she told the page.

'Thank you,' Mary acknowledged. 'I shall not delay long. Come, Peter.' She turned, and led the way back upstairs to the apartment of the Ladies-in-Waiting.

Hay closed the door behind him, and stood looking at her. His clothing was spattered with mud, and flecked with foam from a hard-driven horse. There was a tension about him that was unusual and not to be mistaken.

'What is it, Peter?' Mary demanded. 'There *is* trouble, is there not? It is not Vicky? The Duke?'

'No. He is well enough. With the King and Bothwell. It is . . . other.' Putting a hand into the deep pocket inside his riding-cloak, he drew out a bundle of papers, letters, all mud-stained and dirty, some still sealed, some opened. Laying them down on the table, he pointed to the topmost, opened, soiled and crumpled. 'No doubt I should not show you these,' he said, 'but you have a better head than any I know. Besides, you are in some way concerned. You can tell me what to do.'

Frowning, she looked from the young man to the untidy papers and back. 'What is this? What have you done?'

'I was sent back, from Hailes. With a half-troop as escort. To fetch the Queen,' he explained, jerkily. 'Crossing the Gled's Muir, this side of Haddington, we came on trouble. Fighting. Or the end of it. A bad place it is, for cut-purses and broken men – miles of it, wild and empty. These were robbers – some of Bothwell's own damned mosstroopers, I shouldn't wonder, running loose. Lacking employment. Six of them. They had waylaid and cut down two men. Travellers. They were ransacking their bags. One was opening these letters when they saw us. They bolted as we came up. We were too many for them. They threw down the letters as they went. No doubt they got the purses. Other things, maybe.'

Mary's eyes were on that topmost letter. 'I know that hand-

396

writing,' she said tight-voiced. 'And those seals, broken as they are.'

'Aye. As do I. They are the Master of Gray's,' the other agreed grimly. 'One of the travellers was dead. The other died as we sought to put him on a horse. His blood, this is. Run through again and again. The one better dressed I recognised. He was a creature of Sir Richard Bowes, the English envoy. I have seen him about the palace here. The other would be guard and servant. Couriers, clearly. Heading south. For England. With letters and dispatches for the English Court. For my lord of Burleigh and Sir Edward Wotton.'

Mary shook her head. 'How cruel! How wicked a deed! God rest their souls. But . . . ' Stepping forward she picked up the top letter. 'This, of Patrick's, was with them?'

Hay nodded. 'It was within an outer paper. Both opened. The outer was in a different writing. And with plain seals. Addressed to the Lady Diana Woodstock. In care of the Lord Burleigh, Lord Treasurer, at the Palace of Saint James, London. This other was within it. I knew the hand. I have seen many letters from the Master to the Duke. It was sealed with the Gray seals. They had been broken, also.' He paused. 'I can well guess to whom it is written!'

'Yes.'

'Read it.'

Troubled, the young woman searched the other's face, before, clearly reluctantly, she conned the letter. It read:

'Dearest and Fairest Lady,

I acknowledge, with devotion and gratitude, the last sum of £500 remitted by the usual source. I have put it, like that which went before, to good and effective use. I think that you will not deny it. Unlike certain other doles which of your kind heart you see fit to dispense, these remittances are put to excellent purpose, for your causes as for mine. As I take no doubt but that your good Master Bowes, newly knighted, will sufficiently inform you.

Now I hasten to acquaint you that all is well, very well, in the great matter which we planned. The ineffable Bothwell fell most sweetly into the trap, and now struts the stage, calling himself Lieutenant of Scotland, no less. Believing that all the event was his own doing, he now works mightily and happily his own doom. Meanwhile, as foreseen, he works also our ends for us, most obligingly. The Papists are put down. Parliament may no longer be packed with mock bishops and prelates. The Hamiltons are in fullest flight. It will rejoice you to know that the unmentionable Maitland is at last unseated, and I have plans to keep him so. Cockburn, his lumpish good-son, likewise. Your siller is well spent, Lady?

As for your esteemed young coz, he is, I promise you, learning his lesson. I am in a position to know, for he places his fullest confidence in your unworthy servant, privily informing me of his secret mind, little knowing who was the architect, with your aid, Fairest Dian, of his present humbled estate. He will flirt no more with Huntly and Spain, of that rest assured. Nor will he again allow any lord to dominate your mutual borders, once Bothwell is down. So your peace is buttressed on two fronts. I continue with his instruction, and shall not spare the rod, like a good tutor, should need arise. As advised.'

Thus ended the first sheet of paper. Mary looked up, to meet the other's gaze. Her dark eyes were clouded, as though with pain. She said nothing.

'Read on,' Hay urged, handing her a second sheet. 'This was within the first.'

Almost as though it might burn her, Mary took it. This read:

'I used the threat of Hamilton's desire for second place in this kingdom, with the ire at Moray's death, to unite the Stewarts and bring all this about, Madam. Alackaday, perhaps I something wronged poor Hamilton, who has insufficient wit I fear to desire anything thus vigorously, other than a wench and a flagon. But the fact is that our friend the young Duke is more truly smitten with that same sickness. He supported the enterprise the more readily in that he desires to see the Hamiltons laid low and his own claim to second place and heir established. Indeed, it goes further than this. I have reason to know that, once his claim is accepted – Parliament has remitted it to the next sitting – he plans to have your poor coz proclaimed insane and crazed, and unfit to reign. Himself then as Regent. Then, later, King in his stead, no less. I fear that the lad has grown over-ambitious. Can you, great Diana, contemplate Esmé D'Aubigny's son as heir to England? But fear you not. I shall deal with Master Vicky in due course. I have my plans prepared.

A further dispensation of your liberality would much aid me, I would mention.

Meanwhile, may the good God prosper all your affairs, as they now prosper here, and grant you health and well-being to match your wit and beauty. Until these poor eyes feast upon your loveliness again,

I remain, sweet lady, your humblest and most devoted servant and adorer,

P.'

'Well?' Hay demanded, when he saw that she had finished reading.

Mary moistened her lips, but for once had no words.

'You see what he says? What it means? It is lies – all lies. You know it, as do I. He knows it also – the Master of Gray. But it could mean my Duke's head, nevertheless.'

'It . . . is . . . ill . . . done,' the girl said slowly, each word standing alone.

'It is worse than that, by God!' the young man cried. 'This is as good as an assassination! Written to Elizabeth of England, who hates the house of Lennox. She will inform the King. Nothing is more sure. Higher treason than this could scarce be thought of. And all lies. My master no more desires the throne than, than . . . '

'I know it,' Mary said quietly. 'This shall not be.'

Something about her voice calmed him. 'What can we do?' he asked.

'I shall do what I should have done, long since,' she told him, levelly. 'God forgive me that I have waited this long.'

Doubtfully he eyed her.

'Patrick is still at Hailes, with the King?' she asked.

'Yes.'

'I shall see him, then, tonight. You said that you escort the Queen there, forthwith? This afternoon?'

'Yes. But what can you do?'

She did not seem to hear him. 'Peter,' she went on, 'take these letters to Sir Richard Bowes. All save this of Patrick's. Tell him what happened.' She leafed through the other letters. 'These are no concern of ours. Do not tell him of this one. If he knew aught of it, and asks you, you know nothing. The robbers must have taken it. You understand?'

'Aye. You will keep it?'

'Meantime, yes. And, Peter – when you have taken us to Hailes, I think that I may have a further task for you. If you will do it? Weary as you will be . . . ?'

'Anything, Mistress Mary,' he assured her.

'My thanks. Now, to the Queen. And then, while she prepares to ride, to Sir Richard Bowes' lodging.'

'Aye. You know what you will do?'

'God granting me the resolution, I do,' she said. 'Come.'

In a stone garden-house of the pleasance of Hailes Castle, in the gorge of Tyne, the only place it seemed in that crowded establishment where she could be assured to privacy, Mary Gray turned to face her father, pale, set-faced.

'This will serve I think, Patrick,' she said.

'I should hope so!' Patrick, although he laughed, considered her shrewdly. 'I warrant half the Court is watching this so secret assignment! And debating the wherefore of it. As I do also, moppet, I confess. Rejoice as I do in your company therefore, my dear, I bid you be discreetly brief. In here. Lest your reputation suffers – and I, I am labelled even worse than I am! A man who would corrupt his own daughter!'

'Would that was all that you could be labelled!' she told him flatly.

'Eh . . . ?' Startled now, he stared. 'What a plague do you mean by that?'

'I mean, Patrick, that I have come to know you for what you are. At last. I can no longer blind myself.'

Still-faced, he waited, unspeaking.

'Davy warned me,' she went on, in a curious, unemphatic,

factual voice. 'Others also, to be sure. Times a-many. But I believed that they wronged you. Deep down, they wronged you. I believed that I knew you better – because I knew myself. And loved you. We were out of the same mould, you and I. So that I understood you, as others did not. I saw the gold beneath the tarnish. But it was I who was wrong. There is no gold there. Only . . . corruption!'

Taut-featured now as she was herself, he stood motionless, scarcely seeming to breathe. Only his delicate nostrils flared, as a spirited horse's will flare. As did her own, indeed. Never had they seemed more alike, those two. 'Yes?' he said.

'You betray all with whom you have dealings,' she told him, and the unemotional, level, almost weary certainty of her utterance made the indictment the more terrible. 'You betray always, for love of betrayal. Davy said that you were a destroyer. I know now that you are worse than that. A destroyer can at the least be honestly so. A lion, a boar, a wolf – these have their parts. But you – you seek men's trust and love, in order to destroy them. You charm before you betray. You, Patrick, are not even a wolf. You are a snake!'

'God's passion!' Blazing-eyed the Master took a step towards her, fists clenched, knuckles white. Almost it seemed that he would strike her. Only with a tremendous and very apparent effort of will did he hold himself back. Panting, his words came pouring out, his voice no longer musical and pleasingly modulated but harsh, strident, staccato. 'How dare you! You young fool! What do *you* know? In your insufferable ignorance! None speaks me so – you, nor any. Do you hear? Christ – you, of all!'

She stood, head up, unflinching, meeting his furious gaze, not challenging or defiant, but with a calm resolution, sorrowful but sure. She actually nodded her head. 'I know – because this time you have betrayed yourself,' she told him. 'This time it is your own words that condemn you. Written testimony.'

That gave him pause. He drew a deep quivering breath. 'What mean you by that?' he asked thickly.

'I mean that you have gone too far in betrayal. Even for my indulgence, Patrick. I did not believe that you had betrayed Mary the Queen, to her death. Now I do. For I have proof

401

that you have betrayed the King. And intend to do so further. You betrayed Moray, again to his death. Bothwell here, also. The Hamiltons. Even Huntly, and your Catholics. For money. For power. For revenge. For amusement, sport, no less! And now, God forgive you if He can, you have betrayed Vicky.'

'A-a-ah!'

'I warned you,' she went on inexorably. 'At Dunfermline. I warned you to cast down no more men. If you touched Vicky, I said, I would no longer forget my duty.'

'Vicky!' He spat out the name. 'That young blockhead! For him you speak me so! For that ducal dolt you would discard me? *Me*, your father! He has turned your silly head.'

'Not my head, Patrick,' she corrected. 'My heart, perhaps, but not my head. The head that I heired from you. The heart, I pray God, I heired from my mother!'

'You insolent jade! You interfering hussy! Foul fall you – are you out of your mind? Are you, girl . . . ?' The man's words faltered, however, as something of the quality of his daughter's strange certainty tempered the heat of his fury. 'What is it? Out with it! What lies has Lennox been spilling into your foolish ears?' he demanded.

'None,' she told him. 'I have not seen Vicky for three days. The lies, Patrick, are all your own! Written lies. In your letter to Queen Elizabeth.'

His lips parted, and he drew a long breath, but spoke no word.

'That evil letter will not reach Elizabeth,' she went on. 'It was . . . intercepted. I have read it . . .'

'Great God! Who . . . ? Who intercepted it? Who has seen it?' Patrick grasped her arm in his sudden urgency. 'Where is it, Mary? Not . . . not Bothwell? Or the King . . . ?'

'Would you be here, a free man, this night, had either of these seen it?'

He moistened his lips. 'Who then? I warn you, girl – do not seek to cozen me!'

'Who intercepted it matters not, Patrick. Only one other, and myself, have seen it . . . as yet.'

'Where is it, then? Who holds it?'

'I hold part of it.'

'Part? Only part?'

402

'There were two sheets, you will recollect. Within the plain outer paper. Written with your own hand, and sealed with your seal. That in which you betray Vicky, I hold. The other is . . . elsewhere.'

'Elsewhere . . . ?' He swallowed. 'Damnation – where?'

Mary shook her head. 'Where you cannot reach it.' Her voice quivered now. 'Patrick. I have brought you here to say goodbye.'

He stared at her. 'What nonsense is this? You mean that you are leaving Court? Going back to Castle Huntly? I' faith, it is not before time, I think! It was my folly ever to have brought you.'

'*My* going is of no matter. It is yours that is important. *You* are leaving Court, Patrick. Leaving Scotland. Forthwith.'

'Christ – are you crazed? What a plague means this? Have you clean lost your senses, girl?'

'It is my sorrow that I have been lacking my senses for so long, Patrick. That I forbore to put a halt to your evils long ere this. As I could and should have done. Because I loved you. Because I believed that there was good in you – that there *must* be good in you. How wrong I was! It is . . .'

With an impatient gesture of his hand he interrupted her. 'Enough of this puling folly! Think you I must stand and listen to your childish insults?'

'You must do more than that, Patrick. You must go. Leave all.' Almost without expression she spoke. 'I warned you. If you touched Vicky, I told you, with your, your poison, I would set my hand against you.'

'So! You esteem Vicky Stuart higher than you do me, your father?'

The word was long in coming. She raised her head until her small chin was held high. 'Yes,' she said at last, simply.

Something seemed to crumple in the man, then. He turned away from her, to gaze out of that little summer-house to the towering bulk of the great castle, stained with the reflection of the sunset, his beautiful features working spasmodically.

In her turn, Mary's own hard-won resolution cracked a little. 'Oh, Patrick,' she cried, her voice breaking, 'why, oh why did you do it? How could you? To Vicky, who was like a son to you. Or a brother. Whom you brought to this land, from France. Who worshipped you. Who used to esteem you little less than a god. How could you so turn on him? To write those lies about him to Elizabeth. Knowing that she hates and fears the house of Lennox, which is too near to her own throne. Knowing what she would do. That she would be certain to tell King James.'

'Vicky has been riding too high,' the Master jerked, thickly, still not looking at her. 'He presumes. He interferes. Since Moray's death he has set himself against me . . . '

'With cause, has he not? Did not *you* kill the Earl of Moray, Patrick – even though it was Huntly's hand that struck the blow? You planned his death?'

'Not his death. Only his fall.' The Master sighed. 'Moray had to go. For the sake of the realm. He had stolen the Queen's affections. The greatest evil could come of that. For Scotland. Even for England. Can you not perceive it? For doubts as to the father of James's heir could keep him out of Elizabeth's throne. Many in England are against his accession, in any case. Elizabeth herself is hesitant. Moray had to go.'

'His death was ordered by Elizabeth? And paid for with her gold?'

'Not his death. His fall and disgrace. Banishment, perhaps. Until James should have an undoubted heir. Huntly went too far.'

'So you betrayed Huntly, through Bothwell? You plotted Bothwell's attack on the King. Now you are betraying Bothwell. Again with Elizabeth's money. He is working his own doom, you wrote. You released him from Edinburgh Castle for this! And the Lord Hamilton. He is broken and disgraced, put to the horn, for no other reason than that you could use his name to unite the Stewarts to aid Bothwell's attempt against the King . . . '

'Lassie! Lassie!' Patrick Gray interposed, almost wearily. 'Can you not see? Can you not understand? The rule and governance of this unhappy realm is balanced as on a sword's edge. The throne is insecure, and has no power, no strength. Any blustering lord can command more men than can King James. The country is at the lords' mercy, torn with strife and jealousy and hatred. Catholics and Protestants are at each others' throats. War is ever around the corner – civil war,

404

bloody and terrible. Then thousands would die – innocent, poor folk. That is what I struggle and scheme to save this land from, always. Better that an arrogant lord or two should die, than that. Can you not see . . . ?'

'I see only betrayal and bad faith, deceit and lies. Even though you name it statecraft.'

'Aye, statecraft! What else? The ship of state is an ill craft to steer when its master is a weakly buffoon and its crew pirates with every man's hand against another. For the sake of the realm, of our people, I have set *my* hand to steer this ship, Mary – for want of a better man, or a surer hand. Can you name any that could do it better? So I am a Catholic one day and a Protestant the next. One day I support Bothwell, the next Huntly – when either gets too strong. I cherish the Kirk – and when it becomes overbearing and would weaken the throne, I bring in the Jesuits and Spain. Elizabeth's gold I use, yes – but for Scotland's weal. The throne must be supported, buttressed, always. Somehow. For only it stands between the lords and the people. How may a king like James be sustained, save by setting his enemies against each other? How think you that James has kept his crown all these months? By my wits, girl – *my* wits!'

'Yet you betray James also, to Elizabeth!'

'Betray! What fool word is this that you prate like a parrot? One day, Mary, with God's help and these wits of mine, Scotland and England shall be one realm, with one monarch. Strange fate that it should be drooling Jamie Stewart! Then there shall be an end to wars and hatred and fighting. That united realm shall be great and powerful enough to hold all Europe in check. Spain shall no longer threaten it. Nor the Pope. Nor even France. Law and justice shall rule it, from a strong and wealthy throne, with nobles tamed and a church less harsh. To that end I work. For that I plot and scheme, raise men up and bring them low – that James's throne may survive until then. I would have thought, Mary, that you, of all people, would have had the head to see it! For that greater good, we must suffer the lesser evils . . . '

'Such as achieving the destruction of your friends? Causing the deaths of those who trust you? Selling one who is as good as a son to you?'

'Tcha! God in Heaven, Mary – can I not make you understand? Are you blind?'

'No, I am not blind, Patrick. Not any more. You have blinded and dazzled me for too long. I see clearly now. I see that my father . . . that Davy Gray was right. He said that you had a devil. I believe it, now. I believe now that even Granlord was right – that you were the death of our Queen Mary. And . . . and I swear, Patrick, that you shall not be the death of Vicky Stuart! All for the weal of the realm!'

'Tush, child – I wish no hurt to Vicky. Only a warning . . . '

'You accused him of highest treason, to Elizabeth – of having James declared insane, and himself made Regent. Then King in his place. Knowing that Vicky has no thought of power or rule. Knowing too that Elizabeth must tell James. And that, hearing it, he could scarce do less than have Vicky's head, for so great a treachery and threat. And none to know that you, his friend, were behind it!' The young woman's dark eyes flashed now. 'For that, Patrick, no words will suffice. Only deeds.'

'And what deeds, pray, do you intend to perform, Mary, to suffice your maidenly ire?' The Master's scimitar brows rose mockingly. 'Perhaps I deceive myself – but I believe that I may just be able to withstand your direst darts, my dear!'

She shook her head, but sadly, with nothing of triumph. 'The deed is done, Patrick,' she said. 'Past recall. You are too late to save yourself.' Mary looked out at the last of the sunset. 'Tonight, possibly even at this moment, a trusted messenger hands the first sheet of your letter to my Lord Maitland, the Chancellor, at Thirlestane Castle in Lauderdale. He will know well what to do with it.'

'Merciful Christ!' For once that melodious voice was no better than an ugly croak. 'Maitland! You did that? You sent the letter to Maitland? Maitland, of all men! My chiefest enemy . . . '

'I sent it to the Chancellor of this realm. He still is that. Whose duty it must be to take action upon it. I cannot believe that he will fail to do so. And promptly.'

Appalled, aghast, the Master searched his daughter's face. 'Do . . . you know . . . what you . . . have done?' he demanded, from a constricted throat.

'I do. I did it of set purpose. This is what the Chancellor requires. To raise himself up again. And to bring you down. It cannot fail to do so.'

'It cannot fail to lose me my head, damn, burn and blister you! In that letter I said . . . I said . . .'

'You said that you would not spare the rod, on King James. That you were the architect of his present humbled state. That he informed you of his secret mind, which you then disclosed to Elizabeth. I cannot think that this is less than treason.'

'And that you, Mary Gray, sent to Maitland! And you talk of betrayal!' The words rose to a cry that verged on the hysterical.

'I am the daughter of the Master of Gray,' she told him quietly, her voice so very flat in contrast to his. 'Perhaps betrayal therefore comes naturally to me, also!'

'Precious soul of God! This – from you!'

'Yes, Patrick. But at least I only hold the noose before your eyes. I do not put it round your neck and draw it tight! As you have done to others. I have left you with time to escape. Maitland is no young man. He will not ride through all the wild hills between Lauderdale and Hailes at night. You have time to reach the Border before he can act. England. From whence comes your gold and your orders. You will be safe there, will you not? Your fond Elizabeth will cherish you. Or may she no longer esteem you when your usefulness here is past? That you must needs discover.'

He said nothing.

'Perhaps you will fare better in France? Or Spain?' the girl went on, in the same inflexible voice. 'You will not lack employment, I feel sure. Meantime, a fast horse will take you to Berwick and over Tweed in three hours and less.'

'You . . . you are very thoughtful.' Somehow he got it out. 'But have you, in your lofty wisdom, considered Marie and the child? Whom you also have professed to love – God help them!'

'Marie knows all. I spoke with her before leaving Holyroodhouse. Even now she will be on her way to Berwick, with Andrew.'

'She will? Sink me . . . !'

'Marie agrees with what I have done. She said that I was to tell you so. That she believed it to be for the best. She longs to see an end to this evil. She has tried to halt you, but you would not heed her. It required your own flesh and blood to halt your course, Patrick – another such as yourself. So . . . this is goodbye.'

'You think, you believe, that you have halted me? A chit of a girl! You conceive Patrick Gray held by such as you? Lord – was there ever such insolent folly!'

Sighing, she shook her head. 'You have no choice,' she said. 'You *are* held. By noonday tomorrow, if you are not out of this realm, you will either be warded for treason and trial, or else outlawed, put to the horn. Your letter reveals your betrayal of all. You cannot flee north – for will Huntly or the Marischal save you now? In the south, Bothwell will hunt you down. Will Hamilton in the west spare you? Or the Master of Glamis? Or Mar? You are held, quite. When you penned that letter, Patrick, you wrote your own doom. When you turned on Vicky, you signed it.'

The man opened his mouth to speak, and then closed it again. Mary Gray had him silenced.

'Goodbye, Patrick,' she said then, huskily, unevenly.

He drew himself up, to look at her, to consider her all, every delectable inch of her. And looking, his expression changed, eased, softened. 'Mary, Mary!' he all but whispered. 'What have I done to you? What have we done to each other? You and I? God pity us – what are we? So close, so close – yet we destroy each other.'

'I do not know,' she answered, emptily. 'Save that we are the Grays – and fate is hard on us.'

'A-a-aye!' That came out on a long sigh. He held out a hand, open, empty, pleading. 'May I kiss you, child? Once. Before . . . before . . .'

'Yes – oh, yes!' she cried, and without hesitation flung herself upon him, eyes filling with tears. 'Yes – for I cannot but love you. Always.'

For long moments they clutched each other close, convulsively, passionately, murmuring incoherences. Then abruptly, almost roughly, the man thrust Mary away from him, swung about, and hurried out of that pleasance-house, slamming the door behind him.

The girl sank to her knees over the carved stone bench and sobbed as though her heart would break.

Chapter Twenty-five

IT was grey morning before Mary saw Lennox. The previous evening she had deliberately avoided all contact with others, after coming in from the summer-house, even pleading a headache to excuse herself from her duties with the Queen, and retiring early to the bed which she was to share with the Lady Beatrix Ruthven, to hide herself if not to sleep. Now, darker-eyed than ever and just a little drawn and wan, she sought out the Duke in the little high turret chamber which was all that Bothwell had found for him in that crowded house.

Surrounded by his usual untidy clutter of clothes and gear, the young man was in his shirt-sleeves, brushing dried mud from his tall riding-boots, as the girl knocked and entered.

'Mary!' he exclaimed. 'I sought you last night – when I heard that you had come. With the Queen . . . '

'I was tired, Vicky. I went to bed.' She glanced around her. 'I see that Peter Hay is not back yet – since you clean your own boots.'

'No. It is strange. Where he is gone, I know not. He came with the Queen, and then . . . '

'It was my doing, Vicky. He went on an errand. For me. He rode to Lauderdale. Last night. To the Chancellor's house at Thirlestane.'

'To Maitland? Peter? For you? Sakes, Mary – what is this?'

'It was necessary. Something that I had to do. It . . . it is an ill story, Vicky.' Involuntarily she was picking up and smoothing out and tidying the strewn clothing of that little apartment, as she spoke. 'Patrick is gone.'

'Patrick? Patrick Gray? Gone? Gone where? What do you mean – gone?'

'Gone away. Left Scotland. Last night.' Listlessly she said it. 'He rode for Berwick.'

Astonished, he regarded her. 'But why? What is this? Is it some new plot?'

She told him, then, baldly, in jerky broken sentences. She did not spare Patrick, nor yet herself. Starkly, she declared what she had done to her father, and why.

Ludovick heard her out with growing wonderment, his blue eyes devouring her strained face.

'I' faith, Mary – here is a marvel!' he declared. '*You* did all this? You brought him low. Unaided. And . . . by all that is wonderful – you did it because of me?'

'Yes,' she admitted, simply.

He stepped forward, to grip both her slight shoulders, to stare down at her. 'But . . . what does it mean?' he demanded. 'What does it mean, that you should do this? Tell me, Mary.'

'It means many things, Vicky. But, for you, it means that my eyes are open. That I have made my choice. At last.'

'Mean for me . . . ?'

'Yes. You have been very patient. So faithful.'

He moistened his lips, although his grip on her tightened. 'I do not understand you, Mary. Speak me plain, for God's sake! What do you say?'

'I say that you were right, Vicky, and I was wrong. Not only about Patrick. About the life of the Court. About what is best for us, what is good and right and fair. I mean that I am done with courts and kings and queens. Done with deceits, intrigues and glittering follies. I want no more of it. I have finished with this life, Vicky – finished.'

'You mean that you are going home? To Castle Huntly?'

'No. Not unless I must. I had thought to go to another castle than that. To Methven Castle, Vicky.'

'What . . . !' Mary! What are you saying? Dear Lord – what are you saying?'

'I am asking that you take me away, Vicky. Will you take me away from it all? To your quiet green Methven. There to stay, to abide. You and me, together. As you have wished for so long . . . '

She got no further. The young man's arms enclosed her, swept her up off her feet, crushed the breath from her lovely body, held her fast, while he gabbled and gasped endearments, joy, praise and utter foolishness – when he was not closing her soft parted lips with his own urgent ones.

So different an embrace than that of the night before.

At last, breathless and panting, even trembling a little, Ludovick released her at least sufficiently to allow her to speak.

'My heart! My love! My sweet Mary!' he cried, 'So you will marry me, at last? Oh, my dear – we shall be wed. Soon. At once. Here is the most joyful day of my life. Here is . . .'

Shaking her head, but smiling, Mary extricated one hand, to raise it and place a forefinger over his eager mouth. 'Not so fast, young man,' she told him, tremulous only in her breathing. 'A truce, Vicky – one moment! Hear me, please.' And as he began to nibble at her finger, her face grew grave. 'I will not marry you, Vicky. I cannot. You are still the Duke of Lennox, the King's cousin. And I am still Mary Gray, the bastard. Nothing is changed, there. If we marry, in despite of the King and the Council, our marriage would be annulled forthwith. They would part us. They must. You must see it? So long as we do not marry, none will part us. None will see shame in a duke taking a mistress; but to marry out of his rank and style – that would be unforgivable!'

'But . . . but . . . I care not . . .'

'But nothing, Vicky. My mind is made up, quite. You want me. I want you, likewise. Take me, then. Take me to Methven with you. I shall be your wife in all but name. I shall keep your house for you. I shall cherish you always. I shall bear your children, God willing. But . . . I will not be Duchess of Lennox.'

'Heaven save us – this is beyond all!'

'No. Heed me, Vicky. I have thought long and deep on it. In God's eyes we may be man and wife, I pray – but not in man's. I shall cleave to you, never fear. Always. I shall keep your from the life of the Court as much as I may – for it suits you nothing. But some business of state you must perform, for you are born to it. In that I shall not interfere – for I have learned my lesson. I . . . I . . .' She swallowed. 'I shall endeavour not to be jealous when you marry again – as assuredly you shall. You must. To some lady of high degree.

411

To produce an heir to your dukedom . . . '

'Damnation, Mary – have done!'

'Hear me,' she commanded. 'I shall need help, then, Vicky – for I am only a weak woman. And she, whoever she may be, must have her rights. Although she must know, before she weds, that I am what I am.'

'A plague on it!' Almost he shook her. 'Do you know what you say? What this makes you? A courtesan, no more. That is what all will name you. Lennox's courtesan!'

'Why not? That is what I shall be, indeed. There are worse things, I think. Can you not stomach the title, Vicky – for me? Is it too high a price to pay for our happiness? Tell me – is it?'

Helplessly he stared at her. 'God knows,' he muttered at length. 'I do not.'

'God knows, yes,' she agreed, firmly, decisively. 'And there you have it. God knows what we are to each other – and I care not what any other says or thinks. So long as we are together, you and I. You will take me to Methven, Vicky, my love? On these terms. It is a compact?'

He drew a long breath. 'Aye,' he said. 'If that is your will, Mary.'

'I shall make it yours also, my heart,' she whispered.

NIGEL TRANTER

LORD AND MASTER

First in The Master of Gray Trilogy

Patrick, Master of Gray – the most devilishly handsome man in Europe.

Born of one of Scotland's noblest families, Patrick was fascinating, irresistible, ambitious and ruthless. He won all hearts by his strange personal magnetism. Involved in daring plots to free the imprisoned Mary Queen of Scots, in the intrigues of Elizabeth's court and the dramatic conflicts of war-torn Scotland, he strode imperiously across the turbulent stage of European history.

The great events of the sixteenth century provide a colourful backdrop to this stirring tale of love and adventure.

POST A LITTLE HAPPINESS

Post·A·Book

A Royal Mail service in association with the Book Marketing Council & The Booksellers Association.

Post-A-Book is a Post Office trademark.

NIGEL TRANTER

PAST MASTER

Third in The Master of Gray Trilogy

Mary Gray and Ludovick, Duke of Lennox – young lovers caught up in the Master's plotting.

The end of Elizabeth's long reign was in sight. Patrick, Master of Gray, was determined that James VI should succeed to the English throne. Nothing could be allowed to stand in his way. Patrick was even prepared to sacrifice his own daughter's happiness. So she found herself caught up in a savage game of power politics, shaped by personal ambition and religious bigotry.

Patrick showed himself to be a past master of the art of political intrigue. But even he wasn't prepared for the final twist of fate which showed that his mastery might be past indeed.

HODDER AND STOUGHTON PAPERBACKS

NIGEL TRANTER

COLUMBA

Columba, royally-born Saint.

Colum mac Felim O'Neill, Abbot of Kells and Derry, prince of the Northern O'Neills, descendant of the mighty Niall of the Nine Hostages, offered the High Kingship of All Ireland. Who chose rather to serve a church still struggling against the dark, pagan forces that surrounded it.

Unwitting cause of civil war, the deaths of 3,000 on his conscience, his missionary penance was to fight a blood-soaked, human-sacrificing heathenism and bring Christianity and peace to the Picts and Scots.

Columba, a very human saint, tough but fallible, a natural leader, struggling sometimes to remember that humility is a virtue, a great fighter in tumultuous times. A man who could fall from grace but yet convert two nations and make Iona the centre of Celtic Christianity, the burial ground of kings and a place of pilgrimage.

HODDER AND STOUGHTON PAPERBACKS

MORE TITLES AVAILABLE FROM
HODDER AND STOUGHTON PAPERBACKS